Praise for *Lost*

Michelle Griep's wonderful Gothic novel, *Lost in Darkness*, transported me back to 1815 England and entranced me with well-developed characters and a vivid setting. Griep's superpower is her rich prose so reminiscent of the classics. I'll never look at Frankenstein the same way again. Highly recommended!

—Colleen Coble, USA Today bestselling author
of the Pelican Harbor series

With the despairing elements of Frankenstein, Griep takes her readers into the twisted alleyways of greed and malicious intent. A monstrous applause for Michelle Griep's latest read *Lost in Darkness*!

—Jaime Jo Wright, author of *On the Cliffs of Foxglove Manor*

Lost in Darkness is Gothic fiction at its finest with characters so flawed yet endearing you'll count them friends. With her unique signature style, Michelle Griep delivers a broody, romantic tale of Regency intrigue that makes the pages fly. Her best yet!

—Laura Frantz, author of *A Heart Adrift*

An absolutely captivating story, brimming with tension and suspense. While set on a Gothic stage, *Lost in Darkness* explores timeless questions relevant for every generation. The best and worst of humanity come together in these pages, turning on its head what it means to be either monstrous or heroic. As ever, Michelle Griep writes with courage and authority, weaving truth throughout the tale.

—Jocelyn Green, Christy Award-winning
author of *Shadows of the White City*

Lost in Darkness is the perfect blend of mysterious and romantic. The characters are so complex, each one strong in some ways and yet tenderly vulnerable in others. I was rooting for a happy ending for them all, even though I couldn't imagine how Michelle Griep could pull it off. And the homage to Mary Shelley was perfection.

—Erica Vetsch, author of The Serendipity & Secrets series

Tense and heartrending, with echoes of *Frankenstein*, Griep is at the top of her game in Gothic romance with this one! It will suck you in and keep you up half the night with the need to find out what happens. I don't know how she keeps getting better and better, but she does!

—Shannon McNear, 2014 RITA® nominee, 2021 SELAH winner,
and author of *Daughters of the Lost Colony: Elinor*

Griep's latest is a unique, standout story that evokes all the deliciously eerie tones of Gothic classics, but with generous doses of hope and beauty. Tender moments stand in beautiful contrast to the shocking and terrible events that play out, and

I never knew what to expect from one page to the next. Griep pens noble yet broken characters unlike any you'd find in other books, and carries them through the most surprising, amazing circumstances. A light-filled twist on Shelley's *Frankenstein*, *Lost in Darkness* is a read-all-night sort of book!
—Joanna Davidson Politano, author of *A Midnight Dance*
and other historical novels

Michelle Griep's *Lost in Darkness* is an atmospheric page-turner packed with romantic tension, faith, and shades of *Frankenstein*. Fans of Jaime Jo Wright won't want to miss this one.
—Julie Klassen, author of *Shadows of Swanford Abbey*

Never one to shy from sympathetic, flawed characters, Griep's prowess shines in *Lost in Darkness*. Fans of Mary Shelley's Frankenstein character will fall in love with gentle giant Colin Balfour. This book is not to be missed!
—Elizabeth Ludwig, USA Today bestselling author

Michelle Griep once again stuns with this spellbinding tale of love, loss, and acrifice. *Lost in Darkness* left me breathless with every turn of the page. A powerful story that reveals the monsters some keep inside…and the gentle beauty of those the world rejects. This is a masterpiece I'll not soon forget!
—Tara Johnson, author of *Engraved on the Heart*,
Where Dandelions Bloom, and *All Through the Night*

Reminiscent of *Beauty and the Beast* with a twist, I was captivated by this "what-could-have-been" tale from page one and not released—even after I turned the last page. I can't stop thinking about the characters.
—Ane Mulligan, author of *In High Cotton* and
the bestselling Chapel Springs series

Hauntingly brilliant and masterfully written, *Lost in Darkness* is yet another example of how Ms. Griep never fails to entertain, to romance, and to take one on a journey not soon forgotten. Her characters are deep, her prose exceptional, and her storytelling provocative. Another not-to-be-missed novel from this remarkable author.
—MaryLu Tyndall, award-winning author of
the Legacy of the King's Pirates series

LOST
IN
DARKNESS

LOST iN DARKNESS

MICHELLE GRIEP

BARBOUR
PUBLISHING

© 2021 by Michelle Griep

Print ISBN 978-1-63609-065-8

eBook Editions:
Adobe Digital Edition (.epub) 978-1-63609-229-4

All scripture quotations are taken from the King James Version of the Bible.

This book is a work of fiction. Names, characters, places, and incidents are either products of the author's imagination or used fictitiously. Any similarity to actual people, organizations, and/or events is purely coincidental.

"A Sailor's Song," featured in chapter nine, is taken from *Fugitive Verses* by Joanna Baillie. First published in 1840 and now in the public domain.

Cover Design: Kirk DouPonce, DogEared Design

Published in association with the Books & Such Literary Management, 52 Mission Circle, Suite 122, PMB 170, Santa Rosa, CA 95409-5370, www.booksandsuch.com.

Published by Barbour Publishing, 1810 Barbour Drive, Uhrichsville, Ohio 44683, www.barbourbooks.com

Our mission is to inspire the world with the life-changing message of the Bible.

Member of the
Evangelical Christian
Publishers Association

Printed in the United States of America.

DEDICATION

To my brother, Bradley Reid,
because brothers always hold
a place in a sister's heart;
and as always,
To the Saviour of my Soul,
the One who owns my heart.

"He was soon borne away by the wave and lost in darkness and distance."

Mary Shelley, *Frankenstein*

ONE

"There is something at work in my soul which I do not understand. I am practically industrious—painstaking;— a workman to execute with perseverance and labour:—but besides this, there is a love for the marvelous, a belief in the marvelous, intertwined in all my projects, which hurries me out of the common pathways of men, even to the wild sea and unvisited regions I am about to explore."

⌇

London, 1815

There was something glorious about the first day of June. The time of year when the earth exhaled a warm breath, coaxing tender shoots and delicate emotion. And for one blessed moment, Amelia Balfour surrendered to the wonder of it, lifting her face to the sunshine beaming through her bedroom window. Surely this was how heaven would feel.

But for now, the grind of wheels and soot-flaked air of London beckoned. Snapping out of her reverie, she primped her bonnet bow tight beneath her chin then scurried out of her bedroom. God may still sit on the mercy seat, but her editor would pace a deadly cadence behind his desk if she were late.

Near the front door, Amelia gave her portfolio a final peek through. Manuscript, check. Proposal for a new travel handbook, double check.

Lucky Egyptian Ibis feather…

Wait a minute.

Plunging her hand in deeper, she fingered around for the white plume with a black tip. She could've sworn she'd set it in there last night before retiring. This would never do.

"Betsey?" She peered down the corridor, hoping to spy a sturdy grey gown. If asked to do so, her maid and faithful companion could find a singular grain of peppery-pink sand amidst an entire Menorcan beach. "Have you seen—?"

A rap on the front door echoed through the foyer as Betsey rounded the corner. Everything about the woman was robust, from the dense stripe of silver hair that refused to conform to the rest of her dark locks, to the wide cut of her shoulders and thick waistline. She was a battleship. Formidable. Durable. Not to be trifled with. And Amelia loved her with her whole heart.

"I'll get that for you, miss." Betsey tipped her head towards the door, her heavy shoes thudding like distant cannon fire with each step.

Amelia held up a hand. "Thank you, but no. I'd rather you find my Ibis feather."

"Your—oh! I know just the place."

With a snap of her fingers, Betsey turned on her heel, and Amelia turned to the door.

A cadaverous man in a lawn-green frockcoat loomed on the stoop, sunshine glinting off his spectacles. Amelia blinked, not for the brilliance of reflected sunspots but for the incongruity of seeing her editor at her home instead of ensconced in his paper-strewn office. An unprecedented action, for Mr. Moritz never ventured outside the publishing house save for a late-night dash to his home for a few hours of sleep. What on earth was he doing here?

He dipped his head in a curt bow. "Good day, Miss Balfour."

"Mr. Moritz." She tucked her chin in greeting. "What a surprise. I was just on my way to see you."

"I suspected as much, but I felt a private setting would be more appropriate for our meeting."

Her throat closed. This couldn't be good. Forcing a smile, she stepped aside. "Do come in."

After he passed, she retrieved her portfolio then scuttled ahead of him. "This way, please." She led him into the sitting room and stopped near the bellpull. "Shall I ring for tea?"

"You may wish to ring for something stronger when I tell you why I am here." He doffed his hat, the flat line of his lips giving away nothing. "Perhaps you should take a seat."

The milk she'd taken with her breakfast curdled into hard lumps in her belly. She'd been right. Only ill could come of a superior deigning a home visit to one of his writers.

Willing her fingers to keep from trembling, she pulled out her manuscript and closed the distance between them, offering it over. "Perhaps you would like to read this first?"

He took the bound papers, yet shook his head, not one pomaded hair straying from the movement. "No need, Miss Balfour. I trust every I is dotted and T is crossed, for such is your perfection." With his free hand, he reached into an inside pocket, but paused before producing anything. "Are you certain you would not like to sit?"

She swallowed. Maybe she should, especially since Betsey had not yet returned with her lucky feather. Still, if she were going to be dismissed, ought she not suffer such a disgrace with all the poise and dignity she could muster? It wasn't as if she'd never been in dire straits before. Straightening her spine, she tucked her elbows tight to her side. "Whatever you may say, Mr. Moritz, can be heard as well on my feet as on my sofa."

"You are a singular woman, Miss Balfour, a trait which has earned you this." He held out two rectangular documents not much bigger than his hand.

She narrowed her eyes on what appeared to be tickets. Two berths on the HMS *Blackwell*, sailing June 8, 1:00 p.m., port of Southampton, bound for Cairo.

Cairo?

Her breath caught. "You are not letting me go?"

"Actually, I am—to Egypt." He chuckled. "All expenses paid for you and your maid. The ship sails in a week. Are you up for the challenge?"

Of all the ludicrous questions! Her jaw unhinged, quite unladylike but totally unstoppable. "I assure you, Mr. Moritz, it is no challenge whatsoever to write of veiled ladies with their turbaned sheikhs. In truth, sir, it is a particular dream of mine."

"As I well know." He stretched forward, peering at her from kindly grey eyes. "Which is why I put my neck on the chopping block for you. It took a fair amount of arm twisting with old man Krebe, yet I prevailed. Lucky for you, I am all muscle." He flexed his arm, pride lifting a thin bicep and his sharp chin.

"Oh, Mr. Moritz…" She clutched the tickets to her chest. "How can I ever thank you?"

"By saving the neck I risked and penning the most brilliant journal in the history of travel writing."

"Which is what I always aspire to." She tossed back her shoulders. "Don't worry, sir, I will not let you down."

"I should hope not. Or both our heads may yet roll." He tugged at his collar. "Krebe made that inordinately clear. And with that cheery thought, I bid you adieu. I imagine there is a certain amount of packing you will wish to be about." He clapped on his hat as he strode to the door. "No need to see me out, Miss Balfour. Good day."

Of course he was entirely wrong. It wasn't just a *good* day but a dazzling one. Magnificently auspicious. The sort of day she'd hoped and yearned for these past seven years. Finally—*finally!*—she'd been good enough for God to notice, to answer, to shed His grace and favour upon. She gazed up at the ceiling.

"Thank You," she whispered. "Your blessing means the world to me and I—"

Another rap of the door knocker ended her prayer. What had Mr. Moritz forgotten?

"Don't trouble yourself, miss," Betsey called from the corridor.

Before Amelia could tuck away the tickets, the maid ushered in a wisp of a man dressed in a blue coat so somber and dark it might as well have been black. "Miss Balfour, a Mr. Walton to see you." Introduction made, Betsey vanished out the door, apparently still on the hunt for the feather.

"Mr. Walton." Amelia curtseyed, all the while examining the man and the name, neither of which sparked any recognition.

"Miss Balfour." He nodded, his short stature giving her full view of a bald patch on the crown of his head. "I am here on behalf of your father. Perhaps you'd like to take a seat?"

Father? At once she sank onto the sofa, as if the man himself had issued the order. And if she listened hard enough, she could hear his commanding voice as distinctly as the day he'd sent her on her way with naught but a curt goodbye and the promise of a yearly stipend just to be rid of her.

She clutched the Cairo tickets all the tighter. "I trust all is well?"

Mr. Walton took the chair adjacent, his feet barely skimming the carpet, so short were his legs. Setting his brief-bag on his lap, he clicked open the lock, the report of it as sharp as the hammer of a pistol.

Amelia winced, as much from the sound as from the way his dark little eyes met hers. There was something foreboding in his gaze. Like a sinister shadow glimpsed from the corner of the eye and knowing in your gut that it was coming for you.

"I am afraid I bear upsetting news, Miss Balfour. Three weeks ago, your father suffered an apoplexy, one from which he did not recover. In short, I regret to inform you that Grafton Balfour is deceased and has since been buried in the family plot at Clifton."

The announcement made no sense. Father, that domineering force of nature whom no one dared cross, was gone? Just like that? Without a farewell. Without any amends. She drew in a ragged breath, trying not to crumple the tickets in her hand. "Why am I hearing of this now? Why was no word sent sooner?"

"My apologies for that. The letter my clerk drew up somehow got shuffled in with other papers and was never posted. It was only recently discovered as I was making my preparations to travel here."

She bit her lip, stopping an inappropriate smile, for the irony of the situation could not be denied. Father—that stoic man who insisted on precision at all costs—was likely rolling in his grave over the misplacement of his death announcement. Truly, she should be weeping for the loss of him, but though she might try, no tears could be forced.

Sweet heavens! Is this what she'd become—as callous towards him as he'd been to her and her brother?

Still, the information was so new. Grief would likely come calling in the dark of night when she least expected it. She met Mr. Walton's gaze. "This is very sudden. My father's health was never an issue, least-wise not that I was aware."

"Indeed, Miss Balfour. I worked with the man these past five years. Never a sniffle. Nary a cough. Though I suspect he felt this coming on."

"How so?"

He retrieved a folded paper. "The day before your father passed, I was summoned to Balfour House. He gave me this letter with the express directive that should anything happen to him, I was to personally deliver it to you. And so I am here. And so here you are." Mr. Walton held out the missive.

But Amelia didn't move, the temptation to live in blissful ignorance just a moment longer too strong to overcome. Her father had been domineering in life. Was he to be as officious in his death?

"Miss Balfour?"

Duty called. As it always had a way of doing, knocking, rapping, pounding on the door of her heart. There was nothing to be done for it, then. Father wrote the letter. She must read it.

She pulled the paper from Mr. Walton's fingers, folded open the page, and gazed at the recognizable bold lines of her father's pen.

> *Amelia,*
>
> *But a few grains of sand remain in the hourglass of my life. Would that I could turn the hateful thing over, for never are regrets more poignant than during one's last breaths. Yet I will not trouble you with the requisite pleas for mercy and forgiveness. You are not heaven's gatekeeper.*
>
> *Instead, I charge you with the guardianship of your brother, leastwise until the revolutionary surgery I have scheduled for him can be carried out. At such a point, you will be freed of all familial responsibilities if you so choose, for at last Colin will be able to face the world as his own man. I have arranged for him to arrive in Bristol by dark*

of night, June 8. My solicitor, Mr. Walton, will supply you
with the appropriate details and means for your travel to
Balfour House.

To avoid a case of too little, too late, I will not suffer
you with trite words of apology or endearment. But rest
assured, Amelia, that you have been, and I trust forever
will be, the most obedient of daughters a man could ask for.

As always, your father,
Grafton Balfour

Father? What a farce.

Obedient? As ever.

But guardianship of her brother? She bit her lip. She'd always feared this day would come.

Amelia stared at the note, a scream welling up from the depths of her little girl heart that had only ever wanted unconditional love. Everything shook. Her legs. The letter. The tickets to Cairo. In one hand she held her future. In the other, her past.

And between lay the present's ugly decision of who to disappoint—her editor, herself, or the man she'd called Father.

TWO

"I often worked harder than the common sailors during the day, and devoted my nights to the study of mathematics, the theory of medicine, and those branches of physical science from which a naval adventurer might derive the greatest practical advantage."

Bristol

Any dream worth pursuing required toil and hardship, but must it also entail the ruination of a perfectly good pair of trousers? Graham Lambert scowled at a gash in the fabric and slight sting on his calf. Pacing in the shadows had seemed like a good idea until he'd snagged against that cursed nail. He ought to have waited in one place. Stood still. Dash it! Must rash behaviour always be his downfall?

He anchored near the lamplight pouring out the window of the Llandoger Trow public house. Neither the steady stream of sailors from the nearby docks nor the actors exiting the Old Vic Theatre captured so much as a bat of his eye. Instead, he focused on a white-haired gentleman in a Paris beau hat who conversed with two other fellows until a gig was brought 'round. Whoever said women were long-winded harpies had clearly never suffered a half-hour parting from three men who'd spent the evening swapping tales inside a tavern.

At long last, several hearty goodbyes traveled on the night air, and the men parted ways. Graham pushed off the wall and closed in on the white-haired fellow paying off a stable hand for retrieving his gig. "Mr. Peckwood, a word, if you don't mind. I promise to be brief."

Uriah Peckwood, a prominent and—as some claimed—rather provocative surgeon, turned on his heel. His hat dipped low over a wide swath of forehead, his sharp blue eyes narrowing as he dissected Graham's face. In person, the intelligence of the man's gaze far outshone that of his image in quarterlies and journals. "Do I know you?"

Graham nodded. "Somewhat."

"I've never cared for cryptic conversation, sir. State your name. Make it plain."

"Graham Lambert, at your service." He dipped a bow.

"Lambert?" His name rolled off the surgeon's tongue like the tasting of a foreign sweetmeat—neither familiar nor entirely unpalatable. But then the man's dark eyes brightened, and he lifted a finger. "Ahh, yes. Graham Lambert. I know the name, for you see, I *never* forget names, yet I am unable to place your face."

"Through no fault of your own, sir. We have never formally met." Graham stepped closer to be heard above a particularly boisterous ditty leaching out the tavern's door. "I submitted a proposal for partnership several weeks back."

"That's right." Mr. Peckwood stroked his clean-shaven jawline. "Did you not receive my correspondence on the matter, Mr. Lambert?"

The mere mention of the letter was a fresh punch to the gut, but defeat was not an option he'd willingly embrace. A trait that had served him well over the years. Mostly. "I did receive your letter, this very afternoon, in fact. Hence my immediate need to speak with you. I tried your office, but—"

"My office is always closed on Thursdays."

"Yet it *could* be open, were you to take me on as your partner." Graham flexed his fingers then clenched them tight. Would the man welcome such boldness or scorn it as a sign of ill breeding? Peckwood's unwavering stare gave no clue to his reaction, which put Graham off balance. An unnerving sensation for a seasoned seaman.

"Mr. Lambert, I believe I was very clear in my letter that I am not interested in a partnership. And with that, I wish you well and bid you good night." He turned to his gig.

In one swift move, Graham sidestepped him and blocked his way. "Please, I simply ask that you hear me out before you drive off. That's all."

Peckwood turned, clearly annoyed, then heaved a great sigh. "Very well, Mr. Lambert. You have my ear."

Graham retreated a step. This was it. His final shot. The one that would either make or break him. It took every jot of willpower not to grab hold of the man's shoulders and impress upon him the importance of his acceptance.

"I am a diligent worker, Mr. Peckwood, a surgeon and an apothecary. Dependable to a fault. In my years as a naval surgeon, I learned to push past the usual physical limitations, developing innovations in technique and acquiring the skill to think quickly on my feet. I have seen diseases most have only read of in textbooks and am a practiced hand with injuries of any sort. Though you may look far and wide, you would be hard pressed to find another candidate as well qualified to work alongside you."

"Therein lies the heart of the matter." Peckwood shook his head. "I do not now, nor ever, wish to partner with anyone."

No surprise there. The man's letter had revealed as much. Graham clenched his jaw. If he could not persuade this visionary of medical thinking, there'd be no way to convince a more traditional surgeon to associate with him, and he'd be on his own. Without funding to furnish a full practice. Left with no choice but to roam about as a traveling healer, offering legitimate services to a distrusting public.

There was nothing for it then but to fire his biggest gun. Would that it might not misfire! He clenched the lapels of his coat. "Taking me on, sir, would free you up from your office commitments, and your work at St. Peter's would move forward at an exponential rate—a work we both know could change the field of medicine forever."

The older fellow gaped. "What the devil would you know about that?"

Graham swallowed. Exactly. What did he know other than that

he'd spied the man coming and going at odd hours from the warden's office at the asylum? Still, he'd not learned to bluff a hand of cards in the wardroom for nothing.

"Come now, sir." He patted Peckwood's arm. "You think I would so easily invest my life's savings to associate with a man I did not first research?"

Peckwood harrumphed. "You are canny, Mr. Lambert."

"I am determined, Mr. Peckwood."

"That is more than apparent." The man smiled, then sobered, his gaze locking onto Graham's. "But you should know I am a greater force with which to be reckoned. While your former captain highly recommends your work and your character, enough so that he was able to save you from the disgrace of a dishonourable discharge, it seems even his good word was not enough to thwart your administrative dismissal from His Majesty's Navy."

Air whooshed from Graham's lungs. Blast! The man had done his due diligence as well. Fighting the urge to tuck tail and retreat into the public house, he planted his feet. "I own my past sins, yet in the future I vow that no matter how righteous, my anger shall never best me again."

"I commend you for such an indomitable resolution." Peckwood sniffed, his long nose wrinkling. "Yet intention never negates risk."

"No man can claim to be risk-free, and if he does, he lies. I am no saint, Mr. Peckwood. I am a surgeon, highly skilled and ambitious, two traits which will serve you and the practice well."

"Your candor is refreshing." Peckwood eyed him with a sharp gaze, and Graham got the distinct impression the fellow examined and diagnosed every fault he could find, from the crooked knot in his cravat to the scuff on his left shoe.

"But I am curious, Mr. Lambert. There is a plethora of other surgeons in this wide world of ours. Why such dogged resolve to add your name to the shingle above my door?"

A fair question, one that Graham had given weeks of research to before deciding whose fate to entwine with his own. "It is no secret you are a visionary." He shrugged. "Your work with Sir Humphry Davy on the anesthetic properties of nitrous oxide is revolutionary. The article you wrote did not receive the recognition it should have, and I daresay if it had, even now the medical community would be pursuing a more humane way of conducting surgeries."

Peckwood's jaw dropped. "Are you an avid reader of obscurity, then?"

"I am an avid reader, period."

A great chuckle rumbled in Peckwood's throat. "So serious, Mr. Lambert. I wonder if your bedside manner is as grim."

"I am exemplary with patients, I assure you."

"Hmm," Peckwood drawled. "I suppose that will prove out."

Will prove? His heart faltered a beat. "Sir?"

For a long moment—one that could suck the soul right out of a body—Peckwood stared off into the night sky. As the man's silence prolonged, hoots and hollers rang from the public house. Tackle clinked and clanked on ships moored for the night. All the while, hope and trepidation rocked Graham's gut like contrary waves battering either side of a vessel.

"Well, Mr. Lambert," Peckwood said at length, "being that you come with the highest of praise from your captain and, I suspect, will continue to hound me should I refuse your proposition, I agree to a three-month probationary period, at which point either I shall take you on as a full partner or send you on your way and pocket your deposit. But know this…"

A different man looked out from Peckwood's eyes. Nay, a demon. One that crawled under Graham's skin and burned a trail down his spine.

"There is a reason I have never had a partner, for I am a particularly private man. My personal life and my current medical research at St. Peter's have no part in our agreement and are off-limits to your inquiry. Is that quite understood?"

"Without question." And without hesitation. If Peckwood were occupied in his own pursuits, there'd be less chance he'd muddle about in Graham's. "Besides, I imagine I will be more than busy with office calls and home visits."

"Ha ha! Not to mention manning the surgery on your own each Thursday. I suppose with you about, it will free me up to pursue investors for a certain procedure I am developing."

Graham shoved out his hand before the fellow could change his mind. "Will you shake on it, then?"

Peckwood gazed at his fingers, mind clearly whirring, before finally clasping his hand. "See you tomorrow morning at eight sharp, Mr. Lambert, at which point we shall iron smooth the financial and other details. Good night."

Bypassing Graham, the older surgeon hefted himself up into his gig.

Graham tipped his head at him. "Good night, sir."

He stared down the road long after the carriage departed, unused to the suddenly buoyant feeling in his gut. He hadn't felt this light since the day he'd left home as a lad of fifteen. But this time, it was a legitimate joy. A decision he'd not carry around like the ball and chain he already wore—one that tethered him to a weighty regret.

THREE

"I had often, when at home, thought it hard to remain during my youth cooped up in one place, and had longed to enter the world, and take my station among other human beings."

⌒

Clifton, a suburb of Bristol

If houses had souls, this one was clearly bound for Hades. Amelia hesitated on the carriage step and frowned up at her childhood home. Early evening shadows added to the dreariness of the soot-darkened yellow brick, and the more her gaze roamed from foundation to soffit, the more her brow scrunched. The whole facade of Balfour House needed a good scrub down. As did the windows. Rows of mullioned glass stared at her with dull, empty eyes. Black. Devoid of life. Not a particularly warm homecoming after twenty years. This close to twilight, why were no lamps lit? Surely Mrs. Kirwin had received the correspondence detailing her arrival.

Then again, a letter was no guarantee the old housekeeper would remember even had she read it. A dear woman. An industrious labourer. But the sort who sometimes forgot what she was doing while in the midst of doing so.

Amelia descended to the pavement, followed by Betsey, when a queer prickling spidered along her spine. Securing her bonnet with a firm grip, she whirled, only to find the street behind her empty in the waning daylight. Strange. She would've sworn to a magistrate that someone stood at her back, eyeing her with a ferocious scrutiny.

No doubt fatigue from the long journey plagued her. She dropped her hand. Though the London to Bristol mail coach had made good time, such a cross-country trip taxed even a seasoned traveler such as herself. Add to that the recent sleepless nights, during which a surprisingly recurrent grief for her father hit in waves, and it was no wonder she imagined things.

She started to turn back to Betsey when the odd sensation tingled afresh. This time she snapped her gaze upwards. And there. Behind the first-story window of the neighbouring house, a drapery swung unsettled, as if suddenly set free. Amelia pursed her lips. Clearly someone took an interest in her arrival. Hopefully that someone was not Mrs. Ophidian. But no. After all these years, the old woman must surely be at rest in St. Andrew's graveyard. Immediately, Amelia drew a cross over her heart in reverence of the dead.

"—to your chamber. Miss?"

The tail end of Betsey's words wagged against her ear. Snubbing the neighbour's window, she faced her maid instead. "Pardon?"

Betsey narrowed her eyes, probably searching for the cause of such blatant woolgathering. "I said I shall oversee the unloading and have your things brought directly up to your chamber. Mayhap a hardy cup o' tea will set you to rights after such a bone-rattling ride. I'll be along shortly thereafter, if you please?"

"Yes, thank you." Amelia dashed up the few steps to the front door, giving no quarter for any further examination from Betsey. She reached for the knocker just as the door swung open to a mobcapped, pale-eyed spectre from her past.

"Oh, my stars! Can it be?" Mrs. Kirwin slapped a hand to her chest. "Let's have us a good look, now, shall we? Why, it's my little Miss Amelia all grown up. And the very image of your saintly mother, no less. Come in. Come in, child!" She stepped aside, fingers fluttering. "Mercy! I'm giddy as my Great-Aunt Gusta. I have so longed for this house to be a home again, like when your dear mother graced these halls. And now with you and Master Colin returning, why…I'm certain these walls will once more ring with laughter."

Though she very much doubted that, Amelia smiled at the old housekeeper as she entered. She had no idea what she'd face when she met her brother at the docks tomorrow night, for she hadn't seen Colin these past seven years. What sort of man had he grown into?

"Thank you, Mrs. Kirwin." She handed over her hat, already thinking ahead. If she could schedule Colin's procedure for early next week, she just might make it onto the next ship to Cairo. "As lovely as it is to see you, I feel it fair to inform you I will be staying only for the duration of my brother's surgery and recuperation, which hopefully won't be too long."

"I'll take you both for as long as possible and be glad for it. This is a dream come true, all these dear people and, well, bonnets, even!" She waved Amelia's hat in the air, a big grin adding creases to her lined face. "When your father—God rest him—was in town, he were out till all hours and then off in the morn with naught but a sip of coffee. Oh! Fiddle-faddle! That reminds me."

Hiking her skirts, the housekeeper dashed past Amelia, bonnet bobbing against her thigh. Did she even realize she yet held it? "I've forgotten to instruct Cook on breakfast for the morn," she called over her shoulder. "Your room's been aired, miss, and…"

The woman's voice faded as she disappeared down the corridor. Amelia couldn't help but smile while she pushed shut the front door Mrs. Kirwin had neglected to close. The old servant was exactly as Amelia remembered her.

But the house wasn't. She unbuttoned her spencer as she wandered first into the sitting room then to the dining room. Though this was by no means a small residence and was certainly larger than many could afford, neither were the rooms as cavernous as she recalled. She ran her finger along the waxed mahogany table where, as a child, she'd never been allowed to eat. Things could not help but be different all these years later.

No domineering father.

No mother lying dead in her bed.

A brother, now a man, whose face caused children to scream.

She snatched back her hand. Enough with the morose. A mischievous quirk twitched her lips, and she scurried down the back passage and out the door into the jungle. The rainforest. The outlying reaches of Northern Mongolia. Or anything else her seven-year-old mind imagined while listening on the top stairs whenever Father and Mother entertained. And, surprisingly, the back garden was still all those things, minus the frigid clime of the Mongols, of course.

Picking past ankle-high horseweed and overgrown ivy, she hurried to the iron trellis near the rear wall, her favourite place in all the world. Unmindful of her gown and the damp soil, she dropped to her knees and peered into the space hidden by a screen of clematis with glossy green leaves. She couldn't fit into her hidey-hole anymore, but that didn't stop her from closing her eyes and breathing deeply of dirt and moss and memories. How many times had she squirreled away here, dreaming of voyages to the farthest reaches of the earth? Sailing on uncharted seas and journaling about species undiscovered or foreign races no white man had ever seen. Even at such a tender age, she'd known she was never meant for a life of smothering convention.

The overhead churring of a nightjar popped her eyes open, and she sighed. So much for wandering the wide, wide world. For now, anyway.

With her sight acclimated to the growing darkness, a patch of red caught her gaze on the ground between trellis and wall. What was this? She pulled out a wooden ball covered in chipped paint and frowned at the child's toy. She'd never owned one, and Colin had been far too young for such a plaything when they'd quitted the house all those years ago for the country.

Rising, she brushed the creases and stray soil from her skirt as she surveyed the area. The wall behind and the one to the south were both in good repair, too high for a small child to scale. The back gate appeared sound and properly locked. Pivoting, she faced the north wall.

Aha.

Ball in hand, she strolled to a crumbled pile of rock, then peered over the jagged edge of the broken barrier into the neighbour's yard. A pretty bench sat beneath the branches of a Spanish chestnut, surrounded by manicured lawn and a border of blushing pink peonies. A child could have climbed the breach or even tossed the ball over the wall with a wild throw, but judging by the state of the pristine garden, no children lived there. She gazed up at the windows. Did anyone? It was dark as a tomb—as were the gathering shadows. She could explore more tomorrow.

Tossing the ball from hand to hand, she worked her way to the house. Just the thought of a soft bed loosened the tightness in her shoulders. But first, a nice cup of chamomile.

Inside, she barely made it past the dining room when Betsey plowed down the corridor, her steel-grey skirts swooshing in time with her heavy steps. "What's that?" She nodded at Amelia's hand.

"Nothing of consequence." Amelia held out the toy on one palm. "Some child must've lost his ball. I found it next to the trellis. Perhaps you could give this to Mrs. Kirwin and she'll know whose it is."

"She might know and have plenty to say about it, but will she remember to return it? Granted, I scarcely know the woman, but she strikes me as a bit fluffy in the attic." Betsey's fingers closed around the plaything.

"Hardly here a quarter of an hour and already you've pegged her like a sheet on a drying line." Amelia grinned. "So, are we unloaded, then?"

"We are. And I've got the maid filling a bath for you. Scrawny little thing. Might take her awhile." One grey brow arched. "I may give her a hand. Meantime, you can enjoy your flowers in the sitting room."

She angled her head. "Flowers?"

"Just arrived." Betsey headed for the stairs.

Odd. No one could possibly know she was arriving today…unless Mrs. Kirwin had unthinkingly babbled the news while in town. But no, the old housekeeper hardly ever left the house.

"From whom?" Amelia called up the staircase.

"Far be it from me to poke about for a card." Betsey winked over her shoulder then rounded the landing and ascended the next level of steps.

Amelia's mouth twisted awry. Hah! Either she knew and wasn't saying, or there'd been a wax seal, for her maid owned an insatiable appetite for intrigue. A boon while traveling in a foreign land and writing of the experience. But here? Her lips flattened. Time would tell, especially once Colin arrived.

By now, Mrs. Kirwin had lit the lamps, and the sitting room glowed a warm welcome. On a pedestal near the window, green fronds and bloodred roses filled a crystal vase. Amelia inhaled the sweet fragrance, then looked about for a note. Nothing on the stand. Nothing on the silver salver near the tea table either. She spun in a circle on the off chance the housekeeper had mislaid the card, but from mantel to shelves in the corner, there was no sign of a handwritten sentiment.

Amelia returned to the flowers, a fresh wave of unease creeping up her backbone. Who had sent such a beautiful bouquet? And were they for her?

Or her brother?

FOUR

"Oh! No mortal could support the horror of that countenance.
A mummy again endued with animation
could not be so hideous as that wretch."

⟳

Darkness. Thunder. Ironically apropos. Colin Balfour smirked up at the cabin timbers.

Truly, God? A bit dramatic, is it not?

Outside the porthole, a flash of lightning lit the night, and Colin snagged his cape off a peg. If his sister didn't arrive before that storm hit, they'd both be drenched. It would save time if he waited at the end of the wharf instead of remaining holed up in the ship, but such a public move was a risky venture, even at midnight. Despite the hour, in a city the size of Bristol, there was sure to be an unsuspecting man or woman about. Scads! But he was weary of this.

How much longer, Lord? Have I not borne enough screams? Abided enough horror? Am I never to know peace this side of death?

A sharp knock rattled the door just before another thunderous boom shook the hull. "The carriage is here, Mr. Balfour."

He crossed the cabin in three strides and spoke against the wood. "Thank you."

Straining his ear, he waited for the footsteps to disappear and, for a long moment, listened for any breath or other sign of life. His hand fell to the knob. Was he ready for this? Precautions or not, even the best stitched plans sometimes had a way of fraying into threads—a wretched truth he'd learned when most lads knew only of catching toads and skipping rocks. But it was too late to back out now. Father had made sure of that, with a will that even from the grave would not be thwarted.

Colin flipped up his hood before stepping into the narrow passageway. The width of his shoulders scraped against each side. Though most of the crew had long ago fled ashore for women and rum, he still shunned the lanterns hanging at intervals, turning his face from the light—an old habit that would not die.

He ascended the steep steps, lungs growing heavier with each rung gained. Though he ought to be used to it by now, hefting a giant's torso was no small feat, especially when each passing year increased the load. Would that he could simply spend the rest of his days in the effortless solitude of the Devonshire family manor. He'd not been able to convince Father of such, but Amelia? Perhaps he could persuade her that this was a waste of time. She could go her way, and he, his.

Hoping for just such an end, he drew in a deep breath of damp air as he cleared the final step.

Lightning cut across the sky, followed almost immediately by a loud bang. The metallic taste of it zinged his tongue. No rain yet, but a torrent lurked like a beast in the shadows, just waiting to spring.

Three paces from the gangplank, footsteps approached. "Carry your bag, Mr. Balfour?"

Before he could flee to the dock, wind gusted. His hood flew back. A most inopportune time for the next flash of electric white to paint the world in stark relief.

The sailor's scream was brassier than the approaching tempest. "Lawks a-mercy! A bleedin' monster!" With a flail of hands and no doubt trousers freshly soiled, the man tore off in the opposite direction.

Colin huffed as he yanked up his hood. The sailor's words were nothing but air and vibrato. He'd heard them all and more. What annoyed most was the flare of the man's nostrils. The terror widening his eyes to an unnatural proportion. And worse, the accompanying gape of maw and twisted mien. Gripping his travel bag with whitened knuckles, he stormed down the gangplank, the thick board threatening to break with each step. Man's inability to see past fault never failed to irritate him—which irritated him even more. He should be used to this by now.

He strode along the darkened wharf towards the twin lights of a carriage and the silhouette of a gown standing beside it. The closer he drew, the greater the snarl of emotions knotting in his gut. Disappointment. Sympathy. Longing. Love. How many years had it been? Six? Nay. Seven. He'd been on the cusp of manhood the day he'd last embraced his sister, the only one save God with whom he'd ever bared his soul.

Grabbing handfuls of her skirts, she scurried towards him. "Colin?"

Another blaze of lightning lit the night. Dark eyes. Pixie nose. Red lips and the strong Balfour jawline. Yet more than that. Time had been overly gracious, softening what had been angular lines to feminine curves. This woman was *his* sister? They were yin and yang. Beauty and beast. Why in all of God's green earth had no man laid claim to her?

"Yes, Amelia. It is I, at long last." He hesitated a moment, then set down his bag and opened wide his arms. It was a gamble, this vulnerability. One that could sting. Would she consent to the touch of an ogre as she had all those years ago?

A garbled cry came out throaty, and she flung herself into his embrace, nestling her face against his waistcoat. The intensity of her reaction caught him off guard. If she'd missed him this much, then why the sporadic and ofttimes absent correspondence?

She nestled all the closer with the next outrageously loud peal of thunder, and he wrapped his arms tighter, protecting her from the sound. She was naught but a twig against his ungainly trunk as he rubbed one big hand along her back. What a change of roles, when as a child she'd been the one to comfort him during storms. Ahh, but it was good to love and be loved, a balm to his soul, healing wounds that he'd not realized still bled.

After a last shuddering breath, she dabbed her eyes with her sleeve. "Thank you. I don't deserve such a warm welcome."

Remorse? Apparently there had been more behind the scarcity of her letters than a lack of love for himself. Though he knew the effect to be hideous, he couldn't stop a huge grin and sank all the farther inside his hood to prevent her from seeing it.

"We are family, are we not?" He picked up his bag. "Though I didn't like it, I understood your need to be away from Father. God knows I'd have left if I could."

"I have missed you, Brother, more than you can possibly know." She stepped closer as the next white zigzag cut the sky. "Let me have a look at you, then."

No. Immediately no!

He bit back the words and turned away. He could barely keep from shuddering any time he chanced a look in a mirror.

"Time for that later," he explained—though even to his own ears it sounded false. "A storm brews, and I would not have you catch your death." There. That was better.

Yet a surprisingly strong grip pinched his arm. "Don't forget I out-rank you seven years, three months, and a day. I will not be moved until I assure myself the brother I love stands before me."

He clenched his jaw, stopping a profanity he'd heard aboard ship. Stubborn woman! The Balfour curse.

After a glance to be sure no one else could see, he pulled back his hood. "Satisfied?" The question flew out harsh and bitter.

"Oh, Colin." Rising to tiptoes, she cupped his cheek, her fingers barely spanning the curve. Nothing but love burned in her gaze. "You are all grown now, the handsome man I've kept in my heart suddenly come to life."

He snorted. "Liar."

"Well, I am a writer, after all." She withdrew, mischief quirking her lips.

"And about to be a very wet one. Shall we?" He swept his hand towards the carriage.

She dashed to the coach and pulled herself up, then paused on the stair. "Oh, I forgot to say—"

Thunder cracked.

The horses spooked.

Amelia's body jerked and, though she flailed for balance, she tumbled to the ground, skirts splaying—where the turn of the wheels would easily crush her leg.

Graham loved it best when night brooded stormy at the midnight hour. There was something wild about the twangy scent and bass rumbles that crawled inside the bones. He leaned over the harbour-side wall, filling his lungs with the approaching squall. Filling his soul. Some of his best—and few—moments of glory on the sea had been during such evenings as this, when the greatness of the One who ruled the heavens raised a mighty arm and revealed His strength.

A pity He didn't always do so.

Raking his hand through his hair, he briefly lamented that he'd forgotten his hat at Peckwood's surgery. But no wonder. Fatigue hung on his frame like a sodden wool blanket; he was lucky he'd thought to grab his coat. Now he knew exactly why Peckwood absented himself every Thursday. It was the busiest shipping day of the week, pouring a glut of sailors into Bristol who required care that ship surgeons had either neglected or hadn't the knowledge to tend. Owners were notoriously lax in hiring skilled onboard doctors. The more proficient, the higher the wages—and the less profit. Peckwood ought to have cautioned him, but the man had been curiously absent since the day they'd come to terms. Were Graham a wagering man, he'd bet ten guineas the surgeon was engrossed in his research at the asylum. He'd see him tomorrow though, when they attended a patient together—which was a strange change of Peckwood's habits. Was the doctor hoping to pawn him off on some peevish old rheumatic?

He shoved away from the wall just as a ragged shout not far down the road snagged his attention.

"Amelia!"

Graham squinted to where a great hulk of a silhouette pulled a body from beneath a carriage, barely a second before the horses bolted. A woman's cry rent the night. He broke into a dead run.

"I'm a doctor," he called. "I can help."

The man—nay, a giant—cradled a woman in his arms, her face pale against the wicked darkness and all-consuming black of the man's cape.

"No!" she gasped. Her eyes were overlarge, a sure sign of distress that belied her refusal. "I require no help."

"The strain in your voice says otherwise." Graham stepped closer, and immediately the man retreated with her deeper into the shadows. A curiosity, that. Why was he afraid—a man who bested him by at least six stone and stood a full foot taller?

Another peal of thunder boomed, and the woman clutched a handful of the fellow's cape. "Please, leave us. I am perfectly fine in my brother's care."

"Oh?" Graham peered up at the monstrous man, whose cavernous hood fully hid his face even in the next flare of lightning. "Are you a surgeon? Or physician, perhaps?"

"I am neither." His voice was as deep as the din of the oncoming storm.

"I do not need a doctor." The woman twisted in the man's arms, craning her neck past his shoulder. "Look, our carriage returns to carry us home, where the wonders of a good night's sleep will render me whole."

"So you admit to being hurt." Once again Graham edged closer, as he might to a skittish mare. "Where? What pains you?"

The first fat drops of rain splatted loud and wet as the carriage stopped behind them. The woman looked up at her brother. "Colin, please. This is too much of a risk and you know it."

Risk? Him? Graham stifled a snort. A man that size could squash him beneath his heel and not even realize he'd snuffed out a life. "Sir, madam, you have nothing to fear. I assure you I am well trained and qualified as a naval surgeon."

A gust of wind blew in off the harbour, rippling the man's hood as he gazed down at his sister. "Are you certain? I would not have you suffer on my account."

"We shall all suffer if we do not seek shelter." Her dark eyes turned to Graham. "Good night, Doctor."

"But—"

The man wheeled about, the tails of his cape flapping like the wings of a freakishly large bat. The carriage listed heavily to the side as he stepped up, his sister grunting in pain, and deposited her on the seat. Graham watched, perplexed. Clearly the man cared about her, so why such a stubborn refusal to have her examined by a medical professional? What did the fellow have to fear? Was there any more he could have possibly done to put their minds at ease and aid the woman as she so obviously needed?

The big man reappeared, snatched his bag from the ground, then called for the driver to make haste. The sky opened the second the whip cracked, and the carriage lurched into motion, disappearing into the dark of the rainy night.

By the time Graham trotted to his small apartment on Flagg Street, there was not a mite of him that didn't drip or chafe. He peeled off his wet garments piece by piece, then settled into a nightshirt. Sinking onto the thin mattress, he reached for a worn copy of *The London Medical and Physical Journal*, too overtired to sleep. Not that reading this would do any good. He'd already memorized it word for word. He needn't even crack open the cover.

Blowing out a long breath, he returned it to the stand then leaned back, lacing his hands behind his head. What a strange day. What a strange life.

Unbidden, his gaze strayed to the small bookshelf on the opposite wall, its sole occupant a Bible, worn, torn, and far too long unread. His mother's. A gift he didn't deserve, sent along with a message written inside the cover just before her demise. He could read that. He *should* read that. But he turned aside his head and blew out the candle.

He'd been no more able to help his own mother than he had the woman tonight.

FIVE

*"She looked steadily on life, and assumed
its duties with courage and zeal."*

"This is a bad idea."

Amelia hid a smirk at her maid's judgment and clutched all the tighter to Betsey's shoulder as they hobbled out of her room and down the corridor. "So was that second helping of *vetrnik* when we were in Prague last spring, but I don't recall you raising a fuss then."

"Pastries are one thing, your well-being quite another. You aren't even able to put on your shoe." The bend of her maid's brow indicted as much as the hot pain in Amelia's foot.

She pressed her mouth shut. There was nothing to argue about. Betsey was right. Two of the toes on her right foot were purple, and a bruise spread over the top. The swelling was too large to accommodate anything but a stocking. An excruciating setback, for she was determined to make that next ship to Cairo in a week, but in spite of it all, a certain amount of gratitude welled in her heart. Thanks to God—and Colin—she'd suffered naught but some crushed toes. It could have been much worse.

At the top of the stairway, Betsey pinned her in place with a stern eye. "I should think if you're not fit enough to go down to breakfast, you're not fit to go down at all."

Hiding a grimace took all of Amelia's concentration, but crippled or not, she must go. She would not endanger her father's final wish no matter what it cost. Besides, as the eldest—and only other—Balfour, it was her duty to see that Colin's surgery was arranged and performed, and she would do so with head held high. Now, if she could just make it to a chair in the sitting room before the surgeon arrived, no one would be the wiser of her injury, and then she'd prop up her foot for the rest of the day.

With her free hand, she patted her pocket to make sure the Ibis feather hadn't dislodged in all her gimping about, then tipped her chin at Betsey. "Are you going to help me, or shall I hop about like a lame rabbit? For with or without you, I will attend the meeting with my brother and the surgeon. So what is it to be?"

Heaving a sigh, Betsey shored up Amelia as they limp-stepped from stair to stair. "You're the one who needs a surgeon," she muttered under her breath.

"Grumbling about the matter will not change my mind."

"Pah!" Betsey snorted. "There's no denying that. You do know your own mind, miss."

Amelia cocked a brow at her. "As do you."

"Well," Betsey chuckled as she maneuvered them off the final step, "we are quite the pair, are we not?"

A terse truth—yet Amelia would have it no other way. Working as a lady's maid for an independent travel writer was not for the faint of heart, which was why she'd hired the stalwart woman to begin with. Still, even iron-boned Betsey might wither when she laid eyes on Colin.

As they neared the sitting room door, Amelia lowered her voice. "I should tell you that my brother—he…" What to say? He's a monster? A freak of nature? That perhaps she ought to leave off here and let Amelia hobble in alone?

Betsey glanced at her sidelong, a no-nonsense twist to her lips.

Amelia searched for the right words, carefully gathering them as she might a bouquet of posies. "There is a reason for my brother's upcoming surgery that I've not yet told you. He suffers from a disease that causes uncontrollable and abnormal growth. He is misshapen, overlarge, and to make matters worse, he suffered a horrible burn to the face and upper chest as a young boy. In short, he is hard on the eye, abysmally so, but if you can look past that, a kinder soul you will never meet."

Deep creases carved into the sides of Betsey's mouth. "I am no wilting flower, miss."

"No, you are not. I only thought it fair to prepare you for what you are about to see."

Yet even with her warning, the second they entered the sitting room and Colin turned from the hearth, Betsey stopped dead in her tracks. Not that Amelia blamed her. Seeing his shocking visage last evening in the dark of night had been bad enough, but with sunshine streaming in the side windows, her brother's malformation was revealed to be far more advanced than she'd credited. Amelia's heart squeezed.

Oh, my brother. Would to God the world could see you as I do, could know the tender heart that lives inside such a hideous ruin.

But no one could look past the ape-like face with the impossibly large forehead. His lower jaw was grotesquely enormous, and one of his cheeks was offset from the other, as if bludgeoned by the flat side of a hatchet. Rippled skin pulled tight on the left half of his skull, from temple to nose and on down past his neck. His arms hung long, sporting hands the size of mutton chops, and he stood a full seven feet tall on shoes that had to be specially cobbled. The longer she studied him, the more tears burned Amelia's eyes. There was not a mortal on this planet who wouldn't be shocked.

Yet she loved him fiercely, and she couldn't help but smile. "Good morning, Brother."

"Not for long." He shot a pointed glance at the mantel clock, where the hands closed in on noon. "I was beginning to wonder if you were to join me at all."

"Nothing could keep me from this meeting." She pulled away from Betsey, but when a white-hot flash of pain shot from foot to thigh, she clutched her maid's shoulder all the tighter.

Colin frowned. "You should sit before you fall. Shall I help you?"

"No need." She nodded towards a chair. "Over there, Betsey."

Her jaw nearly cracked from the strain of keeping in a scream as she limp-hopped over to the chair. Ahh, but it was heaven when she sank into that cloud and Betsey gently rested her foot on a cushioned stool.

Keeping her distance from Colin, Betsey looked at her alone. "Will that be all, miss?"

A disappointing response from the normally unshakeable maid, but undeniably reasonable. "Yes, thank you."

With her back to the door, Amelia could not watch her retreat, but Colin's eyes did. "Quite the brave woman," he murmured. "When Mrs. Kirwin saw me in the breakfast room, she broke into tears, and the poor little maid fainted straightaway after opening my drapes this morn."

"Oh, Colin." Sorrow panged sharp in her chest. The raging pain in her foot was nothing compared to the rejection and horror her brother faced on a daily basis. "Soon enough you will no longer have that effect on others. In fact, the sooner, the better. We shall have your surgery scheduled immediately, hopefully tomorrow, and by the end of next week, this will all be behind us."

"About that…" In two long strides, he crouched at her side. "I know it was Father's wish for this procedure, but I—"

"The surgeons Mr. Peckwood and Mr. Lambert are here to see you, Miss Amelia, Master Colin." Mrs. Kirwin's voice entered the room, along with the thud of heavier footsteps.

Two doctors? Why would that be necessary for a simple scheduling meeting? Amelia angled her head, but the tall and wide chair back prevented so much as a glance over her shoulder.

Colin rose. "Gentlemen, do come in. I am pleased to make your acquaintance."

Gripping the chair arms, she eased her wounded foot off the footstool, intending to meet head-on the men who held Colin's fate, but her brother shook his head at her.

"You will forgive my sister for not rising, sirs. She is momentarily incapacitated. Please, sit down." He skimmed his fingers towards the adjacent settee.

Though it pained her, Amelia refused to prop up her foot in the presence of these strangers. To remain sitting was breach of etiquette enough.

Yet she needn't have given that a second thought. The white-haired man who strolled into her circle of vision took no note of her whatsoever.

"Oh, my…" he murmured as he orbited Colin. "Simply magnificent!"

Magnificent? Amelia's brows shot skyward. How unusual. Then again, the fellow dissecting Colin was decidedly unusual himself. The doctor was of compact build, soft in the face and white of hair, like a great pile of cotton batting heaped upon a warehouse floor. A peculiar scent wafted from him, a mix of peppermint and ammonia. Sapphire eyes sat wide atop a nose with an alpine slope, and he wore his cravat tied tight to his chin, as if any sort of loosening might cause his head to tumble off.

He circled again, analyzing Colin with continued mumblings, not once glancing in her direction. No surprise though, really. Her brother was far more remarkable. She was as common as a door latch, or so she'd been told many times by her father. He'd never thought her marriage-able material—a blessing to her career, but her self-regard? Hardly.

Colin endured the doctor's perusal with his usual grace, allowing the fellow to get his fill, which apparently he gained upon completion of his third round. "I am pleased to meet you at long last, Mr. Balfour. I must say you are even more marvelous than your father described in his correspondence. Oh! Dear me. What a boor."

He pivoted her way so fast, his shoulder-length hair flew about his ears like a cloud of dandelion fluff. "I am afraid it is I who must beg your pardon, Miss Balfour, so rudely have I ignored you, especially after your brother clearly stated you suffer from some sort of malady. Tell me, dear lady, is there anything I can do for you that may correct your incapacitation?"

No. Absolutely not. The more time spent fussing about with her, the further put off was Colin's procedure—and the less chance she'd have of making that ship to Cairo. She smiled up at the doctor as if the blazing fire in her foot didn't exist. "No need, Mr. Peckwood. I suffer nothing but a trifle. Let us speak only of my brother's upcoming surgery."

"As you wish." He dipped a small bow. "Then allow me to introduce my newly acquired partner, Mr. Lambert, recently of His Majesty's Naval Service."

A tall man—though still thoroughly dwarfed by Colin—strode forward. "Mr. Balfour. Miss…" His eyes widened as he locked gazes with her. "You!"

Him?

Amelia bit her lip to keep her jaw from dropping. The man from the dock last night—the one who'd not been so easily put off.

Casting aside any modicum of propriety, he immediately crouched at her side. "I knew you were injured, and this time I will not take no for an answer. If I do not miss my mark, your foot grieves you. Am I correct, Miss Balfour?"

Hazel eyes stared into her own, more brown than green at the moment, yet she got the distinct impression they could change at will, for such was the determination in his commanding tone. He was not handsome per se, not in a worldly sense. Nothing about him smacked of style or refinement. Yet he was not altogether unpleasing to the eye and, in truth, was attractive in an earthy sort of way. Decidedly masculine, with his defined brow, thick, wide lips, a slightly crooked nose, and a trimmed beard. Obviously, the doctor cared nothing for convention, for most Englishmen would wear only long side-whiskers, not a full face of dark bristles. He could do with a good haircut as well, for untamed locks hung loose against his neck.

Botheration! What a rabbit trail. Why and how Mr. Lambert chose to present himself to the world was none of her business. She straightened her spine, taking care not to jostle her leg. "My toes are bruised, sir. Nothing more. And since I will not consent to a leeching, there is no need to speak further on the matter. Besides, we are gathered here to discuss my brother."

Colin frowned down at her. "Even so, Amelia, it would put my mind at ease if you would let the doctor render his opinion. It is all I ask."

"And you may put *your* mind at ease, Miss Balfour, for I don't happen to have any leeches with me at the moment." Mr. Lambert winked at her.

Winked!

She sucked in a breath. How astoundingly brazen of the fellow.

What sort of shameless man was this Mr. Lambert? Were all of them? Surely they didn't expect her to take off her stocking here in front of God and man.

She shook her head. "I hardly think this is the place to—"

"We are medical men, Miss Balfour, and he is family." Mr. Lambert tipped his head at Colin. "There is no indiscretion, only concern for your well-being."

Her gaze drifted from one man to another, all three unwavering in their resolve. She slid her hand to the feather in her pocket, expecting the thing to have vanished. But no. What kind of luck was this? Her familiar talisman was still there yet, surprisingly, no help whatsoever.

"Very well," she huffed. "Examine me if you will, but please do not allow this to detract from the scheduling of my brother's procedure. That is, after all, why we are here."

Mr. Lambert's dark eyebrows lifted skyward, and though the expression ought not rankle her, it did. She knew that look. She'd seen it too many times. The man thought her too forward. Too independent and outspoken. The very reason no man would take her as a bride. But so be it.

Her duty was to Colin alone.

⁂

Of all the pluck! Miss Balfour's resolve was as extraordinary as her brother's abnormal physiognomy.

Graham stared unabashed at the sprite in the chair as she gingerly rolled off her stocking, taking great care to keep her leg hidden. What an odd mix of propriety and bullheaded determination, one he wasn't quite sure he ought to admire. For certain, she was no sheepish miss. In fact, the raven-haired Miss Balfour was as disconcerting in daylight as she had been the previous night.

But this time he would help her whether she liked it or not, which clearly she didn't, if the pucker of her lips were any indication.

At length, she perched her bare foot on the stool. "You may proceed, Mr. Lambert." Then, apparently done with him, she peered up at Peckwood. "It was my father's last wish and is of the utmost importance that my brother undergo your procedure as soon as possible. Does tomorrow suit?"

Plucky indeed. He hid a smile.

"Amelia!"

Graham carefully inspected her bruised toes. Breath hissed through her teeth. From his touch or the reprimand in her brother's tone?

"Mr. Peckwood is not one of your baggage handlers to be ordered about," the big man grumbled. "Once again, Doctor, you must pardon my sister."

"No need." Peckwood chuckled. "She merely asked a question. An inquisitive mind is never to be condemned."

Graham peeked at Miss Balfour's face, but no hint of embarrassment pinked her cheeks. Her big brown eyes merely held steady upon the men in front of her, though there was no denying the glassy sheen to her gaze. Nor did he miss the perspiration glistening on her fair skin or the white knuckles gripping the chair arms. His methodical prodding clearly hurt, yet not a whimper escaped her lips. He'd seen yeomen squeal for lesser grievances.

Satisfied with his prognosis, he gently eased her injured toes to the stool. "You are lucky, Miss Balfour, that your entire foot didn't break, or worse, considering the weight of that carriage. You could have been permanently maimed. I did not detect any broken bones, but that does not necessarily rule out some small fractures, especially judging by the amount of bruising and swelling. You'll lose several toenails, I'm afraid, but after a week or two of immobility by elevation and padded wraps, you should see vast improvement."

"But that is impossible." Her doe eyes blinked, completely dumbfounded. "I cannot remain stationary for such a length of time."

"Oh? Have you some pressing matters to attend?"

"Yes, I—I mean, Colin will need me." Her lips flattened, and then she did blush in full, perfectly pink and stunningly becoming against her previous pallor. Bending, she hastily worked on her stocking, jaw clenched tight.

Interesting. Graham narrowed his eyes, studying her movements.

Was she concealing something more than a throbbing foot?

"Mr. Peckwood." Colin Balfour's deep voice drew Graham's attention from sister to brother. The man massaged the back of his neck with a meat hook of a hand, clearly agitated. "I have a few questions before agreeing to the surgery."

Miss Balfour sat ramrod straight. "But, Colin, you know Father wished—"

Her brother held up his hand, staving her off, and faced Peckwood. "What is it that you intend to do?"

Graham looked from sister to brother. Were they not in agreement on the matter?

"In layman's terms, Mr. Balfour, I shall set up Mr. Lambert here"—he tipped his head at Graham—"with equipment to administer a series of treatments to prepare your mind and body for what will be an innovative and, I daresay, historic operation. Afterwards, I fully expect your deviant growth not only to stop but to be reversed. You and generations following will own the hope of a perfectly normal life."

Mr. Balfour frowned, the crevices on his face folding into deep crags. Quite the ghoulish effect.

"Pardon, but how exactly is that to be accomplished?" Concern sharpened Miss Balfour's tone.

Graham rose from his crouch, eyeing the man. Naturally, excess skin could be removed. Some straightening of bones accomplished. Perhaps there could even be minimal success with the right ointments and salves to relax the rippling on half of his face. But Peckwood expected this man to live a normal life by shrinking him to a standard size? How could he possibly achieve that?

"If you wouldn't mind taking a seat, Mr. Balfour." Peckwood strolled to a table behind the sofa and indicated that Colin Balfour should sit directly in front of him—which he did.

"My associate, Mr. Lambert, will visit daily to administer pinpointed electrical shocks here and here." The doctor's fingers skimmed the thick eyebrow of the man's left eye, then slid his touch over to the puckered skin near his temple. "Hmm. This scarring could prove a challenge. How long ago did this injury occur?"

"I was a child at the time," said Mr. Balfour. "Three, I believe."

"Four," his sister corrected.

"Of course. You should know better." A slight smile wavered on the man's wide lips before disappearing. "I'd wandered into the kitchen and pulled down a pot of boiling water off the range."

"Which frightened the life from us all and nearly cost my brother his." Miss Balfour pinned Mr. Peckwood with a direct stare. "Will the scarring be a problem, Mr. Peckwood?"

"Yes, but not one I cannot overcome. My method, combined with an elixir that thickens the blood and loosens the skin, will lay the groundwork for the day I will remove a portion of Mr. Balfour's skull and disconnect the faulty gland that is responsible for such a deformity. At which point, I will replace the bone, sew you up"—he patted Balfour on the shoulder—"and in a month or possibly two, your body should return to the size and shape of a regular man."

Graham rubbed his jaw. He'd known Peckwood to be a vanguard in the medical field, but *this*? "Have you performed such a procedure before, Doctor?"

The instant the question flew from his tongue he knew it was a mistake. Possibly a fatal one, considering Peckwood's black glower.

"Of course, Mr. Lambert. I have found it to be highly effective in reducing abnormalities in rats."

"My brother is not a rodent, sir." Miss Balfour looked from Peckwood to her brother, doubt leaching the previous enthusiasm from her tone. "How can we know this will not cause irreparable harm? That he will not end up at an asylum, broken in mind and body?"

"Dear lady." Peckwood rounded the sofa to collect her hand and pat her fingers. "It is my job as a surgeon to do no harm. I have every belief that the preoperative measures I shall train Mr. Lambert to administer will guarantee the success of the surgery. You do wish for your brother to live out his years in happiness, do you not?"

"Without question." She pulled away her hand.

"And," Peckwood continued without missing a beat, "as I discussed over many months of correspondence with your father, that is exactly what I intend to give him."

"Who is to say I was not happy in my country refuge?" Mr. Balfour asked.

His sister stared up at him, head tipped to a curious angle. "But, Colin, do you not wish to lead a normal life?"

"Normal is but a state of mind, Sister."

Graham clenched his hands, fighting off a strong feeling of unease. Miss Balfour may desire the best for her brother, and Peckwood surely had good intentions, but did neither of them notice Mr. Balfour's hesitation? Were intention and desire enough reason to proceed with such a dangerous surgery? He shook his head. "This is quite an undertaking. I wonder if any of us are ready for it."

Balfour heaved a great sigh. "My thoughts exactly."

"Now see here, my friends." Peckwood advanced, standing front and center of them all, hands clasped behind his back. An orator's stance—one that instantly put Graham on edge.

"Great achievement," Peckwood began, "is never obtained without great risk. This is more than just an operation on one mere man, but a whole new revolution for those who suffer from the same malady." He lifted his chin at Mr. Balfour. "You do the world a service, sir, by consenting to a treatment that is sure to be life changing. And for your daring, you will be given a new visage. An entirely new beginning. The question is will you accept the challenge? For such did your father assure me of your courage."

The speech landed like rotten meat in Graham's gut, sickening him. He'd heard such monologues before—preceding a battle wherein he was left with mutilated bodies and buckets of blood.

Mr. Balfour appeared unmoved, his cool stare unwavering. "I understand, Mr. Peckwood. It is a big decision. I should like to take the day to think it over."

Peckwood inhaled so sharply, his nostrils nearly closed. "As you wish, but I must warn you that time is of the essence. I have my own upcoming research project to attend, so if we do not begin the ministrations within the next week, your surgery will by necessity have to be put off for several years. Such is the magnitude of my next venture. So, you see, *now* is the time for your transformation." He pulled out a folded paper and set it on the tea table. "We will move forward once you sign this document of agreement, and with that, Miss Balfour, Mr. Balfour"—he nodded at each in turn—"I bid you good day."

He strolled from the room without so much as a backwards glance, leaving them all in an awkward silence. Both Balfours swiveled their heads to Graham.

How was he to salvage this? He clenched his hands to keep from loosening his collar. "My colleague is…we have other patients, and…"

And what? There was no defending a man in the throes of a tantrum. He stepped near Miss Balfour's chair and peered down at her. "If your pain increases, miss, do not hesitate to send for me. Good day to you both."

With a sharp nod, he exited, only to face a thundercloud in a black serge suit pacing on the front stoop. "If you ever question my practices again, Mr. Lambert, especially in front of a patient of such distinction, you may take your bag and seek elsewhere for a partnership. Am I quite clear, sir?"

Hmm. Quite the churlish if not childish response. Apparently, the doctor's sentiment of "an inquisitive mind is never to be condemned" did not extend to him. Though it never came easy to admit defeat, he dipped his head. "I beg your pardon, Mr. Peckwood. I misspoke and I deeply regret the matter."

"Well." Peckwood sniffed. "Very good, then." Retrieving a slip of paper from his pocket, the doctor handed it over.

12 Pinnell Street, Redcliffe

Graham looked up. "What's this?"

"Your next patient. Oh, be a good man, would you, and lock up the surgery when you're finished tonight? I shall be indisposed for the rest of the day. And by the by, I shall be taking the gig. Good day." With a pat on his hat, Peckwood strode off.

Graham watched him go, trying to disregard the rising unease he felt about the man. Perhaps this partnership had been a bad idea. Not only was he doing all of the work, but the work that Peckwood *did* do could very well be questionable at best. And at worst? Criminal.

Especially if Balfour did not survive the man's revolutionary surgery.

SIX

*"Life, although it may only be an accumulation
of anguish, is dear to me, and I will defend it."*

Wh`W`hat was one to do when handed two sacks—one filled with ambiguous promise, the other with the unspoken risk of premature death? Colin flexed his fingers. The doctors had left both outcomes in the sitting room, forcing him to choose between the two, neither desirable. Saints above! He cracked his neck one way then another. How he longed to get back on the ship that brought him here and sail into oblivion.

"You are troubled, Brother."

His sister's sweet voice drew him around. "As is to be expected, I should think. My life is at stake, Amelia."

"Yes, there is genuine risk—a risk I dearly wish you didn't have to take. It's not right or fair that you must face such a decision." She leaned forward in her chair, as if the movement might drive home her next words. "But Mr. Peckwood is the first doctor to offer you hope. Is living in hiding, shut away from everyone and everything, really living at all?"

Touché.

He sank onto the sofa opposite her and plowed both hands through his hair. "It is all I know." Blowing out a long breath, he looked her straight in the eye. "Especially since you left. I was thirteen, Amelia. Thirteen! Not a boy and not yet a man. You were my only buffer against

Father, and I…"Too many emotions stuck in his craw. Too many years of seeing the disappointment in his father's eyes with no one to cheer him or lend a kind word.

After a gruff clearing, he tried again. "I was at such a loss when you went away. I don't think you realize how much I depended upon you."

"Oh, Colin—" Her voice caught, his name as broken and jagged as his face. "You know I couldn't stay. Father would have made me a prisoner every bit as much as you."

True. And for that he could not—would not—begrudge her. Still…

"I know, Sister. I really do know. Yet that does not account for your sporadic and, as of late, absent correspondence." He shook his head, fighting against a rush of bitterness. She had no idea how the lack of her letters bludgeoned, repeatedly, when he asked daily for the post, only to be told there was nothing for him.

"I lived for those letters," he murmured. "You were my only tether to the outside world."

She looked away. "I had no idea."

"Maybe not on the surface, but deep down, I think you did."

The accusation snapped her gaze back to him. "What do you mean?"

For so long he'd pondered the why of her erratic communication, but dare he tell her the results? As his dearest—his only—confidant, she deserved to know.

But he doubted very much she would like it.

Rising, he paced the rug, from hearth to tea table, then back. "I suspect you drifted away from me not on purpose but from a necessity, of sorts. More than likely, your work engrossed you, and rightly so. Traveling about all day. Writing of your journeys at night. It is hard enough for a man to make it on his own, but a woman?" Wryness twisted his lips. "You have drive, Sister. More motivation and backbone than anyone I know, and you are a constant role model to me for the days when I wish nothing more than to cover my head with the counterpane and let the world go by. Your preoccupation with your career is completely understandable, for without it, you would not be the success you are today. But there is more to it than that."

She cocked her head. "How so?"

The question greeted him like an old friend. He'd had seven long years shut away in isolation to ponder that very thing, suffering a vicious circle of emotions from rage to hurt and shame, then back again to start the malicious cycle all over. Eventually, he'd landed on a highly probable motivation for why his sister hadn't written, and he'd made a fragile peace with it…but was he right?

He faced her. "I can only suppose that by busying your mind with work, it became easier to think less of home. To think less of Father, and as a result, less of me. To ignore the uncomfortable portion of your life that is less than perfect, the part you are helpless to make flawless. I am a constant reminder of all the ugly and defective things in your life, am I not?"

"Colin, no!" She clawed the arms of the chair. "Never think such a thing. I love you, no matter how you look. The outside of you does not define the intelligent, compassionate heart that I know beats inside your chest."

He drank in her words like a vagabond too long on the road, parched for a single drip of water. Father cared for him, providing for his every need, but never once had he given any soft words of affection.

Casting aside his restlessness, he knelt at her side and collected her small fingers between his two monstrous hands. "I care for you, Sister, with equal fervor, yet that is not what I am talking about. Look at you. Sitting here with ruined toes, acting as if you are whole even when the doctor poked and prodded. This need of yours to appear perfect will be your destruction. We all have monsters within. Is it not time you slay this particular dragon?"

Her eyes glistened, and she reached up to tenderly caress his cheek. "How did my little brother become so wise?"

Kind of her, but a load of claptrap. Were he actually wise, he'd have risked striking out on his own and left his father behind years ago just as she had, even if it meant facing the contempt and derision of mankind. He pulled away and stood. "I have observed much from the shadows in which I live."

"But that's just it. You don't have to live in shadows anymore. The sooner you sign that paper the doctor left behind, the sooner Mr.

Peckwood can begin to make you whole."

A bitter laugh bubbled up from deep in his chest. "You speak as if I am but a fragment, a collection of splinters to be glued together and crafted into a new creation."

"Your outside will change, yes, but inside you will still be the same man—a man the world will not scorn. Do you not wish to live happily amongst humanity?"

"Why does everyone think I am not happy?" He flapped out his arms, mindless of their ungainly length, and upset a vase. Glass crashed. Water splashed. Bloodred roses lay dead on the carpet.

Scowling, he wheeled about, turning his back to the mess, and speared his sister with a sharp stare. "I am sick to death of others' definitions of what happiness must look like. Of what *I* must look like. Yet I am content, Sister. No matter my outward appearance, I am happy with the man who lives inside me"—he stabbed his thumb into his chest—"which was never good enough for Father. Can you honestly say that it is good enough for you? Why so eager to change me?"

Her backbone stiffened. "Never question my constancy for you. There is no man I love more in all the world. My desire is for you to have a good life—nothing more, nothing less—which is what Mr. Peckwood offers."

"And you seriously think this surgery will accomplish that? What proof do we have?" The question he'd poked at for so long finally flew past his lips. Oh, how he wanted to hope, to believe the surgery would make him a new man…but would it? Dare he imagine life without deformity?

A great sigh deflated her chest. "All I know is that Father wished for the procedure and tasked me with carrying it out. And as you well know, Father was never one to be denied. But I have done my part in coming here and meeting with the surgeon. What happens from here on out is up to you."

He closed his eyes, her words a balm to his bruised soul. "Thank you," he murmured.

"For what?"

His eyes flicked open. "Acknowledging that the choice is mine."

"As it should be. I am not Father to order you about. I daresay neither of us grieve the loss of his overbearing will." A sad smile wavered on her lips. "Which is not to say that we don't each grieve his passing in our own way. But the question remains…what will you do?"

"I do not know. I have never been allowed to decide things for myself." He pressed Peckwood's document to his side, not quite ready to read the thing. "It hardly seems just that my first decision must be between a risky surgery or continuing the rest of my life as a hermit."

～

If ever there were a portal to hell, the slum of Redcliffe was surely it. Lethargic children sat on the filthy streets like little lepers, bony hands outstretched, half-savage cries begging for coins or crumbs. Women with bent shoulders and sallow skin trolled about, lugging rag baskets or sacks of rubbish they'd collected after a good scavenging on the riverbanks. But the men…sweet, blessed Saviour, the men! Graham's chest tightened and he focused straight ahead, avoiding the empty eyes staring out of doorways and alleys. He'd seen that look one too many times on sailors given to hopelessness as they lay dying on a cot, ticking off the hours until death released them from a life sentence of pain.

No wonder Mr. Peckwood didn't wander into this neighbourhood. But why had he taken on a patient here at all? Peckwood liked his Spanish cigars and aged port too much to operate on a *gratis* basis. How would a Redcliffe resident be able to pay a fee?

Sidestepping an oily puddle, Graham turned onto Pinnell Street, found door number twelve, and gave it a careful rap—too hard and the whole thing might cave in.

The wood opened a crack and a single eyeball appeared. "You be the doctor?"

He dipped his head. "I am Mr. Lambert, associate of Mr. Peckwood."

Instantly, the door slammed shut.

Graham blinked. *What the deuce?*

He lifted his hand to knock again when the door flew open and a young woman sailed out, cheeks cinder-smudged and garbed in a gown sewn of burlap. She quickly pulled the door shut and held out what appeared to be a large chunk of a broken fireplace screen. "Here. Ye'll be needin' this."

He hefted the thing in his free hand, keeping a tight grip on his medical bag in case this were some sort of distractive swindle. "What is this for?"

"Ye'll see." She gave a backwards nod, towards whoever or whatever resided inside the crumbly brick hovel.

He squared his shoulders. Danger may be real, but fear was a choice. "Who is the patient and what is their ailment?"

"Granny tangled with a feral cat, sir. Scratched her face fierce, it did. Here and here." The young woman pointed to her cheek and chin. "We tried a mud poultice and a snail and spiderweb plaster, but it's bigger 'n ever, swelled up like a bladder full o' water. I used all our savin's to fetch the best doctor I could find—that bein' Mr. Peckwood. Leastwise, Mr. Waldman over at St. Peter's said he were the best."

The warden at the asylum? Graham looked past the girl to the scarred oak. What the devil was he going to face on the other side of that door?

"Oh, don't fret none, sir. Granny t'aint mad. Her mind's more corky than you and I put together. I works at the asylum, so that's how I know the warden." She stepped aside, allowing him passage. "I'll wait out here."

He glanced at the flimsy hunk of broken shield in his hand. Was this to be used for quashing vermin while he worked? Or perhaps some sort of barrier to make the old woman feel more comfortable in the presence of a man? Whatever, he put his shoulder to the door, then paused before pushing it open. "What is your grandmother's name?"

"Bap, sir."

His brows lifted. "She's named after a sweet roll?"

The girl smiled, her front tooth chipped to a sharp edge, but at least none were missing. "People used to travel far and wide for a bite of one o' my grannie's Colston buns…till she fell on hard times, that is. Good luck, sir."

He shoved open the door and stepped inside, blinking in the spare light. "Mrs.….em, Bap?"

Whack!

Pain cracked into his skull, and he jumped backwards. "Ow!"

Ahead, a slip of a white-haired woman wielded a broom handle, wheezing for air. "I knew it! That girl were awful cagey. Out you go!" She struck again.

This time he raised the hunk of fireplace screen and fended off the blow. "Listen, Mrs. Bap, that granddaughter of yours cares about you. She's hired me to take a look at your scratch, and I mean to do so, broomstick or no. Though this will be a much more pleasant experience if you'd be so kind as to lower your weapon."

"Don't need a look. Don't need a doctor. God's got His eye on me." With her free hand, she aimed a gnarly finger at the ceiling.

"Very true, madam." He edged closer. "But it is also true that sometimes God uses human hands and feet to accomplish His purposes."

"Ha ha!" Approval lilted in her voice. "You got me there."

Pressing his advantage, he lifted his black bag and waved it about. "I assure you I am fully prepared to do the will of God."

She laughed, a discordant yet somehow delightful chortle. "I like you. I do!" But she didn't set the broom handle down and, in fact, clutched it to her chest. "Even so, I'll not let go o' this."

"I would have it no other way. Any woman—or man—should always be on guard in this wicked world of ours." Carefully, lest he spook the old woman, he set down his makeshift shield and his bag, then pulled a wooden chair away from the hearth and set it in front of the only window. "Would you mind taking a seat?"

She narrowed her eyes for a moment, studying him, then circled about and sank onto the chair, never once letting go of her stick.

"Thank you, madam." He bent closer to her in one smooth, careful movement. My, my. Her granddaughter had not been exaggerating. Two murderous red welts swelled large, one on her cheek, another near her chin. The woman's washed-out blue eyes glazed feverous, and even without touching her, he could feel the heat radiating off her thin bones. Quite an impressive infection.

He frowned. "I hope the cat paid for these transgressions."

"See for yourself." She jiggled the broom handle upwards.

He hesitated. Did he really want to see some rangy furball hanging from a rafter? Slowly, he peered up at the ceiling, only to meet the luminous green gaze of a fat feline who perched upon a joist, tail swishing.

"Ha ha!" The old woman slapped her knee. "The look on yer face! How oft', I wonder, do God see that same bewilderment from me?"

Half a smile rose to his lips. Her granddaughter had been right—the old woman was sharp as a lancet. Retrieving his medical bag, he pulled out a jar of ointment and worked off the lid. "I was told the cat was feral."

"He were, till I filled his belly a time or two. But that first meal were a real fight, I don't mind tellin' ye."

"Yet you kept him?"

She patted him on the sleeve, knobby fingers rife with rheumatism. "That's what mercy is all about, young man."

His jaw dropped. He'd not heard a more powerful sermon in years. Gathering his wits, he dipped his finger in the salve and tenderly applied it, first to her cheek, then her chin, and—hold on. With his other hand, he tipped her head just so and eased down her fichu, exposing a neck nearly twice the size it should be. Such a swelling in this area had nothing to do with a cat scratch.

He set down the ointment and dug out his surgeon's *vade-mecum*, paging through symptoms, causes, and diagnoses until he landed on the one that most concerned him. The more he read and compared the words to Mrs. Bap's condition, the more his stomach hardened into a knot.

"What's this?" She leaned closer and eyed his small book. "Am I to get a scripture reading as well? Ha ha! I truly do like ye."

He sighed. Would that this were a volume of encouragement instead of life-threatening illnesses. Forcing a half smile, he tucked the thing away. "I am afraid not, madam. Tell me, how long have you had trouble breathing?"

The whites of her eyes rounded large. "Be ye a prophet, sir?"

"Hardly." He snorted. "Do you mind if I listen to your heart? If I am to be certain of your condition, then I must put an ear to your chest, but I swear nothing more." He slapped his hand to his heart. "You may swat me with your broom if I do not keep my word."

She edged back in her chair. "I dunno 'bout that."

"Please, Mrs. Bap." He softened his tone. "I think we both know your scratch isn't your only ailment."

Her lips rippled shut and, clutching her broom handle with two hands, slowly she nodded.

He pressed his ear to her breastbone, then held his breath, mostly to hear but also to avoid inhaling her odd smell of fish and lye. Instead of the regular lub-dub, an irregular lub-lub-lub-dub repeated sporadically, as off-kilter as a pebble shaken in a dented can. He straightened. Knowing what was wrong was often a boon but—as in this case— sometimes a curse.

Mrs. Bap cocked her head. "Well?"

He inhaled deeply. "I suspect you suffer from dropsy, ma'am, but not to worry." He forced a smile as he swiped up the ointment jar and screwed on the lid. "I shall return tomorrow with a mixture of foxglove granules, to be administered over the next several days."

"Sticks and stones!" She wheezed and shook her broom handle at him. "I won't be needin' that. All I be needin' is in God's hands, and I'll thank you for what's in yours. Namely, that salve. I won't be payin' for anything more."

He handed over the jar, but as she grabbed it, he wrapped his other fingers around hers, boldly grasping not only her hands but her attention. "This ointment is yours, Mrs. Bap, as are my services, free of charge."

"Why…I never heard o' no doctor fixin' up some old Redcliffe woman without no cost to it."

"You said it yourself, that's what mercy is all about."

Her hands trembled beneath his. "But why me?"

Because I wish to God that someone had shown my own mother mercy during her final days.

He clamped his jaw shut. As much as he liked this feisty old woman, there was no way he'd expose that bitter sentiment.

"Let's just say you are my wild cat, and leave it at that." He winked and rose, swiping up his medical bag on the way. "I'll call on you tomorrow."

He wheeled about, heart heavy. He would visit her over the next several days and hopefully for weeks to come—but even with foxglove, her breaths were numbered, and there was nothing he could do to stop it.

Any more than he could have been at his mother's bedside when she'd succumbed to an odious death.

SEVEN

"This was strange and unexpected intelligence;
what could it mean?"

❧

June was a fickle lover. Amiable one day. Sullen the next. Leaning heavily on the crutch Mr. Lambert had so kindly sent over on Saturday, Amelia hobbled into the backyard, as disagreeable as the pewter sky.

Even after propping up her foot for the past three days, the thing still throbbed and refused to bear weight. Between Betsey's exhortations to simply *give it time* and Mrs. Kirwin's endless expositions on wrappings, poultices, and something about hog-nettle tea boiled with doornails, Amelia was exhausted and not just a little vexed. Mostly with herself, though. Had she driven Colin to accept a surgery he didn't wish? He'd signed the document, and the doctors would be arriving in an hour for the first treatment, but was Colin merely doing this for her and Father…or for himself?

She breathed deeply, the faint honey scent of the linden tree promising a tantalizing perfume in a week or two. Apparently she'd be here to experience the blossoms. The doctor had said Colin would require at least a fortnight—perhaps more—of daily ministrations before the surgery could take place. She'd immediately posted a letter to Mr. Moritz, asking for a month-long extension on her Cairo assignment. He'd likely agree, but his superior, Mr. Krebe, was notoriously cantankerous. It would take some negotiation on Mr. Moritz's part to convince him—if Mr. Krebe didn't dismiss him on the spot.

The hairs at the nape of her neck suddenly lifted. Crippled or not, she did her best to whirl about and glance up at the window of the neighbouring house. Just like the day she'd arrived, nothing but a lace curtain stared back at her, slightly riffling back and forth. She narrowed her eyes. The flimsy fabric could have easily been disturbed by the passing of a servant. Yes, that was it. Better that than to believe the ghost of Mrs. Ophidian watched her every move.

She turned her back on the house and limped over to the wrought-iron bench beneath the linden. Leaning the crutch against the arm, she sank onto the seat and pulled a small psalter from her pocket. Carefully, she smoothed open the book and leaned over the pages as she read. It wouldn't do to have tree sap or other foreign objects defile the scriptures.

"I will behave myself wisely in a perfect way."

She paused, Colin's words of a few days ago pushing their way into her devotions. He'd equated the perfection she aspired to as a monster in her heart, yet did not these words contradict his admonition?

"O when wilt thou come unto me?"

The question unfurled like a whip, stinging her conscience. The psalmist may have longed for God to visit, but did she truly desire the same? How could she know if God would come as a compassionate friend, warm and loving, or as a stern lawgiver, pointing an accusing finger?

"I will walk within my house with a perfect heart."

And there it was again. The very word for which Colin had indicted her. Was it wrong to strive for perfection? The psalmist did. And was not scripture given for instruction?

A frown weighted her brow. Obviously she'd do nothing but find more questions than solace in God's Word this morning. She closed the book in time with the shutting of the neighbour's door.

Tucking the psalter inside her pocket, she rose clumsily as wheels ground against gravel on the other side of the garden wall. A small cart, perhaps? A trolley for hauling wood? Whatever it was, it clipped along at a good pace.

"Miss Mims!"

Amelia froze, the name sailing right over the wall and piercing her heart. She'd all but forgotten her mother's pet name for her. What spectre from the past could possibly know such an intimate detail? No one. Unless—

"I would confer with you at the gate, if you please."

Hesitating, Amelia gripped her crutch with white knuckles. She recognized that voice, as distinct as the scrape of a bow producing an off-key note. But how could it be? Mrs. Ophidian had seemed breaths away from the grave twenty years ago.

Though common sense screamed for her to hobble into the safety of the house, Amelia obediently worked her way to the back gate. Even inside four walls, there'd be no escaping Mrs. O if the woman were bent on conversation.

One-handed, the latch took some jiggering, but eventually Amelia pulled the gate open, then planted her crutch firmly to keep from retreating. Before her sat an old frog of a woman, green-tinged, waxen skin stretched taut over a crooked-spine skeleton reclining on a blue-velvet Bath chair. Warty growths dotted her face, and colourless eyes with no lashes fixed her with a stare that sucked the marrow from Amelia's bones. Behind Mrs. O, the dog-faced servant operating the invalid chair was no less intimidating, what with her mannish stance and broad shoulders. Pushing around such a contraption all day no doubt accounted for her muscular build.

Amelia dipped her head. "Good day, Mrs. Ophidian."

"My, my! Despite the crutch, you are the very image of your mother...and I am the likeness of a humpbacked toad perched upon a rock, am I not?" She cackled.

For an awkward moment, Amelia wasn't quite sure how to respond. Should she smile? Nod? Wiggle her finger in her ear and pretend she hadn't heard?

"Tell me, Miss Mims." Retrieving a handkerchief, Mrs. O dabbed the corners of her wide mouth. "How do you like the flowers?"

Amelia glanced around, but nothing currently bloomed in the yard other than an untended bed filled with some washed-out astrantia. "I am not sure—"

And then it hit her. The vase of roses Colin had clumsily knocked over. *Those* had been sent by Mrs. O. She smiled back at the woman. "Yes, of course. The blooms are exquisite. Thank you for the kindness."

Mrs. O nodded, an unsettling sight, for skeletons ought not move. "It was the least I could do in light of your father's recent demise. Of course, you have my condolences. You and Master Colin must attend me for dinner. Tonight suits."

Amelia teetered on the crutch. How could the woman know Colin was here? He'd arrived in the darkness of the wee hours. "While I appreciate the generous invitation, I am afraid that will be impossible. My brother is not well."

"Nothing serious, I hope." She leaned forward, chair creaking—or was the eerie crackling her bones? "Though that does account for Mr. Peckwood's recent visit to Balfour House, which I'd assumed to be for your lame foot."

A dull headache pulsed in Amelia's right temple. From here on out, it would be a challenge to obscure things from the woman's all-seeing eyes—and ears. She lifted her chin. "My foot is but a trifle. My brother's condition, however, is serious enough to warrant his not leaving the house."

"I see." Mrs. O cocked her head like a raven about to peck. "I suppose we can put it off a few weeks, though he shall definitely have to miss the tea when the new neighbours arrive, for I expect them any day." She lifted a bony finger, indicating the house with the immaculate lawn. "Quite the scandalous pair, I am told. One questions whether they are legally wed or not. And you, Miss Mims?" Her anemic gaze returned to Amelia. "I see no husband has accompanied you to Balfour House, though you are seven-and-twenty."

Amelia stifled a gasp. The woman's tongue was as unmanageable as a gypsy pony she'd once ridden. She searched deep for the will to force a smile. "I suppose I have been too busy to settle down."

"Ha ha!" Mrs. O slapped the arm-rail on her chair. "Too busy gadding about the world, are you? Prague, most recently, was it not? Naturally, I must have a signed copy of your *Rambles through the Bohemian Crown*."

"I will be happy to accommodate." She dipped a small curtsey. "But for now I am afraid I must bid you good day, madam. I am required in the house."

"I imagine so. That young scamp must keep you on your toes." She nodded. "Good day, Miss Mims."

Brow wrinkling, Amelia maneuvered the gate shut. While Colin was a good seven years her junior, he was no young scamp. Perhaps the sharp-minded Mrs. O was beginning to slip a bit, which sadly could work to their advantage. If the woman did chance a glance at Colin and spread gossip about his horrific visage, perhaps not many would believe her.

Heartened, Amelia left behind the grey day for an even greyer corridor, working her way towards the sitting room, where a small spot of scarlet near the baseboards caught her eye. Balancing with her crutch, she bent to swipe up the object. Lying on her palm, a soldier saluted her, one leg broken off and his shako completely missing. Another toy. But this time inside the house. How had a young boy's plaything landed here in a passageway that was swept clean every night?

And more importantly, to whom did it belong?

❧

Perplexing. Graham's gaze followed the coils of wires from one voltaic pile to another. How the contrivance would actually help Mr. Balfour was beyond him. Though he had a rudimentary understanding of the process, a lecture here and a journal reading there were scarcely enough to sufficiently explain how an electrical charge could alter a human brain for the better.

Peckwood, however, methodically connected one tall glass tower to another, each movement confident. The whole assemblage looked like a medieval torture device, and Graham inwardly shuddered to think of what pain it might inflict. But it didn't seem to bother the doctor in the least. The older fellow hummed an old bawdy tune while he worked, as if he were merely setting up for a rousing game of whist.

Graham kneaded the back of his neck. Perhaps the pang in his gut was for nothing. After all, the surgeon bested him by more than two decades of experience. Surely he knew what he was about. Besides,

Graham himself understood better than most that oftentimes agony preceded a full and complete healing. Did not the removal of a gangrenous leg, while hurting like devil's fire, preserve the life of the infected man?

"Watch carefully now, Mr. Lambert." Peckwood held up a brass hook attached to a silk-wrapped cord, then caught it through a corresponding metal loop on the top of a rod at the center of the five towers. "It is very important the connection here is secure. Otherwise, the energy will discharge into the air instead of into Mr. Balfour's skull, which could result in injury."

Graham bent, peering closely at the assembly. "In what way would it injure him?"

"Not him, Doctor. You. Without the disbursement pads"—he pointed to a series of felt-covered discs attached by cables—"a concentrated arc of such magnitude would sear the flesh in an instant and cause blindness should it catch the eye."

Graham backed away instinctively.

A disturbing leer stretching his lips, Peckwood rubbed his hands back and forth. "And now we are ready."

While the doctor summoned the housekeeper to alert the Balfours, Graham once again studied the machine. Carefully. After today, he'd be solely responsible for administering the treatment. A formidable task, that.

He turned at the sound of voices and swish of a gown. Colin Balfour dwarfed his sister physically, yet the resolute way Amelia Balfour held her shoulders, the adeptness with which she managed her crutch—and particularly the keen mind he'd detected at their last meeting—made her every bit as notable as her brother.

Mr. Peckwood ushered them into the room with a flourish of his hand. "We are ready to begin. Miss Balfour, Mr. Lambert, this shall suit as the best place for your viewing." He indicated the sofa. "Mr. Balfour, over here in this chair, if you don't mind."

The big man frowned. "And if I do mind?"

"Come now." Peckwood patted the high back of the cushioned seat. "Are you not eager to begin the journey to normalcy?"

"*Eager* is not quite the word I would choose. Nonetheless, the sooner we begin, the sooner this shall be over with." He closed the span in two great strides.

Graham pulled a stool close for Miss Balfour's foot before he sat beside her. Though she'd made use of the crutch he'd sent over, he doubted she'd taken his "stay put" advice to heart.

She leaned towards him, voice lowered, a fine knit of lines worrying the skin between her eyebrows. "It is a bit daunting, all those glass tubes and wires and such."

"Not to Mr. Peckwood." Shoving aside his own earlier doubts, Graham gave her a small smile, hopefully putting her more at ease. "I assure you the doctor is in complete command. Did you know he worked with Sir Humphry Davy?"

Her eyes widened. "The famous lecturer?"

"One and the same."

"I was told that a one-way system was put into place on Abermarle Street just to cope with the traffic his discourses generate."

Clearly the woman was up-to-date on the minutiae of London. Exactly how much intelligence resided behind those striking brown eyes?

"That is true." He nodded. "Though with Sir Humphry's recent travels, he hardly has time for speaking anymore. I did have the pleasure once of attending a lecture of his, though my view was abysmal and the crush of the audience intolerable."

"Now then." Mr. Peckwood cleared his throat, drawing their attention. "In effort to loosen the skin so that it will more easily conform to the new size and shape the skull is soon to be, I have formulated my own special unguent, which is to be applied before every treatment." He lifted a brown jar on his open palm and began to massage a pasty balm into Colin's skin.

Miss Balfour leaned forward. "What ingredients make it so special?"

"Tut, tut, Miss Balfour. Your father paid me to perform my healing arts, not to give away my formulations." Peckwood dipped out one more fingerful before screwing the lid on with a flourish.

Graham hid a smirk at the man's theatrics. Judging by the tingling in his nose, he'd bet his pocket watch the special blend was nothing more than camphor and peppermint oil mixed into a healthy amount of goose fat. Not harmful, but certainly not an agent to loosen skin… unless the calming qualities of both suggestion and scent were his underlying goal?

While Peckwood finished his ministrations, Graham faced Miss Balfour, making the most of the opportunity to speak with her. He enjoyed this woman's conversation, her quick mind, her willingness to speak her insights. Though he'd only known her several days, he'd come to learn she knew what she was about, yet with an air of humility, and such a quiet confidence was altogether fascinating.

"How is your foot faring, Miss Balfour?"

Her gaze turned to him. "Still grievous, but nothing I cannot live with, especially thanks to the crutch you sent over."

"I suspected that crutch or no, you'd be ambling about."

One fine brow lifted. "You hardly know me, Doctor."

"No, but I do know myself. I'd rather take a bullet to the head than to have to sit still for days on end."

Her other brow climbed to meet its mate. "So you think us kindred spirits after only a few meetings?"

"Suffice it to say I noted that you are one who is not given to warming a couch cushion for overlong. Neither am I."

"Then perhaps we do have much in common." A smile curved her lips, the effect at such proximity so alluring he averted his gaze lest he stare. Well. This was quite the pleasant change of pace from working with crusty seamen.

"And, now." Peckwood set down the jar and picked up a large pair of calipers. "Before setting the conductors, it is important I take a series of measurements in order to determine the best placement. Mr. Lambert, your assistance, please."

Leaving Miss Balfour, Graham rose and retrieved a small notepad from his pocket. As Peckwood called out numbers, he wrote them down. Through it all, Mr. Balfour sat still as a sphinx.

"Thank you, Mr. Lambert. Next I shall indelibly mark the touchpoints." He held out his hand. "The marking device."

Graham handed over a thick, pen-shaped utensil, then collected a squat glass bottle of thick black ink.

Mr. Balfour glanced at him and Mr. Peckwood, a wry twist to his wide lips. "I never thought to be a canvas for artwork."

"When I am finished with you, Mr. Balfour, you will be a true source of inspiration." Stooping, Peckwood set about drawing a series of small *X*s at what appeared to be random intervals, then straightened and returned the pen and ink to Graham. "And there we have it. Now, for the first session. Mr. Lambert, pay particular attention."

The doctor gathered the octopus of felt pads and, one by one, painted the rims with a sticky substance smelling of pine. Some sort of gum, no doubt. He placed them over each mark, until all were attached and Mr. Balfour looked like he was tethered to a monster that could siphon the soul from his body.

Peckwood turned to Graham. "Step back, if you please, Mr. Lambert."

He retreated, close enough to be of service and observe the process, yet far enough that should something go wrong, he'd not be burned or blinded.

A series of dials lined a small control board. Graham watched intently as Peckwood twisted one after another, but curiously, the doctor's hand paused on the last. His index finger twitched slightly, then he turned the knob nearly all the way to the right.

Into the red zone.

So high an intensity for the very first treatment? Graham cocked his head, about to comment on it, when Peckwood whirled about and faced the Balfours.

"And now I am ready to begin, Miss Balfour, Mr. Balfour." Peckwood nodded at each in turn. A bead of sweat escaped and slid into his collar as he reached for the switch.

Alarm prickled down Graham's spine like a pin-blister rash. Was all the doctor's confident and boisterous talk of his cure just that...

talk? But no. Surely he knew what he was doing. The man had far more experience and connections than Graham could ever hope to obtain.

A high-pitched humming ensued, followed by a throbbing bass drone. Something sizzled. The air crackled.

And Mr. Balfour convulsed into a series of jerky contortions.

EIGHT

*"The surgeon gave him a composing draught
and ordered us to leave him undisturbed."*

" **S** top! Stop it at once!"

Amelia shot to her feet, then immediately reached for the sofa arm as blinding pain ripped up from her injured toes all the way to her throat. A deep cry tore past her lips, blending with Mr. Lambert's shout.

"Turn it off, Doctor!" Mr. Lambert lunged towards her brother, whose eyes rolled to the back of his head.

Amelia's blood ran cold at the sight.

Mr. Peckwood flung out his arm, barring Colin from receiving any help whatsoever. "Leave him! This is all part of the process."

Process? No! This was utter madness. Could the man not see how her brother writhed and foamed?

She hobbled to Mr. Lambert and grabbed his sleeve, not caring if her fingernails punctured his skin. "Mr. Lambert, make it stop. Please!"

Without hesitation, he wheeled about and struck the switch.

"What the devil are you doing?" Mr. Peckwood flung the rebuke on a wave of spittle.

Amelia paid them no mind whatsoever. All that mattered now was her broken younger brother, who'd already borne a lifetime of pain.

"Colin?" She dropped to her knees at his side.

His mouth stretched into a razor-sharp grimace. A great shudder shook his big frame, and his chest rose and fell with a gasp for air. Then finally, blessedly, serenity draped over him, and his grip on the chair arms loosened. His head drooped her way, and it took him several tries to lift his eyes to her face.

"I am fine, Sister," he rasped.

"You most assuredly are not!" She yanked out her handkerchief, then inhaling deeply, gently dabbed the sweat from his brow and moisture that had seeped out at the corners of his mouth. What had ever possessed her father to place his trust in such an incompetent doctor?

She glowered up at Mr. Peckwood. "I hold you personally accountable for my brother's torment, sir. Yours is an inhumane and barbaric practice."

His blue gaze swiveled her way, eyes as cold and dark as the North Sea. "What is barbarous, Miss Balfour, are your objections and Mr. Lambert's insubordination. This inhumane practice, as you call it, is the only way to ensure your brother's survival on the operating table and ultimately the success of the procedure. As I feared, today's session has clearly been too much for your feminine mind to manage. I invited you to join us only because of your insistence, but if you continue to behave in such an obtuse fashion, I shall be forced to ban you from all future treatments."

Stunned, she blinked. Surely the man didn't seriously think he could evict her from her own home. Fisting her hands, she opened her mouth to tell him where he could take himself and his torture devices, but Mr. Lambert's voice rang out first.

"Miss Balfour has every right to be at her brother's side, sir. Mr. Balfour is her own flesh and blood. It is only just and fair that family be together."

Mr. Peckwood frowned. "I grant you grace in this instance, Mr. Lambert, being you've only ever worked with hardy sailors and naval officers, but trust me when I say the fairer sex holds weaknesses you have yet to experience. I will not willingly take part in provoking hysteria in Miss Balfour nor suffer to see her committed to St. Peter's."

A deep flush spread up Mr. Lambert's neck like a bruise. "I would never endanger Miss Balfour in such a fashion, but allow me to say"—he lifted his chin and stared the man down—"I think you discredit her stamina and owe her an apology."

Mr. Lambert's defense, while kind and well meaning, didn't do much to assuage the irritation pounding with each beat of her heart. Must men always speak as if she were not in the same room?

"I require no apology." Grasping the chair arm that Colin no longer used, she pushed herself to her feet and leaned heavily on her good leg. "Rather, I wish you to leave, Mr. Peckwood. Take this contraption back to your office"—she flicked her fingers at the hated machinery—"and instead prepare for my brother's surgery."

"This *is* preparation, and I insist you absent yourself from this day on." He removed his spectacles and pulled out a handkerchief, rubbing a lens as if his glasses were of the utmost importance.

"I will not be told what to do in my own home, sir." She clenched her hands so tight her knuckles ached. "Neither will I stand for your condescending—"

"Enough!" Colin pulled off the tethers attached to his head and rose, towering above them all. "It is the four of us who began this process, and it is the four of us who will see it through to the end. I will have it no other way, nor will I brook any further discussion about my sister's presence. If she wishes to be at my side, so be it."

Mr. Peckwood peered up at him, his jaw clenching rock hard. Did the short fellow really think to stand up to her fearsome brother? Colin could break him in half without exerting any effort whatsoever.

"As you wish," Mr. Peckwood ground out, then shoved away his cloth and reseated his spectacles. "Whatever puts you most at ease."

"Good. Now, if you will excuse me, I believe I shall go lie down. I feel a bit jittery." He pivoted, but hardly a step later, his left foot dragged and he stumbled.

Before Mr. Lambert could reach him, the older doctor rushed to Colin's side, shoring him up with a strong arm. An odd sight, that, the pygmy supporting the behemoth. "I will accompany you, Mr. Balfour. A sleeping draught is in order today, I think. The first treatment is always the worst."

Amelia watched them go, heart squeezing. Had she made the right choice in enforcing her father's wishes, or was this all a horrible mistake? And if the latter, could she even talk Colin out of it, now that his mind was set on the course?

"Here, Miss Balfour." Mr. Lambert's low voice tugged her gaze away from the door. He stood inches from her, crutch in hand, worry in his eyes. "Are you quite all right?"

She reached for the crutch. "Nothing a stout cup of tea won't cure."

But that was a falsehood. Not even a cup of tea would soothe the underlying worry. She tipped her head towards the towers and cables on the table. "Must my brother endure such violent spasms?"

The doctor shook his head. "I fear Mr. Peckwood, in all his enthusiasm to bring about great change, neglected to begin at a more temperate level."

Hmm. Would such exuberance transform Colin or ruin him?

"Perhaps this was a bad idea," she murmured.

"Pardon?"

Heat flooded her cheeks. There was no possible way she could explain such double mindedness to this man of science. She barely understood such conflicting thoughts herself. Turning her face, she limped over to the contraption and touched one of the tethers. "Will you show me how it works?"

"Of course." He joined her side, his scent a curious mix of sage and lemon. "These glass towers are voltaic piles, sometimes called electrical cells or batteries. When two metals and brine-soaked cloth are arranged in a circuit such as this"—his finger followed from tower to tower—"an electric current is produced."

She bent, her gaze skimming the discs behind the glass. "Light and dark," she murmured, then straightened. "Copper and zinc?"

His eyes widened. "Very astute, Miss Balfour."

"I am no great mind, sir. My travels have simply taught me to pay attention and absorb as much as I can."

"Then I revise my opinion." Pleasure deepened his tone. "You are astute *and* humble."

His kind words went deep, and it took an effort of will to keep her eyes on the glass-and-metal puzzle before her. Most men scorned her intellect. Ridiculed or outright shunned her for speaking of anything other than needlepoint or flowers as proper ladies must. Even Mr. Moritz, her champion at Krebe Books and Journals, ofttimes slanted her a demeaning frown when she let too much information pass her lips. What made Mr. Lambert so different?

"So, now that you know where the power originates, you can see that it travels via this wire, which attaches to the conductors that connect to your brother's head. It is actually a pretty simple machine."

"Yes, not as formidable as it looks, I suppose." She looked from the silk-wrapped wire to the doctor. "Yet I fail to understand how it prepares Colin for his upcoming surgery."

"Besides the issue of your brother's scarred skin, it is Mr. Peckwood's belief that his yellow bile is out of balance and must be brought back into harmony before the surgery can be safely performed."

"Air. Water. Fire. Earth. Yellow bile is…" She bit her lip, searching her scant knowledge of medicine, then glanced at Mr. Lambert. "Fire?"

He flashed an approving smile, altogether handsome and addictive. "You are familiar with the four humours, then. Yes, it is fire that associates with yellow bile. And electricity is a far safer form of heat, more concentrated, easier to pinpoint. And this, right here, is where the intensity is adjusted." He pointed at the farthest dial of three.

The information surged fresh hope through her veins. Perhaps Colin didn't have to suffer after all. She stared at Mr. Lambert, fearful yet compelled to know more. "Then might not the intensity be turned down? Would Mr. Peckwood agree to such an alteration?"

The doctor said nothing as he brushed his knuckles back and forth along his jaw, his fingers bristling his shorn beard. Each pass, each consecutive moment of silence shaved layers off her newborn hope. And rightly so. After the way Mr. Peckwood had berated Mr. Lambert for interfering earlier, she doubted he'd be the man to persuade the older surgeon to do anything he didn't wish to do.

At length, Mr. Lambert dropped his hand and met her gaze. "Mr. Peckwood was here today for setup and the first treatment. It is his wish that from now on I administer your brother's treatments…which means he need never know what adjustments I make."

Even if she tried, she couldn't stop the smile that spread across her lips. She liked this man. His tempered rebelliousness. His compassion. And why had she not noticed before now that when he grinned, a small crescent-shaped dimple made an alluring appearance just below his right cheekbone? She leaned harder on her crutch lest she sway towards him, for such was his draw. "Then it shall be our secret, Mr. Lambert."

All emotion drained from his face, and he stared at her queerly. "You are quick to make a pact with a stranger, Miss Balfour."

She shook her head. "I find nothing strange about you, Mr. Lambert. It is Mr. Peckwood who concerns me."

❦

Propped against pillows, Colin sat immobile, transfixed by the shadow animals that had been cavorting in his room for the past several hours. Camels. Crocodiles. Bears and weasels. Even a tufted titmouse swooped the perimeter now and again, chased by a red-eyed goshawk.

With a monumental effort, he pinched the bridge of his nose, willing sanity to return. How did one know if one was mad? Did a lunatic believe himself normal? Because other than an underlying light-headedness and a tongue of cotton wool, he felt perfectly ordinary—save for the beasts and birds parading about. Either he'd gone daft from Mr. Peckwood's procedure earlier that morning, or the draught he'd swallowed packed quite a wallop. Regardless, the grit in his throat must be washed down, for there would be no more denying his thirst.

Grabbing the bedpost, he eased his feet over the side of the mattress, then rose by careful increments. The room tilted, but only for the span of a few breaths. He dared a tentative step, and another, pleased to find his legs still worked. Even so, he scowled, fighting the urge to lunge back to his bed when a black bear swiped its claws at his head.

"Go away," he whispered.

Bah! What sort of man pleaded like a little girl cowering in a corner? He threw back his shoulders, sick of this nonsense.

"Begone!" His voice rattled the windowpanes.

Not waiting to see if the phantoms actually slunk back to whatever hell they'd sprung from, he strode to the door and out into the corridor. Bad decision. His gut churned as the world slanted cockeyed. Pausing, he closed his eyes.

Breathe. Just breathe.

Slowly, he blinked his lids open. Late afternoon sun filtered in through the lace panels on the window at the end of the passage. The walls appeared straight. The floor squared. Nothing tilted anymore. Best of all, not one animal had followed him.

Once again he set off, rounded the corner towards the stairway, and ran into a man-of-war in a steel-grey skirt.

A sharp yelp cut through the air, followed by, "Oh! Mr. Balfour. You caught me quite off guard, sir."

"My apologies." He reached for his sister's maid, steadying her with a grip to her arm. "I was—"

Dizziness stirred once again. Harder this time. If he didn't release the woman, they'd both topple headlong. He flung out his hand, shoring himself up against the wall until the swirling faded.

Tentative footsteps edged near. A mix of concern and trepidation clouded Betsey's dark eyes as she peered at him. "Is there aught I can do for you, sir?"

What a lionhearted soul. On his best days, he could scare the fur off a rabbit. But after his harrowing morning and lying abed most of the day, he surely must be a sight. No wonder his sister didn't hesitate to travel the wide world with such a stalwart woman at her side.

Still, a layer beneath her fortitude, a very real fear of him could not be hidden. Heaven and earth, but he was tired of this. Weary of the horror he birthed and the resulting loneliness. Weary of life, really. As much as he despised Mr. Peckwood's awful machine, if it did work and he came out on the other side a changed man, no longer frightening women such as this, it would be worth it.

With a last deep inhale, he straightened. "Actually, yes, there is something you can do for me. I was on my way to hunt down a drink, but I think I should like to have one brought up instead. Could you arrange it?"

"Why, I'll do so straightaway myself, sir." After a stiff nod, she turned and disappeared down the stairs.

Colin eased himself around. No sense making the world spin on purpose. He edged along the wall, taking his time in case the vertigo returned, when his toe hit something and an object skittered against the baseboards. He bent slowly, for it was a long way down to the floor for him, and swiped up the forgotten item. When he held it at eye level, his heart stopped.

A cat.

A toy cat.

But was this animal real or just another imagining?

He wrapped his fingers tight around the carved tortoiseshell and squeezed. When the sharp edges of the ears cut into his flesh, he was more disturbed than ever.

Wheeling about, he whaled the thing down the corridor, not caring in the least if it broke the window or nicked the plaster. Children did not live here! Just him and his sister and a handful of servants. All were well beyond toy figurines.

To believe anything other was insanity.

NINE

"He is an Englishman, and in the midst of national and
professional prejudices, unsoftened by cultivation, retains
some of the noblest endowments of humanity."

Strange how little changes oft seemed the most monumental. A hole in the heel of one's stocking. A corn hull caught between gum and molar. The absence of a raven-haired woman who never failed to brighten a room with her thoughtful observations.

Graham glanced at the sitting room door, keenly aware of Miss Balfour's absence this morning. In the past two and a half weeks, she'd never missed one of her brother's treatments. Why today?

And why the odd hollow in his chest that strangely yearned for her presence?

"You are distracted, Doctor."

Colin Balfour's bass voice pulled Graham's gaze from the door. "So I am. My apologies."

Even sitting, the big man was nearly eye-to-eye with him, and far too much shrewdness glimmered in that knowing regard. "Is there a certain woman on your mind, perhaps?"

He smirked. He'd not admit aloud it was Miss Balfour who occupied his thoughts of late—which was an entirely new phenomenon. Other than a passing glance at a well-curved skirt, he didn't usually dwell on females. His first love was—and always had been—medicine.

He rummaged about in his bag on the tea table, bypassing the hated fleam that Peckwood insisted he use. Graham never did, nor ever would. Though many sang the praises of bloodletting, he had yet to see results that confirmed such a necessity.

Retrieving the ointment jar, he turned back to Mr. Balfour. "You are correct. There is a woman on my mind. After your treatment today, I am off to care for a high-spirited snip of a white-haired lady who I daresay could run circles around us both were her heart not failing."

"Is that so?" Mr. Balfour arched a brow at him. "And here I suspected it might be my sister for whom you pined."

Oh, no. He'd not touch that barb even if he wore a padded leather glove. He dipped his index finger into the salve and scooped out a generous amount just as a rustle of skirts swished into the room.

Since the accident, Amelia Balfour had graduated from a crutch to a cane, but even with the walking aid, she moved with grace. Each step poised. Assured. Which, after a solid fortnight in her presence, Graham suspected was a front. There was a curious vulnerability hiding behind those enormous, childlike eyes. Something, he suspected, she would not admit even to herself.

Mr. Balfour turned his head her way. "The doctor and I were just speaking of you, Sister."

A pretty shade of pink spread over her cheeks. "Is that what comes of leaving the two of you alone?"

"It was either that or devise ways to get out of Mrs. Ophidian's dinner party tomorrow night."

Miss Balfour frowned, and Graham didn't blame her. Experience had taught him to avoid such gatherings like a fresh outbreak of typhus. Rubbing the ointment between his hands, he warmed the gel until it softened, then began applying it to Mr. Balfour's puckered skin.

Miss Balfour stopped near the sofa, head tilted. "What dinner party?"

"An assemblage of meddlesome horn-blowers, no doubt." Disdain rumbled in Mr. Balfour's tone. Apparently he scorned socializing as well—and with good reason.

Mr. Balfour's great jaws moved beneath Graham's touch as he spoke. "The invitation is there, on the tea table."

She first reached for Graham's medical bag and set it on the floor. He stifled a wince. By now he knew she expected a certain order in her home, which his carelessness had just violated. She didn't comment on his lapse, though, and quietly retrieved the card. Graham covertly studied her. While her eyes tracked down the page, her brow dipped into a frown.

"This is a problem," she murmured, then placed the paper back on the table and lifted a brilliant smile towards him and her brother. "But not even that will spoil my mood. Not today."

"You are excessively buoyant, Miss Balfour," he observed.

"The doctor is right," her brother chimed in. "What sort of sunshine did you imbibe with your breakfast, I wonder."

She crossed over to the sofa and sat, her green skirt billowing atop the cushions. "I just received word from my editor, Mr. Moritz. My proposal for a short piece regaling my recent travel on the mail coach from London to Bristol has been accepted."

Graham grinned at the note of pleasure in her voice. "Congratulations. And I have further good news. Before I left the office, Mr. Peckwood informed me that he shall attend your brother on Monday for an assessment. If all looks well, the surgery may take place next Tuesday."

"Those are glad tidings for such an auspicious day as this." Rising, Miss Balfour crossed the rug and squeezed her brother's hand. "Happy twenty-first birthday, Brother."

"Thank you, Sister."

Allowing the two a moment of familial intimacy, Graham turned away and picked up a cloth, then wiped off the remaining salve sticking to his hands. "I had no idea today was your birthday. You have my well wishes, Mr. Balfour."

"Oh, but he shall have more than that." Mischief skipped along the edges of Miss Balfour's voice, a lilting quality he'd not heard before. One he'd like to hear again. "I insist you join us for dinner tonight, Mr. Lambert."

He instantly recanted of his wish. Using supreme effort, he schooled his face to a pleasant mask and tossed down the cloth. "Thank you, but no. I am afraid that is not possible."

"Of course it is." She flashed a smile far too charming for such a dangerous topic. "You simply knock on the door at seven o'clock and Mrs. Kirwin will usher you to the dining room. An easy procedure, Doctor, especially for one so learned as yourself. Unless you have a previous engagement?"

The question escorted him to the brink of a cliff. He could jump off and embrace a free-falling lie, which would prove easy enough to end the conversation without hurting anyone's feelings. But the cost to his conscience would open a vein, a conscience that had a pitiful amount of remaining lifeblood.

He reached for the felt pads. Better to busy himself with work than with mulling over a possible deception. "I have no engagements," he admitted.

"Then you must come." She practically bounced on her good foot. "My brother and I have grown fond of your company."

"She speaks truth, Lambert," Mr. Balfour cut in.

Such sentiments warmed his soul. Though he'd spent years aboard different ships, he'd forged no lasting friendships. He enjoyed the Balfours' companionship, but the urge for caution in a patient-doctor relationship ran strong in his veins. He methodically began placing the felt pads onto Mr. Balfour's skull. "I am honoured, but—"

"But you intend to disappoint us, sir?" Miss Balfour stepped near, lifting her face to his. "Surely you know that you are the only person whom we can invite, other than Mr. Peckwood, that is. Yet he is not nearly as quick-witted as you."

Something sparked in those fathomless eyes of hers. What? A smidgeon of desperation? Maybe. Or was it fascination? She did seem to enjoy an exchange of clever banter, but no good would come of encouraging such an interest. She was the patient's sister. This was a professional relationship. Nothing more.

"I thank you for your kind invitation, Miss Balfour, and even kinder words, but I do not think it would be a good idea for me to associate socially with a family of your standing."

"Claptrap!" Colin Balfour frowned up at him. "My sister wishes you to dine with us, Mr. Lambert, not enter into a blood oath. I expect you at our table at seven sharp. Now, are we to move this treatment along or fritter away the rest of the day with a pointless to-dine-or-not-to-dine debate?"

He sighed. Balfour was right. Besides, if Peckwood heard of his refusal to one of his highest-paying clients, he'd suffer worse than a tongue-lashing and just might be given the boot.

Rock. Hard place.

Inhaling until it hurt, he turned away from the duo's expectant stares. "Very well," he choked. "Seven it is."

His fingers quivered as he reached for the first dial. He hadn't dined with anyone since that ill-fated night he'd gotten kicked out of service, when a heated discussion arose between courses and he'd struck an officer of His Majesty's Royal Navy.

And all because of a woman.

Somewhere between the chestnut soup and marchpane cake, Amelia was smitten. Not in a flighty way. Not the sort that drove reason from the mind and fluttered the heart. She was too old for such absurdity and Mr. Lambert too conventional to inspire such a frivolous response. But all the same, she'd nearly dropped her knife when she realized the depth to which he'd invaded her thoughts.

She speared one more bite of her pudding and slipped the man a furtive glance across the table. There was something about him that unmistakably wooed her attention to the careless way his dress coat stretched across his shoulders and how that dark swath of hair broke rank and brushed across his brow. Though he'd been quiet throughout dinner, there was an intensity about him. An underlying ruggedness completely unsoftened by cultivation and unapologetic about it. Never before had a man so impressed her. And she wasn't quite sure what to do with that.

Especially when his head swiveled her way and his hazel eyes caught her in the act of gawping.

She set down her fork and pushed away her plate. The strange twist in her stomach would not tolerate a morsel more, even though well over half of Cook's famed confection yet remained on her plate.

"Well, I must say, gentlemen"—she affected a breezy smile—"this has been the most serene birthday celebration I have ever attended."

Mr. Lambert's dark brow arched. "You speak as if that's a bad thing."

"I confess I had hoped for something a bit more..." What? Colin was hardly a child. Surely she couldn't have expected ponies and jugglers to liven things up. "I suppose I anticipated our dinner to be something more memorable."

He leaned forward in his seat, his low voice for her alone. "Beware what you wish for, Miss Balfour, for it may come true."

Colin waved his hand at their guest. "We are but Englishmen, Sister. I doubt Lambert here or myself could live up to the colourful characters you have experienced in all your travels."

"Hmm..." She tapped her bottom lip with her finger, her glance drifting from Colin to Mr. Lambert. "I suspect you have traveled much more extensively than I have, Doctor. Your associate, Mr. Peckwood, made it plain you served as a naval surgeon. Surely you have a tale or two with which to regale us."

A humourless smile played across his full lips. "Nothing I should like to repeat in polite society."

"But those are the best sorts of stories, are they not?"

Both his brows shot skyward.

"Forgive my sister," Colin grumbled. "Her scandalous tongue often gets her into trouble."

"True, but not this time. I meant what I said in the best possible sense. You see"—she took a sip of ginger water before continuing—"when I journey to foreign lands, if I limit my conversations to only what is acceptable to the upper class, I would never sell a story to my publisher. Readers want—nay, expect—to escape into a world unlike their own, if only for an hour or two."

"And do you feel the need to escape right now, Miss Balfour?" Lamplight caught the green flecks in Mr. Lambert's eyes.

"I don't know about Amelia, but I wouldn't mind escaping to the comfort of a softer chair." Colin rose, his great frame bumping against the table and toppling the salt cellar in front of her.

Scrambling, she snatched the thing into an upright position, then pinched some granules from the spilled pile and lobbed them over her left shoulder. No sense inviting lies and disloyalty into their lives.

Across the table, Mr. Lambert eyed her with an enigmatic stare. Had he never seen anyone toss salt before? She stood.

So did the doctor, not once varying his gaze. "After you, Miss Balfour."

Grabbing her cane, she passed him, breathing in his now-familiar scent of sage and lemon. Out in the corridor, Colin's long legs disappeared down the length of the carpet runner instead of turning off into the sitting room. He glanced over his shoulder, catching her eye, then disappeared through the farthest door.

What in the world? She followed, a small frown pinching her brow as she entered the oak-paneled library. A fire was laid and sconces glowed. An intimate setting. Far too personal and relaxed to entertain a guest, breaking all the standard protocols. "Would not the sitting room be a better choice, Brother?"

Colin sank into the overstuffed wingback near the hearth, a great *oof* whooshing out of his lungs and the cushion as he landed. "I think we've all seen enough of that particular room. Besides, these chairs are more comfortable."

Mr. Lambert's voice rumbled at her back. "I have purposely kept my talk of medicine to a minimum tonight; however, I cannot help but ask you now, how are you feeling, Mr. Balfour?"

Her brother's mouth twisted. "How would you feel after more than a fortnight of taking jolts to the head?"

Amelia studied the deep lines that spidered out from the corners of her brother's eyes, her heart breaking. He should be attending house parties, riding in hunts, and smoking cheroots with other young men, not bravely hiding his hideous face and the pain of a daily procedure that wrecked him.

She smoothed her hand along her skirt, working out her anger. "Colin, if this is too much, we can call it an evening."

He snorted. "I am as tired of my bedchamber as I am of the sitting room."

His words, while valiant, frayed at the edges, belying his fatigue. She glanced at Mr. Lambert, pleading with her eyes. If he suggested they retire, perhaps her brother would be more inclined to listen.

But he did not meet her gaze. Instead, he reached for his white cravat and began untying the long band of fabric. "Well then, how about you allow me to regale you with a diversion?"

Amelia gaped as his collar fell open, exposing the skin of his neck down to the hollow between his collarbones. Scandalous! *This* was his idea of entertainment? She should look away. Turn her back. At the very least order him to return his neckcloth at once. Yet her mouth dried to ashes and her eyes refused to stare at anything other than the hint of black hair peeking at the top of his shirt. Oh, my. Why was it so infernally hot in here?

Of all the inopportune times, he looked at her then, no doubt noticing the warmth that burned on her cheeks. The mouth she couldn't seem to close all the way. The skirt she clutched in her hands.

The gold flecks in his eyes flashed with undue humour. "I believe your best viewing advantage would be on the chair next to your brother."

She retreated a step towards the door. If he began unbuttoning his waistcoat, she'd fly to Betsey and have her strong-armed maid usher the man out.

As if reading her mind, a rogue smile lightened his dark features, half-pirate and half-king-of-the-world. "Don't fret, Miss Balfour. I assure you my neckcloth is all I will be removing."

Colin burst out laughing. "I say, Lambert! I have no idea what your intended diversion is, but the look on my sister's face is the best birthday amusement you could have possibly devised."

Lifting her chin, Amelia hobbled over to the chair with as much poise as she could summon. Let them have their laugh. She would show them both how a dignified person ought to act. "Please, by all means, go on with whatever it is you intend to show us, Mr. Lambert."

"Right, then." He gave her an approving nod while winding his cravat into a long, ropelike shape. "It is no secret that sailors are renowned for their knot tying, and I learned several that ought to amuse, especially accompanied by a poem you may be familiar with, 'A Sailor's Song,' by the

Scottish authoress, Joanna Baillie. Will that suit?"

That he'd chosen literature warmed her heart, but that he'd selected a piece by a female made her positively giddy. Forgiving the doctor's recent teasing and his open collar, Amelia couldn't help but smile. "That should suit very nicely, sir."

"Then we begin." His fingers worked the makeshift rope as his low voice filled the room.

> "While clouds on high are riding,
> The wintry moonshine hiding,
> The raging blast abiding,
> O'er mountain waves we go,
> We go, we go, we go,
> Bravely we go, we go."

He held up the rope, and sure enough, the knots he'd formed looked like a frothy ocean bed. Then once again he lowered it and began reworking the thing as he spoke.

> "With hind, the dry land reaping,
> With townsman, shelter keeping,
> With lord, on soft down sleeping,
> Change we our lot? O no!
> O no! O no! O no!
> Change we our lot? O no!"

This time when he held it up, the knots had squared into what looked like a bed with a ropy man sleeping atop it. Amelia leaned forward in her seat, as did Colin. How on earth had the doctor managed to create such a thing?

Before she could ask, Mr. Lambert's deep voice continued.

> "On stormy main careering,
> Each sea-mate, sea-mate cheering,
> With dauntless helms-man steering,
> Our forthward course we hold,
> We hold, we hold, we hold,

Our forthward course we hold, we hold."

A knotty sailor dangled from his fingers, and Amelia could imagine a brawny seafarer shouting into the wind of a tempest as the captain held the brig on a straightforward course.

The doctor's hands once again flew to work.

"Their sails with sunbeams whitened,
Themselves with glory brightened,
From care their bosoms lightened,
Who shall return?—the bold;
The bold, the bold, the bold;
Only the bold! the bold!"

A series of knots formed a ship's hull, and while he shook the fabric, he held up the two ends as if they were sails billowing in the breeze. Amelia clapped a hand to her chest, astounded at the man's skill. As a surgeon, of course he must be dexterous, but this? Absolutely amazing!

He pulled the two ends, and just like that, the whole thing came apart. Once again he held nothing but a limp cravat in his hands.

"Bravo, Mr. Lambert!" Amelia clapped, her applause matched by Colin's beside her. "Bravo!"

"Well done, Doctor," her brother rumbled. "You are quite…quite the…"

"Mr. Balfour!" The doctor's neckcloth plummeted to the floor as he sprinted forward.

Amelia jerked her gaze aside, horrified to see Colin slumped in his chair. Only this time he wasn't convulsing. His eyes were not rolled back. He was still.

Deathly still.

TEN

*"...at the top of the house, and separated from
all the other apartments by a gallery and staircase,
I kept my workshop of filthy creation..."*

⚜

"Hold still just a moment more."

With one hand, Graham steadied the little boy's chin, and with the other, fished about in the lad's ear using the tip of a long-handled hemostat. A simple procedure. One that would have a satisfying ending, unlike Mr. Balfour's mysterious collapse the previous night. Oh, the man had come 'round well enough after a pinch of smelling salts beneath his nose, but it was the *why* of the matter that yet haunted Graham. There'd been no reason for Balfour to have so instantaneously languished in such a fashion. A puzzle Graham had been unable to solve as he'd roamed Bristol's streets well into the witching hours, and after that, pored over his medical journals until the break of dawn.

The metal tip he gently guided in the boy's ear hit something hard, where no bone should be, driving away thoughts of Balfour. Carefully, Graham followed the solid shape until the narrow forceps hit a soft wall of tissue. The boy squirmed, but he didn't cry out. Brave fellow!

"Hold on now. Just a moment more and—" In one swift movement, Graham pinched the object and pulled out a big seed showing the first signs of sprouting. "There we have it."

He held up the navy bean for all to see, the boy, his mother, and the small girl that hadn't let go of the woman's patched skirts since he'd ushered them into the surgery.

"Grimmety grouse!" The boy's mother popped her fists onto her hips. "Charlie, I told you time and again to stop playing blow-the-bean with them neighbour boys."

"Your mother is a wise woman, Master Charles." Graham pointed to the tiny white finger of a root just breaking through the shell. "Had this grown any further and lodged in your ear, you would have lost your hearing. So listen to your mother while you still can, eh?"

The lad's face blanched. "Y–yes, sir."

Graham sighed. Hopefully the boy would act on his word, for he had no idea the haunting sorrows that would attend him if he didn't. How different things might've been had he listened to his own mother when she'd pleaded with him not to join the navy.

Shrugging off the old regret, Graham clapped young Charlie on the shoulder. "Good man." He dropped the bean into a porcelain bowl with a plink then helped the boy off the table.

"Thank you, Doctor." Charlie's mother fumbled with the draw-strings of her reticule. "What do I owe you?"

"Five shillings, ma'am."

Her mouth pinched as she rooted about in her bag. One by one she pulled out pennies and farthings, pushing them about in the palm of her other hand. Her lips moved as she silently counted. The small girl buried her face in the woman's skirts, and Charlie set about walking the perimeter of the room, eyeing all the medical instruments while keeping the heel of one hand pressed against his sore ear.

"I, em…" A great lump traveled the length of the woman's throat as she peered up at him, her face as ashen as young Charlie's had been just moments ago. "I don't seem to have five shillings, Mr. Lambert. If you like, I could send Charlie here to work for you until my debt is fully paid. Times is tough, sir, and my man's not been home since he sailed nigh on eight month ago."

The distress folding her brow weighed heavy on his chest. Was that how it'd been for his mother after Father had been lost at sea, leaving her to her own wits?

"Oh, did I say five?" He feigned a distracted shrug. "My mistake, madam. I meant to say three."

The weight of the world fell from her shoulders, and she stood a full inch taller. "Very good, sir. Here you are." She offered her handful of coins.

He pocketed the money, knowing full well he'd have to make up the difference from his own dwindling funds. A sore spot, that. After a month of service to Mr. Peckwood, he ought to be seeing some remuneration, especially since increasing the man's business. When the doctor returned later today, he'd have a word with him.

The woman lifted the small girl to her hip, then held out her free hand towards the boy. "Come along, Charlie."

"Allow me to see you out." Graham crossed to the door and ushered them into the receiving room, where a bristly-headed man sat on the waiting bench. A stink wafted about him, like a cloud of thick fog, smelling so strongly of gin that the little family whisked past him in a trice.

"Mama, why does that man smell—"

The clatter of the door shutting cut the boy off.

Graham stepped forward. After years of living amongst unwashed sailors who reeked of bilge water and damp rot, the odour didn't bother him. "May I help you, sir?"

"Yes." The fellow rose, surprisingly steady on his feet. Other than the bulbous nose pitted from years of blue ruin and the eye-burning scent of spirits oozing out of his pores, nothing else gave so much as a hint of intoxication. Apparently, he was an even-keeled sort of drunkard. The kind that could imbibe daylong without so much as the tremor of a hand.

"I should like to see Mr. Peckwood."

Graham shook his head. "I am afraid he's gone out."

"We were to meet here at one o'clock." He tugged the chain on his pocket watch, sliding out the gold timepiece, then flicked open the lid. After a glance, he tucked the thing away and lifted washed-out blue eyes to Graham. "It is now five past the hour, sir. I cannot abide tardiness."

Graham frowned. Strange. Had Peckwood returned while he'd

been busy de-beaning young Charlie? "Very well. I shall go look for him. Whom may I say is calling?"

"Mr. Emmanuel Waldman." The fellow's thick shoulders squared to attention. "Warden of St. Peter's."

Graham gave him a sharp nod and turned on his heel, hopefully hiding the unstoppable lift of his brows. *That* was the warden of the asylum? He'd expected someone older. Someone more academic in appearance. Maybe with a quizzing glass pinned to his waistcoat and sporting neatly trimmed grey side-whiskers. Not a tippler with a penchant for punctuality.

Bypassing the surgery, Graham strode down to the study. Upon finding it empty, he continued searching the remaining rooms on the ground floor. Mr. Peckwood inhabited none of them. On the off chance, he peeked from the back door into the small yard and even quick-stepped to the stable for a cursory glance. Nothing but the horse greeted him. Apparently Peckwood had not nicked off on a medical call with the gig.

Graham went back inside, then paused at the back staircase. With one hand on the railing and a foot on the bottom step, he called upwards, "Mr. Peckwood? Are you about?"

Only the tick of the clock in the hall answered...or did it? He cocked his head. Above him, floorboards creaked, but only once.

"Doctor?" Though the man had forbidden him to tread foot in his private quarters, he ascended the stairs anyway. A quick call at the top of the stairwell wasn't exactly trespassing. The door on the right of the landing gaped open an inch. Perhaps the older fellow had closed his eyes for a few moments and dozed off.

"Mr. Peckwood? Are you in here?" Graham tapped the wood with his knuckle.

The door swung wide, the hinges clearly greased with an inordinate amount of lubrication, and though he shouldn't, Graham couldn't help but gape. This was no bedchamber.

Shelves lined one wall, loaded with all manner of glass jars that were filled with varying colours of liquids and body parts. In the corner sat a cage of white rats, red-eyed and gnawing at the bars. A big desk stood in front of an even bigger window, bearing a vast amount of papers stacked in neat piles, though some were wadded up and littering the floor near the chair.

None of that interested Graham so much as the slab in the middle of the room where a sheet outlined the figure of a body. An incongruous sight, one that raised more questions than for which there could possibly be answers. These were Mr. Peckwood's private quarters, not a school of anatomy or a deadhouse!

Unbidden, he strode inside and stopped at the raised table. Despite the covering, the stench of death hung heavy in the air. Not a particularly fresh body, but neither had putrefaction fully set in. Grasping the corner of the stained sheet, Graham slowly peeled away the fabric, revealing a naked grey corpse. Male. Middling of years. Malnourished and with a morbidly cleft palate. Abrasions marred the skin at wrists and ankles, but nothing that would have factored into the man's demise. Nothing else appeared out of the ordinary. So how had the man died? Who was he? Why was he here? And how had Peckwood gotten the body up the stairs on his own?

"What the devil are you doing in my private quarters?" As if the very thought of the man had conjured him, Peckwood's voice nailed Graham between the shoulder blades. "I told you never to pry into my affairs, Lambert!"

Dropping the sheet, Graham wheeled about, annoyed with the censure in the man's tone. It wasn't as if he'd been purposely on the prowl to snuffle about in the doctor's business. "There was no prying involved. The door was open and I assumed you were in here."

A murderous flush spread up the man's neck and spread over his face like an angry rash. "I always lock the door."

No wonder, what with an illicit cadaver lying about. Graham bit the inside of his cheek to keep the retort from slipping out. Silently, he counted to ten before answering. "I do not care to be labeled a liar, sir. You must have forgotten to secure the latch."

Peckwood's blue eyes iced over. "Get out."

Two words. Just two. But the rage in them filled the room with a palpable threat.

Graham stalked towards the door, debating all the while what to do. Finding a corpse in a senior partner's office wasn't something he could just ignore. It was illegal. Unethical. Wrong on too many levels. But if he went to the authorities, he might very well get tangled in Peckwood's web by implication alone, simply by virtue of being the man's partner. Becoming embroiled in yet another scandal would seal the fate of his already ponderous career.

Heaving a disgusted sigh, he paused on the threshold. Ought he let the fellow keep his secrets? They were none of his business, after all. A man's privacy ought to be just that—private.

Still troubled, he spoke without looking back. "There is a Mr. Waldman downstairs, waiting for you, which is why I searched you out."

Steps clipped. Fingers dug into his arm, yanking him around with an inhuman strength.

"If you breathe a word of what you have seen to Mr. Waldman," Peckwood seethed, "I will not only end our partnership, I will have you arrested for trespassing. Is that clear?"

He gave a sharp nod. "Quite clear."

Graham spun away, the lie rancid on his tongue, for nothing was clear about the situation. Not the dead body that belonged in a grave nor the body parts that had been severed and saved. Not the violent reaction from a man who'd been trained to heal bodies instead of acquiring them illegally for dissection in the privacy of his own quarters.

And especially not Peckwood's desperate wish to keep all of this a secret from the warden of the local insane asylum.

❧

Lunacy! Of all the bizarre and peculiar sights Amelia had experienced on her travels abroad, nothing compared to Mrs. Ophidian's sitting room.

She barely disguised a scowl as she perched on the end of the settee. Birdcages hung from hooks on the wall, chain swags attached to the ceiling, and even from a homemade ladder-type contraption with branches sticking out of it. How the woman maneuvered about in her wheeled chair took a miracle of navigation. Other pens crowded the floor, housing heavier fowl that didn't fly. Which, all in all, wouldn't be so bad if Mrs. O didn't leave the cage doors open. All of them. All of the time.

Ducking the swoop of an orange-beaked finch, Amelia set down her nearly full cup of chamomile on the newspaper-strewn tea table. There'd be no drinking it. After one sip, a downy feather had floated through the air and landed in her cup. She never should have come here tonight. She should have sent her apologies and stayed home with Colin, though likely he was faring better than she. Since his strange attack the previous evening, he'd been perfectly fine, save for complaining of a slight headache.

Which was nothing compared to the throbbing pulse inside her head at the moment. Oh, that she might be allowed to arm Betsey and herself with brooms and dustpans and tackle the cleaning of this menagerie.

"—evening, Miss Mims."

She jerked her gaze to the ancient lady across from her, whose skin, by lamplight, looked even more green than in full sunshine. "I beg your pardon, Mrs. Ophidian. What was that?"

"You just proved my point, dearie." The older woman fluttered her fingers in the air, brushing away a yellow-rumped warbler. "I noted you are quite preoccupied this evening."

Of course she was. Who could think when there were cages to be cleaned and feathers to be swept? Yet there was nothing she could say about it. Mrs. O had made it quite clear these birds were her companions. Nay, her children. Each one named and loved and pampered.

She curved her lips into what she hoped would be a pleasant smile instead of a grimace. "There is much on my mind of late."

Mrs. O cocked her head like a woodpecker searching for a juicy insect. "Such as a certain dashing doctor?"

Her cheeks burned. There was no stopping it. But that didn't mean she'd allow Mrs. Ophidian to gloat over her direct strike.

Rising, Amelia sidestepped a duck and picked her way to the window, then peered out at the lit street. "I am concerned for your other guests.

They are late. I hope nothing has gone wrong to detain them."

"I shouldn't think they'd meet with any trouble on the short trek from two doors over."

Amelia turned away from the window, fighting a tickle at the back of her nose. If she sneezed now, how many birds would she startle? "Did you not say it was only a few days ago the new neighbours arrived? How did you make their acquaintance so quickly after they moved in?"

"I haven't actually met them. I heard about the couple from the owner, Mr. Lavenza, who let the house out to Mr. Shelley. Naturally, I sent my maid over there immediately with an invitation."

"Well…" Amelia glanced at the sitting room door, wondering how many more birds she'd encounter when they finally did retire to the dining room. The sooner this evening was over, the sooner she could go home and brush the molted feathers from her hair. "Perhaps they are too exhausted after their move and have changed their minds. Maybe we should—"

The front door rang, the clang of the bell infiltrating from the corridor and rousing a chicken with a squawk.

"Here they are now." Mrs. O arched a triumphant brow, then manipulated her chair about to face the doorway.

In walked a brown-haired young woman, far too young for such a grim-lined mouth and drooping shoulders that barely kept her black shawl from slipping to the ground. She was a mite of a thing. A pebble that'd been kicked one too many times. Sadness radiated off her, a sorrow so thick it sucked in light and air, pulling at one's heart.

The petite woman stopped just inside the threshold. Completely ignoring the cacophony of tweets, chirps, and peeps, she graced a proper curtsey. "Good evening, ladies. I apologize for my tardy arrival. I misplaced my left shoe and did not wish to hop over like a one-footed wombat."

Amelia stared. So did Mrs. O. What a strange little lady!

A small chortle warbled in Mrs. Ophidian's throat. "Not to worry, Mrs. Shelley, though I hope your husband didn't meet with the same fate."

"I am neither a missus nor a Shelley, for now, at any rate, though

I suspect my dear Shelley will revise that, eventually." A hollow smile rippled across the woman's lips. "My name is Miss Mary Godwin. And I regret to say that Mr. Shelley is gone for London, so you find me alone."

Another silence followed, which was quite remarkable. Never had Amelia seen Mrs. O twice-over rendered speechless.

The older lady sniffed. "Then without further ado, Miss Godwin, allow me to introduce you to Miss Balfour."

Amelia dipped her own curtsey. "Pleased to meet you, Miss Godwin."

"As am I, but do call me Mary."

"Ha ha!" Mrs. Ophidian clapped her hands. "I daresay we shall all be the best of neighbours. Do have a seat, ladies."

Amelia took one side of the settee. Mary, after unsuccessfully trying to shoo a pigeon from a high-back chair, ended up smoothing her skirts next to her on the long cushion.

"Had I known it to be just us ladies tonight, I would have instructed Cook to make a more extravagant pudding." Mrs. O leaned forward in her chair, a conspiratorial twinkle in her eyes. "Women do like their sweets, hmm?"

"Oh, I think we can manage something a bit more scandalous than that, can we not?" Mary folded her hands primly on her lap. "Without the censorship of the male of the species, we ought to partake of Madeira at the dinner table and smoke cheroots like three chimney stacks."

Amelia stifled a gasp. What would Mrs. O say to such a shocking suggestion?

But the older woman's shoulders merely shook with mirth. "I've been saving a bottle for just such an occasion, though I cannot abide cheroots. They give my darlings here a smoky odour for days." She fluttered her hand through the air, ruffling a nearby cockatiel. "But I could manage to pass around my snuff box."

This time Amelia did gasp.

Mary laughed. "You surely do know how to live with zest, Mrs. Ophidian."

"By the time you reach my age, dearie, you realize what a wisp life is. I have a word for you, ladies. Do not live your lives looking over your shoulder, wondering what others think of your behaviour. It is God you will answer to one day, not society. And as for me"—she winked—"I am fully prepared to explain to my Maker how I never read one verse of scripture forbidding a hefty pinch of snuff. Now then, I shall see about dinner."

With a small symphony of grunts and *oophs*, Mrs. O wheeled herself around the grouse cage, shooed away a parrot, and vanished out the door, leaving Amelia with the paradoxical young lady in the midnight-blue gown.

Mary turned to her. "I applaud you, Miss Balfour, that you neither swooned nor scowled when discovering what an unconventional woman I am."

"I have learned never to be quick to judge, for not all are as they appear at first meeting. Take Mrs. Ophidian, for instance. Who would have ever guessed a well-advanced lady in a wheeled chair might house such an avian sanctuary...or entertain a pinch of snuff?" She smiled. "And please, call me Amelia."

"I think we shall be great friends, Amelia." The dark pools of Mary's eyes glimmered. "As my mother often wrote, the most holy band of society is friendship."

"A kind sentiment. Your mother is a wise woman."

"She was." Mary looked away. "She died shortly after my birth."

Amelia bit her lip. What a faux pas. "Forgive me. I am sorry for your loss."

The little lady shook her head, the tight ringlets framing her face attracting the attention of the dove perched on the back of the couch. "Do not fret for me." She swung her gaze back to Amelia. "I live my mother's ideals every day of my life, as do many other women. Perhaps you've heard of her works? *A Vindication of the Rights of Woman*? *A Vindication of the Rights of Men*? Or perhaps, as is most commonly known amongst polite society, *Letters Written during a Short Residence in Sweden, Norway and Denmark*?"

Amelia's mouth dropped open. "Do not tell me your mother is Mary Wollstonecraft."

"Very well. I will not." Mary leaned close and whispered, "But you have guessed it correctly."

Amelia slapped her hand to her chest. "Why, she is a particular heroine of mine! Your mother's travel writing is exquisite. I can only aspire to such well-crafted prose, for you see, I am a travel writer as well."

"Are you?" A pixie-like smile graced her lips. "Well, if you like, I have some of Mother's other writings that were never published—yet. Should you find yourself in need of inspiration, I am happy to lend them to you, though obviously I should expect them back."

What a boon! Not even the constant flutter of wings annoyed her anymore. "That would be lovely."

"I often find my mother's words inspiring. I dabble with the pen myself. Haunting tales are my specialty." Her voice dropped to an eerie tone. "Ghost stories, if you will."

Not surprising, really. Not with the way the woman seemed to exude a dark shade of melancholy. Amelia countered with a lightness in her voice. "Then Bristol is a good place for you to be. The streets here are rife with ghoulish history."

"Are they?" Mary tipped her chin. "And how would I find out about such legends?"

"I would be happy to share with you what little I know." As soon as the words passed her lips, Amelia recanted. It wasn't as if she could host the lady for tea, not with Colin about. "Unfortunately, I fear my time is filled and I don't usually have the wherewithal for social visits. Tonight is an exception on behalf of Mrs. Ophidian's, umm, persistence, shall we say?"

"Think nothing of it, for I have just thought of the best idea." Folding her hands in her lap, Mary leaned towards her. "You should write it down, Amelia. Get your own little book of morbid folklore published. I cannot be the only one interested in such stories."

Strangely enough, the idea lodged in her mind like a grappling hook, and she sank back against the cushions with the weight of it. Perhaps writing down tales of Bristol's history would give her something to do other than worry about Colin. Maybe even give Mr. Moritz something with which to pacify Mr. Krebe until she could finish the Cairo project. Besides, she wouldn't be—and hadn't been—sleeping much anyway, not with her brother's upcoming surgery.

But would it be wise to fill her head with thoughts of dark intrigue when she ought to be focused on tending Colin?

ELEVEN

"How all this will terminate I know not."

❧

Never had a sky looked bluer, despite being viewed through the curtains of the sitting room window. Colin fixed his gaze on that promise of freedom instead of paying attention to the pokings and proddings of Mr. Peckwood. Oh, to be outdoors beneath that azure dome. Flying free. Soaking in the warmth of the sun instead of enduring a salve that burned and jolts that singed. But it was not to be. Not now, at any rate.

"That's troublesome," Mr. Peckwood murmured, then stepped away from him and folded his arms. "Your progress is not as advanced as I had hoped."

Colin's lips curled in a derisive snort. "You sound like my old Latin tutor."

His poor attempt at humour did nothing to ease the wrinkle in Amelia's brow. If anything, it deepened, which concerned him as much as the crescent shadows beneath her eyes. Apparently she'd been sleeping as well as she'd been eating—which was minimal and troubling.

She skewered Mr. Peckwood with a pointed stare from her seat on the sofa. "What does that mean, Doctor?"

The thud of Mr. Lambert's shoes grew louder from behind, until the man himself entered Colin's peripheral vision. "More precisely, what specific progress did you expect?"

"The skin—especially that covering the zygomatic and temporal bones—here and here"—the doctor unfolded his arms and pointed to Colin's cheek and temple—"is not loose enough to guarantee the shrinkage that will be needed once the cranial capacity is reduced."

Lambert's brows suddenly mirrored Amelia's. "Can the skin not simply be surgically removed?"

"Of course it can." Peckwood flourished his fingers in the air. "But with the increased risk of scarring and blood loss, I should like to avoid as much unnecessary cutting of Mr. Balfour's body as possible."

"So would I." Colin frowned. The recovery would no doubt be brutish enough as is, without further slicing and dicing.

Amelia smoothed out the lacy handkerchief square she'd been toying with all morning. Was this talk of blood and gore getting to be too much for her? Admittedly, his elder sister was no fainting flower, but even she must have her limits.

"I think we are all in agreement that the less invasive the surgery performed on my brother, the better, but Mr. Lambert raises a valid point. Would it not be more expedient to remove the excess skin during the procedure instead of having him suffer through these daily treatments?"

"I am afraid," Mr. Peckwood said, "such intricacies are beyond the feminine psyche to comprehend."

"Now see here, Doctor!" Lambert crossed the room to her side, sweeping out his hand in a protective manner.

Colin hid a smile. The man was proving as defensive of his sister as he.

"Miss Balfour is as capable of understanding your explanations as I, and so I echo her question. Why continue this"—with a nod of his head, Lambert indicated the pile of medical contraptions on the table—"when it is possible to cut, remove, and suture any extra tissue?"

Peckwood's chest puffed out several inches as he gripped the lapels of his suit coat. "Because after extensive research and practice, this is the way I deem best, not to mention this procedure is the one I presented to the patriarch of this family before his demise. Who, by the way, was in full support of giving me control over any and all medical decisions, the extent of which I have in writing. So either we do this my way or not at all. Mr. Balfour?" His blue gaze sharpened on Colin. "Are you in agreement?"

Though something in his gut twanged, he met the man's gaze and nodded. "I am."

The sharp angles of Mr. Peckwood's face relaxed. "Good. Then you shall require two more weeks of my prescribed regimen, three at most, and I shall require a banknote of forty pounds for the extra time and effort involved."

Amelia shot to her feet. "Forty pounds!"

"So much?" Lambert grumbled beside her.

Colin blew out a long breath, annoyed at them all, but mostly with himself. He never should have come here. He should've ignored Father's wishes. Stayed in Devon. Shut himself away from humanity. Spared his sister the diminishment of their inheritance and the rise and ebb of hope that wreaked havoc with his own peace of mind.

Rising, he faced Peckwood, anxious for this to be over. "My sister will see that you are paid."

"But, Colin!"

The distress in her voice struck a nerve. He crossed to her and pried the now wadded-up handkerchief from her hand. After smoothing out the bit of lace, he refolded it into a neat square and handed it back, patting her hand before he let go. "It is only money, Amelia."

"Forgive me. Of course it is only money." Her palm rose and rested gently on his cheek. "I merely wish to end this daily suffering of yours."

"And soon it shall be." Pulling from her touch, he nodded at Peckwood. "If you'll excuse me, I bid you good day, sir." His gaze drifted to Lambert. "Until tomorrow, Doctor."

Leaving them all behind, he strode out of the room and stalked to the rear of the house, then paused with his hand on the back door. Going outside was a risk, one Amelia would no doubt take him to task for later. But hang it all! He needed a moment—just one—to feel normal again instead of like a specimen caged for experimentation.

He twisted the knob and stepped out into freedom—and didn't stop until he was halfway into the yard. Lifting his face, he filled his lungs with fresh air and the leftover sweetness of spent linden blossoms. Surely this was heaven. The *chacker-chacker-chacker* of a starling. The quivering green leaves high overhead, swooshing in the breeze. The scrape of wood and scuffle in the shrubbery at his back.

The what?

He wheeled about. In the wild tangle of an overgrown weigela near the corner of the house, the whites of two eyeballs peered out at knee level. Human eyes. Or were they? Was this just another laudanum-induced delirium? Pressing the heels of his hands to his own eyes, he rubbed, then squinted and looked again.

The weigela remained, but nothing gazed back at him.

Colin advanced then crouched and parted the greenery, the sharp branches scratching the backs of his hands in the process. The way the lower branches were bent, it was conceivable something had squatted here recently, but not a man. There was no way a grown human could fit into such a small space.

He sank back to his haunches, frowning. Perhaps it was a good thing the surgery had been pushed back. Clearly he was not mentally ready for such a major procedure, not with hallucinations like this.

How could Peckwood's operation possibly end well if he weren't sound to begin with?

A slow burn simmered in Graham's gut as he pounded the pavement of Bristol's streets. Thunderation! He was sick of being angry. Again. All the time. This was the very thing he'd hoped to escape by settling in a town where no one knew him. Where he thought he could forget about the injustices meted out by impudent naval officers whose only care was for their own insatiable appetites. But then Peckwood happened. A doctor every bit the blackguard as Lieutenant Clerval had been.

And it was his fault for signing a contract with that devil.

Clutching his medical bag with a death grip, he turned off the main street and entered the Redcliffe slum, barely registering his surround-ings. How could he pay attention when his thoughts were stuck in a rut of indignation? It wasn't right that the doctor belittled Amelia Balfour's intelligence to her face. She'd proven herself more scholarly than most men he knew. Nor was it right to prolong Colin Balfour's suffering. Oh, he bore it well enough. Such a dauntless fellow. A man of integrity who would've made a fine naval officer. Graham enjoyed their daily conversations immensely. In truth, he'd never realized he possessed such a keen need for a brother until Balfour quietly and thoroughly filled that empty space deep in his soul.

As he turned onto Pinnell Street, a maggot-quivering pile of rotted cabbages blocked his way. But instead of sidestepping the mess, he kicked it. Churlish but satisfying, especially when he imagined the refuse splattering against Peckwood's immaculate trousers. The greedy goblin! Bleeding the Balfours by demanding an additional sum. He was already making a year's worth of salary from them. And what would he use the money for? Paying off resurrection men to haul in more fresh corpses?

Graham stopped mid-lane. Feet itching to turn right around and report Peckwood to the police even if it meant trouble for himself. But of course there was no way to prove the man's indiscretions. By now, the corpse was gone, and wily old Peckwood surely left no trail to whoever provided him with bodies. Or did he? Perhaps another visit to the man's makeshift laboratory was in order.

That settled, he continued on his way to Mrs. Bap's, when several curses and a moan crept out of a narrow passage to his right. Shading his eyes, he peered into the shadows.

Ten or so paces ahead, a pile of rags huddled on the ground. Two bigger boys kicked at the heap while a younger one pillaged amongst the fabric. A flap of the cloth lifted, revealing a swath of skin. Graham narrowed his eyes. That was no cast-off mound of material.

It was a man.

"Leave off!" he roared as he tore into the thin space.

All three boys jerked their gazes towards him, then without a word, pivoted and sprinted in the opposite direction, their laughter ringing sharply off the brick walls. Shards of gravel flew in their wake. Graham was of half a mind to hurdle the fellow on the ground and pursue them to mete out a justice of his own, but a groan doused that desire.

He dropped to one knee beside the injured fellow. "Here now, I'm a doctor. Let me help."

Wild eyes met his beneath a flop of hair, grey and matted. Blood snaked out the corner of his mouth. The reek of ale and human waste wafted strongly as the fellow edged away from him. "Don't need no help."

Stubborn man. Graham shook his head. "You may have broken ribs after that thrashing. At least allow me to examine you for internal injury."

Turning aside, the vagrant spit out a stringy wad and a series of profanities that made the boys' earlier oaths seem like nursery rhymes. "Ye'll make no coins off'n me!"

"I seek no payment, only to give you aid." Graham opened his bag and pulled out a roll of bandages. "See? I only wish to bind your chest should you need it, which—judging by your shallow breaths and the way you're clutching your side—you do."

"Skimmin' and scammin' is all yer good fer. Begone!" With another groan, the fellow dragged his body back another foot.

Graham frowned. Though everything in him yearned to help the man, the wall of mistrust between them was too great to breach. Nor could he blame him for such wariness. Medical charlatans preyed on victims such as this. How many times had the poor fellow been duped out of whatever pennies he owned for the sake of a fake cure?

Setting the dressing on the ground, Graham rose. "So be it, then. But this is yours for the keeping. At the very least, take it and bind those ribs yourself."

The man's gaze shifted between the bandages and him. Back and forth. Like a whipped hound deciding whether or not to snatch a bone. The sight cut Graham to the quick. There was no cure for fear or despair, leastwise not in his bag of tools.

"God's mercy on you, sir." Graham wheeled about and, after a few steps, was pleased to hear a rustling as the man snatched up his offering.

But the pleasant feeling didn't last long before the low-grade anger inside him once again blistered. That vagrant would just as soon sell that binding for a nip of gin than use it to care for his own body. How could God stand it? This world that turned men into animals through want and need and misery? He could barely suffer it himself.

Wadding up all the morning's fury, he stuffed it down, cramming the black emotion into a dark crevice deep in his heart. Perhaps he'd sort it out later. Review the injustice of the world in the quiet of his chamber by the light of his mother's Bible. A virtuous thought—if he actually carried it out.

He pounded harder than necessary on Mrs. Bap's door.

"Come in, Doctor. I know it be you."

Crossing the threshold, he pinned a smile into place, one that nearly slipped off several times as he examined the old woman. Her ankles were the size of small melons and her heart lub-dubbed an off-beat rhythm. The foxglove wasn't working. Neither was the hawthorn tea or motherwort poultice on her chest.

With a sigh, he turned back to his medical bag and rummaged about, looking for another answer. A new method or treatment idea. Something must be tried. Had anyone worked this hard for his mother when she lay dying?

Ouch!

Pain stabbed his index finger. In reflex, he lifted the offended digit to his mouth and sucked away the blood. Of all the incompetence! He should know better than to dig into a bag of sharp instruments.

The woman eyed him knowingly. "Something rankles ye today, Doctor."

Wiping his finger on his trousers, he faced Mrs. Bap with a smile that felt too tight. Would she notice? "Nothing to concern you."

"I weren't talking 'bout me." Gripping the chair arms, she leaned forward in her seat. "What is it that ails you?"

The old woman's heart might be failing, but her mind was quick. There'd be no hiding the truth from her…though he could downplay it a bit. He gave a careless shrug. "Life, I suppose. The general unfairness of it all."

"Pish-posh. A man of your years. Why, I should think ye would know by now that life here on earth ain't fair." She chuckled, her breaths wheezing on the output, then sobered. "But God is just. Always."

He cocked a brow. "You sound like my mother."

"Then she is a wise woman."

"She *was* a true saint." He clamped his mouth shut. Funny how after five long years, sorrow still lingered on his tongue whenever he spoke of her.

Her wrinkled face smoothed peacefully. "Perhaps I'll meet her soon."

He shook his head. "I am doing everything in my power to keep that from happening, Mrs. Bap."

Leaning back in her seat, the old woman eyed him with a soul-searching gaze. "You are a goodly doctor, Mr. Lambert, but you try too hard. Dying is not the end. I neither fear nor despise it. And I daresay your saintly mother didn't either."

A bitter laugh choked him. "We will have to agree to disagree on that point, for I have no idea of the fear and desperation she may have felt. My mother died alone, and it was my fault. I willfully left her to fend for herself. There. What do you think of your good doctor now?"

She didn't so much as flinch. "I think ye are human. Weary with compassion. One who clutches on to regrets too tightly."

The anger he'd tried so valiantly to tamp down flared once again. "And for good reason, madam! I should have been at her side, caring for my mother as I care for you, doing what I could to heal her. And though I pleaded in prayer, God made no provision for me to attend her, to her detriment and my eternal shame. She suffered for *my* rebellion. So yes, I find it hard to willingly let go of such an offense."

His booming voice echoed in the small room, but Mrs. Bap didn't shrink from it. On the contrary, she clucked her tongue as if he were naught but a wayward child. "It's a twisted view ye hold, Doctor. One that's been eating at ye a long time, if I don't miss my mark."

He sucked in a breath. The woman was far too insightful.

And he'd said far too much.

"Forgive me." Picking up the pieces of his smile, he once again pinned the thing back in place. "I have waxed far too philosophical for one visit."

Finished with the discussion, he turned and gathered the salve jar and began packing away the rest of his tools.

Yet Mrs. Bap was clearly not done. If anything, her volume

increased the more she spoke. "I'll allow ye that perhaps your mother's death could have been a result of yer actions, leaving her on her own, as ye did. But God did not punish her for yer fault. We are each accountable for our own deeds, deeds that will eventually be weighed and measured. For good or for bad, God will have His justice in His time, not ours!"

Footsteps crept up behind him, and a gnarled hand rested on his shoulder. "Besides, dearie, your mother didn't really die alone. God was with her till the last breath left her chest. Even had you been there, you couldn't have healed her, not with all your medicine or equipment. God alone numbers our days. God alone heals, and He did—the very moment your mother stepped into heaven. Of that, ye can rest assured."

His throat closed. Completely. No air in or out, for such was the power of her words. He'd never thought of it that way. He glanced up at the rafters where the green-eyed cat stared down at him, and for the briefest of moments, he closed his eyes.

She's right, God. Though I did not hold my mother's hand, You did. You were there. I ought not have been angry with You, and I beg Your pardon, here and now.

A weight lifted off his shoulders, and for the first time in years, he breathed freely. Almost lightly. All because of a faithful old woman who didn't fear to speak truth. Without turning to her, he laid his hand atop hers. "Thank you."

"Ha ha! It's I what should be thanking ye. Stopping by like ye do without a penny to show for it. Why, no doubt I'll be kickin' up these old feet o' mine in no time, and all because o' yer faithful ministrations."

He stiffened. Her faith in him was misplaced. She would not be leaving her confinement anytime soon, not with the way her heartbeat continued to limp along. Though he desperately wished her words were true, a full recovery wasn't likely.

And buried in his soul, beneath a rock he'd rather not lift, that same suspicion wriggled for Colin Balfour.

TWELVE

"Thus ended a day memorable to me:
it decided my future destiny."

⚬⟋⟍⟍⟍⟋⚬

I f yawns were coins, Amelia would have enough to bless every last child in Bristol with a shiny new penny. She stared aimlessly out the sitting room window, stifling yet another jaw-stretcher with the back of her hand. Thank goodness Mr. Lambert hadn't arrived yet to witness such unladylike behaviour.

With one finger, she slid back the lace curtains. Morning light bathed her face in golden warmth, adding weariness to weariness. She could blame her sluggishness on the sun, for even cats napped in such balmy patches on the carpet. But that would be a lie. Fatigue dogged her from staying up until the smallest hours of the night, writing down all she knew of the city's history. Not her best idea, which Betsey had remarked upon when she'd opened the draperies and seen the smudges beneath her eyes. But it was better than acknowledging—even to herself—that she wouldn't have slept anyway due to fretting about her younger brother. Twelve more days. Just twelve. Then the surgery could happen. Colin would be transformed. Life would go on as if—

Thwump!

For one horrible eternity, a black, beady eye stared into hers. Dark as night. Empty as death. Feathers mashed against the glass, barely an inch from her face. She jerked backwards as a bird plummeted to the ground.

No!

Amelia limp-ran out of the house, fingering the lucky Ibis feather as she rounded the front stairs. *Please, little bird. Please be all right.*

She stopped in front of a sparrow lying on the pavement. Ever so slowly, she withdrew her hand from her pocket and let her arm hang limply at her side. So much for luck.

The bird was dead.

And that's when it hit. Standing right there on the street for all to see. A grief so wretched and real that it clawed up her throat and demanded release. She bit her knuckle to keep the awful thing inside. It'd been a month—a *full* month—since she'd first heard of her father's demise. She'd shed some tears in those early nights. Felt a bit of sadness. But nothing like this.

She pulled in a shaky breath. How could the fall of a defenseless sparrow remind her so acutely of a powerful man who never loved her as a father should? Hot tears leaked out of her eyes. One after the other.

Oh, Papa. Would that things had been different between us.

She bit down harder on her knuckle. Though she'd thanked him often via letter for the monetary support he'd provided over the years, she should have visited him. Thanked him in person. Expended more effort to make him see her as a daughter worth loving rather than one to simply support with monthly banknotes for food and lodging. But it was too late now. He was as dead to her as the tiny bird at her feet.

"It is good to see you out amongst the living rather than shut behind the walls of Balfour House."

Mr. Lambert's deep voice curled over her shoulder, and she stiffened. Of all the inopportune times for the doctor to arrive!

Tugging out a handkerchief she'd tucked into her sleeve, she hastily dabbed her eyes, then turned to face him with a brave smile. Leastwise, she hoped it looked brave and not like a crazed grimace. "Good morning, Mr. Lambert."

"Good morning, Miss—you're crying." Concern creased his brow, and with his free hand, he reached up and wiped away a straggling tear near her chin with the pad of his thumb. "For what cause?"

Huskiness laced his voice—a tone she'd never before heard him employ. All manly and protective. One that wrapped around her and bid her to shelter against his chest. Sweet heavens. What was she thinking?

She straightened her shoulders. Her thoughts may be muddled, but her posture didn't have to suffer for it. "You'll think it silly of me, Doctor, but the cause is nothing more than a fallen sparrow." Stepping aside, she indicated the bird. "It flew into the window as I stood looking out."

His gaze drifted from her to the bird, his face completely unreadable, which unaccountably set her on edge. Did he think her an empty-headed female who was overly passionate for such an underwhelming occurrence?

She clenched her hands. Since when did so much of her confidence depend upon a man's opinion?

"Well…" He rubbed one hand along the bristles of his trimmed beard as he studied the sparrow, then set down his bag and pulled off his hat. "Let us see what can be done."

He knelt and gently guided the bird's body into the crown of his hat, his hand impossibly large next to the tiny sparrow.

Amelia gaped. "It is dead, Doctor. There is nothing to be done about that."

"Have a little faith, Miss Balfour." He rose with a gleam in his eye. "Perhaps all is not lost."

With a wink, he snatched up his leather bag then tipped his head towards the house. "After you."

Puzzled, she led the way, his sure steps following from pavement to sitting room, where he bypassed her and made space on the table with all the medical instruments. Was he seriously thinking he could resurrect the bird?

She joined his side, close enough to breathe in his now-familiar sagey scent. "Are you a miracle worker, sir?"

A pleasant chuckle rumbled in his throat. "Hardly."

Pulling a handkerchief from his pocket, he dabbed away the tiny bit of blood near its beak. "Nor do I make any grand promises. But who knows? The little fellow appears to still be breathing."

"It's alive?" Unbidden, her fingers strayed to her pocket, her finger-tip brushing against the silky smoothness of the Ibis feather. "Perhaps good luck did prevail after all," she murmured.

"Luck has nothing to do with it." He straightened. "As my mother would have said, God alone appoints the number of our days—even a sparrow's. And with some care, God might not yet number this little one amongst the fallen. I suspect it may be stunned, that is all, as long as that small amount of blood doesn't indicate further internal bleeding. With that in mind, I shall think on a course of treatment."

She pressed her lips tight to keep from gaping once again. What an absolute anomaly of a man. Modifying her brother's regimen so that each day would not be agony for him. Defending her against Mr. Peckwood's cutting remarks by standing up for her intelligence. And now, tenderly caring for a bird that most men would kick aside and be done with.

She peered up at him. "You are a very kind soul, Mr. Lambert."

"Others would beg to differ." He smirked.

"Your former captain, perhaps?" The question flew out before she could snatch it back—a trait that served her well when gathering information for a travel piece. But now? She bit her lip. What business was it of hers to inquire after his personal life?

"No," he murmured as he tucked away his handkerchief. "Not my captain. A certain lieutenant, rather."

Now she was intrigued. She'd heard stories of naval officers' exploits whispered by giddy females in London parlours. But she'd never heard of a surgeon entangled in such deeds, especially not one who appeared to be as upright as Mr. Lambert.

"What happened?" she asked, this time without one bit of remorse for her boldness.

Averting his gaze, he reached for his medical bag. "It is not a tale meant for a lady."

"Come now, Doctor. We both know I am made of sterner stuff."

"True." The glimmer of admiration in his eyes twanged a response deep in her belly.

"Very well." He shifted a wad of bandages from one hand to the other. "Though allow me to make our friend here a suitable resting place other than in my hat."

"I have just the thing, for now, at least." She padded over to the mantel, and though her foot still ached, what freedom there was not to have to depend upon a crutch or a cane. She removed an ornamental bowl with little blue sampans painted around the circumference and returned to Mr. Lambert. "I shall trade you this for a story."

"Not a very fair trade, I'm afraid. Our friend here is the one who shall get the better end of that deal." He smiled as he accepted the container, the captivating dimple making an appearance on the right side of his cheek.

"We anchored in Barbados to take on supplies." He began to unwind the tightly wound cloth strip. "Which allowed plenty of leave for the sailors before a solid eight-week voyage. The night before we were to depart, I was called upon to tend one of the islanders' daughters."

All pleasantness drained from his voice, and a stranger looked out from his eyes, fierce and foreboding.

"The woman had been brutally abused. She claimed her attacker was one of ours and that she'd scratched the left side of his face quite severely. I filed a report and turned it in to the captain, then waited on board for the returning sailor to visit my quarters for care. None came."

Amelia frowned. "Had she perhaps been mistaken? Surely other sailors roam those same streets. How could she have known it was a member of your crew?"

"She said the man made sure to impress upon her the name of the ship, that every time she saw it anchor in the harbour to be ready for him, for he'd be back." He jerked the last bit of bandage free. "Of course, the man could've been lying—or she might have been—and that's what I began to believe when no sailor came to my quarters to have his face tended. The next day passed in the flurry of setting sail, but that evening at dinner…"

A great sigh deflated his chest, and he said nothing more. Just padded layer after layer of the dressing inside the porcelain dish. Once it was all deposited, and with more tenderness than ought be possible with his strong fingers, he laid the sparrow carefully on the cloth bedding.

"What happened then?" she gently prodded, trying to put him as much at ease as he attempted to provide for the bird.

"Lieutenant Clerval arrived in the wardroom with severe lacerations on his cheek. His *left* cheek. I questioned him. He made up a thinly veiled excuse, which later changed after liberal amounts of brandy. So I marked up the other side of his face with a left hook." Mr. Lambert stepped back from the bird and fixed her in place with a stare so intense, she felt it to her toes. "There. Do you still think me kind, Miss Balfour?"

She shook her head, trying to make sense of the self-condemnation running rampant in his tone. "But the man deserved it. Why were you dismissed when the lieutenant was the true villain?"

The lines of his face hardened, sharpening into a fury she couldn't begin to understand. "Because Clerval was a society man. The son of a baronet with large pockets."

His words stole her breath. "How horribly unfair!"

"Indeed." A muscle at the side of his jaw jumped. "But never fear, Miss Balfour. I am told God will have His justice in His own time."

"That He shall. And, if you'll forgive my forwardness, it seems to me the self-reproach I detected in your tone is highly unwarranted. You did the right thing."

Something behind his eyes moved then, like the closing of a great pair of shutters. Gone was the righteous anger, and the calm-mannered doctor once again appeared. "Well, it is behind me now, and there are more important matters at hand, like your ailing sparrow. When it wakes, you should…wait. I'll write it down."

He pulled out a notepad from his pocket, then retrieved a pencil from his bag. After scratching his instructions, he ripped off the small sheet of paper and handed it to her. "Here is a prescription for full sparrow care."

"Thank you."

"Oh, and one more thing. If you will allow me?" Grasping her chin—his touch as gentle and firm as he'd employed with the sparrow—he tipped her face to the sunshine streaming in the window. "I should like to examine you. I fear you may be taking on too much."

Good thing he wasn't listening to her heart. That traitorous organ fluttered like one of Mrs. O's free-ranging birds. She could feel the heat of him, so close did he stand, and couldn't keep from admiring his fine strong nose and the handsome cut of his jaw.

"Hmm," he murmured, an altogether pleasing sound, the sort that set the world right simply by the vibration of it.

She leaned towards him, drawn by his magnetism—until a throat cleared at the door and she jerked away.

Mrs. Kirwin frowned on the threshold. "Betsey asked me to let you know she's gone to the milliner about your hat."

"Very well." Amelia dismissed her with a nod.

But the woman didn't move. "Is there aught I can do for you or the doctor? Maybe tidy up in here a bit?"

"Nothing at all, thank you."

"Well, if that changes, just ask." The housekeeper narrowed her eyes. "I'll be nearby the whole while."

Of course she would.

"Thank you, Mrs. Kirwin." Amelia smiled sweetly and waited until the housekeeper's skirts swished away before facing the doctor. "Well, what is your diagnosis?"

"That your housekeeper is overprotective and that you will live." A faint smile ghosted his lips. "But you do look a bit peaked. Fatigued, I would say. There are shadows beneath your eyes and your skin is pallid. I suspect another prescription is in order."

Once again, he scribbled on his notepad, then tore off the sheet. "This is for you. See me when you are ready for it to be dispensed."

Curious, she lifted the paper, and her cheeks grew warm as she read.

Balfour, Amelia
Recommend fresh air and exercise
by walking, prn, escorted by Graham Lambert

❧

An evening breeze blew in the window, flickering the lamplight and casting crazed shadows around the tiny office. The coolness, while welcome, could—and no doubt would—wreak havoc with the papers on the desktop. Papers Graham had been desperately trying to tend since the last patient had left nigh on four hours ago.

Leaning sideways, he closed the sash, then sank back in his chair and pinched the bridge of his nose. What a long day. So many patients. So much need. His head hung heavy, his bones as weary as Amelia Balfour had looked earlier that morning.

And then it hit him again, the very ignominy he'd been trying to banish all day. He slammed down his pen, rattling the inkwell. Whatever had possessed him to such boldness with the woman? Inviting her for a walk. What had he been thinking? He didn't stand a chance with Miss Balfour, not a man like him, a doctor in need of his own practice. What had he to offer her but long hours away from home, tending to the sick and needy? It was a wonder she'd not tossed him out on his ear the second he'd handed her that prescription. Yet instead of balling up the paper and throwing it at his head, she'd graciously tucked the ridiculous remedy into her pocket and given him an enigmatic smile before promptly changing the subject.

Outside the door, footsteps clipped, and a moment later, Peckwood's grey head peeked in, his hat clutched in his hands. "What's this? You are still here?"

Graham straightened in his seat. The man had every right to be surprised, for he should've finished this paperwork long ago. And he would have, if not for a certain raven-haired lady plaguing his thoughts.

"Guilty as charged, sir. I have been working on formulating a new calming draught for Mr. Victor's dyspepsia. Ginger tea and peppermint balm are not doing the trick."

The old surgeon pursed his lips, lamplight casting odd shadows on his face from the movement. "I assume you've ruled out gluttony."

"Naturally."

Peckwood pulled out his spectacles and perched them on his nose, then peered at the formula Graham had been working on. "What have you got?"

With one finger, he pushed the paper closer to the doctor.

"Charcoal. Chalk. Fennel. Mmm, very good." Peckwood leaned

closer. "White oxide of bismuth?" The doctor straightened, as did his brows. A gleam of appreciation flashed in his dark eyes. "Very progressive of you, Lambert."

Graham soaked in the man's praise. These moments of appreciation didn't quite make up for the times Peckwood railed at him for insubordination, but they did soothe those abrasions and were, he suspected, the very reason the doctor kept him on instead of dissolving their partnership.

He swiveled in his seat, facing the man. "Not too far out of the realm of plausibility, I hope."

"On the contrary. I have recently read of an American doctor who not only wrote a thesis on the compound but has since had much success with it. Not to mention notoriety."

"I read the same, which is where I got the idea. Apparently Mr. Samuel Moore is making quite a name for himself."

"Which goes to show that journal publications can make or break a surgeon's career. One wrong article, and you are anathema." He pushed the paper back across the desktop. "But if you present something innovative, with the research to back it up, well…you'll have the Academy knocking at your door, offering money and prestige. All it takes is the proper publicity."

"Perhaps, yet too much money or prestige is a cancer."

"There is a cure for every disease, Lambert. All you have to do is discover it. And if you're the first to do so, you will have the medical community eating out of your hand."

Nine chimes tolled from the great longcase clock in the receiving room, and Peckwood promptly clapped on his hat. "Excuse me, but we'll have to finish this discussion another time. I have a meeting to attend. Lock up on your way out, please. Good night."

Graham dipped his head. "Good night."

The man's footsteps faded. The thud of the front door echoed throughout the empty building. A lonely sound. Melancholy, in a way, for now he was utterly alone.

And yet a charge ran through him. This was the first time he'd been the sole occupant of the building since he'd discovered that corpse in

Peckwood's quarters three days ago. The perfect opportunity to search for a connection to the man's supplier.

He pushed away from the desk and grabbed the lamp, debating all the way up the staircase about the ethics of his actions. Peckwood had told him outright to stay clear of his personal business, yet was it personal when it involved a medical illegality? Was it not his duty as a citizen to expose those who had committed a crime? For if Peckwood had been supplied a body by resurrectionists, then there was more at stake than just the private life of one man. That body had belonged to someone who trusted their loved one rested peacefully beneath the earth, not lay naked upon a wooden slab.

At the top of the stairs, he stopped, the door inches in front of him. A load of confliction weighed heavy on his back. Did the end justify the means of trespass? Stumbling into the room as he had last time didn't equate with the willful entrance he was about to commit.

Well, God? What of it? Am I once again trying to bring justice ahead of Your time?

He received no answer but the flickering of the lamp flame. This was ridiculous. Either he ought to charge ahead or forget the whole matter once and for all. He put his hand on the knob, then paused, unsure. No doubt the thing would be locked, and he'd have to work to unlatch it, which would add crime upon crime to his account.

So what's it to be, God? Am I Your instrument in this matter or simply another sinner bent on doing his own will?

And...nothing. No guidance whatsoever. The same uncertainty churned in his gut. How had his mother ever heard God's voice so clearly?

He turned away, but the scuff of his fingers on the knob sent the door creaking open. Not much, but enough that Peckwood would discern he'd been up here nosing about. In his great haste for his meeting, had the man forgotten to lock it...or was this a trap?

He reached for the knob, intent on ending this fool's errand, but this time his lamplight ran ahead of him and illuminated a portion of the room.

The very *empty* room.

Graham pushed the door open all the way and entered, golden

light landing on naught but a Turkish carpet at center. Not a slab. Not a body. Just a rug. He swung his gaze to the wall of shelving. Where once jars of body parts sat row upon row, now books lined up like little soldiers. The only thing that remained the same was the big desk near the window.

He padded over to it, set down the lamp, and fingered through some assorted papers, making sure to keep them in the exact order as he found them. Yet document after document, slip after slip, not one thing even so much as hinted at a connection between Peckwood and resurrectionists. He blew out a disgusted breath. What an imbecile. What was he expecting? A proper receipt? Still, that didn't stop him from a quick once-over of the rest of the desk.

From the lowest drawer, he pulled out a wrinkled sheet of paper that'd been crammed to a back corner. Holding it close to the lamp, he squinted at the invoice for lamp oil. A red PAST DUE was stamped across the top, the date received several weeks ago. Was the man not paying his bills? But why? He not only had the funding Graham had deposited for half the practice but the fat payment from the Balfours as well. Not to mention the increase in patients and the resulting income from their care. Where was Peckwood's money going?

He rubbed his neck. Troubling, that. He was going to have to discuss it with the man but in a way that wouldn't reveal he'd nosed about in his private quarters. He nestled the invoice back in its resting place and shut the drawer.

Swinging about, he cast a last glance at the bookshelves. Medical references, all. Nothing odd whatsoever there, save for the alignment of the last four titles on the far right at the top. The spines sat at the edge, as if the doctor had removed them for inspection then shoved them back without taking the time to line them up with the others. What had Peckwood been researching of late?

Graham pulled one off and inspected the title. *The Anatomy of Humane Bodies with Figures Drawn after the Life.* Pish. No great surprise here. Graham himself owned this one. Reaching, he shoved it in place, or tried to. The thing would not set right, having hit something hard. Pulling the book back out, he set it down and lifted the lamp.

Something was blocking the way, and by the looks of it, a great sheaf of paper.

He removed the other books then pulled down a three-inch stack of documents. The top sheet was clearly a letter, but undated and with no address other than *Dear Sir*. Scanning the contents, he frowned. This was a query for publication, yet without a title. Was this what Peckwood had been spending his time on?

"Present something innovative, with the research to back it up, well… you'll have the Academy knocking at your door, offering money and prestige."

The doctor's words suddenly made sense. So did the cadaver Graham had spied earlier. But what exactly was the man researching? He flipped to the next page.

> *Transsphenoidal (or Transcranial?) Removal of a Portion of*
> *the Frontal Lobe*
> *A Remedy for the Complete Reversal of Madness*
> *and Full Restoration of the Human Psyche*

Apparently Peckwood hadn't decided yet on the best approach to his innovative new procedure, because the title was in question. Either way, quite the morbid procedure—unless it actually worked.

Graham replaced the papers on the shelf, filled with more questions than when he'd come in here. Was this the reason for the doctor's excessive amount of time at St. Peter's? For his close relationship with the warden, one that allowed his access to the inmates?

And if so, how many inmates had suffered for the sake of this research, for Peckwood's quest of money and prestige?

THIRTEEN

"This was strange and unexpected intelligence;
what could it mean?"

∽

Some mornings, it took more than a prebreakfast cup of strong black tea to face the world. It took cold-blooded courage. Particularly when Betsey stood near the bedroom door with a glower that could make a saint cower behind a crucifix.

Undeterred, Amelia gently picked up the small box with the sparrow inside and cradled it in the crook of her arm. The container jiggled a bit, the tiny bird moving about, more than ready to fly free. Twenty-four hours of following Mr. Lambert's instructions had worked wonders. Apparently the man wasn't only talented at caring for humans but for all of God's creatures.

She crossed the rug, ignoring the sudden rush of warmth from thinking of the good doctor. Nor would she pay any heed to the endless concerns Betsey had been voicing since she'd opened the draperies and helped her dress. Amelia paused near the scowling matron. "Chin up, my friend. You worry too much."

"Me?" Betsey snorted. "You're the one who frets endlessly about your brother. Who's awake till all hours, writing your fingers to nubs in an effort to appease a publisher who is capricious at best. And now this." She threw her hands in the air. "Dawn's hardly broken and here you are, escorting a sparrow as if it were a child in your arms, anxious for its release. Summer or not, you'll take a chill this early in the morn, and then who will care for you?"

Amelia grinned and pertly lifted her nose. "You, of course. But I think the true heart of the matter is that you're jealous."

"Of what?"

She held up the box, cautious not to upset it overmuch. "That our fine fellow here did not have to awaken as early as you."

"Miff-muff!" Her maid's fingers fluttered towards the door. "Off with you."

Amelia chuckled as Betsey turned away, but three steps later, the matronly servant pivoted back with an arched brow. "Unless you'd like me to attend the going-away ceremony?"

Amelia shook her head. "No need. Sit yourself down with a cup of tea. What with Colin's morning treatment, I don't think I shall be needing anything until later today."

"Right. Good luck, then." Betsey nodded at the box.

"Thank you."

One hand on the railing to steady herself, Amelia toted the sparrow down the stairs. Despite Betsey's outspoken ways, a compassionate heart beat beneath that sturdy grey bodice.

Armed with her lucky Ibis feather in one pocket and Mr. Lambert's prescriptions in the other, she shoved open the back door, though she needn't have bothered with the doctor's written instructions. She'd memorized his details on how to release the bird, and as for the other recommendation to take a walk with him as needed, well…there was absolutely no reason to carry that about other than she found it strangely charming. How was it that a man, other than her brother, would not only take note of her fatigue but also make such a personal offer to remedy it? Dare she hope Graham Lambert took interest in her, not as a patient, but as a woman?

She stopped beneath the canopy of the linden and knelt, nestling the box in the grass. Silently she counted to ten, allowing time for the bird to get used to the lack of movement. If this didn't work, she would simply have to add the poor thing to Mrs. O's feathered menagerie.

"Are you ready, little one?" she whispered. "It won't be easy, but I am cheering for you."

Her brow scrunched. Did God ever murmur the same to her despite her imperfections? Strange idea, that the Almighty might view her efforts to please Him as a child's fumbling attempts to walk or a bird's hesitant endeavor to fly. She wasn't sure she altogether enjoyed the comparison.

Gripping the top of the container, she lifted the lid then sank back on her haunches and waited. The tip of a beak appeared. Wings rustled. And then the sparrow lifted its head and took off on a breath of morning air.

Amelia's gaze followed the bird's route, bypassing branches and leaves, up into the blue. Flying free. Doing what it was created to do. Being exactly how it was supposed to be, without apology.

Soon Colin would be able to experience the same.

"I've often thought we might fly too, if only we would let go of that which weighs us down."

Amelia shot to her feet, startled to see Mary Godwin's thin face regarding her through the breach in the garden wall. How long had her neighbour been watching? She dipped her head in greeting. "Wise words, Miss Godwin."

"Mary, please." A small smile played on her lips. "Formality makes for good politicians, not friends."

"You speak truth, Mary." Amelia grinned in full. "I daresay this world could use more friends and fewer politicians."

"Hear, hear! But do tell." She lifted her hand to the sky, pointing to the sparrow's route. "Is this a pastime of yours, freeing birds and wistfully watching them go?"

So she had witnessed the whole event. Amelia gathered the box and held it up. "This is my first—and hopefully only—venture. I've actually been spending more time working on your suggestion of the other night."

"Excellent! The shadowy tales of Bristol, eh? I should dearly love to read it when you are finished." She clasped her hands in front of her, quite the picture of innocence in her white lawn gown, morning sunshine blessing her nut-brown hair like a benediction. A sharp contrast to the gruesome history the petite lady wished to read about. "Perhaps your stories will inspire me to explore my new neighbourhood. Oh! That reminds me. Hold on a moment."

She disappeared into the house, leaving Amelia standing with an empty box and a head filled with questions. What a queer little woman.

Moments later, Mary reappeared and held out a sheaf of papers bound with string. "Some inspiration for you."

Tucking the box back under her arm, Amelia strode to the crumbled rock wall and retrieved the bundle. Fine penmanship graced the top sheet. Strong. Bold. Elegant. Amelia peered over at Mary. "Your mother's writing?"

"The very same."

Amelia smoothed her fingers over the cool sheets of parchment. "I shall take great care of this. Thank you for your kindness."

"No need." She angled her head. "No, wait a minute. There is, perhaps, a tangible way in which you could show your gratitude."

Oh dear. She should have known. Though she frequently tried to deny it, no one gave anything away without cost, just as her father had taught. And so she'd experienced in her travels. Why had she expected Mary to be different? "What is it you think I can do for you?"

"Not you, per se." Mystery twinkled in her eyes. "Allow me to hire your boy. I am on my own until Mr. Shelley returns, and there are certain errands to run and things about the house to do that I have not been able to attend. I have not been feeling well, you see— hence my early morning turn about the garden. Fresh air is so healing, is it not?"

Amelia studied the woman's face. A shade on the pale side, a bit drawn, but all in all, nothing else about her appeared sickly. "I am sorry to hear of your illness. Should you have need of a surgeon, I highly recommend Mr. Lambert."

"Thank you. I shall keep that in mind, but I don't think what I suffer requires medical intervention. Nine months or so ought to do very nicely."

Amelia blinked. Mary was with child? Should she offer congratulations or condolences, being the woman was admittedly on her own and not yet married? She held Mary's earnest stare, forbidding her gaze from slipping to the woman's middle. "Well then, I look forward to meeting your new little one someday."

"Yes, hopefully. Though one is never guaranteed any number of days or…" A faraway look glazed her eyes, and her shoulders sagged. No, her whole body did. As if a hole had suddenly been carved into her chest and her heart removed, leaving nothing but a shell, a frame so fragile, it might give way at any moment.

Alarmed, Amelia stepped toe-to-toe with what remained of the wall, ready to leap through the gap should the small woman swoon. "Mary? Are you all right?"

"What?" Her gaze snapped back to Amelia. "Oh. Pardon. Yes, I am fine. Well then, about your boy. May I hire him off you?"

The question did nothing to ease her worry for her new friend. Clearly the woman was confused. "We employ no boy," Amelia explained gently. "Balfour House is minimally staffed at the moment."

"Really? Then I beg your pardon. I had no idea he was your son."

Hah! A spinster such as she? Amelia couldn't help but chuckle. "I have no child."

Small creases lined Mary's brow. "So, just to be clear, there is no flaxen-haired boy, say five or six years old, of yea height"—she lifted her hand to hip level—"all arms and legs, who lives in your home?"

"No, there is not."

"How curious, for I often see him coming and going."

Mary's eyes shone blue. Clear. No hint of jesting or humour. Were hallucinations part of early pregnancy? Perhaps Mr. Lambert ought to examine the young lady.

Amelia smiled to put her at ease. "Probably just a neighbourhood lad, roaming about like a stray cat. In fact, when I first arrived, I discovered his ball behind the trellis over there." She lifted her free hand and indicated the overgrown clematis.

Mary's gaze drifted to the corner of the yard. "Yes, of course. My mistake. Think nothing of it, then."

Her explanation was wholly sufficient. It was an easy enough error to overlook. Even so, Amelia turned away as the full weight of the woman's words pressed in on her. Normally she wouldn't give such a blunder another thought.

Were it not for the toy soldier she'd found *inside* the house.

Colin stared out his bedchamber window, watching his sister kneel on the lawn. A touching sight, the way the first rays of sunshine blessed her bowed head. She took infinite care in setting the little box gently on the ground. But even so, the short hairs at the nape of his neck prickled to attention. So did the hairs on his arm. Was he the watcher?

Or was he the watched?

He spun, fully expecting to see a servant at the door. Or at the very least, perhaps a mouse observing him from the safety of a hole in the baseboards. His gaze drifted from one wall to another, floor to ceiling, until he was satisfied there was no other life-form in the room.

He turned back to the window, but the unease remained. Some might say the room was haunted, and in truth he'd heard a servant girl whispering as much to Mrs. Kirwin. But he knew better. The only spectre that troubled Balfour House was himself.

Outside, Amelia lifted the lid, and he pressed his face to the glass, heart suddenly beating fast. Something was wrong. Why did the bird not immediately soar free? Rise to the heavens and never look back? Lord knows he would…but would he really? Even when Peckwood did eventually perform his miracle, after a lifetime of living shut away, would he have the fortitude it took to walk freely amongst mankind?

Then the sparrow flew, wings stretched, catching the wind, passing near the window as it circled about, and a sob burned in Colin's throat. If a bird once broken could fly, he ought to be able to do so as well. Yet who knew if the upcoming surgery would work? Or if he'd even survive it? Broken or not, he ought to be man enough to fly free like that bird right now!

He wheeled about and grabbed his hooded cloak off a hook near the door. The day was young enough that few souls would be roaming about. He'd return before his treatment, and no one would be the wiser.

"You're up early. Be ye going somewhere, Master Colin?"

Mrs. Kirwin's voice stopped him before he reached the stairway. The mobcapped housekeeper shut the door opposite his behind her. Why was she not seeing to the downstairs staff as she should be?

"I will be stepping out for a few moments," he explained, then lowered his voice for her alone. "And I'll thank you to keep this excursion between ourselves."

"Pish-posh! What's this? A secret, then?" Her pale blue eyes sparkled merrily as she clapped her hands together. "I do love a good intrigue, sir."

Rot and bother! That'd been the wrong tack to sail. The goosey housekeeper would be honking of his absence for all to hear if she thought this a game to be played.

"Forgive me, Mrs. Kirwin, for clearly I have misled you. Keeping silent in regard to my absence is not a secret, but rather a gesture of mercy. For, you see, I would not want my sister to worry."

"La, such a notion!" She hooted, her shoulders twitching with mirth. "Why, once that fine young doctor arrives, I daresay he won't be giving Miss Amelia a chance to fret about anything at all, not even you."

Colin stiffened. What on earth had Mrs. Kirwin seen that would prompt her to say such a thing? "What do you mean?"

"Oh, don't mind me. I suppose this may be one of those gestures of mercy you were talking about." She fluttered her fingers in the air as she bypassed him and scurried towards the staircase, pausing with one foot on an ascending step. "Off with you, then, and godspeed on whatever it is you're about. I've gone and lost my larder key, and Cook is red-faced about it, so I must be off as well. Only one more floor to search."

Colin flung his cloak over his shoulders, pausing to tie a knot at his neck and ponder Mrs. Kirwin's unexpected intelligence about his sister and Lambert. There was an undeniable attraction between the doctor and his sister, but was their relationship advancing to an impropriety? He liked the man well enough. Still, he'd not see Amelia hurt. God knew she'd been maimed enough by Father's harsh words. He tugged the bow tight. Perhaps he'd have a word with Lambert. Search out the man's intentions. Make sure he understood that his sister was not to be trifled with.

That settled, he trotted down the stairs and fled the house, flipping up his hood as he emerged into the morning air. This early, pedestrians were nonexistent. Even so, he set his face towards the Avon River gorge, preferring the seclusion of greenery and cliff to the commerce of Clifton.

It didn't take long to leave behind the houses and turn onto a trail that led into the woods. Birdsong accompanied him, as did the hum of insects. The farther he traveled, the narrower the path. City folk didn't travel this far from the hub of town, so it caught him off guard when he heard voices on the breeze.

"Davey!"

"Come back, lad. Daa-vee!"

Colin tugged his hood forward and upped his pace. They'd be hollering for more than just a wayward boy if they chanced a look at his face. Only when the path emerged from the trees and emptied onto a stretch of flatland did he slow. To his left, a field of purple speedwell in full bloom hummed with bees and white-winged butterflies. A stunning masterpiece, yet he turned away from it and stepped off the path, closer to the edge of the cliff, and welcomed the gust of wind that cooled his face.

Below him, honewort and rockcress clung to the rugged surface, dazzling splashes of green and white all the way down to the black river snaking through the bottom of the gorge. Tenacious little plants, clinging to the sharp crags of limestone. Refusing to give up and plummet to a sure death. This high up, the sound of the rushing water could not be heard—but laughter could. Childish laughter.

He snapped his gaze aside, pulling his hood as far forward as possible. Ten yards down the path, a small boy, arms outstretched, chased a butterfly, giggling. Chubby legs pumping. Tow-coloured curls crowned his head, wispy as milkweed silk. A heartwarming sight—were the child not running straight towards the brink of the cliff.

Colin took off at a dead run, jamming his hand into his pocket and fishing about for something—anything!—to lure the child to him. "Aye there, boy! Over here."

The lad stopped, feet perilously close to the edge. One gust of wind could take him. But at least his stare was no longer fixed on the butterfly.

"Wha's that?" The sweet, high pitch of innocence sang in his voice.

Colin slowed his pace as he dangled his pocket watch. Rushing the child could cause a retreat—one from which the lad would never recover. "This is for you, boy. A gift."

"Me?" The boy jammed his thumb into his chest so forcefully he wobbled.

Sweat beaded down Colin's brow, stinging his eyes. So close! If he lost the child now, he'd never forgive himself.

"You are Davey, are you not?" Two more steps. Just two.

The boy's eyes widened, impossibly blue. "Tha's me! Did you see my butterfly?"

Swinging out his arm, the boy pivoted on one foot. Too fast. Too forceful. The top half of his body flipped over the ledge.

Colin swiped, snatching the child's waistband. Yanking him back to safety. Clutching him to his chest, he staggered backwards. For the first time in his life, he thanked God for arms too long and hands too big.

The boy giggled. "Do it again!"

Colin let out a huge whoosh of air, draining the jittery unrest in his muscles. Shifting the lad to one arm, he held out the watch, fully entrancing the boy. "Not now, Davey. Here. This is yours."

Tiny fingers snatched the golden trinket from his hand. "Oooh, pretty," he purred, then he flung his arms around Colin's neck and squeezed. "Thank ye!"

For the briefest of moments, Colin gave in. Nuzzled his misshapen cheek against the boy's downy head. Breathed deeply of the child's pure scent of earth and grass and all things little boys should smell of. An ache throbbed deep inside, in the cavern of his heart, for want of his own child. His own little man whom he could love and be loved by. A son born of passion, by a woman who would delight to bear his child. Who would delight in him.

"Day-vee!" A woman's ragged voice filtered out of the woods.

The boy straightened, face snapping towards the tree line. "Mama?" Just like that, the spell was broken.

"Yes, young Davey, you are missed." He swung the child up to his shoulders, taking great care to keep his own face hidden in the shadows of his overlarge hood, then tramped back along the path. "Call for your mother."

"Mama!" Davey hollered.

As they stepped from the sunshine of field to the shadow of forest, a brown-haired woman, braids unpinned and flitting about her shoulders, ran headlong towards them. "Davey! Naughty boy. You gave me such a fright." Fear and longing, anger and relief, all bled out in her words and the great heave of a sigh as she stopped in front of them.

She peered up at Colin, and he instinctively recoiled deeper into his hood. "Thank you, sir, for finding my son. Please, come back with us, and I shall feed you breakfast for your good deed."

"No need, madam. My own plate awaits me at home."

"Look, Mama! Look!" Davey bounced on his shoulders, his little hand dangling the pocket watch by its chain and bobbing it in front of Colin's eyes.

Horror folded the woman's brow. "Give the man back his watch, Davey. You cannot keep such a thing."

"It is no longer mine, madam, for I gave it to your son. A reminder, of sorts, for young Davey." He swept the child off his shoulders, shifting him to one arm, and pointed to the watch. "This is to help you remember to never again run off alone. Do you understand, boy?"

Davey nodded, mumbling a solemn, "Aye, sir."

The woman gaped. "But we cannot possibly accept such a fine gift. You are too kind."

"I insist." He wrapped Davey's fingers around the watch, then held the child out.

His mother reached for him just as Davey launched into her arms, but in so doing, the boy's foot kicked Colin's hood, knocking it off. Exposing his face.

He swiped for the fabric.

Too late.

A scream rent the air. Loud as a siren's call. The woman's eyes bulged as she staggered backwards, face grey as death. "Help! A beast!"

The boy squirmed, twisting in her grip, and when his gaze landed on Colin, his high-pitched wails joined hers, along with a torrent of fat tears.

All the earlier communion he'd felt with the boy, the fledgling hope for a child of his own and woman to love, shattered into jagged shards. Cutting brutal. Cutting deep.

"Mary! Davey!" A man's voice bellowed off to Colin's left. Footsteps pounded. Crushing undergrowth. Coming fast.

Colin spun the other way as a shot rang out. He sprinted, praying to God he could outrun a bullet between the shoulders, yet knowing that no matter how fast he ran, he could never outpace the gruesome ugliness of his face. Breathing hard, he pumped his legs all the faster, racing pell-mell away from the awful screeches and howls, the blast of another shot, and now—more than ever—he was sure of one thing.

Whether it killed him or not, his only hope to ever be out in public again was Peckwood's surgery.

FOURTEEN

"I greatly need a friend who would have sense enough
not to despise me as romantic, and affection enough
for me to endeavour to regulate my mind."

❦

A full day after setting the sparrow free, Amelia herself flew from Balfour House, much to Betsey's chagrin. Her maid had engaged in a proper fit over it, her lips all pinched. She'd mumbled about how she should be the one to run an errand, not to mention that someone with barely recovered toes ought not be trampling around town. Yet Betsey *had* mentioned it. Even now Amelia couldn't help but smile at the gruff maid with a heart the size of Brighton.

But Betsey had also been right. Though Amelia tried to ignore it, there was a residual ache in her foot. Still, every step of the short walk from Clifton to Bristol had been worth it. Summer was short, pledging but a fleeting friendship, a companion she would keep company with for as long as possible.

As soon as she entered the small, brick post office, the clerk behind the counter lifted a face as flat as the bottom of her shoe. His nose was a straight line, his lips nearly nonexistent. But when his smile broke, two large front teeth protruded quite nicely, yellow as a rodent's. "Can I help ye, m'um?"

"Yes, please." She set her carefully wrapped manuscript on the counter. After a week of late nights writing until the ink would not be scrubbed off her fingers, she'd finished a rough draft of Bristol folklore. "I should like to have this sent on the next possible mail coach."

"Very well." The clerk set the package on a nearby scale. Leaning close, he squinted at the numbers. "That'll be a bob, m'um."

She fished in her reticule, then set a shilling on the counter while the fellow removed the parcel and stamped it with a postmark.

His eyes narrowed again, this time on the return address. "You be Miss Amelia Balfour, m'um?"

"I am."

He faced her with another smile, and she forced herself to keep her gaze on his eyes instead of his rabbity teeth.

"Why, then, I've got a letter for ye. It'd save ol' Freddy the trouble o' bringing it up to the house if ye don't mind me fetchin' it now."

"I'll be happy to wait." And she would. Colin had already received his morning treatment, so there was nothing pressing her to return home.

"Very good." The clerk disappeared through a door behind the counter. The whole time he was gone, Amelia shuffled through possibilities of what the letter might contain. Had Mr. Krebe changed his mind about her and written a formal dismissal? Perhaps her father's solicitor had yet one more legal document pertaining to her or Colin? She tapped her finger on the counter as she waited. More than likely it was simply a greeting from one of the many acquaintances she'd made during her travels.

"Here ye be, m'um." The clerk reappeared and held out a creamy envelope.

"Thank you." She collected the missive and went outside to read in private, on a little bench painted red just to the side of the door. Smoothing her skirts, she sat and broke the seal.

Dear Miss Balfour,

Hopefully the weather you are experiencing is better than the current thunderclouds which darken the office here in London. Be thankful you are in Bristol. Mr. Krebe has been in a particularly foul disposition of late.

That being said, I suggest you use the enclosed tickets

without delay, for I assure you, there will be no more extensions.
I wish you safe travels and many productive hours of
writing.

Sincerely,
Mr. Justin Moritz

Frowning, she refolded the paper. Hopefully her peace offering of the eerie tales of Bristol's history would pacify Mr. Krebe for now and make life easier for Mr. Moritz. She pulled out one of the tickets. Monday, July 31, 10:00 a.m. Just a little over three weeks away. Would Colin be sufficiently on the mend by then?

"I see you've taken my advice to heart. The fresh air suits you well."

Mr. Lambert's deep voice drove away any further thought of Colin or Mr. Krebe or—surprisingly—Cairo. How could a few simple words from this man do such a thing, especially when she'd already spoken with him earlier that morning? Or was it the nearness of him that affected her so? The way the hem of his trousers nearly brushed the trim of her skirt, or the pleasing waft of sage and lemon and man that made her pulse race so?

Giving herself a mental shake, she tucked the ticket back inside the letter, then peered up at the doctor. My, but he was tall, especially with her sitting. Even as she rose, the top of her head came barely to his nose. Still, that didn't stop her from tipping her face and admiring his good looks. Yet as she did so, her smile wavered. Something was off. His usual bright eyes seemed a bit bleary, his shoulders not quite as squared. He looked as if work and life and possibly the weight of the universe weighed him down, and her heart squeezed at the sight. Clearly the man had been working too hard, for Colin and for who knew how many other patients.

"Yes, Doctor, I did take to heart your instruction of fresh air and exercise." She looked him straight in the eye. "And may I say what is good for the patient might be good for the doctor as well."

"It might—*if* the sick didn't have an adverse proclivity for my attention whenever I chance to close up shop early." He winked.

A trademark gesture of his, one she should be used to by now, so why the strange twinge in her belly that made her gasp for air? What a base reaction. She gripped her reticule to keep from fanning her face. "Well, I suppose you cannot turn down a patient."

"Not if I wish to be a doctor of integrity."

Ahh, but he was, and to the detriment of his own health no less. Mr. Lambert worked himself ragged—the thought of which birthed a wonderfully preposterous idea, one that quirked her lips into a smile. "I might just have a way to keep your integrity intact while taking in a bit of air and exercise yourself."

He cocked his head. "What have you in mind, Miss Balfour?"

She tucked her letter into her pocket and pulled out the slip of paper he'd written for her days ago, then offered it over. "Have you time to fill this prescription now?"

As he pulled the paper from her fingers, she bit her lip. Would he think such a brazen act too forward?

Graham held the prescription loosely, wary of giving too much meaning to the fact that Amelia Balfour had toted the thing around these past few days. Or had she simply forgotten to remove it from her pocket? Perhaps…but that wouldn't account for the way her brown eyes gleamed up into his, half-hopeful, half-embarrassed. It'd been a long time since a woman looked at him with such earnest expectation. Pah! He stifled a snort. Who was he fooling? After years a'sea living amongst jack tars and swabbies, no woman had looked at him at all.

A breeze teased the corner of the tiny paper, and he pinched it tight. He could use a walk, especially with the beautiful Miss Balfour. It might serve as a remedy for the frustration festering inside him—or at least a little of it. As of yet, he'd not figured out a way to question Peckwood about the cleared-out room and unpaid bill he'd discovered in the man's office without incriminating himself.

"Of course, if you are too busy, Doctor, I fully understand." She cinched her reticule drawstring tight, a prim smile sliding ambiguously across her lips.

Sudden loss punched him in the gut, and against his better judgment, he shook his head. "I am never too busy for you, Miss Balfour, though I do have one stop to make before I am free. Would you like to come along?"

"That depends upon where." Her nose lifted like a hare sensing danger—a quality that no doubt served her well during her travels to foreign countries, but did she really think he'd lead her amiss?

An unaccountable sadness draped over him at the thought. He shook it off by shoving the prescription into his pocket. "Nothing too disreputable. I was just on my way to the Hatchett Inn, which isn't far from St. Brandon's Hill, a place I've been meaning to explore."

"I cannot refuse St. Brandon's." She smiled in full. "My nurse used to take me there as a young child, and it happens to be on my route home."

"All right, then, shall we?"

She fell into step at his side. "I hope it isn't too serious a case that awaits you at the inn."

"I suppose there's a possibility of someone choking on a fish bone, but other than that, I am merely dropping off this portfolio of notes for a meeting Mr. Peckwood is conducting." He lifted a bound swath of papers. "Afraid I didn't finish them up in time before the doctor left the office."

She peered over at him, brow sinking. "If they are your notes, should you not be staying for the meeting?"

"As senior partner, Mr. Peckwood felt the information would be better received from him. He's angling for investors to finance a new procedure he's working on."

"Well then, I hope he at least credits you for your labours."

Not likely. From what he'd come to know of Peckwood, if there were any glory to be had, the man would garner it all for himself. A little too forcefully, Graham kicked a piece of broken cobble out of the way. The fragment skittered across the street and bounced off a rain barrel.

"Sometimes, Miss Balfour, it is better to remain in the shadows. And here we are." He held open the blackened oak door of the Hatchett Inn.

The strong scent of ale and sausage drifted out, growing stronger as they stepped into a public room so ancient, a worn depression in the floorboards led them directly to the counter. Graham caught the barkeep's eye with a jut of his jaw, and the big-bellied man ambled over.

"What'll it be, sir?"

"See that this is given to Mr. Peckwood at once, please. He is expecting it." Graham handed over the folio.

"Aye, the doctor said as much when he arrived. I'll get it to him straightaway."

"Thank you." Officially finished with his errand, Graham turned to Miss Balfour and offered his arm. "Now then, shall we take our medicine in the great outdoors?"

"Ready when you are." She grinned as she rested her fingertips lightly on his sleeve.

A mere five minutes later, they reached St. Brandon's Hill, a rolling stretch of wildness, dotted with trees and trails, rising ever upwards, impervious to the city surrounding it. As much as he loved the ocean, he could get used to this bit of beguiling green—just as he could get used to the woman at his side.

She peered up at him, her brown eyes luminous in the brilliant afternoon. "You know more about my family than I do of yours. Have you any nearby?"

"None nearby, nor far off, I'm afraid."

"Oh." A wave of compassion washed over her face. "I hope I didn't overstep in asking."

"Not at all. Yours is a genuine inquiry, a sign of your inquisitive mind, not of a gossiper bent on collecting seeds to sow far and wide." He smiled, which widened into a full-fledged grin as her cheeks pinked a most becoming shade. "But in effort to satisfy you, I have no siblings. My father died when I was a small child, and I lived with my mother until I joined the navy at fifteen."

Her fingers pressed into his sleeve. "So young?"

"Other than my mother, there was nothing to keep me on land." He shrugged. "And I figured, why not get paid to learn a vocation?"

She stopped, her head tilting to a curious angle. "I wonder, sir, if you are more a businessman than a doctor."

"To be a success, one must be both in this profession."

He tensed as she studied his face, her brown gaze shifting from one eye to the other. A ridiculous response on his part, for this slight woman could not possibly proclaim him a success or a failure. She hardly knew him. So why the sudden urge to change that? To share with her things he'd never share with anyone else?

"Well." An intoxicating smile lifted her lips. "I am sure your mother would have been proud of you."

A familiar sorrow ached his chest. "I am not so certain, Miss Balfour, but I do know this—family, no matter the size of it, is precious. Never leave a loved one behind."

"That's quite the strong sentiment for a mere walk in the park."

She was right. How on earth had he allowed the conversation to veer so far off course? Tugging at his cravat, he looked away, taking refuge in the squawk of three ravens on a branch instead of digging himself deeper into memories better left buried.

"Oh, dear." Miss Balfour's hand fell away from his sleeve.

"Are you all right?" Graham snapped his gaze back to her, medical instinct on high alert. Her pupils were normal. Her skin was a bit pale, but only because she'd been so long in the house. Nothing about her appeared out of the ordinary. He should know, for he'd watched her closely enough this past month when she wasn't looking, memorizing the curve of her cheek, the swan-like neck, the elegant swoop of her shoulders.

She didn't answer, just kept on staring, her gaze fixed on a point past his shoulder. As the seconds ticked by, a real look of fear deepened the brown in her eyes—and raised the hairs on his forearms.

He wheeled about. Hands curling into fists. Feet spread. Poised to take on whatever threat may come. Leaves rustled overhead. Just off the path, two squirrels played tag, scurrying from one trunk to another. And that was all. No blackguards or cutthroats rushed from the trees. No one else even strolled on this part of the trail. Nothing—not one blessed thing—smacked of any sort of menace.

Perplexed, he turned back. "What's wrong?"

Licking her lips, she jerked her gaze back to his, and once again the collected Miss Balfour appeared, any hint of fear suddenly vanishing. "Forgive me. It was nothing." Tucking her chin, she walked on.

He stood there for a moment, once again scanning the area that had so disturbed her, when wings ruffled and the three black birds took flight.

He caught up to her in a few long strides. "Are you frightened of ravens, Miss Balfour?"

"Not the birds, just their number." She glanced at him sideways. "And I am not frightened, but rather…leery, I suppose. Are you not familiar with the tradition that a gathering of ravens portends death?"

So that's what this was? Naught but another of her superstitions, like the salt over her shoulder and the feather he knew for a fact she carried wherever she went. All the fight instinct in him drained, and he breathed easier. "On the contrary, Miss Balfour, from where I come, it is said that one raven is for sorrow, two is for mirth, and three for a wedding."

She quickly averted her gaze, a pretty blush reddening her cheeks.

He chuckled, supremely satisfied to have flustered her so. "At any rate, it's all a bunch of balderdash." He cut his hand through the air. "No truer than the promises made by the quack selling cure-all remedies on a street corner."

Once again she stopped, but this time her gaze was fixed steadily on him instead of over his shoulder. "You do not believe in the lore of our forefathers?"

"Not to the degree that it changes my behaviour in the here and now. And neither should you." He bopped her gently on the nose. "It is not good for the mind or the soul. Trust must ultimately rest on God, not in folklore, which is flimsy at best and malignant at worst."

"Point taken." She arched her brow. "But not all tales are so morbid. Some are lighthearted, others achingly beautiful. Since we are here, would you like to hear a story from the past of Brandon's Hill?"

"I am intrigued. Shall we sit? That boulder over there is more than big enough for two, but first—" He strode ahead and pulled out his handkerchief, sweeping away a few sticks. "There. All clean."

"Very gallant of you, sir." Smiling, Miss Balfour approached and settled her skirts on the far side of the big rock, then waited for him to sit before beginning. "This hill is named after a chapel dedicated to St. Brendan, which once stood at the summit over there." She pointed to the rise.

His gaze followed the direction of her slender finger. "Brendan?" He cocked his head at her. "Then why is it called St. *Brandon's*?"

Sunshine dappled through the trees, landing soft against her face, the fine curve of her cheeks, the full cut of her lips. How was he to pay attention to a story with such a beauty of a distraction?

The feathers on her bonnet fluttered as she angled her head jauntily. "Names, like people, change over time, hence the current mispronunciation. But the purpose of the saint remains, that being the godly patron of travelers, and in particular, mariners—which is why I thought you might be interested in this story, being you were a man of the sea. Sailors about to depart for all corners of the world would trek up here, seeking favour and blessing, for not to do so was inviting certain doom."

"Mmm," he grumbled. "Sounds ominous."

She rolled her eyes. "Oh, do play along, Doctor."

"Very well." He slapped his hand to his heart. "I vow I shall behave."

"Good." She tugged her gloves snugly over her knuckles and continued. "Now then, there was a certain sailor named Oswyn, a young man who fell hopelessly in love with a village maiden named Gillian, and she with him. Her father, however, was against their union, for a common sailor was no match for his daughter, or so he thought. But, as young lovers often will not be swayed, Oswyn and Gillian married in secret. Naturally, they could not share a home, but that didn't stop them from sharing their love in secret, which rumour has it they did, over there in that thicket of white mulberry trees. Oh, my!" She pressed a finger to her lips. "That was a bit much. I'm afraid I got carried away in the story."

He chuckled, surprisingly honoured she felt comfortable enough with him to share such an intimate reference. "One question. Were ravens involved in this match?"

Once again, the flush of a June rose coloured her cheeks, followed immediately by a flash in her eyes. "Do you mock me, sir?"

"Do you mind, very much?" He laughed, surprised by how good it felt, this mirth. This good-natured teasing. How long had it been since he'd so freely made merry?

She clouted him on the arm. "Do you want to hear the story or not?"

"I do." He forced solemnity to his tone, for to do anything else might end this magic moment.

"As I was saying"—she smoothed her palms along her skirts as she spoke—"Gillian and Oswyn met here as often as they could, until one night when her father discovered their tryst—the very night before Oswyn was to set sail for the Indies, a notoriously dangerous voyage. It is said Oswyn and her father wrestled till the break of day, Gillian wailing the entire time. Finally, Oswyn broke away, with no time to seek favour of St. Brendan before boarding his ship."

Miss Balfour stopped then. So did the movement of her hands. Instead, she clenched her fingers together and bowed her head.

Perhaps he ought not have encouraged such a sad tale, but what exactly was it that moved Miss Balfour to such emotion?

"And?" he prodded gently.

She sighed. "Oswyn never returned to his love. To this day, if you chance a midnight walk when the moon is full and the white mulberry is in flower, it is said you can still hear Gillian's cry—accompanied by that of her newborn child." Her gaze sought his, undeniable pain swimming deep in those brown pools. "The son that Oswyn never got to hold in his arms. A child who was never loved by his father."

Instinctively, he leaned towards her, drawn by her grief, a primal need rising to remove that sorrow. Right her world. Pull her into his arms and kiss away all that lay heavy on her heart. Yet to do so would be a barefaced admission, not only to himself but to her, of a truth he'd been trying to conceal for the past week. Nay, weeks. He was falling in love with her. Hard.

And he had absolutely no idea what to do about it.

FIFTEEN

*"I revolved rapidly in my mind a multitude of thoughts,
and endeavoured to arrive at some conclusion."*

Rainy afternoons were meant for a pipe, a book, and an overstuffed chair. A tranquil remedy for the ills of life, though apparently not for a headache. Colin purposely shoved the pain into a corner of his mind and furnished the resulting space with a treatise on English common law. Pat-pat-pattering droned against the library window. Spent Cavendish tobacco lingered in earthy clouds on the air. If he closed his eyes, he'd drift away. And he nearly did—until the pleasant sound of someone humming Bach swirled into the room.

Amelia practically waltzed through the door, book in hand, her blue skirt swaying about her legs. A faraway gleam shone in her eyes. Judging by the curve of her mouth and heightened colour on her cheeks, whatever filled her head was all-consuming and highly agreeable. He'd wager ten-to-one it had nothing whatsoever to do with travel writing. Twenty-to-one she didn't even know he was in the room.

He closed his book. "You are in a merry mood for such a dreary day."

"Oh!" Her gaze landed wild on him, her free hand flying to her chest. "What a start. I didn't see you there."

He nodded at the volume in her hand, a wry twist to his lips. "Perhaps I ought to read whatever it is that has you so enthralled."

A snort puffed from her nose. "Rather the opposite, I'm afraid.

This"—she shook the book in the air—"is nothing more than last night's sleeping material. I do not recommend it."

"Not sleeping well, are you?" He shifted in the chair. "Is there something occupying your thoughts overmuch? Or should I say...someone?"

She slapped the book against her dress with a scowl. "Don't be daft. Of course there is—a brother who is soon to undergo brain surgery."

"I do not question your concern, and I thank you for it, yet you have been inordinately cheerful since yesterday afternoon. I'd assumed the cause to be good news from your editor after your trip to the post office, until Mrs. Kirwin set me straight an hour ago when she brought me my pipe." He lifted the yellowed pipe by the bowl and shook his head. "The old goose let slip that she'd heard you'd been accompanied home by Mr. Lambert after strolling with him at St. Brandon's." He leaned forward, studying his sister intently. "Is there something I should know about, I wonder?"

"What you should wonder about, Brother, is why you have given such credence to a housekeeper's gossip." This time her snort was not nearly so feminine. "St. Brandon's was on my way home from the post office. The doctor merely tagged along after I ran into him in town. It was a walk, nothing more."

She shoved her book onto a shelf. "Besides, you know as well as I that I am too old for any such schoolgirl whimsies Mrs. Kirwin might imagine."

"It's not like you have one foot in the grave. You are only twenty-seven, are you not?"

His question hit some sort of target, for her shoulders stiffened. Amelia faced him. "I have a career and a brother to attend. Even were a man to show interest in the likes of me, there is no room in my life, and that's all there is to it."

"Mmm," he drawled. "Methinks the lady doth protest too much when it comes to the good doctor."

"You've been reading too much Shakespeare."

"And you parry like a swordsman, especially whenever I bring up the topic of Mr. Lambert."

A deep flush rose up her neck, which she attempted vainly to hide with a toss of her head. "Have I told you lately what a beast you are?"

"No need. I know what I am."

He leaned back against the cushion, unsettled. He knew exactly what sort of monster he was, for the boy's tears and the woman's cries still echoed in his heart. But what he didn't know was Lambert's intentions towards his sister. Perhaps he should've spoken to the man before now. Though his stubborn sister would not admit it aloud, obviously her feelings were already engaged, and he would not see her hurt. Father had done enough of that to last them each a lifetime.

"What has *you* so occupied this afternoon?" Crossing to perch on the arm of his chair, Amelia read aloud the title of the book in his lap. "*The Commentaries on the Laws of England.*" She straightened, an arch to one brow. "Am I to hope that in the near future there will be a Balfour called to the bar?"

A bitter laugh rumbled in his throat. Since childhood, he'd dreamed of donning a black robe and a wig, fighting for right in a world gone wrong. But even if Peckwood's operation proved successful, it would still be years before he could become a barrister. Oh, he knew enough of the theory of law, and was well versed in precedents and principles, but what did he know of the legal society as a whole? Of the powerful men and politics that inhabited the halls of justice? Would he, a hermit who'd been shut away from civilization, be accepted by such men?

He ran his fingers over the book's cover. "That remains to be seen, Sister."

"It shall be." She squeezed his shoulder. "You will be the best lawyer London has ever known, and so I leave you to your studies."

He caught her hand before she pulled away. "You're like her, you know. Leastwise what I imagine her to be."

Tiny creases marred her brow. "Who?"

He gazed up at the family portrait hanging above the mantel, painted before his birth. A raven-haired woman beamed at the young girl on her lap. A man with an iron-clad stare towered over them both. Even before his ogre of a son had been born, Grafton Balfour hadn't smiled, but that did nothing to change the beautiful demeanor of the woman, and Colin felt sure she'd have loved her misshapen child despite his deformities.

He sighed. "I never knew our mother, but I suspect she would've encouraged me much as you do."

"Oh, Colin." Sorrow thickened Amelia's voice. "Though I was only seven when she passed, I do remember her as a radiant beacon that warmed everyone in her path. She'd have been proud of you, as am I. But there is one thing you are very wrong about."

He snapped his gaze back to her. "What is that?"

"It is you who are like her in every way, not I."

She turned and vanished out the door, and just as well. She'd rendered him quite speechless. And he surely didn't feel like reading anymore.

Rising, he reshelved his book and strode from the library. A short lie-down before dinner might relieve the headache that'd crawled unbidden from its corner. The stairs groaned beneath his weight as he trudged up to his room. Might even mundane sounds such as this be forever changed once his body shrank—as Peckwood had assured him it would?

He reached for the knob on his bedroom door, then paused as lightning flashed at his back. Eerie light cast a shadow of his grisly silhouette against the door. Thunder bellowed, rattling the panes of the stairwell window while raindrops plastered the glass like grapeshot. Just a storm. Nothing unusual, especially for a summer day. So why the unease prickling down his backbone?

He wheeled about and scanned the length of the darkened corridor leading to Amelia's room. Another bolt of lightning strobed, reaching in through the window at the end of the passage. Lighting the world in electric white.

And outlining the shape of a child.

❧

The blink of an eye. The beat of a heart. Astounding how fast things could change. One minute, the heavens rent and poured down fury. The next, late afternoon sunshine broke through the clouds like the charge of a light brigade through enemy lines.

Pushing away from the desk, Graham strode to the window. Fat raindrops yet clung to the glass as he threw open the frame, ushering in the fresh scent of a world washed clean. For one glorious moment, he breathed in the promise of a beautiful night. When he finished that pile of paperwork on his desk, another good, long walk would be just the thing.

The front door crashed open, followed by a man's ragged shout. "Doctor! Help!"

So much for a long walk.

He wheeled about, striding from the small office into the reception room, where three dockhands hoisted a body between them, two at the head, one at the feet. Blood dripped in a steady stream onto the floor.

"In here, men." Graham threw open the surgery door, allowing them passage. The smell of sweat, tar, and soured ale followed.

So much for fresh air too.

He tagged after them. "What happened?"

After a grunt and a heave, the men deposited the body onto the examination table, and the eldest of the trio lifted a face full of wiry whiskers towards him. "Chain broke, droppin' a crate o' lampblack and catchin' ol' Hobbs unawares." He dipped his head at the broken fellow on the table. "Crushed him, it did. Can ye save him?"

Two of the men backed away as Graham stepped up to the table. In a trice, he scanned the injured dockhand from head to toe. A bone protruded from the man's left arm, skin ripped open, muscle partially flayed. But even more worrisome was the blood pooling out of his gut on the same side. As a naval surgeon, Graham had seen as much and worse, but time was of the essence, and there was no way he could do this alone.

He met the elder man's gaze. "With a little help, I think your man will be saved." Striding to the door, he addressed the other two. "Light the lamps, men, then wait outside, if you please."

"We be lightin' yer lamps and be glad for it, but we not be stayin.' Broken chain and now one man down, we've a sight o' work ahead of us a'fore it gets dark."

Graham paused, rolling up his sleeves. "I understand. I shall send word when your friend here is on the mend."

He dashed down the corridor, surprised to see Peckwood already clearing the last stair. "I was just about to call you, Doctor."

"I heard the commotion." Peckwood joined his side. "What have we?"

"Dockyard injury. Lacerated arm and abdominal bleeding."

"I'll take the gut. You do the arm."

"Yes, sir." The instant he returned to the surgery, Graham hefted an oak addendum to the table—a smaller slab that connected to two posts beneath—and carefully shifted Hobbs's injured arm onto it. Leastwise as much as he could without causing further damage.

While he attended to the arm, Peckwood had rolled over a small instrument table on wheels, prepared only this morning for just such an emergency. After a dip of their hands into a basin of water and a cursory toweling off of the moisture, they set to work.

At first, neither of them spoke, each too engrossed in stopping the bleeding then deducing how best to put all the man's parts back together. Eventually, though, Peckwood broke the silence.

"Quite the boon the fellow is unaware. Makes the procedure much easier when the patient isn't writhing about like an eel."

"A boon, yes, but sometimes a curse," Graham said as he pushed a string of catgut through the eye of a needle. "I've seen many a successful surgery give way to a patient who never awakens and eventually succumbs to his coma, which rather negates the whole operation."

"As may be," Peckwood grunted, "but at least the poor man will never have known a moment of the agony of surgery. If and when this fellow does come 'round, he may wish he hadn't. The pain will be excruciating."

Graham began the suturing process, deftly tying a neat little square knot to complete the first stitch. "It is pain that lets us know we are alive."

Peckwood squinted at him around his scalpel. "A heady philosophy for a naval surgeon."

"Death is a constant companion aboard a ship." He grasped the needle with steady pressure. "The only surgeons that last are those who cling to hope and entreat their patients to do so as well."

"Perhaps." Peckwood removed a soiled piece of wadding with his forceps and dropped it into a bowl. "Yet I find it takes more than a positive mind-set to hold mortality at bay. Tenacity. Innovation. The courage to do what you know to be right when others nay-say you. These are the marks of a successful doctor, instilling in the patient confidence in the surgeon rather than allowing a tenuous hope in an invisible unknown."

"That smacks of blasphemy, Doctor. A surgeon is not God, a truth I've learned time and again. Though we do our best, skill or not, it is God alone who numbers a man's days." Graham inserted the needle and began a second suture identical to the first.

Peckwood's blue eyes twinkled up at him. "Religious fellow, are you?"

Graham stifled a snort. Perhaps Mrs. Bap was starting to rub off on him. He'd even picked up his mother's Bible the other day—yet still hadn't the nerve to actually open it. No, Peckwood couldn't be more wrong about him.

He bent his head and returned to sewing. "I should say not, sir."

"Just as well. Religion never helped me a whit."

Though the words were lighthearted enough, a certain amount of bitterness clung to the sentiment like a ground fog. Thick and cold. What happened in the doctor's past that soured him so? From all he'd read of Peckwood in the journals, he'd had a banner career thus far.

Once again tying a knot to set the final stitch, Graham snipped the thread with a small scissors. Then he wrapped a roll of bandages around the arm snugly. "I am finished." He turned to Peckwood. "May I be of service to you?"

"No, no. Nearly finished here myself. His gut wasn't as bad as I anticipated, no major organs affected, though he did lose a bit of blood. Still, barring infection, he ought to pull through in no time. Thread me a needle and I'll truss him up right handily."

Graham did so then began removing bloodied instruments and dropping them into a basin. Once finished, he retrieved the bowl of spent wads. Before tossing them into the dustbin, he poked them about and counted out of habit. Only nine? Surely not. He recounted and came up one short again. Odd. Unless Peckwood had missed the basin entirely with one of them.

"And there we have it." Peckwood clipped the thread and tossed the needle and scissors onto the tray. "I leave the rest to you, Mr. Lambert."

"Just one moment, please." Graham crouched, studying the floor. Nothing was by Peckwood's shoes. Save for blood and a few scraps of bandages, the oak boards were clear beneath the table. Rising, he glanced at the tray. Only the scissors, the spool of catgut, and a bloodied needle sat on it. Where was the other wad?

Peckwood cocked his head. "Is there a problem, Mr. Lambert?"

"Yes. There were ten waddings on the tray when you began, yet I only account for nine."

"Pish! That is hardly problematic. I suggest you count again." Pivoting, he strode to the washbasin and began scrubbing.

Graham frowned. How could he have made such an error? He snatched up the basin and again prodded through the wads on the off chance that two had stuck together.

But no. A thorough dissection resulted in the same number. He set down the porcelain bowl and faced Peckwood. "There is definitely one missing, sir. Only nine are accounted for."

Peckwood chuckled while he rolled down his sleeves. "Well, there you have it, then. There must have only been nine on the tray."

"No, I take great care in keeping records." He did. A lesson learned the hard way. As a young assistant on his first assignment, he'd blundered by not documenting what he'd set out on the tray for the ship's surgeon. A silver forceps was not accounted for by the end of the night—and he had the scars on his back from an unjust flogging after being accused of the theft.

He pulled a black leather journal from a shelf. After a quick page-through, he stopped at the current date and held it out for Peckwood's perusal. "See here? There were ten cotton wads on that tray when I readied it this morning. If we do not reopen that man and remove the wad, infection is sure to set in."

Peckwood scowled as he hung up his apron. "I assure you, Lambert, *I* would not make such a novice mistake. Clearly the error is in your accounting. You may have written down ten, but you must have pulled only nine from the jar. Now, if you will excuse me, I have some friends to meet." Straightening his waistcoat, the doctor strode out the door.

Graham's jaw hardened, tight as a woodscrew about to splinter a board. Was Peckwood right? Had he miscounted? Everyone made mistakes.

His gaze drifted to Hobbs, lying unconscious on the slab. The man breathed easily, chest rising and falling in a normal rhythm. The incision stitched by Mr. Peckwood looked like a great-granny's masterpiece of needlework, finely crafted and without one spot of blood leaking out. Was he justified in destroying that handiwork and reopening the man's side? And if he did, would Hobbs sustain more blood loss simply to satisfy his own curiosity?

But what if a piece of wadding were still in his gut? Leaving it there meant certain death. There was nothing for it, then. He readied another tray and grabbed a scalpel. Minutes later, the forceps snagged then pulled out a walnut-sized gob of fouled wadding.

Curse Peckwood and his arrogance!

He threw the forceps, bloody pad and all, onto the tray. This was the final straw. As soon as Colin Balfour's surgery was over, he'd leave—even if that meant becoming naught but a country surgeon operating on miners in Cornwall. But not before he'd reported all of Peckwood's shortcomings to the local magistrate.

Huffing, he once again threaded a needle, this time taking several tries to make the catgut go through. Saying goodbye to Peckwood would be a delight. But as for Amelia Balfour? He tied off a knot with jerky movements. Wishing a farewell to the woman who so thoroughly captivated would maim him in ways from which he might never recover.

Too bad he didn't have a choice.

SIXTEEN

"Sometimes I have endeavored to discover what quality it is which he possesses that elevates him so immeasurably above any other person I ever knew. I believe it to be an intuitive discernment; a quick but never-failing power of judgment; a penetration into the causes of things, unequaled for clearness and precision; add to this a facility of expression, and a voice whose varied intonations are soul-subduing music."

❦

"For by grace are ye saved through faith; and that not of yourselves: it is the gift of God: not of works, lest any man should boast."

Amelia shifted on the merciless pew, vainly seeking respite from the hard wood, harder truth, and a sharp sideways glance from Betsey. Though the vicar's words were meant for everyone gracing the benches of St. Andrew's Church, she felt oddly singled out. Exposed in a way that crawled under her skin and made her wish to scrub with a bar of lye soap. Was that what she'd been doing? Certainly not the boasting part of it, but—perhaps—the works? Was all her good behaviour merely an attempt to win God's favour?

She frowned. Perish the thought! Of course, it wasn't works that had driven her to church this morning. It was the uncomfortable barb in her heart that Graham had planted during their walk at St. Brandon's...

"Trust must ultimately rest on God."

She fiddled with her lacy gloves instead of stroking the Ibis feather she'd purposely left at home—an outward sign of her attempt to depend solely upon God. It wasn't a new truth Graham had given her, but one she'd perhaps been ignoring. Had she been relying too heavily on the skill of Mr. Peckwood to make her brother whole and forgotten to include the Almighty in the process? Was that the root of why she'd not attended services these past five weeks? She ought to know she couldn't expect God to hear her prayers if she didn't make an effort to come hear Him. And she desperately needed her pleas to be received for the success of Colin's upcoming surgery. This had nothing whatsoever to do with her works but everything to do with her brother, which was a self-sacrificial offering. One God would surely smile upon.

That settled, she breathed easier for the rest of the sermon, until they stepped outside and Betsey once again eyed her.

Her maid tightened her bonnet ribbons into a severe knot. "He were a bit heavy-handed today, eh miss?"

Amelia tugged down her sleeves, straightening her cuffs. Apparently, her maid had felt the sting of the sermon as well. "I suppose the vicar must make the most of a captive audience whenever he has the chance."

"I were speaking of God, miss, not the vicar."

"Yes, well…" What was she to say to that? For she suspected her maid was very much in the right. Leaving the church—and Betsey—behind, she turned towards home, but barely two steps later, she stopped.

Ahead, a young girl stood at the curb. Five years old. Possibly six. Hard to tell with street children. They all aged unnaturally. The girl clutched a handful of white poppies, begging the worshippers leaving St. Andrew's to buy her wilted flowers. Nothing extraordinary, really. The poor earned money in whatever way they could.

But this particular girl captured Amelia's heart unlike any other. There was something about her chocolate-brown eyes and the black curls that flopped onto her brow. Beneath smudges of coal dust, the girl was the mirror image of herself at that age. Father had been a harsh taskmaster, but at least he'd richly provided for her and Colin, and she'd never had to face such a cruel existence as this little one.

She called over her shoulder to Betsey. "Wait here, please. I won't be a minute."

Dodging a passing elderly couple, she hurried onward, fumbling with the strings of her reticule. If she emptied the contents into the girl's palm, at least the child would have something substantial to eat today. A good plan—one that stopped short when she bumped into a solid back.

"Oh!" She retreated a step, an apology springing to her tongue, yet it quickly stalled as the man she'd collided with turned. Familiar hazel eyes stared into her own.

"G—good day, Mr. Lambert." Her voice squeaked.

"It is now." He grinned, the warmth of which sent quivers through her belly. "Meeting you on the street is turning into a regular habit, Miss Balfour. A good habit, I might add."

Heat rose, warming her face. "I, erm…"

She fiddled with her reticule strings, stalling for time to pull herself together. Then, blessedly once more in control, she lifted her chin. "I did not see you in church, sir."

His grin faded. "No, I suppose you didn't."

"Then I shall look for you next week."

He clutched his medical bag with both hands, holding it almost like a shield. "Not even the keenest eye can detect that which isn't there."

Now that was an intriguing rock to overturn. She angled her head. "You do not attend services?"

A smirk lifted one side of his mouth, dimpling the divot in his shorn beard. "I am not certain God would welcome a heathen such as myself."

"A true heathen would not acknowledge a God who may or may not welcome him."

"Touché." Admiration flared in the green flecks of his eyes. "Then let us just say I suspect God is aware of my imperfections, which is reason enough not to try His patience by pretending to be a saint."

"But that is exactly why you *should* go. Every breath we draw is a testament to God's patience. I should know, for He's not struck me down with lightning." She glanced at the sky. "Yet."

A chuckle rumbled in his throat. "I hardly think you've done anything bad enough to deserve such a fate."

"We are all sinners at heart, Mr. Lambert."

"Some more than others, I'm afraid." His mirth faded. So did the warmth in his voice. Surely he wasn't speaking of himself...was he?

She opened her mouth to ask his meaning, when a severe voice cut through the air.

"This is the Lord's day, you foul little street rat. Out of my way!"

A girl's cry followed. So did the *whump* of a body hitting the ground.

Mr. Lambert pivoted, and Amelia gawked past him. The little flower seller sprawled on the cobbles, fallen between a carriage and its horses, just as Amelia had the night she'd slipped at the docks. With a great stomp of a rear hoof, one of the beasts flattened the girl's poppies, narrowly missing her head.

A man in a keenly tailored suit disappeared inside that carriage, totally ignoring the child. If he departed now, the grind of the wheels would cut her in half. Instinctively, Amelia fingered for her feather. Absent. Mercy! Of all the days to stop carrying her charm. She turned to Mr. Lambert, but he was already flying towards the girl, his bag lying forgotten on the ground.

By now Betsey had joined her side, her fist shaking in the air at the driver. "Take a care, you cuffin! There's a child on the road."

The driver clicked his tongue. "Then she'd best move. Off with ye, girl!" He slapped his whip against the leather seat with a sharp crack.

The horses jolted, jerking the coach ahead several inches. The girl struggled to crawl out, but her hem was firmly caught beneath a wheel.

"Drive on!" The owner's voice bellowed inside the carriage.

In one great swoop, Mr. Lambert scooped the girl into his arms and yanked her away, the carriage clipping him on the side and causing him to stumble. Amelia reached for them both, but he'd already righted himself. He set the girl on her own two feet.

"An excellent save, Mr. Lambert!" She smiled up at him before stooping to the child's level. "And you, little miss, are you all right?"

Dazed, the girl nodded, still leaning against the doctor's leg.

Mr. Lambert patted her head. "I think she shall be right as rain."

"Aye, sir." The girl's brave words were belied by a quiver of her lower lip—one that broke Amelia's heart.

Once again Amelia reached out, but the child flinched. To what kind of cruelties was she accustomed? "Perhaps after such an awful fright, you should return home, child."

"Ain't got a home, m'um." The girl glanced at the poppies, crushed in a heap on the street. "And now I got me no flowers." Tears sprouted, leaving stark white tracks against the girl's dirty cheeks.

Amelia pulled out her kerchief and wiped them away, making a great smear of things. When finished, she pressed the cloth into the girl's hand. "For you."

The child blinked, wonder wide in her dark brown eyes. "Thank ye."

Rising, Amelia once again fumbled with her reticule, but too late. Mr. Lambert had already retrieved the girl's poppies and now knelt before her on one knee, holding out a handful of coins. "I should like to buy your flowers, young miss."

"But they be ruined now, sir."

"Those are the best kind, don't you know? For it is in the crushing that the strongest fragrance is released." He lifted the flowers to her nose.

She sniffed like a rabbit, testing his theory while poised to sprint should danger develop. Surprisingly white teeth appeared in a wide grin, then she snatched the money from his hand, all her former tears banished by Mr. Lambert's generosity. "Thank ye, sir!"

The girl darted off, weaving through the street traffic like a skittering lamb through the bramble. The remaining churchgoers who'd stood gawking dispersed as well.

Mr. Lambert rose, dusting off his trousers with a few sweeps of his hand. "There you have it. All's well that ends well."

"Does it?" She frowned. "End well for the child, I mean. You were here to protect her this time, but what about the next incident? Life on the street is so precarious."

"Children are more resilient than one might imagine." For a moment, he studied the flattened handful of flowers, then pulled out the single poppy that had managed to remain whole. Stepping close, he tucked the bloom into her bonnet band, then, without retreating, his gaze bore into hers, his breath landing light and warm on her brow. "Beauty has a way of surviving even the harshest conditions."

He spoke of the flower, of course, but even so, her heart skipped a beat. What woman's wouldn't, standing so close to such an attractive man? Breathing in his musky scent. Foolishly believing that maybe—just maybe—he might think her beautiful as well.

As if Betsey read her mind, a thick snuffle sounded beside her. "I don't know about such trifles, Mr. Lambert, but I do know that were a dandy of a catch. The girl's head would've been mashed by that blackguard's carriage and that's the truth of it. Why, you're a regular hero, sir."

He was. Surprisingly, things had turned out all right despite her feather's absence.

"I wouldn't go so far as that." The doctor rubbed the back of his neck, clearly discomfited. Endearing, really, the way he deflected praise.

Amelia changed the subject, lest the man's ears flame bright red from the attention. "Don't forget your bag, Doctor."

"Thanks for the reminder." Backtracking, he swept up the leather case in one grab. "Now then, I believe your brother awaits his treatment. Shall I accompany you home, ladies?"

"That would be lovely, Mr. Lambert."

Leastwise, she thought so. Her maid, on the other hand, protested beneath her breath as they strolled to Balfour House.

"Impractical, I say. And wholly unneeded. You and I are not such dainties that we must be escorted." Betsey huffed. "Why, I've been at your side these past five years, trudging about foreign lands without nary a trouble. Don't see why we need a gent now."

Amelia hid a smile. It wasn't like Betsey to turn so green. Then again, she'd never had cause, facing the world alone as they had. Perhaps she'd been too reliant on her maid?

They turned off the main road and onto the street that led home, when a red-faced kitchen maid came running towards them. "Miss Balfour! Doctor!" The young woman stopped in front of them, doubling over with hands on her thighs and gasping for air.

Fear weakened Amelia's knees, and she reached for Mr. Lambert's strong arm. Had Colin suffered another convulsion? A bigger one? A killer?

"What's happened?" How could the doctor's voice possibly stay so calm?

The girl didn't answer. Just panted, thick and heavy. Amelia wanted to shake her.

"A fall, sir." The words were choppy, but at least they came. "It were bad. Blood everywhere."

"Whose?" Amelia tensed every muscle in her body.

"It is a wonder a heart can still beat when so much blood has been lost. Perhaps I shouldn't have moved the woman to her bed but let her lie as she was."

Balfour's voice resonated in a low vibration around the housekeeper's chamber. Graham cut a length of catgut, then peered across the bed at him. The big man stooped on the other side, pressing a red-stained compress to Mrs. Kirwin's skull. Despite the puckered lines at the side of his wide lips, the man was holding up well. As a young surgical assistant, the first time Graham had witnessed a sailor who'd fallen from the riggings and lay in a pool of gore, he'd turned aside and retched.

"You did the right thing, Mr. Balfour. Head wounds are notorious for putting on a spectacular show. She'll have a headache once she wakes from the laudanum, yet it is not the gash that will keep her abed." Graham nodded towards her leg. "I suspect she has fractured a bone, but that will have to wait until I get her stitched up. Now, gently angle her head this way, if you please. Then on my mark, you will remove the padding and hold the lantern close. If you're up to it, that is. Otherwise, I can manage on my own. It wouldn't be the first time."

"I must daily bear my face in the mirror. I think I can withstand a mere laceration." Slowly yet steadily, Balfour guided the old housekeeper's face towards him.

"All right, then. Ready?" Graham poised his needle above the compress. "And mark."

Balfour removed the bandage. Blood pooled instantly. Soon it would mix with the oils on her skin and add to the twangy odour in the air. Working swiftly, Graham pinched the gash together with one hand, and with the other, speared the needle into her flesh.

"Do you know how it happened?" he asked while he worked. At this point in his career, he could suture up half of Her Majesty's Navy while carrying on a dialogue and never once miss his aim.

"I have no idea, Doctor. All I got from the scullery maid was hysterics, and Cook's nose was so far into a pot of fricassee that she didn't see a thing. I don't understand it. Mrs. Kirwin's been down those servant stairs these past twenty-five years with nary a slip. Perhaps she suffered some sort of fit?"

"Possible." Plunge. Pull. Repeat. Graham drew the thread in and out with steady strokes, placing his knots with careful, if automatic, precision, and considering aloud Balfour's theory. "She is upwards in age, so it's not out of the realm of possibility. Still, from what I've seen on my daily visits, this woman is as spry as a stable cat."

"And twice as twitchy." Balfour heaved a sigh. "A most inopportune time for her to be laid up, what with my own surgery so near. My sister will have her hands full."

Hmm. That wouldn't do. Amelia Balfour had only just started venturing out amongst the living and regaining a healthy colour to her cheeks. Now to be shut away once again? Graham glanced up. "Can you not hire extra help?"

"With this visage?" Balfour circled his free hand in front of his face. "It is hard enough keeping our current staff."

"I am sorry to hear it. Your sister already has enough to manage."

One of Balfour's thick eyebrows rose. "You speak as if you care for her."

Graham swallowed against the sudden tightness in his throat. Dipping his head, he leaned in close to Mrs. Kirwin's gash for the final stitches. "Of course I care for your sister. I wouldn't be a very good doctor if I didn't."

"Is that all it is? Professional courtesy?"

"Should there be anything more?"

"You tell me." The light wavered as Balfour met his eye across the bed. "What are your intentions towards my sister, Lambert?"

Moisture did pop out then, fine and clammy where his hair met his forehead. Thank God he was nearly finished—for he was certainly done with this conversation. Reaching behind him, he felt for the scissors on the nightstand. "What makes you think I have any?"

"You'd better have intentions, and good ones, for my sister already has feelings for you."

A punch to the lungs couldn't have stolen any more of his breath, so stunning was the revelation. Had Amelia Balfour confessed such a thing to her brother? When? And why? Though he'd snipped thousands of knots in the course of his career, this time his fingers shook. He didn't dare make eye contact with her brother. A cowardly move, but absolutely necessary if he were to steady his hands.

"I had no idea," he said at length. "Would you like me to ask Mr. Peckwood to come in my stead for your daily treatments so as to avoid her?"

"What I would like is a straight answer." Balfour's voice sliced as sharply as the scissor blades. "Do you intend to pursue Amelia?"

Blowing out a long breath, Graham set down his tools, then took the time to wring out a rag from the basin and dab away the excess blood on Mrs. Kirwin's brow before reaching for a fresh bandage. The busier he appeared, the more likely Balfour would drop the subject.

"Well, Doctor?"

Blast the man's tenacity! The trait would serve him well during his convalescence, but here? Now? Deuced inconvenient.

With one hand, he propped up the housekeeper's head, and with the other, began wrapping the cloth around her skull, all the while avoiding Balfour's burning stare. "Your sister deserves a better man than I," he said simply.

"Humility is virtuous, sir, yet you take it too far. You are an upstanding surgeon, a partner in a thriving practice. What's more, you are a man of integrity. I believe I could ask for no better match."

"It is I who could ask for no better match," he murmured—apparently loud enough for Balfour to hear.

"If you truly feel that way, then you should speak to her at once and tell her of your feelings."

"No!" He flinched. What was wrong with him? Any more of these theatrics and he'd endanger breaking open Mrs. Kirwin's freshly tied sutures. Gently, he eased her head to the pillow.

Balfour's next question followed him to the washstand. "What is your hesitation?"

He plunged his hands into tepid water, scrubbing off the blood more vigorously than necessary. "The truth is Mr. Peckwood's medical practice may appear to be prosperous, yet I suspect the man is in debt. For what reason, I do not know, and my life savings are now entangled with his. So you see, Mr. Balfour, I have nothing to offer your sister other than poverty, a life I would not subject her to. My mother died a pauper. I will not willingly see that happen again to anyone I love."

"And I would see my sister happy. I know from firsthand experience that living in the finest manor house without any morsel of affection is not living at all. I would rather her reside in a hovel by the dockyards as long as she is well loved. And I believe that you do...love her, that is."

The nail brush dropped from his hands, smacking against the porcelain bowl and plummeting to the floor. For all of Balfour's unconventional looks, his perception was far too shrewd. Graham stooped to retrieve the brush, thankful the man couldn't see the flush that burned over his face. "Love does not put food on the table, Mr. Balfour."

"No, but God does. Have you no faith?"

Snorting, he deposited the brush onto the stand and snagged the towel, practically beating the thing into submission as he dried his hands. "With or without faith, evil men still prosper, and the good are left with nothing but want. I have seen with my own eyes upright, hardworking sailors driven to their death by lazy, arrogant officers who did nothing to ease the pain of those beneath them. Even were I the most saintly of men, there is no guarantee I will prosper in this wicked world, and I will not suffer your sister to sink to the depths along with me."

He glared over at Balfour, who by now had set down the lamp and stood with arms folded.

Balfour met his challenge with an even stare. "In all my years shut away with nothing but books as companions, I have learned this. God *is* sovereign, permitting things for a reason, even if that reason is hidden from man's eyes. Should He allow you—or Amelia—to suffer in poverty, then it is by His good plan. And if you believe that God is not only sovereign but just, then you can be sure no matter how things might look, everything will be made right in the end."

"Hah!" Graham spat out the word as though it were a weevil in his bread. "Lofty sentiment, but not entirely true. Everything was not made right for my mother. She died without the comfort of family at her side. I wonder, Mr. Balfour, if you can tell me how that was just."

"How is this?" He pointed to his face with a wag of his grotesque head. "Yet I find it is not justice so much as mercy that makes all things right. While our Saviour's death on the cross satisfied the righteous wrath of God, the true gift is that Christ allowed Himself to be hung there in the first place. I grant you that we cannot know the mind of God on this side of heaven, but I do know there was a purpose behind the timing of your mother's death, every bit as much as there is a purpose for my deformity."

Balfour's words rushed in, lodging in a far corner of Graham's mind like an uninvited guest—one he desperately wanted to evict but didn't have the time or strength to oust. Clenching his jaw, he instead went to work on the housekeeper's leg, resetting the bone with as firm a resolution as his next words. "I hope you are right."

"Hope is a precious gift." Balfour moved to the end of the bed, offering assistance that Graham refused with a shake of his head.

"You give me much to think on, Mr. Balfour. I will consider all you've said today."

"Don't think too long. Patience is not one of my sister's virtues."

Must everything always come back to that beautiful enigma? Every turn of conversation? Of thought?

He nestled Mrs. Kirwin's now-wrapped leg between two pillows. "I am finished here." He strode to the head of the bed once again and this time lifted one of her eyelids, then the other. Normal pupils. Nothing but slight agitation at the affront. Good.

Satisfied, he retrieved his bag from the nightstand and faced Mr. Balfour. "Your housekeeper ought to be coming 'round soon enough. Have the scullery maid sit with her, offer her water when she does so, then summon me. For now, I'll go prepare your treatment."

He strode to the door but paused as Balfour's quiet words hit him square between the shoulder blades.

"About that…"

"Yes?" He turned.

As if Mrs. Kirwin might hear him, Balfour glanced at her then stalked to the door and lowered his voice. "I've been having a rather odd side effect I thought you should know about."

Graham cocked his head. "Which is?"

"I've, uh…" He looked away, as if finding the courage to speak from some source of strength out in the corridor. "I've been seeing things."

"What sort of things?"

Balfour plowed his massive fingers through his coarse hair, knotting it more than smoothing the dark locks. "At first, mostly moving shadows. Looked like animals at times. But yesterday, late afternoon…" He dropped his hand and faced him. "I swear I saw a child. A boy. Standing at the end of the passageway near Amelia's bedchamber. I called out to him, but he didn't move. Not a whit. So I rubbed my eyes, and when I reopened them, the corridor was empty."

"Well, that is concerning." Graham frowned. "But are you certain it wasn't perhaps an errand boy who'd taken liberties to explore where he ought not have been?"

"I thought as much." The big man shrugged. "Which is why I then went to investigate further. Amelia's room was empty. Unless the boy jumped out a window, there was no way a body could vanish so quickly."

Graham chewed on the information while Balfour paced away several steps. When he doubled back, a terrible fierceness burned in his dark eyes.

Balfour stood silent, clenching and unclenching his hands, as if deciding to fight or flee. It was a pitiful sight.

"I must know, Doctor…am I going mad?"

Graham chuckled, hoping to ease the man's angst. "You're more sane than half the naval officers I worked with. You're not nipping into more laudanum than you should be, are you?"

"No. In fact, after seeing the shadow animals, I cut it off altogether."

"There you have it." Graham cuffed the big man on the arm. "Ending the dosage without first reducing the amount of such a powerful medication can have an adverse effect. Or it could simply have been a trick of the light. There was a storm, after all. Likely you saw nothing more than the play of lightning through glass. But"—Graham looked him straight in the eyes—"let me know if the incident repeats itself."

"Very good." Relief radiated off the man in waves. "I'll go find someone to sit with Mrs. Kirwin and join you shortly upstairs."

They parted ways then, Balfour disappearing into the bowels of the kitchen, Graham strolling towards the servants' stairway. He stopped just shy of the first step, though, a strange glint near the baseboard catching the corner of his eye. Odd. Stooping, he swiped up a small ball of polished alabaster, albeit a bit chipped. A marble? What the devil? He looked from the child's toy to the top of the stairway.

"Mrs. Kirwin's been down those servant stairs these past twenty-five years with nary a slip."

He narrowed his eyes on the plaything sitting on his open palm and wondered aloud, "From whence did you come, you little troublemaker?"

SEVENTEEN

"...and do you not feel your blood congeal with horror
like that which even now curdles mine?"

⁕

Time was a nebulous thing. Each day felt like a thousand, but when Mr. Lambert's steady presence graced Balfour House, the minutes ran like water through a sieve. In the week and a half since Mrs. Kirwin's fall, Amelia had alternately prayed for the hours to speed or to slow.

The very same double-mindedness plagued her now as she perched on the sitting room sofa, wringing her handkerchief. Waiting. Watching. Wondering if this time Mr. Peckwood's assessment would finally result in the scheduling of Colin's surgery. She hoped so. He'd already delayed this examination by four whole days and the ship to Cairo would sail in little over a week. Yet as she sneaked a glance at Mr. Lambert, taking in the lean lines of his body and strong cut of his jaw, her fickle heart had the audacity to wish his daily visits might never end.

As if he sensed her perusal, Mr. Lambert's eyes—more brown than green today—turned towards her, and her breath caught. Mercy! She could get lost in that gaze.

He strolled her way, pulling out a white cloth from his pocket, then offered it over.

She looked from the cloth to his face. "What's that for?"

He nodded at the knotted handkerchief in her lap. "You have strangled the life from that one."

"And so you offer me another?" She arched a brow. "Do you think a doctor should be encouraging such homicidal tendencies?"

Chuckling, he tucked the cloth away and sat beside her. "Mr. Peckwood is merely conducting an evaluation. How on earth will you manage during your brother's actual surgery?"

"I shall be fine." Little by little, she began unwinding the wad in her hand and smoothing the fabric out on her lap. "It is all the waiting that is so agitating."

"Then your brother was right after all." A knowing grin—the sort that hid secrets—spread languidly across his face.

Her hands stilled. "About what?"

"Of all your many virtues, he warned me that patience is not amongst their tally."

She narrowed her eyes. What kind of conversations did her brother and Mr. Lambert partake of when she wasn't around? Colin had been acting odd of late, singing the praises of the good doctor and speaking of the future, but she'd counted it as nothing more than him trying to cheer her spirits as she and Betsey took on many of Mrs. Kirwin's usual tasks. Had there been some other reason for his frequent mentions of Mr. Lambert? Was her baby brother acting the matchmaker?

Though the creases had finally been worked out of her cloth, she scrunched it up yet again. "Why would my brother speak to you about my merits or lack thereof?"

Mr. Lambert's lips parted, but Mr. Peckwood's voice rang out. "Very good, Mr. Balfour."

Amelia snapped her gaze to Colin and the older doctor. Her brother sat stoic, his face an unreadable mask. Mr. Peckwood backed towards them with a large calipers in his clutch. Whatever the older doctor had deemed good was impossible to tell.

"Well?" Amelia rose, as did Mr. Lambert. "Is my brother now fit for your surgery, Mr. Peckwood?"

"He is more than fit." The old fellow popped the instrument into his bag then buckled it shut and turned to her. "Your brother has exceeded my expectations."

Though it was what she wanted to hear, a certain amount of

trepidation for her brother's life caused her fingers to clench her handkerchief all the tighter. "That's wonderful news."

"Maybe for you," Colin drawled. "But it's me going under that scalpel of his."

Mr. Peckwood patted him on one of his big shoulders. "With the progress you've made thus far, I anticipate no problems whatsoever with your upcoming procedure."

"And when will that be, sir?"

The doctor scratched behind his ear, saying nothing. The longer the silence stretched, the more Amelia gnawed the inside of her cheek. Was it really that hard to choose a date? Even Mr. Lambert cast a wondering glance over his shoulder while he packed away the rest of his instruments.

At length, Mr. Peckwood sniffed. "Monday morning, I should think."

She frowned. For the sake of them all, how she wished they were already on the other side of the potentially deadly procedure. "Could you not shorten the time by performing the surgery tomorrow? You said yourself my brother is more than fit."

"And so he is." Mr. Peckwood nodded. "But I have a rather important engagement tomorrow evening, one that requires preparation." He pulled a watch from his pocket, snapped open the lid, and sniffed. "An event I should like you and your brother to attend."

She pursed her lips. Colin never—ever—went out in public, and the grim line of his misshapen jaw declared he wasn't about to start doing so now, even for a doctor who would soon hold his life in his hands.

Colin crossed the rug to a cut-glass decanter. He poured a tumbler of the liquid and, clasping it in his monstrous fingers, faced Mr. Peckwood. "I am sorry to disappoint you, Doctor, but I do not attend social events."

"There is nothing social about it." Mr. Peckwood swung out his arm, indicating the glass towers and conduits on the side table. "I shall be demonstrating the very technique I have been employing upon yourself, and so you see, it is more of a treatment than an appearance."

Colin eyed the man over the rim of his glass, then drank the contents in one big swallow. "Will there be members of the public in attendance?"

"Yes."

"Then my answer stands." He slammed the glass onto the tray, rattling the others and leaving behind an awkward silence.

Amelia exchanged a glance with Mr. Lambert, the press of his lips as tight as hers.

"That's quite the quandary," Mr. Peckwood grumbled. "Though I suppose I could use one of the inmates in your stead."

Amelia angled her head. "Inmates?"

"Mmm-hmm," Mr. Peckwood grumbled again, this time striding over to the machine that had tortured her brother these past five weeks. Piece by piece, he began dismantling the thing, clearly done with the conversation.

Thankfully, Mr. Lambert answered for the doctor as he snapped his bag shut. "Tomorrow evening, after a dinner party of a select group of investors, Mr. Peckwood is performing a demonstration at St. Peter's Asylum. He hopes to increase funding for his research, which in turn would allow our practice to grow. It is his expectation that the procedure he's developed to help Mr. Balfour might also aid those who suffer from other diseases of the brain."

Colin folded his arms. "Are you to be in attendance at this event, Mr. Lambert?"

"As Mr. Peckwood's partner, yes, I am."

"I see." Colin's big brown eyes turned her way. "Well then, Amelia, you shall go in my place."

She clenched her hands to keep them from flailing about in a most unladylike fashion. "Don't be ridiculous, Colin. It wouldn't do Mr. Peckwood any good to hook me up to that machine."

"No, it would not," Mr. Peckwood agreed. "Though…" Carefully setting down one of the coils of wires, he turned to them, a strange light in his dark eyes. "It might work. Actually, it *could* work, and very nicely, I might add."

Amelia's blood ran cold. The man wasn't seriously considering experimenting on her, was he? But why not? He'd certainly had no qualms about employing unknown methods on her brother. She shuddered. Should she have been so insistent that Colin subject himself to Mr. Peckwood?

"Now see here, Doctor. I meant my sister may attend the dinner." Colin strode to her side. "But I will not have her submitting to any of the treatments I have been receiving."

"Nor will I stand for it." Mr. Lambert turned a malignant eye towards Mr. Peckwood. "Your investors will have to be persuaded in some other fashion."

"Of all the misguided notions. You surprise me, gentlemen." The doctor leaned back against the table. "Of course I would not endanger Miss Balfour. I shall use an inmate to exhibit the procedure, one who will benefit from the process. Miss Balfour's words of witness as to the success of the technique should be sufficient to sway the minds of the gentlemen I intend to solicit."

Amelia glanced up at Colin. Sunlight streamed through the window, highlighting the abnormal brow that overshadowed his eyes. Casting an orangish hue on his olive skin. Accentuating the crooked offset of his cheeks and nose. A horrific sight to the unfamiliar eye, but to her, he was still her younger brother, albeit malformed. "He doesn't look any different to me," she murmured. "So how can I publicly say the treatment was successful?"

"Did I not just get done assuring you your brother is now ready for surgery?"

"Yes, but—"

Mr. Peckwood's cheeks swelled as he puffed out air. "Then the procedure was a raging success, and so it is settled."

Not true. The only thing settled was the unease sinking heavy in her chest. It didn't seem right, this circular logic. But what did she know? A woman given to travel writing was no match for the intelligence of a renowned surgeon twice her age.

She crossed the rug and poured her own glass of water, stalling for time. "Even so, Mr. Peckwood, you heard my brother. He will not attend, and it is not proper for me to appear alone at a social event."

"You won't be," Colin rumbled beside her, then faced Mr. Lambert. "Did you not say, Doctor, that you will be in attendance?"

He nodded slowly, curiosity sparking the green flecks in his eyes. "I did."

"Very good."

The glass shook in Amelia's hand, and so did her legs when Colin's gaze darted from the doctor to her, then back again. She knew that look. The slight lift of one side of his mouth. The rubbing of his thumb along the length of his jaw. He was scheming—a trait he'd perfected in the many years of dealing with their father.

"Then it is my greatest wish, Mr. Lambert, that you escort my sister to Mr. Peckwood's presentation."

❦

Graham strode from the Balfours' town house, feet pounding the pavement harder than necessary. Must Peckwood always commandeer the gig? But just as well. He needed air. Space. A chance to sort through the snarl of questions that'd coiled like snakes in a basket ever since Balfour had insisted he accompany his sister to tomorrow's event. The man was more than amenable to the idea of him pursuing her. He'd made that abundantly clear. But why had she agreed to allow him to escort her? As her brother had intimated, did she truly return his hidden affections? Though whether she did or not, how was he to keep Amelia at arm's length when everything in him cried out to draw her close and kiss those full lips of hers?

Amelia?

He kicked a rock. Wind and sea! Since when had he started thinking of the woman by her Christian name? A disgusted sigh huffed out of him. Just one more question with which to contend.

The stench of Redcliffe punched him in the nose as he turned onto Mrs. Bap's street, but it was the wide-eyed, red-faced young lady barreling towards him that really turned his gut.

Emma, Mrs. Bap's granddaughter, skittered to a stop in front of him, fear twisting her lips. "Mr. Lambert!"

He caught her by the shoulders. "Is your grandmother—?"

"Nay, sir! Oh, come quick." She snatched his hand and whirled away, tugging him forward. "He's right bad, he is."

"Who?"

"Ratter."

Emma led him past Mrs. Bap's hovel to the neighbouring door, where a hair-raising howl pealed out. Graham pulled free of Emma's grip and dashed inside, then immediately covered his nose with his sleeve. The place reeked of garlic and burned hair. "What's happened?"

A man stumbled about, bent double, crashing into walls and bumping against a table, all while cradling his head and yowling like a banshee.

Emma's footsteps stopped behind his. "Dunno what happened, sir. Gran and I heard a big boom, and ol' Ratter's been bawling like a stuck calf ever since."

With a quick sidestep, Graham blocked the man on his next pass around the room. "Mr. Ratter? I'm a doctor. I'm here to help."

"T'aint no mister," Emma instructed at his back. "He *is* the ratter."

On one side of his head, greasy grey hair hung in strings, waving back and forth like seaweed. The other was singed in patches to the scalp. He swayed on his feet. "Pain! Bloody awful. Can't bear it."

"Let's have a look and see what may be done."

No chair graced the room, just shards of pottery strewn everywhere and an overturned three-legged stool near a glowing red hearth. "Fetch the stool, Emma."

The girl did so right away. Graham set down his bag then guided Ratter to the seat. He dropped to his knees and vainly tried to pry the man's arms from his head. "I cannot help you, sir, if you do not allow me to examine what ails you."

A great shudder shook through the man. Sweet heavens! Whatever had happened to Ratter's face was not going to be pretty. Graham braced himself and forced the fellow's arms down to his side.

Then hissed in a breath through his teeth.

God, have mercy.

The skin was burned away on one cheek, exposing a portion of raw muscle. And then it made sense. The smell. The broken clay crucible. What sort of rat poison had the man been concocting when it exploded?

"What is it?" Emma's voice curled over his shoulder.

Graham shot to his feet and wheeled about, blocking her view. Digging in his pocket, he pulled out a coin then tossed it to her. "Go fetch a carriage. Make haste."

"But—"

"Now!"

She flinched, but obeyed. Though he hated to be the cause of such a reaction, he had no choice. The girl would never recover from such a gruesome image of ruined flesh and bone. And unless he acted fast, Ratter might not either.

He pulled out a clean cloth from his bag and glanced about for a basin, but he should've known better. Why would a rat catcher bother to wash when he'd just have to go belowground the next night? But at least there was a drinking bucket near the door. Graham dipped the rag and returned to the man, not bothering to wring it out. As poor as it was, it was the only comfort he could offer.

Tilting the man's head just so, he carefully laid the cloth over the mottled burn. "This will soothe for now, but I must get you back to the office for a thorough cleansing and some ointment."

"Can't pay," Ratter whimpered.

"No matter. Coin or not, you have great need."

Only one eye peered at him, the other covered by the cloth. "Ye got yer own office"—air hissed in through his teeth—"yet ye'd tend a lowly ratter?"

"It is a shared practice, but yes, I would tend anyone."

The white of Ratter's eye grew twice its size. "Who ye share with?"

"A renowned surgeon who may be able to offer you even more help than I. Mr. Peckwood is—"

"No!" Ratter's screech lifted to the rafters, louder than ever. "Tend me here!" His hand shot out, his fingers digging into Graham's sleeve. "Tend me here or begone!"

Graham frowned. "Calm yourself, sir. I will not force you from your home, yet it is in your best interest to come with me. I don't have enough ointment in my bag to treat you, and that wound must be washed of any poisonous residue."

"Don't care," the man moaned. "Peckwood is the devil."

He stared at the fellow. What sort of experience did the rat catcher have with the surgeon? "How do you know the man?"

Ratter's single eye burned like an ember in the night. "Peckwood killed my brother."

EIGHTEEN

*"A human being in perfection ought always to preserve
a calm and peaceful mind, and never to allow passion
or a transitory desire to disturb his tranquillity."*

❧

This was wrong. On so many levels. Absently running her hand along the smoothness of her gown, Amelia frowned at the image in the mirror. She'd attended many a dinner and even a fair number of fund-raisers in her day, but never on the arm of a handsome man—and especially not one who did strange things to her heart. But was it really the thought of Mr. Lambert that caused the fluttering in her chest, or was it the knowledge that her life had swerved off her plotted course and just might be heading straight towards a cliff?

"Will that be all then, miss?"

Betsey's voice pulled her around. The woman stood poised to flee out the door, barely concealing a glower. Ever since she'd been summoned, Betsey had been overly belligerent about helping Amelia dress. Suggesting the plain blue gown instead of the brilliant green, pinning up her hair too severely, and insisting on the smallest earbobs instead of the beaded drops. Why such effort to hinder her appearance?

"Just one more thing. Help me with my necklace, would you? The pearl pendant on the pink ribbon, I think." She nodded towards the small jewelry box on the vanity.

Betsey's lips rippled like a clamshell refusing to be pried open, yet she faithfully retrieved the choker. "Wasn't aware the prince regent would be in attendance tonight," she murmured as she tied the ribbon—a little too tightly—at the back of Amelia's neck.

"Just because the event is taking place in an asylum doesn't mean I shouldn't try to look presentable. And a little looser of a knot, please."

A sigh puffed against the skin between Amelia's shoulder blades. "I mean no disrespect, miss, to you or those poor souls at St. Peter's. It's just that it's not right, this going off in the dark, alone with a man."

And there it was. The reason for wishing to dress her as a dull penny…but out of protectiveness or jealousy?

Amelia turned, arching a brow. "You make it sound as if I am eloping with some brigand. It's only a dinner, and it's only Mr. Lambert."

"Humph," Betsey snorted. "What do you really know of him?"

"Enough that you may stop your fretting. He is a man of integrity. My brother has no qualms about him and neither do I."

Her own words doubled back and sickened her. It was true. She had no misgivings whatsoever about the good doctor. It was herself she doubted. Her treacherous heart. And what if that heart jumped sides, giving itself wholly over to Mr. Lambert before she realized it was gone? Would that not be throwing away the independence she'd worked so hard to achieve over the years?

Betsey snapped shut the jewelry box, clearly unconvinced. "I'm still of a mind to chaperone you tonight, were it not for the list of Mrs. Kirwin's chores I'm to manage before my head hits the pillow."

For all her bluster, Betsey was a gem. Despite her hidden disdain of the often bubble-headed Mrs. Kirwin, she had taken over the woman's duties without a complaint. Amelia snatched up her shawl with a smile and settled it about her shoulders. "I have no doubt Mrs. Kirwin appreciates all you've done for her while she's laid up."

"Stuff and nonsense!" She tucked the necklace box into a drawer, then faced Amelia with a twist to her lips. "That housekeeper's taken to that bed of hers like a queen to the throne, ordering me about with a regal air."

"Well, soon enough we shall be out from under her reign and on our way to Egypt." She headed towards the door.

"Your words to God's ear, miss."

Amelia hurried down the corridor, and none too soon, for the thud of a knocker pounded against the front door the moment her slippers landed on the main floor.

"I will answer it, Betsey," she called over her shoulder, lest the woman break her own leg barreling down the stairs to give Mr. Lambert a jaundiced eye and some stern words about returning her mistress home in one piece.

The second she opened the door, she froze. She'd seen Mr. Lambert countless times over the past month and a half, but this fine man? The doctor's usual shaggy hair was tamed back and he'd shorn his beard, revealing an even stronger jawline than she imagined. He wore a deep blue dress uniform with shiny brass buttons, the cut of which accentuated his shoulders and tapered down to a trim waist. The fabric smelled faintly of the sea, of briny fresh air and exotic lands, reminding her he was a traveler, a kindred spirit who silently and irresistibly drew her in.

Sweet mercy. Why was she so hot? She clenched her hands to keep from fanning her face.

His gaze brushed over her from head to toe, the green in his eyes flaring. "You are quite stunning, Miss Balfour."

"As are you, sir."

La! Had she really just said that aloud? She sucked in a breath, wishing to God she could suck in the brazen words as well. What a shameless flirt he must think her.

She tucked her chin. "Forgive me, Doctor. I am not usually so forward."

A knowing grin spread across his face. "Are you not?"

Valid point. She grinned as well. "I am afraid you've come to know me better than most."

"Yet not nearly as well as I'd like to."

He stood so close the warmth of his breath feathered against her brow. Or was it the naked honesty of his words that shot fire through her veins? No, it was the uniform. It had to be the uniform. No man had a right to look that dashing.

"I...uh..." Finally breaking eye contact, Mr. Lambert glanced over his shoulder. "I took the liberty of hiring a coach, which offers a bit more room than Mr. Peckwood's gig. And I thought you might appreciate having a driver—a chaperone, of sorts." Offering his arm, he turned slightly. "Shall we?"

Yes. Fleeing outside was a brilliant idea. She could use some air and lots of it. But feeling the hard muscle of his arm flex beneath the fabric as he led her to the carriage didn't do a thing to relieve the tightness of her stays. If she didn't do something to distract her mind, she'd swoon right here for all of Clifton to see—or at least Mrs. Ophidian, whose pale face peered out the first-floor window, watching their every move.

She focused on the carriage, now just steps away, and willed her thoughts to dwell on something other than the press of Mr. Lambert's shoulder against hers. "Will you speak tonight also, Doctor?"

"No. I am an ornament, merely there to lend Mr. Peckwood credence." He peered down at her. "You are not nervous, are you? I shouldn't think more than a few words would be expected from you."

"No, I am not usually given to jitters." So why the trembling in her knees as he guided her into the carriage? His leg brushed against hers as he sank onto the opposite seat, a jolt charging up her thigh. Clearly repentance was in order for all the years she'd spent silently disparaging the blushing misses she'd witnessed at countless dances, for now she finally understood them.

"I am glad to hear of your fortitude, Miss Balfour, for I've not brought along my medical bag tonight. Neither have I any smelling salts in my pocket." He pounded the wall. "Drive on!"

She eyed him as the carriage lurched into motion. "So tonight you are just a man, not a doctor?"

"For once, yes." A grin flashed in the dim light. "I am merely a man."

Ahh, but he couldn't be more spot-on. In every sense of the word, he was a pillar of masculinity, one she had no business admiring so thoroughly. She shrank into the seat, putting as much space between them as possible. Betsey was right. Going off alone in the night with this man might very well be a mistake from which her heart might never recover.

Two days. Just two. And then what? An entirely new life? Or death on the operating table? Colin grimaced, hand on the door latch. Both presented their own dangers, each as perilous as striding outside right now and baring his face in public. Lord, he was weary of living in a cage. But most of all, he was weary of playing it safe. Hiding. Ever hiding.

He yanked the door open and trotted down the two steps to the backyard. Not exactly a huge risk, traveling a mere six feet from the house, yet it was gamble enough for now.

Lifting his face to the gloom of twilight, he inhaled a lungful of moist air, memorizing the feel of life and breath. If forty-eight hours were all that remained for him, what was the best way to spend them? Though his father would have surely disagreed—nay—scorned his choice, he closed his eyes anyway.

Until my last breath, God, whether that be a moment or years away, I will thank You, for I am how You have fashioned me.

He flicked his eyelids wide open and added, *though I wouldn't mind if You granted me a few years as a normal man before calling me home.*

How long he stood there, a single shadow among many, he couldn't say, but long enough to hear a carriage arrive out front and the linger-ing voices of Amelia and the doctor while they departed. Long enough, as well, for night creatures to rustle about, searching for food, heedless of his presence. Little paws scratching for insects. Little feet creeping through shrubbery and—

Little feet?

Without turning his head, Colin snapped his gaze sideways. The silhouette of a boy emerged from the hedges against the house. Sweat broke out on his brow. This was no play of light nor a laudanum reac-tion, for he'd purposely avoided the stuff these past few weeks. Was this a true hallucination, then?

Or not?

Wheeling about, he lunged for the dark shape, fully expecting it to vanish. But the figure swerved away from him and barreled towards the gap in the broken garden wall.

Stunned, Colin sprinted and snagged the back of a collar, then hoisted a small lad eye-to-eye. His clothes smelled of dirt and mould and hot little boy, with arms hanging past his sleeves and bare feet dangling well beyond the ragged hem of his trousers. He was all knobs and angles, this child. Thin as a spindle.

"So," Colin rumbled. "You are real."

The boy nodded, the whites of his eyes stark against the night and a flop of dark hair hanging low on his forehead. To his credit, the lad didn't cry out. Didn't howl. Didn't squirm. Odd, that. Quite the different reaction than the boy he'd snatched from the cliff.

Colin cocked his head. "Do I not frighten you, child?"

The boy stuck out his lower lip. "No, sir."

Colin gaped. "Why not?"

Thin shoulders lifted beneath his grasp. "I were a'feared when ye first came, sir, but I bit my knuckle bone for to keep quiet."

Gutsy lad. Smart, as well. Colin lowered him to the ground yet did not release his grip. Chasing the child inside the backyard was one thing, but if he bolted beyond the garden walls, answers might never be supplied.

Colin lowered to his knees. Even then he towered above the lad. "Why were you hiding in the shrubbery?"

"I weren't." The boy's bare toes fidgeted in the lawn. "I were hiding in the house, sir."

Colin hid a smile. If nothing else, he was forthright. "Very well, then what were you doing in my house?"

"Being," he mumbled.

Leastwise that's what it sounded like—which made no sense whatsoever. Colin lifted the boy's chin with the crook of his finger. "Speak up, please."

"Being, sir," he belted.

This time a smile would not be stopped. Not only did the boy respond to commands, he did so with gusto. "Being what? A trespassing rapscallion?"

"Dunno, sir." His face screwed up. "Them words is too big fer me."

Of course they were. The lad could hardly be more than five years old. Possibly six. And no doubt he knew only the language of the streets. Colin leaned back and angled his head at him. "Fair enough. We'll try something simpler. What is your name?"

"Sodom, sir."

"What the devil sort of name is that?"

The boy flinched, and no wonder. The harshness of his tone echoed in his own ears.

Yet the child didn't look away, just held his gaze steady with dead-fish eyes, as if he'd gathered all his playthings and run off into the night, leaving nothing behind but a shell.

And that's when the truth punched Colin in the gut. Sickening. Revolting. He yanked back his hand as if the touch seared to the bone. This boy had been groomed to do as he was told, and only God knew what had been commanded of him.

His gut churned. "Your mother did not name you so. What is your true name?"

"Dunno." The boy shrugged. "Only know what Master Monster calls me."

Colin grimaced. What sort of horrors had this boy suffered in his short time on this earth? "You've run from your master then, have you?"

"Aye." The boy's eyes hardened into stones. So did his voice. "And I ain't goin' back!"

A sharp kick jabbed him in the thigh. His grasp slipped, and the boy tore off. Once again, the chase was on. But this time Colin didn't care if he had to pursue the lad clear into the heart of Bristol. Master Monster had seen the last of this child, even if it meant the public saw Colin's monstrous face.

The boy fled over the crumbled wall and into the neighbour's back-yard, little legs pumping hard for the rear gate. Amazing how such a small child could race like the wind.

But so could he.

Colin grabbed him up under one arm, and tucking his chin lest anyone peer out a window, he lugged the boy back to the safety of his own yard. The small body trembled in his grip.

"You have nothing to fear from me, boy," he soothed while he tromped to the house. Or at least he hoped he soothed. What did he know of pacifying children?

He stopped at the back stairs yet did not release the child. "I will not force you to go anywhere other than this stoop, for I should dearly like to finish our conversation. What you do after that is your own business. Are we agreed?"

Though he couldn't see the boy's face, the child's head bobbed.

"Good lad." Colin set him down on one end of the step, then eased his big frame onto the other. The boy immediately scooted as far as possible to the edge, but he kept his word and didn't run.

"So." Colin shifted towards him, quite the feat on such a narrow stair. "How long have you been living here?"

"Some time a'fore you and the pretty lady came."

Of course. With the skeletal staff since his father's demise, it made perfect sense the child had gone undetected...or had he? Were the servants, perhaps, feeding the little mite? "Does Mrs. Kirwin know of you?"

"No, sir." He shook his head, adding to his denial. "Only you, sir."

"How have you evaded detection?"

The boy merely blinked.

Colin tried again. "How is it no one has seen you?"

"Nobody but me uses the secret ways."

"Secret ways?"

He nodded, then shoved back the hank of hair that flopped into his eyes.

The boy seemed in earnest, and it wasn't out of the realm of possibility that an old residence might possess a priest hole or a hidden passageway, but Balfour House? He glanced over his shoulder at the three-story building. "Will you show me?"

"I dunno..."

He gazed down at the boy. How to persuade a rabbity child? "Look"—he splayed his hands—"if you and I are ever to play a game of seek and find, it is an unfair advantage if you know all the best hiding spots."

The boy's lips twitched one way, then the other, until finally he stood and reached for Colin's hand. "All right. Come along, sir."

With impossibly small fingers wrapped around his, the child led him to the shrubbery, then loosened his grip and dropped to his knees.

Colin did as well, trying to shove his bulk into the tangle of leaves and branches, but his shoulders would not cram through the tight weave of greenery.

Ahead, eyes peered at him from the darkness. "You coming?"

"I'm afraid I won't fit, lad." He backed out, but the boy apparently had enough space to turn around, for moments later, his dark head appeared.

Colin sank back on his haunches. "Thank you for showing me. Where does that tunnel through the shrubs lead?"

"To a hole, sir, one what opens into a passage inside. Stairs run from floor to floor on this outside wall." He flailed his little hand at the house. "In a few spots, it opens into rooms, all hid nice-like in the panels."

"So that's how you come and go. But how did you find that tunnel in the first place?"

"I were playing with a ball, sir. One I found, not stole." He lifted his pointy chin in challenge. "All my playthings be found."

Colin chuckled at his courage. He could squash the boy with one swipe. "Tell me then, young master, where do you sleep?"

"The ground, mostly. Inside if it rains."

"That can't be comfortable."

"Better'n what I had, sir." Even in the dark, a shudder could be seen rippling the thin fabric on his shoulders.

Unbidden, Colin's hands curled into fists. What he wouldn't pay for just a moment with the boy's Master Monster to teach the man what fear really felt like.

Taking a few steadying breaths, he forced calmness into his voice instead of the rage that crawled like so many ants beneath his skin. "What do you eat, boy?"

"Whatever I find, sir."

"Is that so? Well. No more, I think." Tentatively, he reached out and patted the boy on the head, and when that small act was accepted, he pushed his advantage even further by saying, "As my new errand boy, you shall have proper meals and a proper bed."

The boy ducked away. "No."

"No what?"

"No, sir."

Were all children this hard to decipher? Did the lad not wish for meals? For a bed? Or did he think the errand running to be too much work? He shifted his weight, the strain of sitting on so small a seat for so long shooting pains through his backside. "What are you talking about, lad?"

"Can't be yer errand boy, sir. Can't no one know I'm here. Not even the pretty lady." Tears thickened his voice. "Master Monster might find me."

Anger flared white-hot. Of course. Though the boy had fled such cruelty, it made sense he'd not risk a return to it. "This master of yours, he is here? In Bristol?"

"Aye, sir. Mostly. Sometimes he be gone when he gets more boys."

Colin rubbed his leg, working out a kink, thinking hard, thinking fast. "All right, then what say you to London? Should you like to be my errand boy there?"

"Really, sir?" The boy straightened like a soldier called to attention. "That be a dream! I seen how kind ye be. Yer not like my other master."

He rose, glad for the child's agreement and the means to be able to whisk him away from such a wicked existence. "Very good, then I suppose for now you can go on *being*, as you call it, beneath my roof, though I insist on providing you a blanket and cushion, and that you promise you'll not stay outside in the rain."

"Oh, aye, sir!" The boy bounced on his toes. "God bless ye, sir."

"May God bless us both." He reached for the door, then on second thought, turned back. "Oh, and one more thing. About your name... For now, you shall be Nemo."

"Nemo." The boy tasted the name like a savory bite of meat pie. "I like it, sir."

"Good. Then *no one* you shall be, as am I, until the day we are both set free."

Once again he reached for the door, but the boy tugged on his trouser leg, his small voice asking, "When will that be, sir?"

"Soon, Nemo. Very soon." He yanked open the door and added under his breath, "Hopefully."

NINETEEN

"But I was in no mood to laugh and talk with strangers,
or enter into their feelings or plans with the
good humour expected from a guest...."

As if riding unchaperoned in a dark carriage with a man weren't improper enough, now this. A lone woman dining amongst a room full of suits. *Only* suits. Amelia kept her gaze pinned on her dish of blancmange. Granted, most of the gentlemen in attendance were white of hair and paunchy at the waist, but that didn't make it any less inappropriate. What were they to think other than she was some sort of trollop?

The only thing getting her through the awful dinner was the constant conversation from Mr. Lambert on her left, which saved her from the wandering eye of the philanderer on her right.

"...not to your liking?"

She blinked up at Mr. Lambert. "Pardon?"

"I asked if your pudding is not to your liking." He pointed his spoon at her plate. "You've not touched a bite."

"I—"

A crystalline *ping-ping-ping* clanged from the head of the table, drawing all of their gazes. Mr. Peckwood continued dinging his glass with the back of a spoon as he rose from his seat. "May I have your attention, please?"

He stood imperially, shoulders thrown back, chin held high, until the chatter melted into respectful silence. "Thank you. Now, as you all know, I have not merely invited you here to partake of a delicious meal—my compliments to your cook, Mr. Waldman"—he nodded at the big-bellied warden sitting at his right hand—"but I requested your presence for a demonstration of a new procedure." His chest swelled as he paused. "However, in its stead, I have a little surprise for you that's so much more than a medical presentation. This evening your eyes will be opened to a whole new era."

Mr. Peckwood's gaze swept from person to person—quite the dramatic effect, one better suited to gaslights and a stage than to a dining room. "Tonight I give to you a glimpse into a world without madness."

Whispers whooshed like an unholy whirlwind around the room. Even Amelia couldn't help but lean aside and ask Mr. Lambert, "How can he make such a claim?"

Mr. Lambert shook his head, his low voice a warm hum in her ear. "I have no idea."

Mr. Peckwood lifted a hand, quieting the murmurs. "I realize such a statement sounds mad in and of itself. But it's true. I am close to perfecting a technique that will eradicate the need for asylums by restoring the mentally infirm to full and complete sanity."

Objections popped like roasting chestnuts from those seated at the table.

"Preposterous!"

"Can it be?"

"Maybe it's Peckwood who needs to be committed."

All these rumblings and more gained in speed and volume until Mr. Peckwood once again *ping-ping-pinged* with his spoon—so forcefully that Amelia winced lest the glass break.

"Now, now, gentlemen, I hardly expect words will convince you. Rather, you shall see with your own eyes. And so, without further ado, I must beg your pardon for a few minutes while I prepare. In the meantime, pass the sherry and enjoy the good company until Mr. Waldman directs you otherwise."

Amelia turned to Mr. Lambert. "I thought he was going to exhibit the treatment you've been administering to my brother."

Mr. Lambert balled his napkin on the table. "So did I."

"Excuse me, Miss Balfour." Mr. Peckwood paused near her chair. "May I have a word with you?"

Though she didn't need his permission, her gaze drifted unbidden to Mr. Lambert, who nodded his agreement.

The older doctor led her to the door, where barely past the threshold, he stopped in the hall and faced her. "Simply a formality, my dear. I thought you ought to know the order of the evening. Before my demonstration begins in full, I shall ask you to say a few words about the treatment I've been giving your brother—how it's prepared him for a successful surgery. How your trust in me has been worthwhile."

Palms suddenly clammy, she ran them along her skirt. "But he hasn't had the surgery yet. How can we know it will be successful?"

"What's this?" Peckwood rocked back on his heels as if she'd struck him. "Do you doubt my capabilities? Have I not extended the utmost care to your brother?"

She pressed her lips tight. It was Mr. Lambert who tended her brother daily, who provided for his headaches and his dizziness—though technically he was following Mr. Peckwood's orders, was he not? Perhaps she was being pettish.

Dipping her head, she peered up at the doctor through her lashes—a penitent look she'd mastered on her father all those times he expected her to agree with him, when at heart, she didn't. "I mean no disrespect, Mr. Peckwood. My brother has been very well cared for indeed."

His sharp blue eyes glimmered. "Then that is all you need say, my dear. Your personal endorsement of my skills will do much to aid the poor souls who inhabit this institution. These men and women need to be cured—nay, *deserve* to be cured—and I am the one who will do it."

His voice rose so zealously a few of the gentlemen inside the dining room craned their necks to see what was going on.

Amelia shrank away from the door, out of their line of sight. Most men—doctors, even—did not care a mite about those who were shut up in asylums and wouldn't spend two minutes trying to better their lives. What made him different?

"You are very fervent about the plight of the insane, Mr. Peckwood.

Not that I don't commend you for it. I do. But I can't help but wonder why." She tipped her head and studied him. "How do you explain such passion?"

For a long while, he said nothing. Just stood there, mindlessly staring. At length, his sharp little eyes focused on her. "Did you know I was once married to a woman with a mind as quick as yours? Or so I thought. Tell me, Miss Balfour, do you know what it's like to watch the one you love slowly slip into lunacy? An inappropriate burst of laughter at odd times. A string of nonsense when least expected. At first you brush it off"—his hand fluttered in the air—"thinking you've missed a jest or perhaps heard wrong. But then it continues, building in frequency, until you drop to your knees and beg God to banish such insanity."

His gaze hardened. "But He doesn't. And she dies. So yes, Miss Balfour, you must forgive me for such passion, as you call it. Since the demise of my wife, my mission has changed from tending broken bodies to fixing damaged minds. And I am very close to doing so. But that takes funding, which is what tonight is all about." The impassioned flush on his face deepened until he inhaled audibly. "So can I count on you to help me persuade these gentlemen to open their purse strings?" He lifted his chin towards the men congregating in the dining room.

She fidgeted with the cuff on her sleeve. He'd shared so much personal information with her, how could she not honour his request? "I will do what I can, Doctor."

"Very good." He patted her on the arm. "Then I shall see you in a few minutes."

He strode down the passageway, coattails fluttering. She turned to find Mr. Lambert, but with every step, her stomach pinched tighter—yet not from the meal. Something else didn't sit right in her belly. She felt like she teetered on a three-legged stool and one of the legs was cracked. But why the unease? Mr. Peckwood was trying to achieve a commendable thing. His heart was clearly grieved over losing his wife, his desire to fix broken minds perfectly understandable, but she couldn't help thinking there was something more to it than that. Information he wasn't telling her.

But what?

Temptation had been nipping Graham all evening, like an annoying horsefly that would not go away. It began the jaw-dropping moment the Balfour House door had opened, revealing Amelia in a green gown, with her hair done up and her cheeks aglow, and continued in the shadowy carriage ride, when every touch of her knee brushing against his was a sweet agony. The woman was a danger. An enchantress. One he should guard his heart against.

But it was too late. The little pixie had already breached his defenses.

His gaze followed her out of the room, lingering a little too long on the sway of her hips, before he snapped out of his trance. Shoving back his chair, he stood. Now that she was occupied by Mr. Peckwood, this might be his only chance to speak alone with Mr. Waldman.

He spied the man off at a liquor cart in the corner, pulling out the stopper of a decanter. Judging by the ripe colour of the man's nose, he ought to be pouring water instead. And as Graham drew closer, it only confirmed his suspicion. Alcohol wafted off the warden in waves, just as it had that day the man had chanced a visit to the surgery.

Graham stopped a few paces away lest he fall victim to intoxication by proximity alone. "Excuse me, Mr. Waldman. Might I have a word?"

Washed-out blue eyes turned his way. "Let me check."

Graham blinked. Check with whom? The man was the highest authority at St. Peter's.

Waldman fumbled about in his waistcoat and produced a pocket watch. He flipped open the lid, held it out at arm's length, then close to his nose, and finally ended up scowling at the thing while tapping his fingernail against the glass face. "Criminy!"

"Is there a problem, sir?"

"Yes." He snapped the lid shut. "Mr. Peckwood asked me expressly to direct these people into the next room promptly at nine o'clock. Not a minute sooner nor later. Then I'm to dim the lights at nine sixteen and restore them at nine thirty sharp."

Graham glanced at the man's white-knuckled grip on his watch. "And your timepiece is not working?"

"Blasted thing. I should have known better than to trust a gift from

187

my mother-in-law. Cheap piece of rubbish." He tossed the thing onto the liquor cart then drained the entire contents of his glass.

"Here." Graham held out his own watch. "You may return it to me at the end of the evening."

"Why, many thanks, Mr. Lambert." A sloppy grin lifted Waldman's thick lips as he snatched up the timepiece and glanced at the face. "You have exactly six minutes, sir. What can I do for you?"

Ever since his chance encounter with the rat catcher—who would live, thank God—Graham had walked the streets, mulling over the man's claims of Peckwood's involvement in his brother's death. According to Ratter, Peckwood had diagnosed his brother with a case of periodic fits and committed him to the asylum—where he died only months later, supposedly at the hands of Mr. Peckwood. Which of course made no sense, for St. Peter's had its own staff surgeon. And yet Peckwood did spend a fair amount of time at the asylum, so it wasn't entirely out of the realm of possibility. But what was Graham to do? Sashay up to Peckwood and ask, "Oh, by the by, have you recently murdered any lunatics?" Ludicrous. Nearly as absurd as questioning a pickle-brained warden who paid more attention to distilled spirits than the souls who inhabited his institution. But what other choice did he have?

Graham glanced over his shoulder. Satisfied Peckwood was yet out in the corridor with Miss Balfour, he stepped closer to Mr. Waldman. "I wonder if you could enlighten me on a certain inmate. A patient by the name of Robert Felix was brought in last year and died a few months afterwards. Do you recall the name?"

"I don't...well, maybe it sounds a bit familiar." The man's gaze drifted to the ceiling, and slowly his head started bobbing. "Yes," he murmured, then louder, "yes, I do believe I remember the fellow. He was one of Mr. Peckwood's cases."

Peckwood's *cases*? Graham rubbed the back of his neck. What jurisdiction did the doctor have at the asylum? "Why was Mr. Peckwood called in? It is my understanding that St. Peter's employs a staff doctor."

"Yes, but you know. Overworked. Underpaid." Waldman refilled his glass, offering the decanter to Graham, who shook his head. "At his leisure and my request, Mr. Peckwood takes on those patients who are not deemed critical. The man is a saint, I tell you, caring for the mad out of the goodness of his heart."

Graham stifled a snort. Did Peckwood possess such goodness? If so, he'd seen scant evidence of it. Not that the old doctor was a hard-hearted fiend, but he did tend to put himself above others. No, Peckwood was no saint. He must be getting some sort of payment from St. Peter's…which did nothing to explain the overdue statement he'd found in the man's office.

"So this Felix fellow." Graham angled his head. "How did he die?"

Waldman swirled the dark red liquid in his glass. "If I remember correctly, it was a purging gone bad. Wait. No, no. That was a different one. In Felix's case, I believe it was a medication mix-up."

"But you said Peckwood only tended the noncritical. Why was Felix on medication?"

"By the stars, man! I am a warden, not a surgeon. You'll have to take that up with Mr. Peckwood." Once again he downed the contents of his glass in one big drink.

He sighed. The man was virtually no help whatsoever. "Do you know what the medication was?"

Waldman set his glass on the cart, then glanced at the watch before shoving it into his pocket. "I'm afraid your time is up, Mr. Lambert. I dare not keep Mr. Peckwood waiting."

Graham grabbed his arm. "The medication, please. What was it?"

"Not singular, but several." Waldman frowned at the grip on his sleeve. "Something to do with Dover's powder and ano-something-or-other."

"Anodyne?"

"Yes, that was it." His gaze shot to Graham's. "Now, release me, or there will be the devil to pay."

Graham dropped his hand, already weary from the late-night walks that were in his future. But this time he wouldn't be wondering if Peckwood were a killer. Apparently he was, whether he'd meant to or not. No, the real question now was why Peckwood had combined a cold and fever drug with diethyl ether. Each was highly addictive in its own right. Had the combination been a simple mistake?

Or was Peckwood carrying out research on a helpless population to establish his own name in the annals of medical history?

TWENTY

"Great God! what a scene had just taken place!"

For a groundbreaking display of curing the insane, the room Amelia entered was surprisingly stark. No operating table. No vials or tubes or medical apparatus of any sort. Even missing were the glass towers and conducting pads used daily on Colin. The space was made up of four whitewashed walls lit by enormous candelabras, a bare wooden floor, and at center, Mr. Peckwood, anchored near a chipped-paint stool supporting two bottles, a spoon, and a glass of what appeared to be water.

Amelia pressed her lips flat, ashamed of the disappointment sagging her shoulders. What had she been expecting? Did an unknown morbid gawker live inside her heart? If so, then apparently the same ghoulish spectator resided inside the ten gentlemen fanned out around Mr. Peckwood. If the whispered consensus were any indication, they were as decidedly unimpressed as she.

Peering up, she searched Mr. Lambert's face to see if he was as underwhelmed. His eyes gave nothing away. Neither did the placid set of his jaw.

She frowned. "I thought Mr. Peckwood was going to demonstrate the procedure he uses on my brother."

"As did I."

She angled her head. "Then what is he going to show us?"

"I don't know. He must've changed his mind at the last minute. Knowing him, it's likely to be something more grandiose...though the setup appears to be anything but."

A sharp clap rang out, preventing any speculation he might have given. Every head turned towards the white-haired doctor.

He smoothed his coat proudly. "Let us begin. As you know, I have had the good fortune to work with many a medical innovator, drawing a wealth of wisdom from some of the keenest minds in all of England. After years—nay, decades—of devoted study and research, I have made several innovations, yet none so great as that which I am on the cusp of developing." He paused long enough to draw a deep breath, then plunged in again. "This, my friends, is why I have requested your presence here tonight. To ask you to join me in changing the world."

Clasping his hands behind his back, he paced over to the gentleman at the farthest side of the room. He continued his methodical gait, making eye contact with each person in the semicircle as he spoke. "Now, gentlemen, I realize a certain amount of trust must be established before you part with any coins. As with religion, I believe there is no better way to fan the flames of faith than with testimony and corroboration. So this evening you shall all be witnesses to the mending of a broken mind." He moved to Amelia and offered his hand. "But first, allow me to present to you the testimony of the lovely Miss Balfour."

His fingers were cold, rigid, and somewhat moist, like sticks that'd been left out in an autumn mist. His touch sent a shiver up her spine. Or perhaps it was just nerves. All the men's gazes locked onto her as if she were the specimen he intended to experiment upon. Her blood really did run cold with that thought. Surely he didn't mean to do so, did he? She cast a wild look at Mr. Lambert, seeking—and blessedly finding—strength in his hazel eyes.

"Miss Balfour." Mr. Peckwood stationed himself at her side. "Would you please explain the treatment I have provided for your brother these past six weeks?"

Panic fluttered in her chest. Why did he not have Mr. Lambert up here, elaborating on the medical intricacies she didn't understand?

Any explanation she might attempt would leave her sounding like a fool.

She patted her pocket, glad now that she'd given in to the last-minute temptation to carry her Ibis feather. Feeling its familiar shape, her anxiety seeped away, and she squared her shoulders. She could do this. Besides, these men likely didn't even care about complicated details.

"You must pardon me, gentlemen," she said, smiling, "for I am not fluent in the language of therapeutic procedures. What I can say is that Mr. Peckwood, with the aid of his associate, Mr. Lambert, has been preparing my brother for what is to be a life-changing surgery of his own design."

She paused, once again uneasy. How much should she reveal about Colin? Too much and she might open a Pandora's box of curiosity seekers. Not enough, and she'd let down Mr. Peckwood. But after two more days, would either of those concerns even matter anymore?

She drew in a breath. "My brother suffers from the rare disorder of *acromegalia*, which is exacerbated by some extreme scarring he received from a burn as a child. These treatments, devised by Mr. Peckwood, break down the weave of my brother's skin, which will make the removal operation not only more efficient, but lessen the recovery time. Leastwise, that is my understanding. If you would like a more technical explanation, I am certain Mr. Peckwood or Mr. Lambert would be only too happy to supply it."

She glanced at Mr. Lambert, who simply nodded in agreement.

"However, gentlemen, what I can speak of intelligently is the hope that Mr. Peckwood has imparted to my brother and myself. In only a few days, my brother begins his journey to entering society, a journey other doctors have laughed at or scorned. I know naught of what the doctor intends to show us tonight, but I have no doubt it will be unlike anything another physician or surgeon can or will offer. Mr. Peckwood is one of a kind, of that I am sure." She dipped a small curtsey. "Thank you."

Mr. Peckwood bowed in return. "And thank you, Miss Balfour."

A polite round of applause escorted her all the way back to Mr. Lambert's side.

He leaned close, his breath warm against her brow. "Very well done."

The admiration in his eyes, the affirmation of his words, sank deep. She all but forgot about the room, the presentation, everything really, save for the attractive doctor caressing her with his gaze. He stood inches from her, with his hair slicked back and clean-shaven face just begging for a touch. She tucked her chin lest he see the heat flushing her cheeks. Until this summer, she'd never blushed so much in all her life.

Thankfully, Mr. Peckwood's voice once again drew all eyes to the front of the room. "For the past year, I have been working with some of the inmates here at St. Peter's. During the course of my labours, I have nearly perfected a radical new treatment to soothe the troubled psyche, remove the oppressive fog of confusion, and revive the tranquility of rational thought. In short, I have discovered the secrets of mending a broken mind. And so tonight, I would have you witness the restoration of Miss Caroline Safie." He swept out his hand, directing everyone's attention to the door.

Shuffling feet and a few grunts accompanied the two men who entered the room, hoisting a squirming woman between them. Her arms were pinioned, a straitjacket tied firmly at the small of her back. She was a wild-eyed creature, her mouth wide yet issuing no cry. No words. Just huffy little breaths and an occasional whimper. It was a jarring effect. Like she desired more than anything to speak but her tongue would not obey. Her hair had been braided, though with the erratic swing of her head, several hanks broke loose and cascaded over her face.

"Thank you, gentlemen." Mr. Peckwood nodded at her handlers. Before they released her, he stepped nearly nose-to-nose with the woman, his gaze burning into hers. Placing his palms on her cheeks, he directed her face to his alone. "Now, now, Caroline, look here. You know me."

The woman stiffened, her backbone a steel post. The light dimmed as the warden went about blowing out several candles. Quite the eerie effect. Amelia swayed closer to Mr. Lambert.

In the semidarkness, Mr. Peckwood spoke low and even. "What

you are about to see is the calming of Miss Safie's universal fluid. I shall interrupt the flow of madness and introduce the rational current of sanity. For this, I require absolute silence."

"Pah!" Mr. Lambert huffed.

Amelia cast him a sideways glance, curious about the sudden spirited response, but she shoved down her question as a thick hush blanketed the room. She'd have to query him later.

Slowly, Mr. Peckwood pulled away from Miss Safie, but not far. Never far. At most, he kept his hands an inch from actually touching her. His fingers traced the entire outline of her body, from the curve of her hips, the arc of her thighs, even the swell of her chest. A queer ripple twinged in Amelia's stomach. This was too intimate, too indecent a scene to be viewing! Especially with a room full of men looking on.

But the more Mr. Peckwood moved about the woman's body, head to toe, toe to head, always maintaining an eye-to-eye connection with her, the more Miss Safie's posture softened. Her lips closed placidly. Her breathing evened. Even the cords of muscles standing out on her neck melted away. So did the wildness in her eyes.

On silent feet, the doctor eased behind her and untied the bindings of her jacket. No one in the room moved. No one so much as inhaled as he carefully peeled it off her. He folded the fabric while once again mesmerizing her with his stare. "Should you like your medicine now, Caroline?"

She lifted her chin and calmly tucked back the loosened hair. "Yes, Doctor."

A sharp gasp filled the room. She'd spoken! Not only that, but with the resonant tone of an angel.

Mr. Peckwood poured a white powder from one of the bottles into a spoon, then exchanged that for the other bottle and pulled out a dropper. Clear liquid fell like raindrops. Two. Three. Four drops. He stopped, returned the dropper, and lifted the spoonful up to the woman's nose.

"Breathe deeply, Caroline," he murmured. "Breathe slowly."

Ever so slightly, she leaned over the spoon, like a flower seeking a sunray. With his free hand, Mr. Peckwood made little sweeping movements, wafting whatever scent the mixture carried directly into her nostrils.

After one inhale, the woman closed her eyes. After two, a smile, so sublime Amelia's heart ached to witness it. And after three, Mr. Peckwood lowered the spoon and mixed the contents into the glass of liquid.

"Open your eyes, Caroline, and drink," he commanded.

She obeyed.

Once she drained the cup, he took it from her and offered his hand. Her fingers rested delicately on his. "Now, would you be so kind as to greet the guests who have come here tonight?"

"Of course, Doctor."

They turned in unison, facing the spectators, and Miss Safie dipped a curtsey elegant enough for court.

"Good evening, gentlemen." She nodded towards Amelia. "And to you as well, my lady."

Amelia's jaw dropped. How could this be the same skittish woman of only minutes ago? The transformation was so complete. So impossible! She turned to say as much to Mr. Lambert.

But he was gone.

Disgust oozed like a raw wound, and no matter how much Graham gritted his teeth or paced the front drive, nothing stopped the festering of it. He'd known all along that Peckwood was not afraid to employ unorthodox procedures. That had been part of the reason he'd sought the man out in the first place. But this?

He kicked up a spray of gravel. Animal magnetism teetered on the very border of acceptability in the medical community. It was more showmanship than substance, leastwise from all he'd read. And because of such a fanciful presentation, the gullible men inside would open their purse strings as wide as their mouths had gaped. What an ill-fated day when he'd pleaded with Mr. Peckwood to take him on as a partner! God must surely be laughing at his stupidity. He glared at the night sky. *Why? Why did You allow me to waste my life savings on that man?*

"What are you doing out here?"

He wheeled about at the soft voice.

Amelia stood at the bottom of the front stairs, the asylum rising behind her like a black monolith in the night. The innocent tilt of her head cut to the bone. Of course she was curious as to why he wore a rut into the drive like a maniac. Why he'd abandoned her in a room full of men. She deserved an answer, and a comprehensive one at that.

But how was he to tell her that Peckwood had just presented a practically worthless medical procedure without planting a seed of doubt in her mind about the man's capabilities? The very man who would be opening her brother's skull in mere days. A few careless words might destroy her hope, obliterate her trust, and crush her dream of a new life for Colin. And possibly not only hers, but the man he'd come to love as a brother. Should he really do such a thing? But Peckwood was not to be trusted! Not after this. He ground his heels into the gravel, taking another lap. No, he couldn't—he wouldn't—shatter her hopes, but he could make sure to watch over Colin's surgery with an eagle eye.

He stopped in front of her, forcing a pleasant tone to his voice—one that sickened his gut. "Forgive me, Miss Balfour, for my abrupt departure, but I believe it is high time we leave. The hour grows late, and your brother will be expecting you home. And so, I have summoned the carriage."

"Pretty words, sir." She folded her arms, her pert little nose rising with the movement. "But I am not leaving until you give me an explanation of why you walked out on what I can only describe as a miracle."

Miracle?

Hot blood surged through his veins. "I assure you, there was nothing miraculous in what Mr. Peckwood did here tonight."

"What do you mean?" Confusion flickered as tangibly as the torchlight across her face. "I saw it for myself. We all did. The woman changed right in front of our eyes."

"The ends do not always justify the means." He plowed his fingers through his hair, uncaring of the mess he was making of it. "What Mr. Peckwood presented was a demonstration of animal magnetism, a highly controversial procedure, one that's questioned by the medical establishment."

"But are not most important innovations causes of contention?" She flung her hand towards the asylum door. "That woman is even now taking tea and conversing with the gentlemen inside, as if she were the queen herself and not a lunatic fresh out of a cell. Whether the procedure is controversial or not makes no never mind, for the effect has left her in a better state. Surely you cannot argue that point."

A bitter laugh nearly choked him. "I did not think you one to be so easily swayed, Miss Balfour."

"I witnessed the transformation, Mr. Lambert." Her eyes glinted, sharp as a steel blade. "As did you."

"Yes, but I knew what I was watching. It wasn't fair of Peckwood to use such dramatics simply to gain some funding." He blew out a long breath, hating to be the one to put skepticism in Amelia's mind against a doctor who held her brother's future in his hands.

But so be it.

He threw back his shoulders. "The truth is that animal magnetism has not been proven to work in the long term. In a few days, perhaps even only a few hours, she will be back to where she began. Besides, how are we to know that woman was mad to begin with and not some playactor fulfilling a role for which she was handsomely paid?"

"Hmm." Amelia eyed him suspiciously. "I wonder if there is not some small measure of jealousy involved?"

"Jealous? Of what?" He slung out his arms. "A man who will do anything to fund his schemes?"

She slowly shook her head. "You disappoint me, Mr. Lambert. I credited you with more of an open mind."

"I disappoint you? *I?*" His voice shook. No, his whole body did, livid with the thought that somehow Amelia held Peckwood—that white-haired showman—in higher esteem than himself.

He grabbed her by the shoulders. "Then see for yourself what a foolish business this is. Stand still, if you please."

She stiffened. "What do you intend?"

"Why?" He shoved his face into hers. "Afraid you are wrong?"

Her chin rose. "Of course not."

"Then allow me to perform the same procedure on you that Mr.

Peckwood employed. You tell me if you feel any different."

She jutted her jaw. "Fine."

He stared deep into her eyes, giving her no choice but to gaze at him alone. Practically nose-to-nose. Their breaths mingling. All kinds of warning bells screamed in his head that this was not to be attempted, not with her—*never* with her—but he wouldn't back down. Not now. Let the woman see for herself what nonsense Mr. Peckwood had perpetuated.

He released his hold of her, just barely, his fingers hovering so close to the fabric of her gown he could feel the heat of her. Slowly, he outlined the shape of her shoulders, down her arms, hesitating at her hips, then tracing the curve. His heart nearly burst out of his chest, so hard did it beat. He should stop now. End this foolishness.

But pride had its hooks in too far. He leaned closer—any nearer and his lips would be on hers—and forced an even tone. "Do you feel anything?"

Her nostrils flared like a skittish horse. "Not yet."

So he continued. Flattening his palms, he placed them in front of her belly, the pounding in his head a primal beat. He moved them upwards—hardly an inch—when reason suddenly punched him in the gut. Sweet heavens! What was he doing? This was insane. Any farther and he'd be crossing the line of decency, if he hadn't already. Besides, had he not proven his point?

"There, you see." His words came out husky. "You feel no different, do you?"

"I—"

Her sharp intake of air charged through him, settling low, lighting him on fire, and he could stand it no more. He reached for her, sliding his fingers up the length of her arms, along her bare neck, and anchoring just behind her ears. "Do you feel different, Amelia?" he whispered.

She leaned into him.

And her mouth landed hot on his.

He staggered from the shock—then pulled her right along with him, pressing her tight, body against body. Guiding her into the shadows against the wall, until it was just her and him and a world that didn't matter anymore.

Life coursed through him from head to toe. Vibrant and wild. So pure it ached. He'd kissed before, but never like this, with every nerve firing, every sense awakened and aware. Just as he'd imagined on many a sleepless night, she fit against him perfectly, as if Amelia Balfour were made for him—*only* for him.

And then he knew, a truth so simple yet so astounding. He'd never love another woman as he did this one.

"Graham." She nuzzled her face against his, the touch nearly driving him to his knees. Her lips moved against his cheek. "Do you feel it? Tell me you feel it too."

His only answer was a groan, one that would not be stopped—and if he didn't stop now, there'd be no turning back.

TWENTY-ONE

"I cannot pretend to describe what I then felt."

What a waste of time. All those years of striving for perfection, of behaving with the utmost decorum and propriety. And in an instant she'd tossed them aside for want of man's kiss? But as Amelia breathed in Graham's earthy scent, reveled in the strength of his arms and taste of his lips, for one glorious, insane moment, she didn't care anymore.

She just didn't care.

The second he pulled away, though, it hit her. Hard. She lifted a shaky hand to her mouth. What had she done? What had *they* done? She peered up at Graham, searching for an answer to a question she wanted neither to admit nor cast aside.

"Amelia, I…" He turned in a tight circle before once again facing her. "Forgive me. I never should have taken advantage of you like that. I am as culpable as Peckwood. No, worse. I should have known better than to have pulled such a foolish act."

She blinked. Here he stood, asking for pardon, when she was the one who'd kissed him! And the fact that he didn't look at her with disgust only endeared him to her all the more.

"Oh, Graham, the blame is not on you alone. I should have stepped away, or at the very least rebuked you."

"Do not think it. This was not your fault." He reached for her, but his hand fell before contact. "I put you into a situation you never should have been in to begin with."

Anguish strangled his voice, and for a moment, the strong, confident doctor transformed into a penitent schoolboy, with his hair mussed and cravat rumpled. The dip of his chin was wholly contrite and beguilingly handsome all at once.

Amelia couldn't help but smile. "Well, I suppose you did prove a point."

He angled his head. "I did?"

"Yes, that you were wrong, sir."

His brow creased, and she clenched handfuls of her skirt to keep from smoothing them away. Such a move would only serve to reignite a passion she was desperately trying to douse.

"Wrong about what?" he asked.

"Your demonstration, this animal magnetism that you so heartily discredited." She rewrapped the gauze shawl that had drifted off her shoulders, then lifted her face. "Clearly it worked."

His head jerked back. "How so?"

"I am changed, sir, in ways I never dreamed possible." She'd meant it as a lighthearted comment. A small attempt at humour, even. But the truth of the words sank deep into her heart. She *was* changed, irreversibly so.

Graham stepped closer, and for one breath-stealing instant, she wondered if he might kiss her again. "As am I."

And there they stood, lost in a gaze, toe-to-toe, heart-to-heart. It was madness, really, to be caught up in such thick emotion beneath the shadows of an asylum.

"So," she breathed, surprised she could even speak for the ache in her throat. "Now what?"

The grind of wheels upon gravel shattered the moment as a black carriage pulled up and stopped on the drive. Graham jolted back a step, then offered his arm with a sheepish grin. "Now, I think, I bring you home."

It was strange, this walk to the carriage. She'd never before been so overly aware of a man's movements. How his coat shifted with each step.

The fine, long line of his legs as they neared the coach. How infinitely tender yet iron strong his grip when he helped her up the step. She settled her skirts, glad for the darkness when he sat opposite her…though he still might see the burn in her cheeks despite the gloom.

For a while, the carriage rumbled and swayed, neither of them speaking. She caught him a few times, glancing at her when she glanced at him, and each time she couldn't help but smile. Were they not both too old for such love-struck antics?

He shifted on the seat, his voice as low as the drone of the wheels. "You asked me what comes next." Leaning forward, he captured her hands in his, his gaze too shaded to read his intent. "I leave that entirely up to you. What do you want, Amelia?"

She gnawed the inside of her cheek, quite taken aback by the question. What *did* she want? A few months ago she'd been so certain she wanted to write of exotic lands, to show the world of men that a woman could have a place other than in front of a hearth. And, truth be told, to make a name for herself as a journalist, an award-winning one at that.

"So many things," she murmured as she pondered the long list she'd compiled over the years.

"Such as?"

Her gaze snapped back to Graham's. None of that could matter at present, for here she was in Bristol with a brother to attend—a brother whose very life would be at risk on an operating table the day after next. "For now, all I want is for Colin to be restored."

Graham's fingers pressed warm against hers. "And then?"

She sighed. Exactly. The question was so enormous it squashed the air from her lungs. "I hardly know," she whispered.

The truth of it was a surprise. She'd been so certain that after Colin recuperated, her future was to set sail on a ship to Cairo. But what of the man rubbing little circles inside the palm of her hand? How did Graham Lambert fit into that plan? She'd never considered marriage. She'd never had a need. Was he even offering such?

"I…" She shook her head, suddenly feeling foolish. Likely she was making too much of this. Far too much. The man had given her a kiss, not a proposal.

"Of course you are right." Graham sank back against his seat. "Our focus should be on your brother's surgery and convalescence. He is what matters right now."

He was. Colin had been her sole reason for coming home. His health. His life. She ought to be glad—and she was—that this doctor cared so dearly for her brother. But all the same, the second Graham pulled away, part of her felt rejected. The selfish part. The space in her heart that desperately wanted to be the one and only thought in Graham Lambert's head.

She bit her lip. *Oh God, forgive me.*

The carriage eased to a stop. Graham exited, his big frame filling the door until he stood outside in the lamplight, gazing up at her, those hazel eyes guarded, like a book slammed shut. A book she desperately wished to read. He offered his hand, and as he helped her descend, for the briefest of moments, she thought she detected a low moan in his throat.

"Good night, Miss Balfour."

She smiled. Though he'd reverted to the formality of her full name, the warm intimacy in his voice could not be denied.

"Good night, Doctor."

He bent over her hand, pressing his lips to her glove for a lingering moment, the heat of his touch burning through the thin fabric. And then he was gone. Vanished into the carriage. Carried off into the night.

Amelia stared after the coach for a long while before floating into the house and gliding up to her room, lighter than the feather in her pocket, even when Betsey popped in with a huff to help her undress.

Betsey eyed her in the mirror as she worked the pins from Amelia's hair. "It appears your night went well."

Absently, she rubbed the back of her hand where the leftover warmth of Graham's kiss yet lingered. "Yes, very."

Betsey tugged out the last pin, releasing a cascade down Amelia's back. "I didn't expect you home so soon."

"There was… That is we…" She ran her tongue over her lips, reliving the feel of Graham's embrace, his scent, his taste.

"My, is it warm in here?" She shot to her feet and strode to the window.

But the curtains already rippled with the night breeze, the sash wide open.

"Mmm-hmm." Betsey frowned. "I knew I should have attended you."

"Don't be silly. I am sure Mrs. Kirwin needed you far more than I." She swung about for her dressing gown.

Betsey beat her to it, holding up the flimsy bit of silk by the shoulders for Amelia to shrug into. "Folding linens and playing a game of piquet with a laid-up housekeeper is not what you hired me to do."

"I hired you as my helper, and for now, the running of this household is my life." She tied the sash.

"And when we leave here, will things go back as they were before? Traveling? Writing?"

A sigh leaked out of her. It seemed the whole world required an answer from her tonight—answers she didn't have.

She faced her maid, giving her shoulder a little squeeze. "Rest assured, Betsey. Whatever the future may hold, you will always have a place at my side if you so desire."

"And for that I am grateful, miss." Betsey's head bobbed. "But it's not my desires that are in question now, is it?"

Amelia turned away, her maid's insight cutting far too close to the truth.

What do you want, Amelia?

The question would haunt her for the rest of the night.

Graham punched open the door to his room, then winced as the knob smacked into the wall. That would leave a divot in the plaster. Just one more offense to pitch atop the heap he'd been acquiring all evening.

After lighting the lamp, he slung off his coat then fumbled with the mess of a knot in his cravat. What a night. First letting irritation get the better of him over Peckwood's theatrics, then abandoning Amelia to fend for herself in a room full of men. And if that weren't bad enough—which it was—when she did seek him out, he'd gone and treated her like a common trollop. What kind of blackguard was he?

Throwing the neckcloth onto the bureau, he smothered a growl, then practically ripped off his waistcoat buttons in his haste to be done with this wretched evening. Now that he'd kissed Amelia, what was he to do? Continue tending her brother and pretend nothing had happened between them? Thunderation! He couldn't. It was too late. That genie had long since fled the bottle.

He tossed his waistcoat over the back of a chair, staring at the thing as if answers might be found in the weave of the cloth. How could he—in good faith—ask Amelia to be his wife? Him. A practically penniless doctor. His hands clenched so tightly, they shook. By all that was holy, why had he not maintained more self-control? The timing of that stolen moment of passion was wrong. All wrong. He should have waited, bided his time until he was financially ready to open his own practice. Become the man Amelia deserved. Yet once again he'd gone off half-cocked, just like when he'd left home for the navy. He'd failed his mother by not listening to her pleas for him to delay enlistment until he was older.

And now he'd failed the only other woman he'd ever loved.

Yanking his shirttails from his trousers, he flopped onto the bed. How was he to make things right? A ragged sigh ripped out of him, just as his gaze snagged on the lone bookshelf across from him. Next to a stack of medical journals, his mother's Bible lay like a fallen soldier, the cover worn, the edges ruffled from overuse—but not by him. Never by him. Yet there it sat. Patiently waiting for him to pick it up. *Daring* him to pick it up. Somewhere deep in his gut, laughter welled, but by the time it surfaced, the sound was repulsive in his ears.

"Well, God," he muttered. "If ever I needed guidance from You, this would be the time, eh?"

His breath hitched as the words doubled back and struck him broadside. Maybe it *was* time he stopped groping his way through this world on his own and instead picked up the faith his mother had clung to so fervently.

Rising, he pulled the book from the shelf then sank back onto the thin mattress. Just touching the thing unearthed bittersweet memories of his mother, sitting by the hearth late at night, reading as if her life depended upon it—which she always said it did. Or how she'd flip through the pages before each meal, finding just the right psalm to pray over their food. He'd been naught but a lad of six when Father had died, leaving her alone to care for him. Many a mother would have apprenticed off her son and gone on with life, but not his mother. She'd taken all the strength and comfort of the words in this book and harnessed them to pull her through the hard times. What a fine, fine woman she'd been.

He cradled the worn leather reverently, then ever so gently he opened the cover, taking care not to crack the now-feeble spine. Inside, on the left-most page, was a list written in his mother's hand, with headings punctuating the columns.

> *When life is heavy.*
> *When goodwill befalls.*
> *When forgiveness comes hard.*
> *When death strikes a blow.*

All those and more were followed by verses, presumably those his mother had clung to for each situation. Interesting, but not nearly as compelling as the note written on the right-hand page.

He squinted, then scooched across the mattress, closer to the lamp. No, this was no note. It was a prayer, and judging by the blotches obliterating the ink on some of the letters, a very heartfelt prayer blessed by her tears. It seemed too personal to read, this act of communion between his dead mother and the God of the universe, but if he listened hard enough, he'd swear he could hear her voice calling across time and space, urging him to continue.

So he did.

> *Oh, Lord, You alone know my heart, how it aches for my*
> *son. My only son. Yet this very pain You are acquainted*
> *with intimately well. It is within Your power to bring*
> *Graham home to me, and how I pray it may be so, that I*
> *may hold him in my arms and feel the beat of his heart*
> *against my cheek just one last time. But more than that,*

Lord, I ask You to bring him home to You, even if I am not yet on this earth to witness it. For there is nothing better than that my boy's heart be turned to You, oh gracious King. Make it so, Lord. Oh, God, I plead with You to make it so.

By the time he finished, a great fat plop of moisture fell from his own face and blended with the stains already marring the page. He closed the book and, clutching it to his chest, dropped to his knees at the side of the bed.

Let her know, God. Please let my mother know, I am finally come home.

TWENTY-TWO

"I never beheld anything so utterly destroyed."

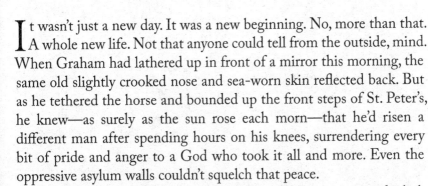

It wasn't just a new day. It was a new beginning. No, more than that. A whole new life. Not that anyone could tell from the outside, mind. When Graham had lathered up in front of a mirror this morning, the same old slightly crooked nose and sea-worn skin reflected back. But as he tethered the horse and bounded up the front steps of St. Peter's, he knew—as surely as the sun rose each morn—that he'd risen a different man after spending hours on his knees, surrendering every bit of pride and anger to a God who took it all and more. Even the oppressive asylum walls couldn't squelch that peace.

The second he entered the warden's office, a pug-nosed clerk looked up from his desk. "May I help you, sir?"

"Yes, could you let Mr. Waldman know Mr. Graham Lambert is here to—"

"No need." The warden stepped from his inner sanctuary, a gold pocket watch dangling from his fingers. "I was just about to leave this with my clerk. I looked for you after Mr. Peckwood's stunning demonstration last night, but rumour had it you'd already called for a carriage."

"Yes, I, uh—" He rubbed the back of his neck, scrambling for an explanation that wouldn't malign Peckwood's presentation. "I had promised to see Miss Balfour home at a decent hour."

Bypassing the clerk's desk, he retrieved his timepiece, just as the swift clack of shoes barreled into the room.

Mrs. Bap's granddaughter, Emma, wide-eyed and skirts a'swirl, slapped a hand to her heaving chest, her words coming out in a burst. "Come quick! One's loose!"

Mr. Waldman shook his head, a rumble in his throat. "Don't tear in here like a wild hellcat, girl, or I shall have you assigned to one of the wards. You know the procedure. Tell a guard!"

Fear flashed in her eyes, but she didn't back down. She was a fighter, this one—a credit to her grandmother.

"Can't, sir." She lifted her chin, still panting for air. "Guard's down."

Graham pocketed his watch. Whatever troubled the girl clearly required help, and quickly. "What do you mean, down?"

"He's right bad, Mr. Lambert. The ward doctor is seeing to him now." A fierce scowl drew her brows into a thick line as she faced Mr. Waldman. "But yer about to lose an inmate, sir, if ye don't act fast. She scrabbled out a window a'fore anyone could snatch her."

"What?" Waldman boomed. "Then lead on, girl! Mr. DeLacey"— he nodded at the clerk—"round up some men."

Emma fled the room, followed by Graham and Mr. Waldman— who snatched a rifle from a rack on his way out. What the devil? Was this not an institution of healing?

No time to ask about it. Emma's feet flew like a nor'easter out the front door and down the stairs, compelling him and the warden to sprint at top speed—which for Mr. Waldman was more like a trot, so large was his belly.

Emma stopped halfway across the front drive and pointed to the ten-foot rock wall ahead. Glass shards were embedded in the top. Anyone fool enough to climb it would shred the flesh from their bones.

And that's exactly what a white-gowned woman was trying to do. A mane of dark hair tumbled down her back as she purchased a foothold in a crevice of the mortar. One more great heave and she'd reach the peak, where razor-sharp edges glinted in the morning sunlight.

Graham opened his mouth to call out, when the cock of a rifle hammer cracked on the air. He snapped his gaze over his shoulder. Mr.

Waldman hefted the weapon, muzzle trained on the escaping woman.

"No!" Graham wheeled about, catching the barrel with his elbow and sending the shot wild.

Waldman glowered. "Now look what you've done."

The woman climbed all the faster, grasping for a hold on the top of the wall and skewering her hand on the glass.

Graham bolted and, stopping just below her, lifted his arms. "Lady, please. Come down. I'm a doctor. I can help you."

She jerked her gaze downward, and when her dark eyes met his, he gasped.

"Miss Safie?"

Lucidity flashed on her face, but only for the space of a breath before a mad demon glared out from her eyes.

"I'm coming!" She hoisted herself higher and grabbed onto the glass with her other hand. "I'm coming, Mr. Peckwood."

She would impale her own hands for the sake of that man? What sort of hold had the doctor created in her mind? For she was mad, driving the glass in deeper with each pull of her body, blood flowing freely. Whatever modicum of sanity she'd gained by Peckwood's procedure was now thoroughly destroyed.

Jumping, Graham made a swipe for the woman's legs and missed by a hand's breadth. Dash it! But if he did manage to pull her down, what then? Would she leave part of her fingers atop the bloody wall?

Shouts bellowed from the asylum doors, where three burly men dashed out, hefting a net between them. If he didn't get Miss Safie down now, she'd be bagged and yanked backwards, adding a concussion to her growing list of injuries.

"I am Mr. Peckwood's associate, Miss Safie. Did you hear me? Mr. *Peckwood's*!" He added a hearty emphasis to the man's name.

The woman gazed down at him, this time with hope flickering in her eyes. "He is here? Where?"

Graham edged as close as he could. "Come down and let us talk."

She loosened one hand and dangled by the other. Blood dripped from the appendage. "My medicine? You have it? I *need* it. No, I need Mr. Peckwood! He is life."

"Miss Safie, please—"

Too late.

The net flew. So did the woman. Backwards. Downwards. Landing hard on the ground. Before he could reach her, Miss Safie was dragged off towards the forbidding hulk of St. Peter's, fighting like a bagged cat, leaving behind red streaks in the gravel, and there wasn't a thing Graham could do about it. Not one. His fingers curled into fists.

Then curled all the tighter when Mr. Waldman clapped him on the back. "Well done, Mr. Lambert. Keeping her talking until the men could bag her. Capital plan! Should you ever find yourself in need of a position, I would be happy to take you on here at St. Peter's, though I daresay Mr. Peckwood will keep you busy enough with the new venture."

Graham stepped away from the man, but not too far. As much as he wished to flee, the warden just might have valuable information. "New venture?"

"Oh? He's not told you?" Waldman's thick lips pursed as if he chewed on a crab apple. "Well," he said at length, "being you are his partner, I suppose the good doctor will inform you soon enough, especially after receiving his needed funding last night."

Graham frowned. "It was my understanding, sir, that the money raised was to be put towards his medical research, not some other enterprise."

"Yes, but oh so much more than that." The warden swung out his arm, indicating the hulking asylum. "Why, he's to take on the whole of the west wing. Just imagine it, Doctor! The ultimate asylum where minds are mended, and it all begins here, under my watch."

A hard pit balled in Graham's gut, growing all the stonier with each of Miss Safie's cries as the men hauled her through the front doors. Mr. Waldman might be thrilled with Peckwood's plan, but there was a slight problem with it. If one could mend the mind, one could bend the mind... and once Peckwood discovered that piece of information, who knew what he'd do with it to garner wealth and fame?

Or power.

The pit sank deeper. Heavier. For an arrogant surgeon who would answer to none, what sort of havoc might Peckwood carelessly wreak while playing God?

❦

Buttered cod, boiled carrots, and Yorkshire pudding. Simple enough fare, yet Colin savored every mouthful as if it were his last, for who knew? It might be. Then again, this could very well be the final time he dined as a misshapen beast. Either way, he'd be transformed, and he swallowed that thought as heartily as the salted fish. He was more than ready for a change.

Across the table, Amelia herded a chunk of carrot around on her plate, shoving it one way and another. He frowned at the pathetic front she put up. Did she really think she was fooling him?

Retrieving his glass, he eyed her over the rim. "I'm not dead yet, you know."

"Colin!" Her fork clattered onto the dish, a wave of horror washing over her face.

He chuckled. She was more than easy to tease, and was that not his obligation—nay, his right—as a younger brother? "Come now, Amelia. It's only a surgical procedure, not a trip to the gallows."

Her brow creased as she reset her fork and laid her knife alongside it, ending any further pretense of eating. "Is it so very terrible of me to worry about you, my only brother?"

"Would it not be better to stop worrying about what might go wrong and instead be eager about what could go right?"

A huge sigh deflated her. "Yes. Of course. You are correct, as always." She lifted her chin and her glass. "To better days, then."

He raised his glass as well. "May they be many."

The wine went down rich and sweet, a fitting finale to a delicious meal.

"Speaking of better days." He set the empty glass back on the table and met her gaze. "We have been so focused on tomorrow's procedure we have neglected to discuss what comes afterwards."

"You mean legal robes and being called to the bar?" She dabbed her mouth with her napkin. A waste of time, for she'd not eaten anything to sully her lips; neither did the action do anything to wipe the smile from her face.

"Those are my intentions, but what of you? What is to become of the intrepid Amelia Balfour?"

Her smile faded, and she paid particular attention to folding her napkin. "Since you ask, I do have a prospect I haven't mentioned because I knew you'd postpone your surgery for my gain and your detriment. But being it's now too late to call off tomorrow's operation, I suppose it is time to confide in you."

Pushing back his seat, he stretched out his legs, cramped from the confinement of the table. He studied his sister while she folded and creased, folded and creased. A strange mix of anxiety and zeal pursed her lips. Whatever she had to tell him affected her in ways he couldn't begin to understand. Then again, what man ever understood the workings of a woman's mind?

At length, Amelia set the tightly pleated cloth atop the table and faced him. "I have been offered a trip to Cairo, fully funded by my publisher. For three months, I will live amongst the Egyptians, sampling their culture, absorbing their history. It is a travel writer's dream, one I have worked hard to achieve."

"Brilliant!" He grinned. "And a well-deserved boon it is."

But his grin didn't last long, especially as he noted the fine lines at the sides of her eyes, and the ever-present shadows beneath them. Truly, his sister had worked hard for her achievements, giving up much for her career. Sometimes too much, in his opinion. Tromping about foreign lands with her maid, casting aside the usual pursuits of women. An unorthodox life for a rather unconventional female, and while he couldn't be more proud of her, he also couldn't help but wonder if she were happy. Was—perhaps—travel writing merely a convenient means to escape from her demons, namely, their father? For surely that's what had driven her to such a vocation in the first place. But now that he was gone, could she not stop running?

Colin leaned forward in his chair. "And what then, Sister?"

"What do you mean? Is that not fantastic enough?" She shook her head. "This could be the pinnacle of my career."

Rising, he crossed to her, then bent a knee and took her hand between his. "Hear me out, please. In no way do I diminish the value of this Cairo trip or your writing expertise, and in fact, I heartily applaud both. But there is more to life than a career. There is family." He squeezed her tiny fingers, taking care not to crush them. "And there is love. While I admit we have had precious little experience with these things, nonetheless, I have come to believe this is what is worth sacrificing for."

"Oh, Colin." Fine, white teeth troubled her bottom lip. "Surely you know I would do anything for you."

"And I for you, but it's not me I am talking about."

She cocked her head, one dark curl bobbing with the movement. "Then speak plainly, Brother."

"Very well, but remember you asked for it." He inhaled deeply, more unsure than ever of her reaction. He'd tried to broach the topic of love before, but the little vixen was as evasive as a fox. "It would ease my mind if I knew you were well cared for, and such as it is, I desire that you might consider Graham Lambert as a husband."

Gasping, she pulled her hand from his. "But I don't need a man to be well cared for! Father left you and me inheritance enough to manage well."

"This has nothing to do with money, Amelia, and you know it." He paced in a circle before staring her down. "Unless, of course, I am wrong and you feel nothing for the man? Do you, or do you not, care for Mr. Lambert?"

She blinked, and though she kept all expression from her face, there was no denying the pretty flush creeping over her cheeks. Strong-headed woman! He couldn't help but smirk at the struggle. If only she'd give in to that emotion, give in to the good doctor.

Averting her gaze, Amelia shoved back her chair. "Perhaps we should retire for the night. We have an early morning tomorrow."

He stayed her with a touch to her shoulder. "Please, Cairo or not, do not discount what Mr. Lambert has to offer."

Her throat bobbed, and a lost little girl suddenly stared out of her eyes, one he desperately wished to protect from all the evils of this ugly world.

"What makes you so sure Mr. Lambert will offer for me?"

"Because I believe he loves you as much as I do." He pulled her into his arms, and it wasn't long before her shoulders shook and tears dampened his shirt.

"What's this?" He held her from him. "My plucky older sister weeping on account of a man?"

"Yes, a man. You! You big oaf." She swatted his arm then swiped away her tears. "I find I am not so very ready to lose you."

"And so you shall not." He tipped up her chin with the crook of his finger. "Where is your faith?"

A small smile quivered over her lips. "I appear to have misplaced it."

"Then allow me to restore it. God's arm is not shortened that He cannot save, and He *is* my salvation, no matter the outcome of tomorrow's procedure. Therein you should take heart."

She nodded, the flicker of a new resolution sparking in her gaze. "I will try."

"I can ask for nothing more." Bending, he kissed the top of her head. "And with that, I bid you good night."

"Good night, Brother."

Her voice followed him out of the room, and though she likely tried to hide the warble in it, an underlying note of worry hovered at the edges—which somehow managed to dampen his own eyes. That she cared for him was apparent, if not dutiful, being he was her only family, yet it moved him deeply. Father had been family too, yet he'd never once shown even a flicker of such love for his only son. How different things might have been had he not been born with such a grotesque visage.

As Colin worked his way to his room, he kept a sharp eye for any sign of Nemo. Since he'd discovered the lad, Nemo had taken to creeping out of the shadows each night and stowing away in his room. The boy had no idea he'd be laid up for the next week or so, and he really ought to explain the matter. Earlier that morn, he'd pulled out his worn copy of *The Odyssey*, thinking to give it to the lad as something to hold on to during his convalescence. Not that the boy could read, but the illustrations might serve to entertain.

He pushed open his bedroom door and lit the lamp inside, but no smudge-faced boy appeared. Even when he shoved up the sash and leaned out the window, scanning the backyard for any sort of boy-shaped movement, still nothing.

With a sigh, Colin backed away, loosening his cravat. The lad was smart, wily enough that he'd not chance being seen when no doubt Amelia would take up residence in this chamber until he recuperated.

He tossed down his neckcloth and padded over to the washstand. After a thorough splashing of water on his face, he grabbed the towel, then dared a peek into the mirror he usually avoided. A monster stared back, the same fiend who always stared back.

Perhaps after tomorrow, if God smiled upon him, that beast would be no more.

TWENTY-THREE

*"My heart beat quick; this was the hour and moment of trial
which would decide my hopes or realise my fears."*

The last chime of seven o'clock rang in unison with a peal of thunder—and a rap on the front door of Peckwood's Surgery. Graham smiled as he reached for the knob and ushered in Colin and Amelia Balfour. This was it. The day they'd all been waiting for. Would that God might smile upon the impossibly large man dripping all over the waiting room floor and the wide-eyed beauty at his side.

"Good morning, Mr. Balfour, Miss Balfour." Graham dipped his head at each in turn, then flipped the OPEN placard to CLOSED before he shut the door. Yet all the while his gaze lingered on Amelia. Since the night of the kiss, he'd not had a chance to speak to her, and though he knew he must, now was not the time.

Colin flung back the enormous hood hiding his face, an overbright sparkle to his dark eyes. "And so it begins, eh, Doctor?"

"Yes, I suppose it does." He beckoned with a tip of his head. "Follow me, if you please."

He strolled past the surgery to the next door, which opened into a recovery room. He'd laid a small fire, hoping the warmth of a hearth on this damp morn might comfort Amelia while she waited. He'd even gone so far as to have a tea tray ready for her use. Small luxuries, but the best he could manage.

"Miss Balfour, if you don't mind waiting in here." He stepped aside.

"All in all, I don't suspect the procedure should last much above an hour and a half, two at most. Please, make yourself at home. Have you any questions before we leave you?"

With a last glance at her brother, she turned to Graham and pressed her fingers into his sleeve, the brown of her eyes burning like dark embers. "No questions, just promise me my brother will live."

Graham's gut twisted. He'd do anything for this woman. Climb the highest mountain during a raging storm. Travel the length of a desert and back. Even give the last drop of his own lifeblood for her if need be. But this? How could he promise such a thing?

And yet what kind of fiend would he be to disregard the desperation thickening her voice?

He laid his hand atop hers. "I shall do my utmost to see your brother returned to you."

Tears shimmered. Her lips flattened into a tight line. Yet she nodded valiantly and entered the room, taking part of Graham's heart with her. She shouldn't have to wait alone, worrying and wondering. He should be there to hold her hand. Give her strength. But all he could do was stride away and leave her in the hands of God. Yet as he was learning—albeit slowly—those were the best hands to leave anyone in.

He led Colin into the surgery, past a row of shelves containing several cloth-draped trays. After preparing the instruments requested by Peckwood, Graham had taken care to cover the tools before the Balfours' arrival. No sense in Colin witnessing what might be construed as torture devices. The sight of a trepanation kit to an untrained eye would surely cause distress. Even he'd flinched when he'd set out the big drill that would soon eat a hole through Colin's skull.

The room was as well lit as possible, with lamps glowing against the dreary gloom of the stormy morning. He stopped near a series of hooks on the wall, two holding long surgical aprons, two empty, and turned to Colin. "You may hang your coat, waistcoat, and shirt here. Keep your trousers on, but remove your shoes, if you will."

Graham reached for his apron as Colin shrugged out of his coat, noting how the big man pressed his fingers against his temple once it was removed.

"Are you quite well, Mr. Balfour?"

Colin dropped his hand and fumbled with the buttons on his waistcoat. "Just a headache, but I suppose anyone facing brain surgery has a fair amount of tension to overcome beforehand. Tell me, Doctor, do you really think it will take all of two hours?"

Good question—one for which he had no sure answer. Graham wrapped the long apron strings around his back and tied them in front before facing the man. "Mr. Peckwood's the man to ask. I am merely assisting."

While Colin finished undressing, Graham retrieved a glass from a nearby shelf. As soon as he pulled off the folded paper he'd used as a lid, a rather astringent apple scent wafted strong enough to tickle his nose. The concoction was his own special mixture of mandrake paste and laudanum, watered down with several fingers of rum to not only deaden the pucker-tart taste but the pain of what was to come.

"Here." He handed it to the now-shirtless Colin. "Drink this and—"

"Ho-ho! Here we are!" Mr. Peckwood rumbled in, pushing a cart with what appeared to be a series of green silk bags the size of melons.

What the deuce? Graham frowned at the nozzle-tipped balloons. Those hadn't been on the doctor's list of equipment.

Peckwood rolled the cart to a stop near the operating table then strode over and clapped Colin on the back. "Tell me, sir, are you ready for a new life?"

"More ready than you can imagine, Doctor."

"Then by all means, make yourself comfortable." Peckwood swept his hand towards the linen-covered slab at the center of the room. "We shall begin posthaste."

While Colin ambled off, Graham pulled Peckwood aside and lowered his voice. "A few things before we begin. First, Mr. Balfour complains of a headache. Should we consider rescheduling the procedure or, at the very least, postpone an hour or two until it subsides?"

Peckwood chuckled, his fingers fluttering in the air. "A minimal concern, Mr. Lambert. Besides, any pain the man may feel now is nothing compared to the headache he'll suffer after surgery."

Of all the callous remarks! Graham glanced over his shoulder to see if Colin had heard the crass words, when the front office door banged open, ushering in another loud peal of thunder and several footsteps. Blast! He should've thought to lock the door instead of simply putting up the CLOSED placard. Now was not the time for a bunion removal or digestive complaint. He stalked to the door.

But Peckwood skirted him and dashed ahead. "In here, gentlemen, and thank you for coming."

Graham gaped as three men entered, two tall and one short. Rain sluiced off each coat, producing a pool of water at their feet. Undaunted, Peckwood guided them close to the operating table. "This will be the most advantageous spot for you fellows."

Every last one of them sucked in an audible breath as their eyes landed on the malformed giant. Though the effects of the numbing drink Colin had swallowed were surely coursing through his veins by now, a fierce glower darkened his face. And Graham didn't blame him, for a scowl tightened his own brow. Did Peckwood seriously think to make today's operation a spectator event? Was there no end to the man's ego?

Graham clenched his jaw. No, he would not allow such theatrics, not at the expense of a man he loved as a brother. "Mr. Peckwood," he boomed. "If you mean to—"

"Excuse us for a moment, gentlemen." Peckwood grabbed Graham's arm, escorting him to the farthest corner of the room. "Those men are journalists," he hissed. "So I will thank you to behave in a professional manner."

"You invited the press, yet you did not think it a courtesy to first get Mr. Balfour's permission?" Disgust blazed a hot trail up his gullet. "Or mine?"

Peckwood tucked his chin like a bull about to charge. "I do not answer to you, Lambert, rather the other way around."

Graham gritted his teeth, well on the way to a headache of his own. Dash it, but he was weary to death of Peckwood's power play. "Even you cannot discount the fact that the Balfours are *your* employer. You should have secured their consent."

"Fine! Have it your way." A murderous shade of crimson crept up

Peckwood's neck as he leaned aside. "Mr. Balfour, have you any objections to the documentation of your miraculous transformation today?"

Colin's big head lolled to one side, his glassy eyes trained on Peckwood. "Do ashhh…you will."

His words slurred. His massive chest rose and fell with heavy breaths. Of course he'd agree now, with so much medication in his system.

"There, happy?" Peckwood's pointy nose lifted a full inch in challenge.

"Hardly." Graham huffed. There'd be no arguing the matter any further now that Colin had consented, but that didn't mean he had to like it. Nor did he like the addition of the equipment Peckwood had rolled in. He hitched a thumb over his shoulder at the cart. "And what, pray God, is in those bags?"

"Nitrous oxide." Peckwood snagged his apron off the hook, as if he'd not just uttered the most preposterous thing Graham had ever heard.

"Nitrous oxide!" he blurted. "Are you mad?"

Behind him, feet shuffled. Curious eyes burned into the back of his neck—but not any hotter than the fiery stare Mr. Peckwood shot his way.

"Keep your voice down," the doctor growled. "It will not do to appear we are at odds."

"But we are at odds!" Graham shoved his hands into his pockets to keep from grabbing hold of the man and shaking him. "What you're doing here is nothing short of a party trick, just like your use of mesmerism the other night. That gas is used for entertainment at high society parties, not for medicinal purposes, and particularly not for use on a patient."

Peckwood tied his apron, all the while glaring at Graham. "You know as well as I it is imperative we keep Mr. Balfour as subdued as possible while I drill into his cranium. Not to mention the need to keep him immobile when I remove the portion of his brain causing abnormal growth. It has been proven that laughing gas relaxes the nerves and even masks pain, an effect Sir Humphry Davy and

I researched years ago at the Pneumatic Institute. I see no harm in employing the method here."

Graham blew out a low breath. Was he being overcautious? Might the gas be as helpful as Peckwood intimated?

He glanced at the green bags. As much as he'd also love to see Colin cured, something in the back of his mind screamed that this wasn't right. Colin deserved more than experimentation. Graham shook his head, unable to dislodge the thought, and turned back to Peckwood.

"I know you've written of such possibilities, sir, but it's never been tried. You don't know for certain if it will harm Mr. Balfour."

"How do you think discoveries are made, Doctor? By playing it safe? By remaining in the same rut worn by time eternal?" Peckwood chuckled, the condescending grate of it noxious to the ears. "I promised the late Mr. Balfour I would see his son cured of his ailment, and I mean to do it, using every possible tool at my disposal."

"Promise or not"—he inhaled deeply—"I must object. Strapped to a table and with his head cut open, Mr. Balfour will have no way of indicating if the gas is too much for him."

"Ish there a problem, Doctors?" Colin's voice, while weak, yet droned as deep-toned as the thunderstorm outside.

Mind made up, Graham wheeled about. "Yes, there is."

The three journalists whipped out their notepads, ready to document the whole sensational scene.

Mr. Peckwood sidestepped him, crooning all the while. "I am afraid my colleague is correct. It appears an important piece of gear was neglected to be delivered with this equipment." He stopped at the cart, flourishing his hand over the green bags. "I see now that a regulator is missing, one which controls a steady flow of vaporous nitrous oxide."

The short journalist's jaw dropped. "Are we to understand you will use the Gas of Paradise on your patient, Mr. Peckwood?"

"Yes!" He rubbed his hands together. "For the first time ever in history."

Pencils flew, capturing the doctor's words while he strolled back to Graham.

"Very clever, Mr. Lambert. I thank you for bringing your concern to my attention, for you are correct. Without that regulator, we could not discern if the amount of gas we administer is too much. And so you must run down to the dockyards and find it. The piece should be in a small box about yea big." His hands spread to six inches wide then half as tall. "Likely it was forgotten in the hold of the *Mary Campbell* or deposited in the Farley warehouse, and so I bid you make haste, sir."

Bid *him*? Graham blinked, stunned. "Send an errand boy. There is still much to be done to prepare Mr. Balfour for his surgery. I cannot leave."

"Neither can I entrust that piece of equipment to some random boy hailed off the street. It's too expensive, too delicate, and far too important to the success of this operation." He stepped so close the peppery smell of the man's shaving tonic crept up Graham's nostrils. "Do not tell me you would endanger Mr. Balfour's life for the sake of an inconvenience."

"Of course not!"

"Good. It shouldn't take you long. In the meantime, I am thoroughly capable of preparing Mr. Balfour myself." He clouted Graham on the shoulder then strode away. "Godspeed."

Graham clenched his hands into fists. Nothing here was going as planned. He tugged at the knot he'd made of his apron strings, tempted to bark at one of the journalists to go get the blasted regulator instead of making the trek himself.

For if Peckwood had neglected to tally his equipment ahead of time, what other essentials might he miss in preparing Colin for surgery?

It was a peculiar sort of in-between, this recovery room, with only a thin wall separating her from the life and possible death of her brother. Amelia paced, from the white-sheeted bed in one corner, over to the stuffed chair in the other, panic welling with each step. What if something went wrong? What if she never saw Colin again? Granted, her communication with him had been scarce these past seven years, but now that they'd been reunited—now that she knew and thoroughly loved the man he'd become—was she possibly to lose him forever? Was this risk Father had set into motion worth such an outcome?

She drew her feather out of her pocket and ran her fingers along the smoothness of it, feeling slightly guilty about bringing the charm as she tried to pray. But what to say? How to put into words the anguish in her soul? There was just no way to explain the fear embedded so deep inside; it was as much a part of her as bone and marrow.

God, please.

Those two pathetic words were all she could manage. Too much emotion lay heavy on her chest. Surely such a flimsy prayer would waft away like smoke before reaching the heavens. The failure of it spasmed in her belly. For a woman of words, she was a dismal disappointment even to herself. How much more so to God?

A door slammed. She flinched. Out in the corridor, footsteps pounded. Had something gone wrong already?

She yanked the door open, only to see Graham's coattails vanish out into the rain. Unease prickled along her shoulders. Where could he possibly be going when her brother needed his skilled hands? When *she* needed him?

She dashed down the passage and flung open the door. Too late. Nothing but sheets of rain hit the pavement, bouncing up like tiny glass beads at impact. The doctor was nowhere to be seen.

Closing out the wet world, she secured the latch then whirled, determined to find an answer—any answer—but preferably one assuring her Colin was all right. Maybe she could even wait with him until Graham returned.

She stopped short of the surgery door, her sudden flare of courage sputtering like a spent candle. What if the procedure had begun and the sharp rap of a knock caused Mr. Peckwood's scalpel to slip?

Hesitant yet undeterred, she pressed her cheek against the wood and called out, "Mr. Peckwood?"

Then a bit louder, in case he couldn't hear. "Mr. Peckwood!"

The door opened to the white-haired surgeon, draped in an apron stained by years of life and blood. "Miss Balfour? Is there a problem?"

"I saw Mr. Lambert hurry off and am wondering how my brother fares." Leaning sideways, she tried to peer past Mr. Peckwood's shoulders. The room smelled of alcohol and something bitter, acrid, leaving a foreign zing on her tongue.

The doctor sidestepped, blocking her entrance. "Nothing to fret over, my dear. Your brother rests comfortably. Mr. Lambert has merely gone on an errand at my bidding. Now, I must insist you return to the recovery room, where your brother will join you shortly, and all your worry will be behind you."

She cocked her head. Surely he didn't mean to begin without Graham to attend him? "But of course you will wait for Mr. Lambert's return, will you not? Until then, I should like to sit by Colin's side."

"My dear." The old doctor patted her shoulder, and it took everything in her not to bat his hand away. Did he think her some child to be so easily pacified? "I fear your choler is rising, which is understandable under these circumstances. Wait here a moment, would you?"

The door shut in her face, the rising choler he'd mentioned now spreading like a hot cancer through her veins. Why would he not let her see Colin? Had something bad already happened?

She raised her fist, determined to pound until her knuckles bled or she was granted entrance. "Mr. Peckwood, let me in!"

Once again, the door opened, but this time the doctor advanced with a glass in his hand, forcing her to retreat several steps.

"Here, now. No need for such a frenzy. As I told you, your brother rests quite comfortably. The surgical theatre is no place for a woman. Tut-tut!" He lifted a finger. "I see you are about to object, but the fact of the matter is I only wish to spare you sights that would increase your agitation. I am sure your brother would desire the same."

Being defined by nothing else than wearing a skirt chafed raw and irritating. Even so, she swallowed the knot of protest wedged in her throat. He was right, of course. Her ever-protective brother would not want her going against the doctor, and Colin's concern would have nothing whatsoever to do with her gender.

She lifted her chin. "Very well. I concede, sir."

"Good. Here." He handed her a glass, half filled with an amber liquid.

"What is this?"

"Just a little something to calm your nerves."

She pushed the drink back to him. "Thank you, but I am fine."

"Oh, but I insist." He pressed the glass against her fingers.

Apparently she had no choice but to take it. Still, that didn't mean she had to drink it. She tucked her chin in what she hoped looked like a posture of submission. "I will trouble you no further then, Doctor."

She turned away, but hardly a step later, a firm hand tugged her around.

"Ah-ah, Miss Balfour. I cannot have you setting down your glass and forgetting to drink what is sure to calm you. Do so now, please, and I shall take the empty cup with me."

She frowned. Why was he so insistent? "But—"

"Make haste, please. Your brother awaits me, and time is of the essence. We cannot have his senses returning during the midst of surgery."

For one unnerving moment, his gaze reminded her of the rats she'd seen in a Bulgarian alley. She blinked, and the intense zeal in his eyes was gone, replaced by the placid and compassionate surgeon whom her brother had trusted with his life. How could she do any less?

She lifted the glass to her lips. Hopefully whatever was in the liquid would soothe better than it tasted, for the metallic tang of it coated her mouth.

And burned all the way down to her stomach.

TWENTY-FOUR

"…that in all the misery I imagined and dreaded,
I did not conceive the hundredth part of the
anguish I was destined to endure."

❧

Rain fell hard and heavy, darkening the world—but no darker than Graham's thoughts as he leaped from the gig. Despite Peckwood's previous experiments with Humphry Davy, he didn't like that the man was about to employ an unknown use of gas on Colin. Neither did he like the eager gleam in the eyes of the journalists, ready and willing to spread Peckwood's fame far and wide. It wasn't professional or safe.

He strode along the planks of the Bristol Dockyard, sidestepped a bollard, and cupped his mouth, hollering up at a sailor in a sealskin coat. "Pardon, but at which berth is the *Mary Campbell*?"

The man shook his head over the gunwale. "Couldn't tell you."

And so began a long and fruitless search for a ship no one could account for. With each inquiry, Graham's apprehension grew. If that vessel had already sailed with the forgotten regulator on board, Balfour's surgery would have to be postponed until the piece could be shipped back to Bristol. Unless, of course, the instrument had been off-loaded and even now sat in a warehouse…but which one? He should've paid closer attention to Peckwood instead of being so focused on his own irritation. Would he never learn to curb his anger?

Flipping up his collar, he wheeled away from the ships. It was closer to tromp to the harbourmaster's than go all the way back to the office and ask about the forgotten warehouse name. Even if the ship had set sail, paperwork would've been filed for unclaimed cargo.

Soaked to the skin, Graham flung open the door to the harbour-master's office.

A pie-faced man with hair the colour of burned crust looked up from a stack of papers. "Can I help ye, sir?"

"Yes, would you be so kind"—squinting, Graham read the man's name placard on the countertop—"Mr. Williams, as to tell me where to find the *Mary Campbell*."

"*Mary Campbell*?" The man shook his head. "I'm not familiar with that name."

"As harbourmaster, should you not be familiar with every ship sailing in and of this port?"

"Harbourmaster? That's a good one." Williams chuckled. "I am only a clerk, and a new one at that. Barely warmed this seat but a few weeks now." He gestured to a stool on his side of the counter.

Graham pulled off his hat, preferring to let the leftover moisture drip on the floor than down his collar. "That being the case, could you check the records, please?"

"Now that I can do." The man rummaged through a series of file drawers. "Not here," he mumbled while he worked. "An irregular, maybe? Mmm. Ha-ha! Not there either."

Graham ground his teeth. He didn't have time for this.

Williams faced him with empty hands. "Can't find it, though could be I looked it up wrong."

"Then look it up right!" he snapped—and instant remorse punched him in the gut. No sense taking out his frustrations on a new hire. He softened his tone. "Forgive me, Mr. Williams. It is imperative I find that information. A man's life hangs in the balance."

The clerk's tiny eyes grew to the size of coat buttons. "All for want of a docked ship?"

"Yes." Graham sighed. He sounded like a madman and he knew it. "I am a surgeon, sir, and there was an important piece of medical equipment aboard the *Mary Campbell* that was either neglected to be off-loaded or has been stored in a warehouse. I must find it posthaste."

"Well…" The clerk scratched the side of his jaw, the roundness of his cheeks rippling with the action. "I shall give it one more try, then, eh?"

"Please do."

The man searched. And searched. Graham shifted his weight from one foot to the other, impatience rising like a blister.

Finally, Williams returned to the counter. "Unfortunately, there is nothing under that name."

Graham shook his head, unwilling to admit defeat. "But the other instruments clearly arrived from said ship. I saw them with my own eyes."

The clerk shrugged. "If you should like to wait until my supervisor relieves me in a half hour, then you may take the matter up with him."

Graham glanced at the clock. Ten thirty already. Thunderation! Without this delay, they could have finished the surgery by now. Balfour should already be on his way to recovery. But what else could he do other than remain here until the harbourmaster arrived?

Gripping his hat, he forced out words through clenched teeth. "Thank you. I shall wait."

He planted himself on one of the few chairs lined against the wall. Each tick of the clock grated. So did the way the low-backed wooden chair cut into his spine. Amelia would be disappointed the surgery would have to be postponed until tomorrow, but it would be worth it to keep Colin safe from an overuse of gas. Gas! To the dogs with Peckwood and his innovative ideas—the very ideas Graham had once thought bold and brave.

At last the door opened, and in strode a tall fellow in a long, dark coat. He was a quintessential old salt, legs bowed from riding the waves on a cargo tub, smelling of kippers and stockings that'd been worn one too many times.

Losing interest in him, Graham glanced at the clock yet again. A quarter past eleven. Dash it!

"Morning, Mr. Henry." The clerk greeted the older fellow, then nodded towards Graham. "This gent here would like to have a word with you."

This worn piece of flesh and bone was the harbourmaster? Then again, with so much obvious maritime experience, he must know this waterway like none other. Graham shot to his feet. "Sir, it is with the utmost urgency I ask you to locate the paperwork on the *Mary Campbell*."

A frown dug deeper ruts into his brow. "Mind if I take off my coat first?"

Graham clenched his hat all the tighter, the felt nearly dry from his long wait. Though he wanted to leap over the counter and flip through the files himself, he merely nodded. "By all means."

Mr. Henry took his time unfastening the long row of pewter buttons on his coat. Eventually, he shrugged one arm out of his sleeve, followed by the other. After hanging the coat upon a hook, he removed a cloth from his pocket and brushed away the leftover dampness along the length of the fabric. Graham ground his teeth. If this snail's pace was the man's standard, no wonder he'd arrived so late.

An eternity later, Mr. Henry stalked towards the clerk, who visibly shrank the closer the man drew. "So, Williams, you were unable to find the paperwork this gentleman seeks? Were you not listening when I trained you in the filing system?"

"Yes, sir. Of course I was, but…" The clerk's head drooped, as did his shoulders. "I beg your pardon, Mr. Henry. It won't happen again."

"No, it will not." The harbourmaster's threat hung thick on the air.

Graham stepped to the counter. Though Mr. Williams hadn't been particularly helpful, neither did he deserve to lose his job over the matter. "Pardon, but to his credit, your clerk here gave it a good try."

Williams shot him a glance, gratitude gleaming in his dark eyes.

The harbourmaster hmphed. "You may leave, Mr. Williams, though I shall expect you back at two o'clock."

The clerk gave a sharp nod, and without another word, he snagged his own dingy brown cloak off a hook and disappeared into the late-morning gloom.

Mr. Henry's gaze followed the man, but as soon as the door shut, he faced Graham. "All right, Mr.…. Who did you say you are?"

"Mr. Lambert, associate of Mr. Peckwood, a surgeon over on—"

"Corn Street. Yes, yes. I know. The doctor has had equipment shipped here before. Now then, what is the vessel you are after?"

"The *Mary Campbell*." He spoke the name crisply, leaving no chance for an error of hearing.

"*Mary Campbell.*" Mr. Henry repeated the name just as his clerk had, then sucked on his teeth as if he might dislodge some information without even looking at the files. "Never heard of her."

Graham crushed his hat to keep from throttling the man. "Will you not even look for documentation?"

The harbourmaster shook his head. "No need."

Queen and country! This fellow was less help than Williams. He slammed his fist on the counter, tired of these games. "Why the devil not?"

Mr. Henry stared at Graham's hand, then eyed him with a scowl. "I should think I have spoken plainly enough, Mr. Lambert. There is not—nor ever has been—a ship docked in this harbour under the name *Mary Campbell*. And I should know. I've been at this post these past twenty-five years. Are you certain you got the name right?"

Was he? He thought back, and…yes. The name was exactly what had flown from Mr. Peckwood's mouth. He squared his shoulders. "I am."

"Then perhaps Mr. Peckwood got it wrong. I suggest you trouble him instead of me. Good day, sir." The man turned away, clearly finished with anything to do with the ghost ship *Mary Campbell* and him.

Graham stood rooted a moment more, a loathsome suspicion rising like yellow bile. Peckwood never forgot a name.

Punching his hat back into shape, he jammed the thing on his head and blustered out into the storm. This had been nothing but a fool's errand, and he was the biggest fool of them all. Peckwood had craftily removed his only source of restraint and was likely even now pushing up his sleeves to present a single-handed performance for his willing audience of gullible journalists. Without Graham's assistance for such a delicate procedure, Colin's life would be in danger. Though he prayed he was wrong, Graham took off at a dead run. Too much time had already passed, and his gut twisted at the thought.

He must stop that surgery before it began. Would that he'd not be too late.

Like he had been for his mother.

She never knew colour had sound. That purple was a symphony. Red, the last gasp of an autumn leaf as it fluttered to the ground. And blue. Ahh, blue. Amelia nuzzled her ear against the hem of her sapphire sleeve, humming along with the melody. Blue was an angel song, majestic in its dulcet tones. Satisfying as a lover's kiss.

And then a cannon fired. Again and again and again. Her head lolled towards the noxious noise, rooting her cheek against the high-back cushion of the chair.

Tree trunks strode into the small room. Tall and black. Black, the irregular beat of a heart bent on dying. Lub-dub. Lub. Pause. D–dub.

The walking trunks—three of them—carried something between them. Something long, draped in white. Her eyes closed, for the haunting note of a viola was too exquisite to do anything but shut out the world and float along on its glorious wave.

"Missss Baal-fourrr?"

The words stretched into a thick piece of taffy, too hard to pull any thinner. She blinked her eyes open. One of the trees knelt before her.

"Caan youu hear meee?"

No. She'd been wrong. Trees didn't speak, and was this not the language of snakes? A shudder shook through her like the sharp slamming of a door.

"Amelia!"

A slap boxed her ears, or was it her cheek? Either way, her head jerked aside, and she gasped. For the space of that breath, the white-haired Mr. Peckwood came into focus.

"Yess, Docc-torr?" Her fingers floated to her lips. Did she speak snake now too?

"The sssurgery wasss…" His mouth moved, his voice droned on, but who cared? Not her. Though she had a deeply embedded suspicion she should care about something. Or maybe about someone.

"Isss that clear?"

She bobbed her head because she was supposed to. Wasn't she? But then the booming started again and a tree lumbered near, towering over her and the doctor.

"Will ssshe beee all right?"

"Yesss. She jussst needs to—"

She flattened her palms against her ears. Snakes ought not to be listened to. That was Eve's folly. And besides, there were too many colours now. Too much noise. The ache of it throbbed in her bones.

The trees thundered away, but it took a long while before she dropped her hands, on the off chance they returned. But the only thing that came back was the sweet, sweet viola music, hovering like a butterfly on the air, compelling her towards its beauty.

She rose—no—floated across the room to gaze down upon the lovely sound, but her heart broke at the sight. She dropped to her knees. "Poor mannn."

She stroked the fellow's face, leastwise the small portion not swathed in glorious white. And the longer she stroked, the stronger a low keen vibrated in her throat. He belonged to someone, this broken man. Someone who should know he had red gasping into the white on his bandage. She should find that someone. Explain he needed arms to hold him and prayers to lift him.

But instead, she laid her head on his pillow, close to his face, and matched his breathing. For now, she would be that someone who cared for him. This hurt man. This lonely one. She reached for his hand, too big to lift, and smoothed her fingers atop his. Everyone deserved a friend.

Even a stranger in white.

TWENTY-FIVE

"I felt my heart sink within me."

Out of breath and short on time—a pox on the traffic blocking Leonard Lane!—Graham blasted into the waiting room of Peckwood's offices. Heart wild, he tore towards the surgery door that gaped open.

Wide open.

Just past the threshold, he stumbled to a stop. Were his lungs not heaving for air, he'd whoop a holler of relief. No woozy giant lay atop the operating table. No journalists or cart of green silk bladders stood at the ready. Peckwood's apron hung limp on its hook and the floor showed no sign of blood spatter from opening a human skull. Thank God! It appeared that for once, Mr. Peckwood had laid aside his need for prestige and postponed Colin's surgery.

But that didn't quench the angry ember burning in his chest. He still needed to get to the bottom of the bootless errand he'd been sent on. He'd mulled on it all the way from the dockyards. Either it had been a ploy to perform the surgery with no further interference by him—which clearly wasn't the case since the operation had not taken place. Or else by some fluke, Peckwood had actually erred when naming the ship and the regulator was yet to be retrieved. If that was the truth of it, then fine, but there was still the matter of being dismissed so casually. He'd not stand for it. Not at the beginning of a procedure and definitely not in front of journalists, whose presence he still disapproved of.

With a last deep breath, he exited the room, intent on seeking out Peckwood, even if his search meant breaking the man's staunch rule of never invading his privacy. He pulled off his hat and shrugged out of his coat as he stalked down the corridor, then paused and cocked his head.

A haunting melody drifted through the recovery room door. Female. Lovely. Frowning, he tossed his wet hat and coat on a side table. Surely Amelia had taken part in the rescheduling of her brother's surgery and gone home with him. But if so, then why the lilting hum of her voice?

He rapped an obligatory knock then shoved open the door. "Miss Balfour?"

The farther he strode into the room, the more his heart sank, until he was thoroughly gutted. Ahead, Amelia's body draped half on and half off the bed he'd prepared for her brother, her cheek sharing Colin's pillow, her fingers entwined with his. Colin's head was swathed in white bandages, a deep stain of blood violating the fabric near the frontal eminence of his skull.

Peckwood had performed the surgery.

Without him.

Graham's hands curled into tight fists. Sweet blessed mercy! Had he killed the man?

He closed the distance with clipped steps, each one a gunshot in the small room. But Amelia didn't so much as glance his way. She just kept staring at her brother, humming her tune, ignoring the world. The poignant image of a woman out of her mind with grief.

Graham pulled his gaze from her to examine Colin's body, the precious little he could see of it, anyway, and his heart began to beat once again. No blue edged the man's lips nor did a grey pallor drain any colour from his skin. In fact, though pale, his flesh appeared to be receiving quite a good amount of blood flow, and his chest rose and fell in even measures. Given the circumstances, there was nothing better to be expected, save for answers to the questions snarling a great tangle in Graham's mind.

Had the procedure been swift enough that Colin's torture wasn't extended, or had he mercifully succumbed to unconsciousness?

Had the gas been abandoned altogether or managed properly despite the absence of the regulator?

How long had he been in recovery?

And—more importantly now than ever—where the devil was Peckwood? How dare he leave Amelia alone with her beloved brother lying comatose in front of her?

Graham plowed his fingers through his hair, knowing full well that now was not the time to interrogate but to comfort.

"Amelia." He spoke as to a wounded child, softly, careful. Anything too harsh might startle and frighten.

She ignored him, neither gazing up nor ceasing her endless humming—and that cut to the bone. Was she angry he'd not been there when her brother needed him most?

"Amelia, I am here now. Will you not acknowledge me?"

Her humming continued.

"Amelia, please." Gently, he wrapped his fingers around her upper arms and guided her to her feet. She gave no hint of resistance, not in word or deed. Just kept humming, humming, humming. Merciful heavens! Had the sight of her brother been too much to bear, breaking something in her mind?

Ever so slowly, he turned her about, and when her gaze finally landed on his face, the crooning in her throat stopped—as did his breath. The pupils in her beautiful brown eyes were small. Abnormally so. Myosis, he'd bet on it.

He rubbed his hands up and down her arms, hoping to snap her back into the real world. "Are you ill?"

Her lips parted, but no words came out. Instead, she lifted her hand and traced her forefinger along the length of his jaw and over his mouth. Her touch arced through him as powerfully as a charge from one of Peckwood's voltaic piles.

"Ssso ssoft," she murmured, then raised to her toes as if to kiss him.

Horrified, he pulled away and snatched one of the lamps from off a table. He held the thing steady, inches from her face. "Follow the light, Amelia."

He moved it left then right.

But her gaze didn't vary. Not a tic.

"Look at it!" He jerked the flame one way and another, but her eyes—those beautiful, velvet-brown eyes—didn't waver whatsoever from staring straight ahead.

Shaking began, way down in his gut and moving upwards, outwards, a rage so pure and distilled that if lit, would blaze over man and beast alike. Clenching every muscle, he returned the lamp to the table. Peckwood would pay for this and pay dearly.

"What did Mr. Peckwood give you?" He swallowed the acid burning up his throat. "Was it a tincture? A powder? Did you drink something or inhale it?"

Strange laughter garbled past her lips. Swaying towards him, she rested her head against his waistcoat. Her arms wrapped around his hips, and she nuzzled her cheek against his chest. "Ssso sssleepy."

Of course she was! Who knew what sort of drugs Peckwood had given her?

He gathered her up in his arms, cradling her like a sick child, and deposited her in one of the chairs near the hearth. Snagging a blanket off the arm of the other, he covered her, then strode from the room, unsure how he'd be able to keep from landing an uppercut to Peckwood's jaw before pummeling the man with questions.

He took the stairs two at a time and rattled the door at the top with a thunderous knock before trying the knob. It gave. So did his temper when he entered to see the white-haired doctor calmly sitting at his desk with pen in hand, as if there were naught more important to do at the moment than scribe a list.

"You have taken things too far, sir!" Graham boomed.

Peckwood swiveled in his seat, a growing scowl cutting lines across his wide forehead. "As have you, Mr. Lambert. You were told never to invade my private quarters again."

Did the man's pride know no bounds whatsoever? Graham drew a deep breath, his rage hardening to a sharp edge. "You think you can hide from what you have done?"

"Hide? From what? Victory?" He flourished his pen in the air, little flecks of ink spraying about with the movement. "What I have done, sir, is perform a life-changing surgery, and I will thank you to leave me in peace to document such for posterity!"

"Oh, you've done far more than that." Graham advanced, unwilling to be bullied by the old dragon. "You turned the office into a stage and sent me on a fool's errand. You drugged Miss Balfour and executed a dangerous procedure single-handedly that could've ended Mr. Balfour's life. And if all that weren't bad enough, you've gone and left them alone in the recovery room, where God only knows what could go wrong without monitoring the patient. Why? On all accounts, why?" He slammed his fist atop the desk, rattling the inkwell. "I can find no rational answers to *any* of these questions."

Peckwood set down his pen and folded his hands atop his belly, so benign it took everything in Graham not to throttle the man.

"And therein lies your greatest fault, Mr. Lambert. You make far too many inquiries for a man of your station."

Graham flailed his arms, a completely juvenile reaction, yet one he could no more stop than a rising tide. "What has my station to do with anything?"

Peckwood chuckled. Chuckled! Of all the condescending responses.

"You frequently forget, Mr. Lambert, that as I am the senior surgeon, you answer to me, not the other way around. And were it not for me taking you on as a potential partner, I daresay even now you'd either be roaming the countryside, prostituting yourself as a doctor for hire, or elbow-deep in disease and filth in some cesspool of a London hospital."

The truth punched him in the lungs, making it suddenly hard to breathe. There was nothing to say for it, no rebuttal whatsoever. The man was entirely correct. He schooled his face, giving nothing away, for to do so would incriminate—and he ought not be the one on trial here.

"I have been more than patient with you, Doctor," Peckwood continued, "yet beware that even I have my limits. Still, I am not an unreasonable man, and for the sake of education, I shall answer your questions one by one." Rising, he lifted his chin as well. "Though in the future, I suggest you present your inquiries with more decorum than one of St. Peter's inmates."

Graham planted his feet, rebuffing the attack. "Go ahead."

Peckwood hooked his thumbs on his lapels, chest swelling as if he were about to address Parliament. "First off, I invited the journalists not for the sake of vanity but to make the public aware of what was accomplished here today. Newsprint is a much faster route to innovation than the hurdling of the bureaucracy which shelters the medical journals. As you know, it can take years and more money than is seemly to publish crucial information."

Graham's jaw clenched and he looked away. It was true. Every last word. But that didn't account for the man's secrecy. He snapped his gaze back to Peckwood. "Even so, you ought to have cleared it with the Balfours first and had the courtesy to forewarn me."

"Which I would have done if the arrangements had not all fallen into place hardly an hour before the procedure." Peckwood paced to the window and back, stirring his peculiar scent of peppermint and ammonia into the air. "Yet, I concede your point, Mr. Lambert. I should have said something. In the haste of the morning's preparation, I neglected to do so."

Graham flattened his lips to keep from gaping. What was this? A concession by the man who rarely gave way to anyone?

Removing his glasses, Peckwood wiped off a smudge before resetting the spectacles on the bridge of his nose. "Secondly, the errand I sent you on was not an entirely false venture. There should have been a regulator built to my specifications and shipped along with the nitrous oxide."

Aha! He had the wily fellow now. Graham tossed back his head. "With or without the regulator, that equipment did not arrive aboard the *Mary Campbell*, for there is no such vessel."

A slow smile spread like a rash across Mr. Peckwood's face. "Exactly."

"What does that mean?"

The doctor pulled down a now-deflated green silk bag from one of the shelves. "I had already determined to use the gas without the regulating instrument, for as I suspected, it was not necessary, and as you saw for yourself, Mr. Balfour survived. Furthermore, a benefit I didn't foresee was that these"—he waved the bag in the air—"provided a convenient excuse to get you out of the way."

The words crawled in, burrowing just below the skin like so many wriggling maggots. "You admit that you willfully banished me from that surgery?"

"Banishment? Such dramatics, Doctor, and a bit draconian at that." Peckwood chuckled as he returned the bag to the shelf. "I merely needed to put a stop to your inquiries, as they cast a pall on what should have been an unbiased presentation of medical prowess to the journalists. I couldn't very well have you tainting what they might write. God knows men of the press are blown about by the slightest of winds. And your absence was no danger, for I am fully capable of managing a scalpel on my own. Granted, it took me longer than if you'd been present, but the outcome remained the same."

Graham shook his head, thoroughly disgusted. "Don't tell me you're saying the end justifies the means."

"In some cases, that adage is incontestable." Peckwood shrugged, then returned to his chair, gripping the back of it instead of sitting. "Lastly, Miss Balfour was in a state of high agitation, and understandably so. As a doctor of strong morals, I can only assume you would have done the same as I: namely, supply a distraught female with a calming agent. Would you not?"

Graham scowled. Once again, Peckwood had nicely shuffled the conversation into a winning hand for himself. To deny would paint him as an uncompassionate fiend.

He narrowed his eyes. "What did you use?"

"A proprietary formula I developed for my wife, God rest her. It is completely safe, so you need not trouble yourself further on the matter." He cut his hand through the air. "And as for leaving the Balfours alone in the recovery room, I had only recently slipped up here to capture a few notes on the procedure before you barged in. And now it is you who keeps me from returning. The longer we play this charade, the longer the patient will remain medically unattended. That being said"—he dipped his head, a bull about to charge—"have you any more questions?"

A sigh deflated all that was left of his fight. The wily surgeon had batted away each of his accusations as if they were nothing but gnats. One by one, his fingers uncurled, fists forgotten. "I suppose there is no more to be said. For now."

"Good." Peckwood threw back his shoulders. "Then I suggest you hie yourself downstairs and monitor Mr. Balfour, though if all goes well, I expect there will be nothing to oversee other than the complaint of a headache when he awakens. Our biggest concern now is risk of infection, so it is imperative we keep the wound site clean."

Scowling, Graham strode to the door, disgusted by the man's clinically cold evaluation.

"Oh, and Mr. Lambert?"

He glanced over his shoulder, brows raised.

Peckwood's blue eyes turned icy, as did his voice. "The next time you question my integrity will be the end of our partnership. Am I quite understood?"

Graham gave him a sharp nod and pulled the door shut behind him, praying to God there would be no more cause to doubt the man.

But that, he highly doubted.

She'd drifted a long time here, in this sea of darkness. Alone. Afraid. But now something stirred those waters. The black depths lightened to the purple of a bruise. The oppressive weight that had been pushing Amelia down released its grip, and she floated higher. Rising, ever rising. Purple fading into grey. Lungs lighter. Life tingling in her hands. Her fingers.

With a gasp, she jerked awake and gripped the chair arms to keep from flying off the seat. A blanket fell from her shoulders, pooling in her lap. Shadows loitered against the walls like so many ruffians in a dark alley. Where was she? *When* was she?

Night, apparently. Across from her, Graham slept in a chair, eyes closed, lips parted. The single lamp glowing on the small table next to him cast a warm glow over half his face. But even asleep, he looked bone weary. As if he'd given all he had and more. But to whom? Her?

Was that why he was here? Keeping some sort of vigil while she'd floundered in the darkness?

She swallowed, tongue thick and fuzzy. A metallic aftertaste soured her stomach. And then it all rushed back. The surgery. The fear.

Colin!

She snapped her gaze aside, desperate to see her brother—then gasped when an intense gaze locked onto hers, so awful it would surely haunt her in nightmares to come. But it didn't matter. Colin lived. He breathed! She pushed from the chair, not caring a whit for the blanket lying strewn in her wake.

Dropping to her knees at his bedside, she reached for her brother's hand and held it tight to her chest. "Colin, I was so frightened," she whispered.

His big lips moved, yet no sound came out.

She shook her head. "No, don't talk, dearest. You don't have to—"

"Ah-me. Ne-mo." His voice was a rusty hinge.

"What was that?" She bent closer.

"Lee-ahhh!" He yanked his hand from her, pressing his palm to his jaw, arm locked, muscles clenched. White bubbles foamed at the corners of his mouth. A frightened little boy looked out through his man eyes. Lost and pathetic.

Her heart broke.

"Shh," she soothed, gently trying to pry his hand from his face. If he jarred the bandage swathing his skull, would he start a bout of bleeding? "Calm yourself, Brother."

Eyes wide, he froze, still as death.

Then bolted upright. Grabbing her close, he roared into her face. Nose-to-nose. Spit hot and sticky against her skin.

Before she could react, she flew backwards, like a rag doll tossed aside. Her head hit the side of the hearth with a sickening thud. Dazed, she lay there a moment, trying to make sense of things. Coming up short. Why had Colin turned so vicious?

She pushed up to sit, and the whole room tilted to a precarious angle. Graham lunged sideways, locked in a struggle with her brother. No, two Grahams. Two Colins. She pinched the bridge of her nose, closing her eyes for a moment, and when she opened them, her brother's big body flopped back against the mattress.

"Amelia?" Worried hazel eyes peered into her own, and with a strong arm about her shoulders, Graham lifted her to her feet. "Are you all right?"

"I…"

Graham split into two again, and she forced a few deep breaths until the shapes melded back into one very handsome, very concerned doctor.

"I am fine," she croaked, surprised at how ragged her voice sounded.

"You are hurt." He pulled a handkerchief from his pocket and, gently holding her jaw, began swabbing her forehead.

"My brother—"

"Don't fret. He is resting now." With a last dab, he searched her face. "But you, how do you fare? That was a nasty spill, and on the heels of what I suspect was a very strong draught from Mr. Peckwood."

His concern warmed her as much as the heat radiating off him. "Yes, rather strong." She cleared her throat and lifted her chin. "But I am fine now."

The rise of his brow labeled her a liar, but this wasn't—shouldn't—be about her. "My brother has never once raised his hand against me. Against anyone. Why did he lash out like that?" She stared deep into Graham's eyes, desperate for answers, craving his strength.

He looked away while he crammed his balled kerchief into his pocket. And the longer he took, the more alarm crept into her heart.

With a sigh, he met her gaze. "My best guess is he experienced a hallucination. Or maybe a drug-induced dream. Honestly, though? I cannot say."

"Will it go away? These dreams. These hallucinations." She grabbed his arm, shoring herself up for whatever may come. "Will my brother be all right?"

A shadow passed over Graham's face, forbidding and dark, and her heart sank.

"In truth?" He blew out a long breath. "I do not know."

TWENTY-SIX

"Ye weep, unhappy ones; but these are not your last tears!"

❧

Sometimes it wasn't merely hard to be thankful, it was downright painful to glean the good from the bad. It took every ounce of Graham's self-control not to wince as he stood next to Colin's bed while Mr. Peckwood examined the man. Yes, two days after the surgery, it was a blessing Colin could prop himself up against the cushions, that he drew breath and his heart beat strong. But one of his arms hung limp, his gaze was empty as a pauper's pockets, and he either grunted or slurred his words when trying to communicate. How was anyone to be grateful for such changes in a man who used to be so robust?

He dared a peek at Amelia, hovering near the door. Half-moon shadows darkened the skin beneath her eyes on a face that was much too sallow. He doubted she'd slept at all these past few days—which reminded him he ought to leave some sleeping powders with her maid.

Across the bed, Peckwood held out his hand. "I'll take that candle now, Mr. Lambert, if you please."

Though morning light blazed through the window, Graham retrieved a brass candlestick from the nightstand.

"Now then, I should like you to do your best, Mr. Balfour, to follow the flame with your eyes, hmm?" Peckwood leaned close, guiding the candle close to Colin's face.

With a whimper, Colin cowered against the pillows and turned away. A man his size could snuff the flame with his fingers and not

245

even feel the burn, yet there he trembled.

Graham rested his hand on Colin's shoulder. Hopefully the touch would soothe instead of irritate. "Be at peace, my friend. There is nothing here to fear."

Colin's gaze shot to the door as Amelia's steps padded near.

"Mr. Lambert speaks truth, Brother. No one wishes you harm."

Slowly—while clutching great handfuls of the counterpane to his chest—Colin faced the candle.

Peckwood moved the light back and forth. Colin's gaze sluggishly tracked the small flame—mostly. One eye lagged behind the other. Graham bent closer, studying the man's pupils. The one that lagged was larger. Abnormally so.

Graham lowered his voice, speaking for Peckwood alone. "The aniscoria is more profound today. His vision appears to be worsening."

"A temporary side effect, Mr. Lambert. Nothing more." Straightening, Peckwood handed back the candle then faced Amelia. "Has he taken any broth since yesterday's exam?"

"Not much, but yes." She nodded. "He's swallowed a few mouthfuls."

The twinkle in Peckwood's eye was strangely out of place with such a ruined man lying in the bed right in front of him. "There. You see, Lambert? That's a magnificent improvement."

An improvement, yes, but magnificent? Graham clamped his lips shut, stemming a sneer.

"Ought not my brother be eating more?" Judging by the pinch in Amelia's tone, she hardly thought the improvement was monumental, either. "It was not his stomach you operated on but his head."

"Perfectly normal. Surgery stresses the entire body, not just the portion that is directly impacted."

She took a step closer, hands spread wide. "But his restlessness—surely that cannot be normal. He doesn't sleep save for a half hour here and there. Not even at night. How can his body heal if his mind is not at peace?"

"Take heart, Miss Balfour; this is all part of the process. I realize that to your untrained eyes, his progress may seem nonexistent, yet I assure you, your brother's recovery is moving along quite swimmingly."

He began collecting his instruments, clearly done with not only the examination but the conversation as well.

Colin put his hands to his ears and swayed back and forth, moaning. His thick lips rippled as he clenched his mouth tight.

Gently—yet firmly—Graham grabbed the man's shoulders, stilling the movement. "Your head hurts, which is to be expected, yet can you tell me where the pain is, exactly?"

Colin leaned towards the right, nestling his big cheek against his palm. "Thissh shide."

Interesting. The opposite of and quite a bit lower than where Peckwood had drilled into the skull. Graham carefully pulled Colin's big hand away from his face. "I shall mix a draught to help with your pain. You'll be better in no time."

Rising, Graham glanced at Peckwood. "With your approval, of course."

Peckwood snapped his bag shut. "It is best to keep him calm, a state which will speed his recuperation." His gaze drifted to Amelia. "Some tepid tea would benefit as well, I think."

"I shall see to it at once." She hurried out the door, skirts swishing.

Just as well. Not that Graham didn't already miss her sweet presence, but it would be easier to discuss the gravity of Colin's situation without her in the room.

But first he stirred a dose of laudanum into a glass of lemon water and turned back to Colin. "Here, my friend. Let's—"

Colin smacked the drink from his hand with a roar. Liquid splattered. Glass crashed. Graham stared, perplexed by the outburst. Fire he could understand, but water? Why such a strong reaction to something so benign?

"Now, now, Mr. Balfour." Peckwood wagged his finger at the man. "We cannot have such brutish conduct. Do you understand?"

Heavy snorts shushed out of Colin's nose, his chest heaving wildly. Whatever was going on inside that broken head of his would not be helped by the wagging of a finger. And what exactly *was* going on? Fear? Rage? Definitely confusion. Graham blew out his own sharp breath. This must be fixed—and soon—but how? He'd be scouring every medical journal he owned tonight…when he wasn't praying for a miracle.

For now, though, he dropped to his knees at Colin's side and collected the big man's hand in his own. "Listen, my friend. I want to ease your suffering, and you want the pain to go away, do you not?"

Colin's mouth opened. No sound came out, but his breathing evened somewhat. The glaze in his eyes lessened by increments. Not huge changes, but good enough. Rising, Graham poured another glass of water.

Next to him, the floorboards creaked. Peckwood drew near, speaking for him alone. "Double whatever you'd intended."

A bit extreme, but he stirred in eight drops of laudanum instead of four, and this time, Colin drank it down without a fuss. After returning the glass to the nightstand, Graham tipped his head towards the window. "A word, please, Mr. Peckwood."

Bag already in hand, the white-haired surgeon followed him, and after a glance at Colin to see he relaxed against the pillows, Graham faced the older fellow. "These extremes in Mr. Balfour's behaviour worry me. Have you dealt with this before?"

"Posh!" A fine spray of spittle flew past his lips, glistening in a ray of sunlight. "I am not fresh from the womb, sir. Naturally I have experienced such oddities after brain surgery. You know as well as I it takes time to heal."

"Yes, but ought we not expect to see daily improvement rather than such marked declines?"

Peckwood chuckled. "You exaggerate, sir."

Hah! He exaggerated? This from the man who claimed the broken-headed giant on the bed was showing *magnificent improvement*? "I hardly think—" He bit back a retort as Amelia's light footsteps tapped into the room.

She paused, tea tray in hand, her shoulders drooping as though her burden were far heavier than a mere pot of hot water and a porcelain cup. "May I offer my brother a drink now?"

"Please do. Mr. Lambert and I are finished." But clearly Peckwood wasn't, for he stepped closer to Graham, his tone quieting. "There is no sense in alarming either of the Balfours. It's been only two days since the man endured major surgery. That he's even sitting up in bed and somewhat able to communicate is a victory, wouldn't you say?"

Graham sighed. The old surgeon's words rang true. Perhaps he was being a bit rash. Expecting too much. Hoping too much, actually. If he could, he'd speed the hands of time and bypass this horrible suffering Colin endured.

"Nooo," Colin roared.

"Colin! Be careful."

Graham and Peckwood pivoted just as Colin crushed the teacup in his hand and threw the shards into Amelia's face.

"Amelia!" Graham's cry blended on the air with Peckwood's, "Mr. Balfour!"

Graham flew to Amelia while Peckwood tended Colin. Wrapping his arm around her shoulders, Graham guided her to the chair near the door and eased her down, then dropped to his knees at her side. She pressed her fingers to her cheek, and when her gaze met his, tears welled in her eyes.

"You're hurt." His voice came out far huskier than he intended, and he cleared his throat. "Let me see."

"I am fine." Her chin quivered, belying her bold statement. "Please, see to my brother."

Though her pluck did her credit, now was not the time for such obstinance, not when she was clearly injured.

Dear God, must this woman bear so much?

He gently coaxed away her hand. "Mr. Peckwood is caring for Colin. Let me tend to you."

Blood oozed from a quarter-inch gash on her cheek, surrounded by smaller nicks that reddened her flesh. Nothing required sutures, thankfully, but the bleeding must be stopped.

"One moment, please." He retrieved some cotton wadding from his bag, then dabbed away the blood. Folding the soiled part inside of itself, he pressed the clean side against the cut. "There. That's better. Just a bit more pressure, no stitches needed."

A single fat tear slipped from her eye. "My brother is not the same man he was."

With his free hand, Graham brushed away the tear. She was right. Colin was not the same.

And might never be.

Amelia sank onto the sitting room chair, pressing her fingers against her temple. Surprisingly, after such a morning, no headache throbbed, but her cheek still stung, a tangible reminder that Colin wasn't himself. He was here physically, but mentally where did he roam? Was her younger brother trapped inside that bandaged skull of his, trying to get out? Was that the reason for his sudden outbursts? She'd tried everything she could think of to allay his restlessness, from lavender sachets to the reported calming effect of grinding lemon balm counterclockwise seven times while humming a lullaby as it steeped in tepid water. Nothing had worked. Not yet, anyway. She sagged against the high-back cushion.

> *Oh, God, this is beyond me. Beyond Mr. Peckwood and Graham. Only You can fix this problem…a problem for which I advocated. This is my fault, Lord. I never should have urged my brother towards such a surgery. Please forgive me, and may Colin forgive me as well. He was happy as he was. Grant that he might be happy once again.*

Heaving a sigh, she searched deeply for scraps of gratitude, and snagged onto the first that came to mind. Thankfully, Colin wasn't in a continual state of unexplainable madness. There were moments of lucidity. Of quiet. Like now. Times when he reached for her hand or lifted a lopsided smile, reminding her he was still in there somewhere.

The front door knocker rapped. Betsey's sturdy shoes thumped in the corridor. Unbidden, Amelia's heart fluttered. Had Graham—perhaps—returned? How lovely it would be to sit by his side on the sofa and just stare into the hearth. To hear his steady breathing. Maybe even to rest her head against his chest and listen to the beat of his heart. What a sanctuary that would be.

Moments later, Betsey entered the room. "There's a Miss Godwin here to see you, miss. Shall I send her away?"

She opened her mouth to say yes, then paused. As tired as she was, and as much as she wanted to keep Colin out of the public eye, still…how lovely to talk with someone about something other than laudanum dosages or broth intake.

"Show her in, Betsey."

Amelia rose and faced the door as Mary gracefully sailed in.

"Good afternoon, Amelia. I was wondering if—oh! Are you quite all right?" She was a bird, this slight woman, one with head cocked and curious eyes fixed on Amelia's cheek.

"I…em…it was an accident, I'm afraid. But just a trifle." The lie tasted like sand in her mouth, but she couldn't very well say her brother—who may be going insane—threw shards of porcelain at her, could she? She looked past the woman's shoulder to Betsey. "Would you see to a tea tray for us, please?"

Mary held up a hand. "No need. I shan't stay long."

"Very good, miss." With a dip of her chin, Betsey continued on her way.

"Will you at least sit?" Amelia indicated the chair.

"I can stay long enough for that." A small smile lit her face.

Amelia took the opposite seat and folded her hands in her lap. "So what brings you to call today?"

"I should like to inquire, being you know this area so well, if you have a recommendation for paths I might venture upon. I dearly love to walk, you see, and I'm not nearly as fatigued as when I first arrived." Though as of yet no telltale bump swelled her dress, Mary rested her hand against her belly. "If only my muse would return as vigorously as my energy, but I find that when I put pen to paper, all I end up with are ink blots and crumpled pages. I thought walking might help."

How well Amelia knew that struggle. After returning from Bohemia with a raging fever that had muddled her mind, she'd had to push past all that to finish her manuscript even though there wasn't a thing in her that felt like writing. Absently, she ran her finger along the chair arm, tracing the brocaded pattern. "It is difficult to write when all one can do is stare out the window. But often we are hardest on ourselves, are we not?" Her gaze met Mary's. "Give it time. There is a season for everything."

The words circled back, and when they landed on her own heart, it was with a wholly different meaning. That was it! She merely needed to give Colin time. He *would* mend. Of course he would.

"You speak the wisdom of Solomon," Mary murmured.

"It is easier to borrow wise words than come up with them myself." She grinned. "Now then, I have a few suggestions. Have you been to Brandon Hill yet?"

"No, but I have heard of it."

"That's a good start. It's a lovely stroll." Amelia tapped her lower lip a moment. What other areas might inspire this young woman? "Oh, I know! There's another walk that's a bit more secluded, but the scenery is beautiful. Take Percival Road until it forks. Go left and continue on towards Clifton Down. Beyond a stand of beech trees is a trail leading into the woods, which opens up to a stunning view of the Avon River Gorge. If that doesn't inspire you, I don't know what will."

"Thank you." Mary beamed. "I shall give both of these—"

Overhead, something crashed. A beastly howl split the air. Mary stared slack-jawed at the ceiling as heavy footsteps pounded like dropped boulders. Amelia shot to her feet, heart in her throat. What if Colin raced down here? Frightened Mary? *Harmed* Mary?

With quick steps, she reached for the woman's hand, guiding her up. "Well, my dear, I am sure you'll want to begin your exploring. If you leave now, you ought to make Brandon Hill and back before the sun sets. Come. I shall see you to the door."

The whites of Mary's eyes were enormous as Amelia ushered her from the room. "Is everything all right?"

"I'm sure it's nothing."

"Nothing? It sounds like a caged monster roams about upstairs."

"Oh. That. Probably just my brother. He...um..." He what? Think. *Think!* She reached for the front door and flung it open. "It's likely just a spider. He's deathly afraid of spiders. Enjoy your walk, Mary."

"But—"

"Thank you for stopping by. Good day." Gently—yet ever so

firmly—Amelia steered the woman out the door and shut it behind her. Whew. That was close, especially since Colin started up a fresh wave of howling. She'd gotten Mary out the door quickly, but the woman had heard enough to spread gossip about the strange doings at Balfour House. Would she?

No time to ponder that now. Amelia had a brother to tend to, and by the sounds of it, a very agitated one.

TWENTY-SEVEN

"Has this mind, so replete with ideas, imaginations fanciful
and magnificent, which formed a world, whose existence
depended on the life of its creator—has the mind perished?"

⚜

A lot could happen in four days. Many a battle had been fought and won in less time. And yet as Graham unhooked the horse from the gig and gave the animal a cursory rubdown, he growled at all the changes that should've happened by now for Colin Balfour. After so much time since surgery, the man should be coherent and able to communicate. He ought to be capable of eating a meal without flying into an inexplicable rage—and that was the whole crux of the matter. The untamable frenzies. The erratic bursts of derangement. The placid, amiable persona of Colin Balfour had been replaced with an animal that frequently strained against the leash. And Amelia bore the brunt of it, a burden she never should have had to carry.

Graham slammed the curry comb onto the workbench, startling the horse. With a pat to the withers and a soft "Easy girl," he calmed the animal, yet it did nothing to stop the fury rising up his gullet.

Forcing a calmness he didn't feel, he retrieved the dandy brush and finished grooming the old bay. It wasn't right that Amelia should have to watch the deterioration of a much-beloved brother, that every day when he attended the man, her big brown eyes pleaded with him for something—*anything*—to be done to help Colin. But there was nothing he could do. The fear in her voice, the worry bending her shoulders, the way her gown hung on a frame much diminished from the healthy woman of little over a month ago, all served to stoke the continual rage burning in his gut.

With a growl in his throat, he flung the brush towards the stable door—narrowly missing a white-haired head.

Dodging aside, Peckwood clutched a leather portfolio to his chest as a shield. "Great heavens! Is it safe to enter?"

In the mood he was in? "Hardly," he ground out through clenched teeth, then turned back to the horse. Better to finish detangling the animal's mane than pop the doctor in the nose.

Footsteps crushed errant bits of straw, drawing closer. "I suspected I'd find you here, but not throwing about the grooming tools like a madman. What has you so frothed at the mouth?"

What sort of game was this? Surely the man had to know. With supreme effort, Graham ran his fingers gently through the horse's mane. "In short, Mr. Peckwood, you are the irritation. No more can I tolerate your ethics, your procedures, your insatiable appetite for power and renown. These things are abhorrent, and I will not remain silent any longer." Stepping away from the horse, he faced the man, mind made up to speak out and hang the cost. "I am done with you, sir, and when the authorities are informed, you will be done as well."

"I see." Peckwood nodded as if they discussed nothing more than which cloth suited best as a bandage. "I suspected something has been eating at you these past several days, hence my reason for seeking you out, but what exactly are you babbling on about?"

Lifting its great nose, the horse snorted, and Graham didn't blame it. He felt like doing so himself. "Did you really expect me not to react to the botched surgery you performed on Mr. Balfour? Or your harmful experiments on St. Peter's inmates? And what about the corpse I saw in your office? We both know that body was there courtesy of lawless resurrection men." Bypassing the doctor, he grabbed a bucket of grain near the door, anything to busy his hands lest he strike the arrogant man. "Any one of those charges is enough to lock you away for a very long time. And don't bother *enlightening* me, as you call it. I won't listen to your twisted truths anymore and, in fact, am of half a mind to inform those journalists who are singing your praises of the real truth about you."

"Tut-tut, Lambert." Peckwood clucked his tongue and let the portfolio fall to his side. "Your claims have no more validity in the real world than an actor's passionate monologue. My work at St. Peter's is sanctioned by the warden, who will attest to the help I have provided in bettering the lives of many of his inmates."

"A *bettering* of lives? That's what you call it?" He grasped the pail so tightly, his knuckles throbbed. "Is creating a dependency on you and your drugs any better than madness? Both your methods and insanity control the mind, causing behaviour that is erratic and dangerous. And what happens when your drugs run out? Or you die? Those inmates will be worse off than before, as evidenced by Caroline Safie. She may never regain the use of her left arm thanks to the mangling she received when scrambling over glass shards to get to you. You did not better her life!"

Graham clenched his jaw, caging the hot fury that begged to spew out in curses he'd later regret. Sensing his unease, the mare stomped the barn floor. Graham stepped a safe distance from her front hooves.

Peckwood dipped his head sadly. "I grant you that Miss Safie's wounds are unfortunate, but they were not caused by me. I was not even present at the time." Peckwood shrugged, the folio in his hands bobbing with the movement. "Surely you know your insinuations will not hold up in a court of law. Anything you say against me and my work at the asylum is mere conjecture on your part. You have no proof."

Gritting his teeth, Graham stalked past the cagey old surgeon. As much as he hated to admit it, Peckwood was right. There was no substantial way to attest to the maltreatment of the inmates, not with Mr. Waldman to say otherwise.

With a pat to the horse's neck, he once again faced Peckwood. "It is true I may not be able to convince a jury of your malfeasance in the case of St. Peter's, especially with the way you have the warden neatly tucked into your pocket, but I do have proof in the case of Colin Balfour. Tangible proof, both in the broken mind of the man and in the testimony of his sister and household staff. You cannot talk your way out of the visible harm you have done to him."

A flicker of fear sparked in the man's gaze, which was quickly snuffed out by a shake of his head and a smirk. "I won't have to, for you will say nothing. The truth is, Lambert, that you came to Bristol in order to link your name to mine, to give you validation as a doctor. If you besmirch my honour, you taint yours as well."

Bah! Had he not already lived through just such a ruination? Graham strode close to the man, lifting his chin in defiance. "You think I care about that?"

"Yes, I think you do. Very much. For therein is your whole career and future—a future that begins today." He shoved the portfolio into Graham's hands. "I trust this will be quite sufficient."

Frowning, Graham opened the folder and leafed through a sizeable collection of banknotes. His gaze bounced between the money and the man. "What is this? How can you possibly have so much money to offer me when you've not even paid the lamp oil bill?"

"Just can't keep your nose out of my affairs, can you, Lambert? I owe you nor anyone else an explanation for what invoices I choose to pay or leave off." Peckwood sniffed. "Not that it signifies anymore. There's enough in that folio for you to walk away and begin your own practice here and now. It is what you have wanted all along, is it not?"

Graham gaped. "You think I can be bought so easily?"

"No, I *know* it. For if you do not avail yourself of my offer and instead go to the authorities, it is I who will ruin you."

"You seriously think to bribe me? What a mockery. Colin Balfour deserves justice!" He thrust the portfolio against Peckwood's chest, forcing the man to grab it. "And I will see it happen, Doctor. You mark my words."

"Justice? Interesting." The doctor chuckled and pulled out a banknote, then stuffed it into Graham's pocket with a swift movement. "Take that and a couple of days to think about this proposition, because who is going to believe the word of a dismissed naval surgeon against that of a respected doctor of more than thirty years?"

Graham stiffened, a sickening twist in his gut clenching tighter and tighter—the same feeling he'd had facing the admiralty board, when the lieutenant's word had trumped his. When he'd been the one who'd lost everything and the guilty man had walked free. Perhaps Peckwood was right.

He'd better think twice before acting.

⸻

A choice must be made. A decision rendered. But for now, Amelia pushed the thought of what to do about Colin to a dark corner of her mind. Would that she might evict it altogether! But something would have to be done. Soon. And as she trudged up the stairs with a tea tray in hand, each step bringing her closer to her brother's room, dread increased in her belly. Would she find him asleep or crouched in a corner, ready to spring?

She set the tray down on the stand in the corridor, then ever so gently rapped her knuckles against his door. The slightest noises or movements seemed to trouble him, so she made sure to keep her voice dulcet. "It is teatime, Brother."

Twisting the knob with a smooth motion, she eased the door open. Late afternoon sunshine didn't visit this side of the house. Still, there was enough light to clearly see nothing but rumpled sheets atop her brother's bed.

"Colin?" She eased inside and glanced about. No monsters lurked in any of the corners. No big shape sat at the desk or in the chair, nor did one loom near the hearth or the window. Her heart crashed against her ribs.

Colin was gone.

A ripple of childish laughter fluttered in through the open sash. Close. In the backyard. Amelia frowned, lured by the sound, and as she approached the window, the pounding of her heart stopped altogether.

Colin knelt on the lawn, towering over a boy—a child who could have no idea of the sort of danger he was in.

Amelia tore from the room. Flew down the stairs. Raced through the corridor and yanked open the back door.

But then stopped, keeping to the inside shadows. She might startle Colin if she bolted out there in a flurry, which could send him into a fit.

By the looks of it, he'd recently suffered just such an episode. His hair stood wild on the unshaven side of his head. The other side sported his exposed stitches, ghastly purple and puckered, his bandage straggling behind him like a limp banner. The edge of the hastily cast-off dressing was caught on the collar of a waistcoat that hung half on and half off his body, only one arm having been shoved through the sleeve hole. His other arm stretched out, his big fingers gripping the shoulder of a sandy-headed boy. One little squeeze would crush the child's bones.

Despite the late July afternoon, she shivered.

Strangely, the lad didn't seem to mind the awful weight on his shoulder or the malformed giant in front of him. He lifted his hand, so small in comparison to her brother's, and pointed at Colin's hideous scar. "Do it hurt terrible much, sir?"

Colin nodded.

Nodded? Amelia gaped. Had he understood the child, then?

The boy's hand dropped. So did his head. "I know all about hurts."

A fierce growl rumbled in Colin's throat, raising the fine hairs at the nape of Amelia's neck. If he lashed out at the child, there'd be nothing she could do to protect him.

Again, the boy didn't appear to be frightened in the least, for he lifted his chin and grinned. "But it do a body good breathin' some air, don't it? I told ye it would."

"Ne-mo good." Colin's massive hand drifted upwards, away from the lad's shoulder, and patted him on the head.

The boy ducked away, rubbing where her brother had no doubt pounded him too hard. Amelia lifted the back of her hand to her own cheek, pressing against the small slice she'd suffered the day Colin had thrown the dish. This had to stop before the boy got hurt.

Gathering the hem of her gown, she glided past the threshold and stopped at the edge of the top step. "It's time to come inside, Brother." Actually, it was past time. One glance out Mrs. O's window and the news of her monstrous brother would be all over Clifton.

Colin and the boy swiveled their heads in unison. Both looked scared and ready to bolt. Colin swung out one big arm and pulled the boy to his side. The lad winced but, to his credit, did not cry out.

Amelia tensed, fighting every instinct to run towards them, yank the boy to safety, and usher Colin from the public eye. God only knew what would happen if she did.

Though it pained her to do so, she slowly swept her hand towards the open door. "Cook has made seedcakes with a fresh dish of clotted cream. There's enough for us all."

The lad peered up at Colin. "Seedcakes is me favourite, sir."

Sorrow folded Colin's face, erasing the years, the deformity, transforming him into the same child who'd pressed his face against the glass as she'd left Balfour Manor all those years ago, begging her to stay…and if she had, how might things have been different?

"Ne-mo come?" Colin rumbled.

"Aye, sir." The boy nodded. "It was you what told me yer sister could be trusted, to run to her should you not be 'round, remember?"

Colin's lips rippled, like a great harvest of words were ripe for the picking yet he didn't have the slightest clue how to gather them. Releasing the boy, he pressed both his hands to his head and shuddered. Sweet heavens! If he snapped now, the lad would bear the brunt of his fit.

"Nemo, is it?" She held out her hand, praying to God he'd take it. "Come along. I'll see that Betsey puts an extra cake on the tray."

"Oh boy!" He skipped across the lawn and plowed up the stairs, entwining his dirty fingers with hers.

Amelia stared, horrified. Had the lad's abrupt movement been too much for her brother to handle? Was Colin even now teetering on the brink of cracking?

But her brother didn't move. Not a smidgeon. He was a statue, palms flat against his ears, a breeze tangling his hair and riffling the dangling bandage.

"Colin, don't you want to come?" She forced a smile. "I believe Nemo is hungry."

Still, he didn't move. Not physically. Only his gaze slid to her. She angled her head towards the house in what she hoped he'd perceive as an invitation.

Moments later, he rose, and once he fully stood, he took off like a hound of hell, sprinting towards her and the boy, never once pulling his hands from his head. She barely had time to yank Nemo aside before Colin shot past them and into the house.

The boy laughed. "He's a fast one, aye?"

Quite the understatement, that. Unsure if she should be relieved or alarmed, Amelia guided the lad through the door and shut it firmly behind them.

As they made their way down the corridor, questions popped up one by one. Clearly the boy knew her brother, and vice versa, but how? Why was the child not frightened of him? How long had they known each other? And then, like the lifting of a dense fog, several answers sharpened into focus.

"So"—she glanced down at the boy—"I suppose I am to understand that all the toys the staff and I have found scattered about belong to you?"

He scuffed his toe on the carpet, a guilty nod bobbing his head, his ragged hair cascading into his eyes. His clothes were too small, his lanky limbs hanging well past the cuffs of shirt and trousers. How had a street boy come to befriend Colin?

"Have you any family?" she asked.

This time his head wagged. "I be an orphan, miss."

"And my brother knew of your existence before the surgery?"

"Aye, m'um. He were gonna take me to London with him. Be his errand boy." Releasing her hand, he dashed up the grand stairway and paused at the top, peering down at her. "How long till ye think he's a'right and we can leave?"

She sighed as she ascended. Oh, for the innocence of youth. "I wish I knew."

Nemo hopped on one foot then the other while waiting for her near the tea tray. The lad was so full of life. So exuberant. As if he'd been freed from a cage and let loose in a wide world of wonder.

And wonder was exactly what pressed in on Amelia, making it hard to breathe. All the wondering, the heavy weight of not knowing what to do. And now with a boy to work into the equation as well.

She paused in front of Colin's door, her own sanity about to snap.

She needed time alone. To think. To pray. To plead for guidance. But how was she to do so with a brown-eyed imp sniffing about the seedcakes?

"Betsey!" she called down the corridor, hoping by some slim chance her maid was even now brushing out a gown in her chamber instead of busying herself below-stairs with Mrs. Kirwin or Cook.

Grey skirts billowed out of Amelia's room. Just the sight of the sturdy maid loosened a bit of the tension in Amelia's shoulders. She could be counted on, this woman, as proven time and time again.

"Yes, miss?" Betsey stopped in front of her, glancing at the boy with a stern eye.

Nemo quit his hopping and darted behind Amelia, still as death.

"Would you mind serving tea to my brother and his guest, Master Nemo? I need a moment to myself."

Betsey dipped her head. "Of course, miss."

Reaching behind her, Amelia shepherded the boy out of hiding. "Go on. Betsey doesn't bite. And if you ask her nicely, she might take you down to see Cook for more seedcakes when I return. Would you like that?"

He gave her a solemn nod, then with a wide berth around Betsey, he sidled into Colin's room.

"Do not leave them alone, my brother and the boy." She tipped her head towards Colin's room. "I shall return shortly."

Betsey's brows arched.

But Amelia didn't give in and instead turned on her heel and dashed to the sanctuary of her own room. How could she possibly answer her maid's questions when she barely had answers herself?

Closing the door, she leaned her back against it and allowed all the excess emotions of the past week to well in her eyes. It was too much. Everything was too much. What was she to do now, with a boy to care for as well as a brother who was often more mad than sane? Would the bouts of lunacy eventually fade?

Please, God!

She pushed from the door and strode across the rug, gathering her handkerchief off her dressing table and pressing the cloth to her eyes. Though she'd had a brief glimpse that the real Colin was somehow trapped inside his ungainly body, the fact remained he was very much out of his mind most of the time. A ruined brain to go along with his ruined body. There was no way she could leave him here at Balfour House to recover on his own, especially since she'd been the one to urge his surgery in the first place. And for what? To satisfy a father who was overbearing to the last of his life? Why had she so willingly gone along with his wishes? A heavy weight of guilt descended, sagging her shoulders.

Setting down the kerchief, she pulled out a small drawer to retrieve the tickets to Cairo, wishing she'd read the departure date wrong. But no. In a mere three days the ship would sail, and if she wanted to be on it, she had no other choice than to commit Colin to St. Peter's, where he'd be watched day and night. For he *must* be watched, lest he stray from the house and frighten half the population of Clifton and Bristol combined.

The only other option was to do the watching herself. She and Betsey. But doing so would be the death knell to her traveling and writing. She stared at the tickets, the ugly dilemma tasting like bile. Should she really give this up? Could she?

What do I do, God?

She crushed the tickets to her chest and closed her eyes. She'd not be given another chance like this. Mr. Moritz had made that painfully clear. It would be so easy to leave. Pack her bags and bury herself in a foreign culture, forget all about her current woes…just as she'd done seven years ago. But then she'd been running from a cruel father and a brother she barely knew. And now?

My, how things had changed.

She bowed her head, the edge of the tickets cutting into the tender flesh between thumb and forefinger. Now she knew the depths of Colin, understood the man locked inside that horrendous body and broken mind. A brother she loved. The only family member she had left.

Graham's words, spoken so soft and low on that glorious day at Brandon Hill, suddenly came barreling back.

Family, no matter the size of it, is precious. Never leave a loved one behind.

Her fingers shook. Her arms. Her legs. All those years of walking in perfection, saying the right things, meeting the right people, advancing in a world of men…none of it mattered anymore. Graham was right. Even now, wondering what people would think if the worst were to happen—if Colin did not regain his faculties—just did not matter. She loved her brother, imperfect, broken, yes, even mad, though he be.

Just as God loved her, as imperfect and broken as she was.

She stalked over to the hearth and dropped to her knees, her skirt billowing like a puff of smoke. Grabbing the poker, she stirred the banked embers, then dropped the iron bar with a clatter. Leaning forward, she edged the tickets ever closer, breathing hard, barely seeing for the tears skewing her vision.

And lit her career on fire.

TWENTY-EIGHT

"...for I was a shattered wreck—
the shadow of a human being."

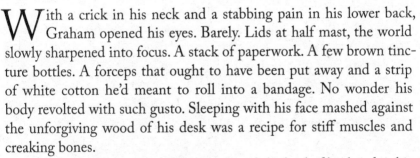

With a crick in his neck and a stabbing pain in his lower back, Graham opened his eyes. Barely. Lids at half mast, the world slowly sharpened into focus. A stack of paperwork. A few brown tincture bottles. A forceps that ought to have been put away and a strip of white cotton he'd meant to roll into a bandage. No wonder his body revolted with such gusto. Sleeping with his face mashed against the unforgiving wood of his desk was a recipe for stiff muscles and creaking bones.

Sitting upright, he immediately pressed the heel of his hand to his brow, pushing back a headache. For the past two nights he'd walked the streets until daybreak, trying to figure out what to do about Peckwood. Turn the man in, and in the process, incriminate himself? Throw away his career and all the years of knowledge he'd worked hard to acquire?

He dropped his hand, the movement so swift, it crinkled the banknote in his pocket that Peckwood had forced upon him. Could he morally take the rest of the money he'd been offered to set up his own practice and do all the good he could for the sick and needy? Yet would that not, in a sense, make him no better than Peckwood? Such a gain would be at the expense of others—like Colin and the asylum inmates who could not speak for themselves. Thunder and turf! Of all the wretched choices to make.

The wall clock began to chime. Three o'clock? He bolted to his feet. How had he managed to sleep for so long? He ought to have called on Mrs. Bap shortly after breakfast...if he'd actually taken breakfast. Even now a terrible growl rumbled in his belly.

But no time for that. He grabbed his medical bag then snatched his hat off a peg near the door on his way out. Thick clouds hung low, not the sort to threaten rain but rather to oppress and dishearten.

He pounded into the stable out back, but the gig was gone. As usual. He'd have to hoof it the nine blocks to Mrs. Bap's. Sighing, he reset his hat all the tighter and set off.

Even without the sun to heat Redcliffe's sludgy gutters, the slum managed to waft its own brand of noxious odours as strong as ever. Were he to take that pile of offered money from Peckwood, he'd have enough to see Mrs. Bap and her granddaughter moved into better housing and ease the old woman's last days.

Raising a fist, he pounded on the flimsy door, rattling the pathetic wood in its frame. "Mrs. Bap? Mr. Lambert here."

Feet shuffled. Hinges groaned. A breath later, teary blue eyes gazed up into his own. Emma, Mrs. Bap's granddaughter, slowly shook her head. Before she uttered a word, his gut hardened.

The young woman's lower lip trembled as she spoke. "She's gone, sir."

Shoving past her, he dashed to the old woman's bedside and dropped to his knees. His medical bag fell from his grip, landing with a dull thud on the hard-packed floor. No matter. He didn't need to listen to her heart or check for breath to know Emma's words were true.

Mrs. Bap's hoary head rested motionless on a burlap pillow. Her grey eyes stared upwards, ever upwards. Chest tight, Graham pulled two coins from his pocket, then gently brushed her lids shut and pressed the cold metal against her grey skin. Deep down, a sob clawed its way up to his throat. Though he knew there was nothing he could have done to prevent her death, still, his heart squeezed. Had he been on time, he might have at least made her final breaths more comfortable.

All the ghosts of his past rose from their graves and pointed accusing fingers at him. He'd failed yet another dear woman. His head drooped.

Oh God, forgive me.

Footsteps scuffled behind him. "Yer not to blame, sir. Granny made sure to tell me so, right before she—"

Emma's voice broke. So did his heart. Surprising, really, after living through so many deaths. He ought to be used to such loss. But losing a patient never came easy, especially one such as this.

Yet duty called. Now was not a time to grieve but to comfort.

Inhaling until his lungs burned, he gathered his bag. "You'll have to let the undertaker know posthaste."

The young woman shook her head. "Got no money for such fancies, sir. Mr. Waldman do say Gran might could be tossed in with their next burial at St. Peter's."

"You and I both know your grandmother deserves better than that, so be at peace, Miss Emma." He squeezed her shoulder. "I will see her buried properly at my own expense." Pulling back, he retrieved Peckwood's banknote and the rest of the coins in his pocket. "Until then, use this for whatever you need in making preparations."

"Thank ye, sir." Sniffling, the girl dipped a quick curtsey. "Yer a good man."

Good? Hah. Would a good man entertain for even a minute the taking of a bribe? Clutching his bag, he strode to the door.

"Oh, sir? I nearly forgot." Emma scurried towards him, pulling a folded paper from her apron pocket.

"Gran wanted ye to have this. Give it to me nigh on a week ago now. Said when she…when she—" A great sniffle ended her words, one that held back a torrent of tears.

"You're a valiant girl, Miss Emma." Graham pulled the paper from her fingertips, offering her a small smile. "Just like your grandmother."

"Thank ye, sir."

He hesitated on the threshold, hating to leave the young woman with the body of her grandmother, yet there was nothing for it. "If you need anything, anything at all, send word for me."

"Aye, sir." Tears welled in her eyes, thick and shimmery. "God bless ye, sir."

He dipped his head, then escaped outside. Shoring his back against the wall, he opened Mrs. Bap's missive.

Doctor,

 If ye're reading this, it means I'm gone to glory, and don't ye fret about it one little bit. Ye did all ye could to comfort me in my last days, and for that I am thankful. Keep yer eyes on God, my son, for surely He keeps His watchful eye upon you. And most importantly, never grow weary in yer well doing, for in due season shall ye reap, if ye faint not.

Until the day we meet again,
Margaret Bap

And there it was. The answer he'd been seeking these past two sleepless nights. Though his heart was heavy over the passing of the dear old woman, his step was lighter as he pushed away from the wall and tucked the note into his pocket. As per Mrs. Bap's request, he would not grow weary in well doing. In this, he would not fail her. Or God.

He upped his pace, setting his face towards the office. He'd gather what information he'd documented on all of Peckwood's doings.

Then go straight to the constable.

⁙

Skitter bugs. No, scatter bugs. Whatever they were, they burned. They bit. They burrowed and nipped and made a big fat rat's nest in his head. He was sure of it. Colin scratched behind his ear like a hound with a flea. Go away. Go. Away!

For one blessed moment, the tingling in his skull abated and he could breathe. Freely. Deeply. Unchained and unbound. Maybe he could actually smile when the kind lady came back into his room instead of growling at her.

Egads!

He bolted upright in bed. They were everywhere now. Crawling up his legs. Tunneling into the webbing between his toes. Scuttling. Buttling. A devilish torment. He roared and raked his nails along his calves.

Then froze.

The voices were back.

A woman's. A man's. What language this time? More often than not, though he tried, he could not understand. Not a word. But then sometimes…this time, perhaps?

He leaped from his bed. Bad idea. Everything swirled like leaves caught in an eddy of wind. Breathing hard, he teetered on one foot then the other until the walls quit spinning. More careful this time, he padded out from his room and stopped at the top of the stairs.

"You'll not be taking him from this house." The words marched up the steps, bristly and sharp as a cornered stoat. "Not under my watch."

"Good lady, I assure you this request is to be expected." A hedgehog this time, chuffing with angry puffs of air. "Though I owe you no explanation, surely you will understand Mr. Balfour requires a follow-up visit to my office after such a major surgery."

"Mr. Lambert's been attending him daily, and neither him nor my mistress has given me any leave to comply with your request." The stoat again. He was sure of it.

The hedgehog huffed. "Produce your mistress at once, and I should be happy to clear it with Miss Balfour herself."

"She is not at home."

"When do you expect her?"

Snag it all! The biter bugs were back. Colin twisted to reach his shoulder blade and gave the creepy-crawlies a good swat, then he stumbled down a few stairs, having missed a portion of the stoat and hedgehog's conversation.

"…cannot say how long it will take for her to retrieve Mr. Lambert."

"Do you mean to tell me your mistress has gone to my office to request medical help?"

Colin grabbed the balustrade lest the hedgehog come tearing up the stairway and try to trip him up. They were sneaky devils. Always zigzagging about, scurrying in front of you when you least expected.

"Yes," said the stoat. "But—"

"Stand aside, woman! Every minute we spend debating means one more minute of possible damage to Mr. Balfour's mind. Do you wish to be responsible for that risk?"

The hedgehog appeared at the bottom of the stairs. Colin gripped the railing tighter. My! He was a big one. All round in the belly and pink of face.

"Mr. Balfour?" The animal's dark little eyes peered up at him.

He glanced around. What was a bal-for and why did this furry mammal want one?

Apparently the hedgehog wanted one really bad, because he advanced and stopped on the same step as him. Did he want help with this hunt?

"Come now, sir." The hedgehog rested his paw on Colin's arm. "I can help you."

Help? With the bugs? Colin cocked his head. Made sense. Hedgehogs ate bugs.

"Let me help you, my good fellow."

Colin opened his mouth to agree, but all that came out was a grunt. Good enough, or must have been, for the hedgehog guided him down the rest of the stairs. The stoat stood near the open door, in a gown of all things! As he passed, he patted the animal on the head. Maybe that would calm the puffed-up little creature.

Outside, the world was grey. Shadowy. Like the gloom might drop from the sky and wrap them all in a tight, black counterpane. His step faltered, but the hedgehog didn't seem to mind the looming darkness at all. His footsteps tapped steady, leading him onward, towards a half box on wheels. But as they neared it, the attached beast flared its great nostrils and screamed. Hooves clacked sharp, grating on his ears.

Hands to his head, he reared back. What if that monster broke loose? Charged him? *Ate* him?

"Help!" he cried. Or so he hoped. By the time the word flew out of his mouth, it didn't sound the same as when it had been in his head.

"Now, now. Steady on." The gutsy hedgehog stepped between him and the creature. "That is what I'm here for. Soon your pain will be over. You would like that, would you not?"

Who wouldn't? He nodded.

"Then up you go." The hedgehog pointed to the rolling box.

With a last glance at the frightful monster in front, Colin climbed up. The whole thing listed dreadfully to the side, and for a moment he feared it might tip over, but it held. Thank God it held!

The fuzzy little hedgehog clamored up beside him and grabbed a set of long ribbons in his tiny paws. He snapped them, and the wheels moved. Colin grabbed the side, stomach roiling. This wasn't good. This was *not* good!

"Be at peace," the hedgehog soothed. "This won't take long."

And it didn't. The box stopped shortly thereafter, near a line of trees. The hedgehog jumped down and held out his paw. "Out you go. Soon your pain will be gone forever."

Colin stared at the tiny claws a good long time before testing the strength of them with a poke of his finger. Spindly and frail, just as he'd suspected. Forsaking it, he instead gripped the side of the box and lowered to the ground.

But still the man held out that paw. "Come along."

Colin shook his head. He wouldn't touch that naked flesh again.

"Very well. Follow that path." The hedgehog swung his arm towards a break in the trees. "I'll be right behind you. It won't be long now."

Good. The nipper bugs were back. Prickling their spiky feet over his scalp, but he'd learned by now not to slap his head. It hurt too much.

He stalked into the woods, and a few paces in, he gasped. He knew this place, but why? How? He upped his pace, flashes of pictures in his mind. A boy. Flaxen haired. Giggling. No. Wailing. A woman screaming. A man with a gun.

A gun?

He bolted.

"Wait!" The hedgehog squealed behind him.

No. No!

He tore ahead, and there was the woman. Brown gown. Grey cape. Braided hair tucked up in a bonnet. What to do? Should he hide?

Too late. Her eyes bulged, her mouth opening into a cavernous O as she stared at him, making him feel ashamed. Dirty. As exposed and vulnerable as the hedgehog's bare paws. A scream rent the air, one that climbed inside him and jiggled his innards. She had to stop it.

Stop it!

In two great strides, he grabbed her by the shoulders and roared into her face.

Then froze. Had her man heard? The one with the gun?

He released her and sprinted ahead, desperate for a hidey-hole. A cave. A yawning maw of earth to fall into and cover himself.

And there. A huge rock. He dashed over a log and crouched next to it, curling into a shape that would fit inside Mother Earth's womb. He could be a rock too. The gunman would never notice.

"There you are."

Only his eyes moved. Sideways. Upwards. Sweat crept down his back along the same path the scuttle bugs used.

The white-bristled hedgehog breathed hard, his little chest rising and falling fast. Once again, his pale, naked paw stretched out. "Come along, my friend. It is time to end this pain of yours."

Yes! Yes! The roly-poly mammal was right.

It was time.

TWENTY-NINE

"Prepare! Your toils only begin...."

❧

So much could be expressed in the grip of a hand. Protection. Compassion. And dare she hope...love? Amelia's cheeks heated as Graham's fingers tenderly wrapped around hers while he guided her down from the carriage. Or was that warm feeling caused by the intimate way he looked at her—and had been all the way on the ride over from his office? A gaze that cherished, treasured, valued.

Her.

Heart fluttering, she clung onto his strength. Oh, how she needed that right now. Needed him. The past days of Colin's fits and frenzies had worn her thin, especially the paroxysm he'd suffered this afternoon.

As soon as her feet hit the cobbles, Graham pulled her close. "Take heart. Now that we are here, I will do all I can for your brother. I won't be a minute while I pay the driver."

He pulled away and she felt the loss. Of all the inopportune times to fall for a man!

Turning from him, she glanced up at Balfour House and inhaled deeply to steady her nerves. What would she find when next she stepped into her brother's room? A wild man thrashing about on the mattress? Or one of the fleeting seconds when lucidity surfaced and Colin looked out of those tortured eyes of his? She sighed. With night shadows advancing, would that he might have already surrendered to sleep.

From the corner of her eye, she spied Graham patting his pockets.

Should he not have already passed the jarvey a coin?

Frowning, she faced him. "Is there a problem?"

"Indeed." His mouth quirked into a sheepish grin. "I'm afraid I used my last coins at my previous house visit, and I've not been home to retrieve more."

Amelia lifted her chin towards the driver. "Please, wait here. I'll send out your payment and a little extra with a servant."

The fellow—as long in the tooth as the old mare hitched to his coach—tipped his hat. "Thank ye, miss."

Clutching his medical bag in one hand, Graham offered her his arm. "Well, that was embarrassing," he muttered under his breath. "I should have thought to—"

"Oh, miss!" Grey skirts flew out the front door.

Amelia's breath hitched. Betsey never *flew* anywhere.

Her maid stopped in front of them, lips pinched into a tight line as she spoke. "I don't blame you a bit should you give me the rough side of your tongue when you hear what I've done. I never should have let him go, and I know it. Whatever got into me? Oh, that man!"

"Betsey, please, get hold of yourself." Amelia pressed her fingers into the woman's arm, hoping to slow her words, not to mention her own racing pulse. She'd never seen Betsey in such a flutter. "What man? What has happened?"

"Mr. Peckwood called, claiming he must escort Mr. Balfour to a follow-up visit at his office. But that don't ring true." Shaking her head, she peered up at Mr. Lambert. "You already make daily visits."

"Blast!" Graham's harsh bark prickled down Amelia's spine. So did the murderous shade of red climbing up his neck.

He stalked to the carriage.

Amelia darted after him, grabbing his arm before he could heft himself inside. "Why was I not told of this follow-up visit?"

"Because there wasn't one scheduled." The sharp edge to his voice cut like a knife. "Somehow Peckwood must have found out I determined to report him, and he's even now getting rid of the evidence to clear his name before the authorities haul him in."

Amelia slapped her hand to her chest, barely able to comprehend the information. "You will report Mr. Peckwood? But why?"

Graham's jaw hardened. "Conspiracy with Mr. Waldman to harm the inmates of St. Peter's, the illegal possession of a corpse, and as you well know, malpractice of the worst sort."

Each accusation bruised, the last of which sickening her stomach so vilely, she lowered her hand to her belly. Though she already suspected the answer, she couldn't help but ask, "What is the evidence you fear the doctor will get rid of?"

Sorrow folded his brow, and he cupped her cheek with his palm. "Your brother."

Fear ran cold through her veins. "Are you saying Mr. Peckwood might harm Colin?"

"Not if I can help it." He reached for the carriage door.

"Then I'm coming too."

"No." He spun back. "It may not be safe, not in the mood I'm in. And especially not if Peckwood has touched your brother. Wait here and I'll—"

"Thank God!" A ragged voice rang out, footsteps pounding hard. Breaths heaving harder. Hair undone and white in the face, petite Mary Godwin tore down the pavement, glancing over her shoulder, and barreled straight into Graham.

He caught her without so much as a stumble, shoring her up while she laboured for breath.

"I cannot…I cannot believe…I outran it!" she panted. "But if it does follow…we must get off the street!"

"Calm yourself, madam. Steady breaths now. In and out. In and out." At length, he released her. "There now. Why don't you allow Miss Balfour to see you inside and tell her all about your trouble?"

Amelia cut him a slanted glance, knowing full well he'd be off the second she turned her back. She didn't have time for this. Colin didn't have time for this, not if Graham's suspicions were true.

Mary shook her head, a queer light burning in her dark little eyes. "No, I've not the time. I must capture the monster's essence on paper before I do anything. His face…oh, God have mercy. What a horribly frightening inspiration. Good heavens!" She clapped her fingers to her mouth, gaze wide. "How mad I must sound," she whispered. "But I think this fiend is just the muse I've needed."

Amelia edged nearer to Graham, seeking his strength. "You saw a monster?"

Mary nodded, her head nearly unhinged with the passion of it. "On the path to the cliffs. He was huge, I tell you. Roared like a lion, no, a demon, and right in my face. I am marked. Marked!" Her gaze drifted from them, a faraway glaze shining incongruously bright in the growing darkness. "I shall never forget such a monster—and neither will my readers."

Amelia lifted her face to Graham. Without voicing a word, the stern lines chiseled at the sides of his mouth agreed with her conclusion. Mary Godwin hadn't seen a monster.

She'd seen Colin.

The carriage bounced and swayed, not fast enough to Graham's liking, but any more speed in this old rig and he might chip a tooth. Thunderation! He should have reported Peckwood days ago. Blast his hesitation.

Amelia jostled next to him, squeezing his hand in a death grip, face pale, staring blankly out the window. In her other hand she clung to a feather, as if drawing strength from the frail thing. A haunting picture. Would that he might spare her from all this. Cover her eyes. Protect her heart. Shelter her far, far away from here. God only knew what they'd find at the end of this crazed ride. For her sake and Colin's, he could only pray he wouldn't be too late.

Please, God, not again.

The driver barked, "Easy now," and a jolt that rattled the bones stopped the carriage. Pulling from Amelia's grasp, Graham flung open the door and leaped to the ground.

"Stay here," he shouted over his shoulder, gravel already crunching beneath his heels. With the bleak cloud cover and threat of twilight, the woods were dark and growing darker. Soon night would fall in earnest. How the blazes had Peckwood and Balfour ended up on this godforsaken trail anyway? The office was as far from this stretch of trees as east from west, leading to nothing but barren cliffs and—

His breath caught heavy in his throat. Sweet mercy! Would Peckwood actually lure Balfour over a precipice, all for the sake of evading public humiliation? But of course he would. Had the man not sent Graham on a false errand, risking a man's life in the process, simply to stop him from planting doubt in a journalist's mind?

"Graham, wait." Footsteps pounded behind him.

He grit his teeth. Amelia. Dashed headstrong woman! Admiration filled him anew. Would he love her so much were she not?

Slowing, he kicked a big branch off the path lest her skirts tangle in it, then reached back his hand. A moment later, cold fingers wrapped around his. Without a word, he squinted into the darkness and guided her through the gathering shadows.

Like the warning snarl of a big cat, an angry growl traveled through the darkness just ahead. Graham sped as fast as he dared. If he or Amelia tripped, they'd be that much farther behind. Such madness, this. Racing the oncoming night, racing against time itself.

Finally, the trees thinned. The path opened. Graham stopped, sweat trickling down his spine. Near the edge of the cliff, two silhouettes were locked in battle—one impossibly large, pushing a smaller, cowering shape. Shoving backwards, ever backwards, towards the hairline edge between land and air, rock and water. Every mewling cry from Peckwood's lips resulted in yet another growl and thrust in the chest from Colin.

Graham's mind whirled. How to stop this? What to do? Any further agitation would only excite Colin all the more.

Amelia pulled from his grip and rushed onward. With a wild leap, he grabbed her arm and yanked her into the safety of the trees. "No," he whisper-growled in her ear. "Whatever we do cannot be abrupt, such is the fragile state of your brother's mind."

She wrenched from his grasp and skewered him with a furious scowl. "Colin will kill Mr. Peckwood if we do nothing!"

"I said we must use caution, not that we do nothing."

"Then what?" Desperation thickened her voice.

0

The same desperation pressed in on him. Plowing his fingers through his hair, he paced in the dark, thinking hard. Praying harder. If they rushed the troubled man, he'd not only send Peckwood to his death, but he might hurtle over the cliff himself. No, that wouldn't work…not directly. But like a warship jockeying to let loose the cannons, they just might be able to pull alongside him.

"I'll come around one side while you—" He turned back to Amelia.

But she was already dashing ahead, hefting her skirts in one hand, the other outstretched. "Colin! It's time to go home, Brother."

The big man stopped.

So did Graham's heartbeat.

"Yes, Mr. Balfour." Whimpering, Peckwood flicked his hand towards Amelia. "Your sister needs you at home. Go!"

Graham riffled through possibilities. If her brother turned on her, one swipe of his hand could crush her skull. Not an ideal situation, but perhaps a situation that might be used. With Colin clearly listening to his sister, Graham could flank him and take him down sideways, eliminating the threat to Amelia and to Peckwood—though that cur deserved to go off the cliff after all he'd done.

Graham crept ahead, giving Amelia a wide berth. Should Colin face her, hopefully he'd not notice his movement.

"Come, Colin," she urged. "Come to me."

Colin snapped his gaze over his shoulder.

Good timing. Graham was already past her and drawing closer to the man. Nearer. Ready to spring should Colin charge towards Amelia or Peckwood.

"That's it. You see me now." Amelia advanced with measured steps. "Take my hand, Brother."

Colin roared.

Graham upped his pace.

"Please, Colin. Nemo needs you. *I* need you." Despite how frightened she surely must be, Amelia's step didn't falter. Fearless girl. "Let us not ever be parted again, hmm? I love you, no matter how you look. No matter how you act. I love *you*, the man I know that's trapped inside."

"Me-lee-ah." Colin's voice scraped the air. His weight shifted. His big body pivoted towards her.

She'd done it! Against all odds, Amelia had broken through the insanity clouding the man's brain. Quickly, Graham changed his tactics. Perhaps violence wouldn't be needed after all, not since she'd—

A crack of wood on bone splintered the air. Colin's knees buckled. The giant pitched forward, his palms grinding into gravel, his head hitting a rock.

Peckwood stood over him, clutching a huge branch, grinning like a skeleton.

Amelia screamed.

God, no!

Graham rocketed ahead, blasting Peckwood with barbed oaths. "Murderer! What have you done?" He dropped to his knees at the giant's still form. "Colin! Come now, man."

Blood oozed from Colin's nose. He lay deathly still, but even so, a faint breath feathered against the back of Graham's hand. He was alive. Thank God, he was alive!

"Let me go. Graham!"

Amelia's cry instantly shot him to his feet.

Ten paces away, Amelia struggled in Peckwood's grip, fingers helplessly trying to pry the man's forearm away from her neck. The blackguard had her in a chokehold—a blood chokehold. Any more pressure and all blood flow to her brain would stop.

Killing her.

THIRTY

*"—that the brightness of a beloved eye can have been
extinguished, and the sound of a voice so familiar, and dear
to the ear, can be hushed, never more to be heard."*

❦

Was this it? The last beat of her heart? Her final breath? Amelia
clawed at Peckwood's arm, but the old surgeon's grip was iron,
and her strength was waning. She could feel it, ebbing like cold seawa-
ter. She'd been frightened before, but not like this. Never like this. Not
even the feather in her pocket could quell the fear pumping poison
through her veins.

She wasn't ready to die! Not yet.

"Release her!" Graham roared, black against black. He stalked
closer, his dark shape murderous in the final gasp of daylight. "You
take things too far, Peckwood."

The doctor's arm jerked tighter. "Stop right there."

Her hands fell away, the fight for air so consuming that any extra
movement was a price she could no longer afford. Not even the added
gust of wind winging up over the cliff was any help.

"You have no one to blame but yourself, Lambert." Peckwood's voice
rumbled in her ear. "You are the one who set this whole charade into
motion. You should have taken the money and let it go."

"No, let *her* go." Simple words. Simply said. Yet unbelievably chill-
ing. "At once!"

"I'm afraid I cannot. Not yet." Peckwood's breath puffed hot against her head—a head that felt like it was going to pop. "Miss Balfour is my insurance you will neither follow me nor go to the authorities until I am long gone from your reach."

Graham advanced, hands fisted. "I swear by all that's holy, Peckwood, I will hunt you down for the animal you are."

"Not another step." The doctor's arm clamped harder.

Black crept in from all sides, like the throat of a tunnel narrowing and narrowing. Her lungs burned for want of air. Need of air. Her head swelled and her legs numbed. Dear God! If she could no longer hold herself up, Peckwood's arm would be the noose that hanged her.

"Stop!" Graham froze, his tone hollow and haunted. "Don't hurt her."

"I am a doctor, sir." Peckwood's words traveled through a dark haze. "I would never willingly hurt anyone."

"But you already have. For pity's sake, man, no more. Let her go." Fear, love, anguish…all bled together in Graham's voice. Breaking her heart. Filling her eyes.

She should go to him. Comfort him. Comfort Colin, who rose behind Graham on his arms and knees, wobbling like a dog about to keel over.

But night fell then. No, wait a minute. She was night. One with the darkness. Slipping further. Going deep. No longer able to fight against the steel band against her neck. No feather—nothing but God alone—could help her now.

"You're killing her!"

Graham's truth rang clear.

Loud.

Then everything faded.

⌘

Death was nothing new, but this? Watching his love, his heart, go limp in the arms of a madman? It was not to be borne.

Graham charged ahead, determined to kill or be killed, driven to the brink of insanity by grief and rage.

Only to be knocked aside. He teetered on one foot, flailing to keep upright.

A primal howl bellowed out of Colin as he shot past. "Me-lee!"

Amelia fell.

Peckwood fled—Colin on his heels, growling like an animal.

But Graham didn't care. All that mattered was the woman on the ground. The pale face. The still body. He grabbed her up, clutching her to his chest, cradling her in his arms. "Please—" His voice broke, a gut-wrenching sob rising to his lips. "Amelia! Don't go. Don't leave me. I cannot live in a world without you."

He pressed his brow to hers, his feverish. Hers cold. She lay still against him. Eerily still.

Closing his eyes, he whispered raggedly against her cheek. "God, please. Do not take her. She is too bright. Too beautiful. Take me instead."

"Graham?"

His name was torn and broken, more guttural than anything, yet the loveliest of music to his ears. He snapped open his eyes. Amelia blinked like a hurt bird, unsure if it could fly, or even if it should try.

Air rushed out of his lungs. "Thank God!"

Though everything in him cried to crush her tighter against him, to never let her go, he carefully set her down, shoring her up with an arm about her shoulders. She needed air and space to recover. A moment to collect her wits.

A moment cut brutally short by a bloodcurdling screech. "Lambert, help!"

"Me-lee!" Colin thundered.

Graham pivoted towards the cliff. There, near the edge, Peckwood stumbled backwards, the heel of his right foot perilously close to the line between life and death. One more shove from Colin and the doctor would plummet into the abyss, body bouncing against jagged limestone until it finally splashed into the dark waters of the Avon. A fitting end. One well deserved.

But an end that belonged to God alone.

As if reading his mind, Amelia faced him, her once dulcet voice now raspy and ruined by Peckwood himself. "Graham, stop him. Stop my brother."

Without any idea of how to do so, he dashed ahead. As much as he would like to see Peckwood reap the fruit of his labours, suffer at the hand of the man whose mind he'd cracked, this wasn't right.

"Colin! Back away." Graham held out his hand, just as Amelia had earlier. "Come with me. Your sister is safe. I will keep her safe, *we* will, you and I, for always."

The big man's head swung his way.

Their eyes met.

Recognition sparked in the last glimmer of day's light, and sweet relief gushed out of Graham in a long breath.

"Me-lee. Love!" Colin pounded his fist against his chest, but then he suddenly arched backwards with a howl. He swung his arm wide, slapping at his back as if trying to smack something between his shoulder blades—yet the only thing he connected with was Peckwood.

The doctor stumbled, grabbing onto the big man's arm to keep from tumbling over the cliff. Colin lifted the man from the ground and shook him off, pitifully crying about bugs.

As soon as Peckwood hit the dirt, he scrambled to his feet, shaking his head and taking a step towards Amelia. Good heavens! Was the man simply trying to get away or seriously thinking of going for her again?

Colin's gaze shifted from the doctor to his sister, then back again. "Nooo!"

He turned and plowed into Peckwood.

❧

"Colin, don't!"

The scream ripped out of Amelia's bruised throat as she charged ahead, stumbling dangerously close to the edge where her brother flew over.

Graham's fingers wrapped around her arm. "Don't look!"

Too late.

She caught the last sight of Colin's huge body hitting a rock far, far below, an instant before that giant of a man slipped into black waters. And just like that, he was lost to her. Her strong, brave brother, lost in darkness and distance.

Forever.

"No!" Amelia threw back her head and raged. "Not my brother!"

Strong arms wrapped around her, pulling her back, turning her around, cradling her against a heart that yet beat and a warm, solid chest—a chest she pounded with her fists until sobs consumed her.

Surrendering, she gave in to tears, hot and fast and stinging. And through all her hideous cries and gulping for air, Graham held her close. Rubbing little circles on her back. Letting her grieve. Keeping her safe, just as he'd promised Colin. Spent, she sagged against him, grateful for the solid beam this man had become to her in so many ways.

When her breathing evened, he crooked his finger beneath her chin, lifting her face to his. "Let me take you home now."

She shook her head, hardly able to comprehend his words for the sorrow that muddled every thought. "He's gone. Oh, he's gone!"

"I know, dear one." He pressed a kiss to her brow, his lips warm against her skin as he whispered, "I know."

In one swift movement, he slung her up into his arms and turned from the cliff. Rogue ends of his loose hair brushed against her cheek as he strode into the woods, his broad shoulders and protective embrace sheltering her from branches all the way to the carriage.

"Balfour House, at once," Graham directed the driver while he hoisted her into the coach.

The moment he sat, she collapsed against him, numb to everything. Time. Space. The beat of her own heart. How could she ever close her eyes again without seeing her brother—her beloved, mad brother—charging over the cliff, thinking he was saving her? The sight would haunt her in nightmares to come, for it was seared into her mind. Looking out the window, she stared, unblinking, into the dark. Seeing nothing but the gentle giant she loved with her whole heart vanish into the gorge.

"Amelia?"

She jerked upright, suddenly aware a warm body no longer shored her up.

Night air curled in the open carriage door. Graham's worried gaze peered in at her, his strong hand stretched up for her to grasp. How had they arrived home so quickly?

As soon as her feet hit the pavement, Graham spoke in low tones to the driver, but their conversation was lost on her. She stared at the house, growing colder by the minute. It would be empty here without her brother. Void. Desolate. She shivered.

"Here." Graham wrapped his coat around her shoulders. "Let's get you inside."

As they walked to the door, she dipped her head aside. Graham's musky scent was woven into the fabric of his coat, caressing her. A tangible assurance, that. Desperately, she tried to recall how Colin had smelled. But she couldn't. And she'd never have another chance to breathe in his presence, to remember, to know.

"Betsey!" Graham bellowed as soon as he ushered her inside, then he turned to her. "Your maid will see you up to your room. You need rest. Promise me you will rest."

A rush of panic weakened her knees, and she clutched his coat tight against her collarbones. Closing her eyes was the last thing she wanted to do. "I don't want to be alone. Stay with me. Please. Stay."

"Amelia." He spoke her name so tenderly, a fresh well of tears threatened to overflow. His palms cupped her face. "I will return soon. I promise. The authorities must be told. Your brother and Peckwood, well…their bodies must be recovered before it's too late to find them."

Voiced aloud, the words added pain upon pain, yet he was right.

"Yes," she whispered. "Of course."

Something like a wince tightened his lips, yet so much love and concern burned in his gaze, it made her want to hide from the raw purity of it.

"I realize now is not the time, but I can no longer contain it. Not after seeing you fall, thinking Peckwood had choked the life from you, that he'd…" His throat bobbed. "What I mean to say is that I love—"

"You called, sir?" Betsey's voice shattered the moment into a thousand pieces.

Graham's eyes slid closed for the briefest moment, then he faced the maid. "Yes. See your mistress to her room, please. There's a bottle on Mr. Balfour's nightstand. Administer a spoonful to her, then sit with her until I return. Is that quite clear?"

"Aye, sir."

Graham turned to Amelia. "You'll be all right. I know you will."

It was a good thing he knew, because right now, she doubted very much things would ever be right with her again. Still, she had to pull herself together. Be strong. Stop this show of weakness and carry on as she always had. Releasing her grip on Graham's coat, she began peeling it off.

His fingers pressed into her arm, staying her. "Keep it for now, if it makes you feel safe."

Her breath caught. How did he know?

With a small smile, he dipped his head at her then vanished out the door. She stood immobile, listening to the lonely sound of the latch catching.

"Come now, miss." Betsey's heels skritched against the tiles. "Doctor's orders."

In a daze, Amelia bypassed her maid, using every last bit of her strength to keep her chin high and march up the stairs with a straight backbone. At the first floor landing, however, she gripped the balustrade with white knuckles, unable to clear the final step.

Colin's bedroom door gaped open. Nemo's blue eyes peeked out, hope lighting his face, an old book clutched in his hands. "Is the master home, miss?"

No. And he never would be again.

Choking, Amelia fled to her room, searching her pocket for her feather, tears once again flowing fast and free. Inside the quiet of her chamber, she stopped, breathing hard, staring fervently at the lucky charm in her hand. It hadn't protected her from Peckwood's attack. It hadn't made Colin's surgery successful or stopped him from plunging off the cliff. It was useless. Senseless. As pathetic as the hope she'd put into it…hope that would've been better spent in trusting for God's provision instead of a feather's—instead of her own.

An ugly sob tore out of her. Merciful Saviour! That's exactly what she'd done, relied not only on an ornamental bit of bird fluff and other assorted superstitions, but on herself, on her own ability to keep her world—and Colin's—in order. In a very real sense, she'd played God. She bowed her head, heart aflame.

Oh God, it seems all I can do is ask Your forgiveness. Again and again and again.

Straightening her spine, Amelia marched to the window, then forced up the sash. Cool evening air wafted in. She leaned out and held up the Ibis feather as an offering. It had done her no good, and never would. And now she knew it was never meant to.

So she let go.

The feather caught a whisper of a draft, floating away and disappearing into the night. Gone for good. For the first time in the past several hours, a small smile ghosted her lips. Never again would she put one smidgeon of faith in luck or in her own means of control, but in God alone.

For if she did not cling to her faith here and now, she would never survive the awful pain in her heart.

THIRTY-ONE

*"Enter the house of mourning, my friend, but with kindness
and affection for those who love you...."*

⁂

How dare the sun rise so merrily? The July sky promise such a beautiful day? It was wrong. Blasphemous. The world had lost a bright and magnificent soul last night. The least it could do was rain.

Sighing, Amelia pressed her forehead against the window, the glass cool, her eyes swollen, and stared aimlessly out over a patchwork of rooftops. Beyond them all, a ship was set to sail this morn. The voyage would have changed her life. But, oh, how irreparably changed it already was.

How I will miss you, my brother, my heart.

Tears should fall now, but none were left. Her reservoir had drained into her pillow during a night of haunted sleep. If Graham had come calling, her laudanum-induced stupor hadn't registered him. But at this moment? Oh, what she wouldn't give to feel his strong arms holding her close and hear his whisper in her ear.

With yet another sigh, she padded over to Colin's bed. The sheets were still mussed from when he'd tossed and turned here only yesterday. Was it wrong to bear such a profound sorrow for him when she'd not mourned so woefully the passing of her own father?

Bending, she pressed her palm to his pillow and smoothed out the wrinkles. Strange that Betsey hadn't ordered the housemaid to haul up a load of fresh linens. Then again, her maid had her hands full with fretting over her now.

"He were a good man."

Her gaze drifted to a small voice at her side. Nemo's blue eyes peered up at her beneath a ragged fringe of hair. How could the child move on such quiet feet? She'd not heard so much as a toe scuff or heel scrape when he'd entered the room.

"Betsey told you, then?"

He nodded, his soulful eyes overlarge. "You want I should leave now?"

"Leave?" She scrunched her nose. Had Betsey asked him to run an errand on her behalf and yet he still sought her approval? "Where are you going?"

He shrugged, his thin shoulders poking up like little knobs. "A new hidey-hole somewhere."

Just when she thought her heart couldn't possibly break more, another chip fell away. It wasn't right that one so young should have to fend for himself in this cold world.

"No." She wove her fingers through his. "We shall both leave. Together."

He pulled away, turning in circles with his arms outstretched. "Ye mean ye're leaving this mansion?" Wonder laced his voice.

Not surprising, really. This was a beautiful home, but she'd flee today if there weren't a body to find and a burial to attend to. How would she ever be able to pass by Colin's door without breaking down? She shook her head. "I cannot live here anymore."

The boy stopped spinning, a knowing look in his eyes far beyond that of a child. "It's not the same without him, is it?"

"No, it is not."

Silence ate up the space between them, connecting their hearts in a way that tethered them to the moment, to each other, to a man they'd loved and respected.

"Well." Amelia straightened her shoulders lest they both tear up. "While I regret it didn't work out for you to be my brother's errand boy in London, I was wondering if, perhaps, you might consider serving as mine?"

"Aye, miss!" Nemo bounced on his toes. "I'd like that very much."

"Good, then after things are settled here, to London we will go." Reaching out, she tussled his hair.

He ducked away with a laugh.

Betsey poked her head in the door. "Mr. Lambert is here, miss."

Finally. Though her hair was a fright and she ought to put a cool compress on her eyes to make herself presentable, she rushed past her maid with a quick "Thank you."

"Oh, miss?"

She turned at the top of the stairs. "Yes?"

Betsey held her hand out to the boy while speaking to her. "You'll find the doctor in the dining room."

Amelia angled her head. "Why did you not ask him to wait in the sitting room?"

"The man looks as if he's not had a bite to eat in days. I told him I'd not summon you unless he first took a bowl of Cook's porridge."

A weak smile lifted her lips. "You are incorrigible."

"I know, miss." Betsey winked. "That's exactly what the doctor said."

<hr />

Fatigue didn't just weigh on Graham, it pressed in on every side, wringing him like an old cloth, and not only physically. For certain, the lack of sleep did sap the vigor from his bones, but the grief of losing a dear friend and the worry of how Amelia fared drained him as well. And bleeding him even more was the fact the authorities had not yet recovered the bodies. How was he to tell her that?

He shoved away the now-empty bowl of porridge just as a light tap of shoes pattered into the dining room. Amelia entered, his suit coat folded over her arm.

Graham shot to his feet and in three great strides grasped her upper arms, pulling her near. "I came as soon as I could. How are you?"

"Better than you, apparently." Resolutely, she lifted her chin. "You look a wreck."

He smirked. Of course he did. Out all night on the water. Wind and mist playing havoc with his hair. Even now he could smell the stink of river water and sludge fouling the fabric of his trousers. A grin quirked his lips, then as quickly faded. How like her to parry a question about her health.

"Truly, Amelia, as a doctor, I wish to know how you fare." He pressed the back of his hand to her brow. Warm skin, neither too hot nor too cold. A blessing, that.

She held out his coat. "I am as well as can be expected, but I should ask the same of you, tromping about all night without your coat. I'm surprised you've not taken a cough." She stepped nearer, her voice growing husky. "And I never got to thank you for all you've done."

He clenched his teeth. The truth was he'd not done enough. He'd failed at recovering her brother's body, failed at stopping the man from tumbling off the cliff in the first place. He'd failed even more by not turning in Peckwood before the doctor's own madness had spawned such sorrow.

He shrugged his arms into his coat sleeves, turning away from the gratitude in Amelia's gaze. "Would that I had done more."

"You did all you were able to. You could not tell the future, any more than could I. We both know it." A light touch pressed against his shoulder. "What of my brother? Did you find him?"

He sighed. As much as he wanted to spare her added heartache, there was no more putting off his odious task—but that didn't mean he had to watch the grief well in her eyes. He stared at the slim fingers resting on his shoulder instead. "I searched all night with the men, rode in the boat, pointed out the place where your brother and Peckwood, where they…"

Pah! Did she really need to hear such morbid details? At the very least he could spare her that. He cleared his throat and tried again. "The bodies haven't been found. Not yet."

"Oh."

A single word, yet so emotion-filled it expanded from wall to wall, squeezing his chest, his heart, his soul.

Pulling away, he snatched his mother's Bible off the table. "You have lost much. We have both lost much. In light of that, I've brought something to share."

Her eyes shimmered. "How thoughtful of you."

"Shall we?" He swung his arm towards the door. "I believe I've eaten a sufficient amount to keep Betsey from spoon-feeding me by force."

Half a smile lifted her lips, and though he wished to restore her happiness in full, it was at least something.

She led him to the sitting room, where she sank onto the sofa. His step hitched as his gaze landed on the chair Colin used to occupy during his daily visits, then again as he strode by the table that formerly housed Peckwood's machine. All that time and discomfort wasted now.

Bypassing such melancholy memories, he sank beside Amelia.

"That looks well loved." She nodded at the cracked-leather cover on the book in his lap.

"More than you know. It was my mother's Bible, and it is my great regret I have not loved it half so well myself."

She reached for his hand, her fingers soft against his. "It appears you are on the way to doing so or you'd not have brought it here to share with me."

Ahh, but he'd never tire of the warm encouragement in her voice—totally undeserved on his part. He shook his head. "Why do you do that?"

Her nose wrinkled, far too adorably. "Do what?"

"Believe the best of me."

"Because you're a good man, Graham Lambert." She reached up and smoothed back his hair, her touch a sweet torment. "A bit worn and weary, but a good man."

He caught her hand and pressed his lips to her palm, wishing to God he could kiss more than that. But now was not the time to take advantage of her emotional state. Or his. Still, such knowledge didn't make it any easier for him to release her.

He flipped open the book cover. "My mother, God rest her, took the time to write me a list of verses for when life turns hard. I thought that perhaps, after everything that has happened, that you…that we could…well, I was hoping it might help," he ended lamely. Maybe this wasn't as good an idea as he had originally thought. "Of course, we can wait until later if you—"

"What's the first verse?"

Heart swelling, he stared at her. How like this woman to hear the hesitation in his voice when he was the one trying to bring her some comfort. Leaning closer to the book, he peered at his mother's spidery handwriting. "Nahum 1:7."

He began paging through, but Amelia immediately stopped him, a curious gleam in her brown eyes.

"'The Lord is good,'" she said simply. "'A strong hold in the day of trouble; and he knoweth them that trust in him.'"

"How do you know that?" He gaped. "I hardly know where to find the book of Nahum."

A sad smile whispered across her lips. "After many days of trouble with my father, that is one verse I have memorized. But, please, do not let me stop you from reading it for yourself." She pulled her hand away. "You'll find it toward the end of the Old Testament, between Micah and Habakkuk."

Ashamed she knew more than he—why had he spent so much time in those blasted medical journals instead of in God's Word?—he thumbed to where she indicated, then frowned.

"What's this?" He pulled out a folded slip of paper...but not just any paper. A banknote for five pounds. Sinking back against the sofa cushion, he stared at the thing. How in the world had that gotten tucked inside?

"That's quite a surprise," Amelia murmured. "You said this was your mother's?"

He nodded, still at a loss for words.

She reached for the Bible. "Do you mind?"

Absently, he shook his head. "Not at all."

Graham scanned the currency, dissecting every word and number, holding it up to the light, even testing the paper for its durability with a few quick tugs. This was no jest. No counterfeit. Where had his mother gotten such a sum to squirrel away?

"Graham, look."

He glanced at Amelia, who held up one more five-pound note. "Another?" He shook his head. It made no sense.

"I suspect there's more." Despite the grief yet shadowing her eyes, a slight twinkle lit her gaze. "It appears your mother left you a treasure in more ways than one. See for yourself."

She held out the Bible, and slowly at first, then faster with each successive find, he worked his way through the list of verses, each one containing yet another sum of money.

His gaze bounced between the stack of notes in one hand and the scripture in his other. "I don't understand it. There's so much. More than a poor widow could possibly possess."

"I don't know your mother, but I do know women. If she took the time to write you a note inside the front cover, chances are she wrote one at the back as well. I know I certainly like to have the last word."

Setting the money aside, he flipped to the end. Why had he not thought of that sooner? Why had he not dug into this book the minute his mother sent it? Oh, how much misery might have been avoided.

Sure enough, written on the last page was a message in his mother's hand, flowing smooth and strong.

> *My son,*
>
> *I trust that since you've made your way to the end of this book, your faith has been kindled afresh, and there is nothing greater I could ask. Use this money for good, yours and others, for it is all the worldly riches I inherited quite unexpectedly when your uncle died. I saved it for you, my son, in hopes that by uncovering the money, you have also discovered something much more valuable.*
>
> *Ever and always,*
> *Mother*

He gaped as he reread her final words. She was right. He had found something more valuable than the funding for a new practice. In one hand he clutched the worn Bible, and with the other he entwined his fingers with Amelia's. The money lay forgotten on the couch cushion.

For he held all that was important to him.

THIRTY-TWO

*"My heart, which was before sorrowful,
now swelled with something like joy."*

One month later

The route to the graveyard was a familiar friend, one Amelia could navigate even were it the pitch of night instead of early morning. The black gate guarding the dead of St. Andrew's stood wide open, and as she strolled through, a wheeled chair ground into the pea gravel, grating to the ear.

Amelia stepped aside and dipped a small curtsey. "Good morning, Mrs. Ophidian."

"Good?" The old frog cackled. The dog-faced maid behind her did not. "A true word, Miss Mims. Every day that begins staring death in the face *is* a good one. Makes a body realize the only thing keeping you on this side of the dirt is God's grace alone."

An accurate sentiment, if a bit odd. Amelia tightened her grip on her bouquet. "Indeed. I did not realize your husband was buried here at St. Andrew's."

"He is not."

"Oh, well…" She cleared her throat, unsure how to salvage that blunder other than to cut things off altogether. "I shall let you be on your way, then. Good day."

She made to pass by, when surprisingly strong fingers reached out and grabbed her arm.

"Tarry a moment, if you please. I have a story for you." The steel in Mrs. O's gaze was as strong as her grasp.

"Of course." Forcing a smile, Amelia pulled away.

Mrs. O folded her hands in her lap, apparently satisfied she wouldn't make a run for it. "There was once a young woman," she began, "right around your age. Every bit as vigorous. Determined as a north wind. Until one day, someone she loved very dearly died prematurely…"

Her words faded off. So did her gaze, until she directed a fierce stare right into Amelia's soul. "Grief is a strange thing, Miss Mims. Sometimes it's shy. Quiet. Crouching in a shadowy corner so that you don't even know it's there. Other times it attacks like a thick, damp pneumonia, smothering the life from you. Most of the time, though—and this is the worst, mind—sorrow is a grey man, hanging off your arm like a needy old uncle you wish to tell to go away, but you know your words will be wasted. He won't leave. He has nowhere else to go." A great sigh lifted her chest.

"So you give in. Shut yourself away with him. Dine with the grey man every blessed night and greet him the moment your eyes flutter open in the morning. Before you know it, years have passed. Many, *many* years. And one day you look at the old hag in the mirror and wonder why you wasted your life on the bones of someone who'd been buried decades ago." She sat back in her chair, an expectant tilt to her head.

"I…er…" Amelia swallowed. What was she to say to that? "That is a very sad tale, Mrs. Ophidian."

"It doesn't have to be." For a moment, the woman's gaze burned like hot embers, then she swiveled her head to her maid. "Well, Simmons, are you going to just stand there or get me to the feed store? My darlings at home shall starve if I don't place a new order for birdseed."

The maid showed no emotion whatsoever, just readjusted her grip on the chair handles and started pushing.

Amelia stepped aside. "Thank you, Mrs. Ophidian."

Mrs. O winked at her as she passed.

More affected than she cared to admit, Amelia worked her way to the tree line, where an ornate fence marked off the Balfour family plot.

The morning breeze shushed through the branches of a nearby pine tree, whispering like an old friend. Or a brother. Amelia listened hard. If Colin could speak to her now, what might he say? Her smile tasted bittersweet, for in her heart, she knew exactly what his words would be…an echo of Mrs. Ophidian's, no doubt.

It is time, my sister. Time for you to move on with your life, to let me go—and in the going, know that you have my blessing.

Bending, Amelia laid a bouquet of white roses—save one—on Colin's grave…right next to the yellow yarrow no doubt laid by Mrs. O. A small smile trembled on her lips. By God's great mercy, his body rested here instead of lodging forever beneath dark waters. His big frame had caught on a rock where the Avon opened into an estuary before spilling out to sea. Mr. Peckwood, however, had not been found, nor likely ever would be. A soul lost in darkness, if ever there was one.

She pressed her hand to the soil, breathing in the raw earthiness. "You are—and ever will be—greatly loved, my brother."

Rising, she trapped a sob behind tight lips, then sidestepped to the next grave. Grass already grew here. The stone was already carved with Grafton Balfour's name. She balanced the last rose atop the black granite and retreated a step.

"Though I cannot truthfully say I greatly loved you, Father, I freely confess that I forgive you." She bowed her head. "And may God grant me forgiveness, as well, for all the years I spent running from you instead of towards you. Who knows what might have changed between us if I had."

"Amelia."

At the sound of her name, she turned.

Graham strode across the small graveyard. Sunlight draped a righteous mantle over his shoulders like some sort of avenging angel garbed for glory. As he drew close, the scent of his sagey soap blended with the fresh August morn. His hair was still damp, with a delightful bit of curl near his earlobes. He needed a trim, and yet somehow, to do so seemed wrong. The devil-may-care length suited him, and despite the unconventionality of the style, it pleased her. She smiled. Oh how far she'd fallen from clinging to perfection.

The green flecks in his eyes were brilliant today. Flashing like gems. Highlighting the browns to a glowing amber, especially as he smiled down at her. "Betsey said I might find you here."

"And so you have."

The longer he silently stared at her, the faster her pulse raced. Highly inappropriate here in this place of solemn rest, yet she could no more control its pace than she could the late summer breeze. Graham had called on her every day since Colin's death, asking after her welfare, sharing what he'd read in his mother's Bible. Always, he caused the same heart-fluttering effect whenever he stood so close.

"I cannot say I am surprised to find you here, for I know you sorely miss your brother." He shifted his gaze to Colin's grave. "I miss him as well. He was a good man."

"As are you, Doctor."

"I hope your opinion remains the same after you hear me out."

She frowned, the jarring call of a nearby curlew as offsetting as his words. "Sounds a bit ominous."

"I hope not." A small chuckle rumbled in his throat, and he loosened his cravat quite savagely, almost as if he couldn't breathe. What could possibly have the usually cool-and-calm doctor in such a state?

"This isn't a very fitting place for me to say what I must." He dropped his hand and drummed his fingers against his trousers. "But then again, perhaps it is."

"How cryptic of you. May I?" She pointed at his cravat, where the tail of the fabric had broken free from the confines of his waistcoat and dangled wild.

He glanced down at the offense, then with a sharp nod, lifted his chin so she could straighten it out.

"I am making quite the muddle of this," he murmured. Red rose up his neck, lodging in his ears.

She hid a smile. "Graham, we are friends. Anything you have to say will do nothing to change that." With a final pat to the cloth, she retreated a step. "There. All is right now."

"I sincerely hope so." He stared at the sky for a moment, then after a deep inhale, he faced her. "I have come to tell you I am leaving, Amelia. That I will no longer call on you daily. There is no future for me in Bristol as a surgeon, not with my name tainted by my association with Peckwood."

It was true. Mr. Peckwood's deeds, the patients he'd maimed at the asylum and the swirling rumours of corpses he'd illegally purchased, had all been aired quite thoroughly in the papers. Not to mention the public knowledge that he'd been responsible for Colin's madness. It would be impossible for Graham to distance himself from such a disgrace without leaving the city. Still…

She gripped handfuls of her skirt. Was she to lose another loved one so soon? For she did love this man. Almost painfully so. A fresh tide of tears welled, but she swallowed them. Deep. And continued swallowing until all the emotion balled up into a hard stone in her belly.

Graham had been the only reason she'd stayed at Balfour House this long. But now? Well, without him, maybe it was time for her to take Nemo and Betsey to London. Try to pick up the pieces of what had been her life. Mrs. Kirwin was recovered enough to manage an empty town house. Completely empty. Just like Amelia's heart.

"Where will you go?" The question slipped out forlorn, like the pleading of a little girl.

"Well, being I have a tidy sum, what with recouping in full the partnership money I'd given to Peckwood and with the inheritance I received from my mother…" A strange light gleamed in his eyes. Not amber. Not green. Something entirely mysterious. "I was thinking I might like to see Cairo before I settle in one place and open a practice of my own."

She sucked in a breath. *Cairo?* The word was a splinter, sharp and jagged, one she took great care not to touch. Of all the places in all the world, he had to name the one city that could cut so deep?

In a single step, he closed the distance between them and collected both her hands in his, giving her a little squeeze of…what? Encouragement? Strength? Comfort lest she collapse?

His gaze bored into hers. "I thought my bride would enjoy such a trip."

Bride?

Her jaw dropped, her fingers suddenly clammy against the heat of his. Was this his way of proposing—or saying that he'd found another? Ought she pull away or lean into him?

He made the decision for her, drawing her ever closer. "That is, only if you agree, Amelia, to be my wife. There is no other love for me but you. No other woman with whom I want to share my life. Will you have me?"

Her breath caught. *Would* she have him? This man of strength and compassion? Of healing and integrity?

"Oh, Graham—" Her voice broke as she rose to her toes and kissed him full on the mouth.

"Yes." She grinned. "But I don't need Cairo. All I need is you."

"Would that I could give you more. More than me. More than Egypt." He skimmed his fingers across her cheek. "I would give you the moon, the stars, the very breath from my body, and, were it in my power"—his brow lowered, along with his voice—"I would give you back your brother."

"Ahh, love. Don't you see? Colin is finally free of all his brokenness and imperfections. How can I wish him back from that? Besides..." She pressed one hand against her chest and the other against his. "He does live on, in both of our hearts."

"So shall it be." His words were husky as he covered her hands with his own.

"So shall it ever be."

THIRTY-THREE

"And now, with the world before me,
whither should I bend my steps?"

One year later, Devonshire, Balfour Country Estate

Time did heal wounds, but not scars. Never scars. The permanent marks on Amelia's heart were sometimes still tender and other times numb, always, though, a reminder of the past—as was the boisterous whoop-whoop-whooping of a boy gone wild beneath the summer sun.

Arching her back, Amelia worked out a kink and gazed past the garden to the pond, where Nemo chased a gaggle of ducklings with flailing arms. She smiled. How many times had Colin done the very same as a young lad?

Next to her, Betsey straightened, the flower basket on her arm swinging with the movement. "That boy needs more chores."

"I suspect you and Mrs. Kirwin will remedy that situation in no time." Amelia raised a brow at her. "But keep in mind Nemo is a child, not a workhorse. Play is the labour of the young."

Betsey batted away a blackfly circling her head. "You dote on him overmuch, I think. Excess kindness will not erase the harshness of the boy's earlier years."

"True. Only God heals the past, but I have learned that kindness makes the present all the sweeter." And it did, for not a day had gone by this last year as Graham's wife in which she didn't cherish his frequent indulgences. A hidden love note tucked into her pocket. Whispered words of affirmation as his head lay next to hers on the pillow. How he insisted on serving her drinking chocolate in bed before her day began. She would always hold a special ache in her heart for her lost brother, but Graham's love had mended and healed in ways she'd never expected or could possibly explain. Her husband was a beam, solid oak, girding her world when all else had collapsed.

Footsteps crunched on the gravel path.

"And so I am graced with flowers amongst flowers, hmm?" Graham's voice was as warm as the June day. He strode towards them, his worn medical bag hanging limp in his grip, his hair ragged and wind-tossed where it peeked out beneath his hat. His suit coat was rumpled. His neckcloth undone. And no wonder. He'd been called out late last night and been gone ever since.

A snort puffed from Betsey's lips. "You're the only bloom that man sees, missus. I'd best hie myself off before my ears burn with what a respectable spinster ought not hear." She reached for the peonies in Amelia's hand then swiped up the scissors lying forgotten on the ground. Tucking the items into her basket, she marched away, dipping her head at Graham as she passed him. "I'll let Mrs. Kirwin know to set your place at dinner."

Amelia smirked. Though her maid feigned a great distaste of their marital bliss, deep down, she knew the woman not only approved but perhaps even longed for the same for herself someday.

"I thought she'd never leave." Graham winked as he set down his bag, then drew her into his arms and kissed her breathless before pulling away.

Amelia couldn't help but grin. "You are wicked to tease Betsey so."

"Me? Wicked?" He lifted his chin. An imperious look. Altogether roguish and handsome. "You may wish to revise your opinion of me, Wife, for I come bearing gifts."

"Oh?" She peered over his shoulder as he rummaged in his bag. There didn't appear to be any brown-paper packages nestled inside.

"Well, letters, actually." He held out two envelopes, his earthy scent of sage and lemon blending with the sweetness of peonies. "I stopped by the post on my way home from delivering the Williams' baby."

She flipped over the first missive. Odd. No return address. Running her finger beneath the wax seal, she peered up at Graham. "All is well with Clara, I hope?"

He went on to explain the details of the birth while she skimmed the short note, and though her attention was divided, his words and those of the letter curved her lips.

"Mother and child—a girl," he went on, "are healthy and happy… and by the smile on your face, you are as well. Good news for the world-famous travel writer, I take it?"

She rolled her eyes. "A favourable write-up in the *Times* hardly makes me world famous."

"How many other authors can claim the same? You told me yourself that particular paper employs the harshest critics." He tapped her playfully on the nose. "Now then, what does your letter say?"

"It's a short note from Mary Shelley."

"Mary who?"

"You remember, the young lady who lived next to Balfour House last summer. Apparently she's married now, with a son, and she sends her congratulations on my Cairo piece. She writes that she hopes to be as successful with an idea for a novel she's working on, something called"—she lifted the paper to eye level and squinted—"*Frankenstein; or, The Modern Prometheus.*"

Graham hmphed. "Kind of her, but why tell you?"

"She says she owes me a debt of gratitude for my friendship and for all the inspiration she received while in Clifton." Amelia looked from the letter to her husband. Husband! She'd never tire of the thought.

She lowered the note. "Those were a tumultuous few months, during which I didn't have much contact with her. I don't remember being particularly inspiring. What do you suppose she means?"

"I suspect you'll have to read her book to find out, quite the clever ploy." He waggled his eyebrows. "And what does your other letter say?"

She shuffled Mary's letter behind the other, which did have a return on it. "This one is from Mr. Moritz." She broke the seal.

Dear Mrs. Lambert,

At long last, I have parted ways with old man Krebe and have established an entirely new publishing venture of my own. Well, I and a very generous patron, that is. It is my sincere hope you might consider penning your next travel handbook for me. Details enclosed.

As ever,
Mr. Justin Moritz

Intrigued, Amelia looked deeper. Sure enough, snugged behind the letter were three tickets. One each for herself, Graham, and Betsey, with two berths reserved on the HMS *Hopewell*, sailing June 8, 1:00 p.m., port of Southampton, bound for Morocco.

"Oh my," she breathed, then pressed her fingers to her lips. How good—how impossibly good—God was despite everything.

"Dare I hope that is a happy *oh my*?"

"A very happy one!" She grinned and held up the tickets. "Mr. Moritz has just sent full passage for us to travel to Morocco."

But then her smile faded. Her hand dropped. She peered up at Graham with what she hoped was a brave set to her jaw and not that of a tot who'd just had a ginger drop taken from his fingers. "But of course we won't go."

"Not go?" Graham reared back. "This is a perfect opportunity."

"For me, yes, but you? The folk around here have come to depend upon you. What are they to do without a doctor?"

"They won't be." A mysterious and far-too-attractive grin lit his face. "I shall write immediately to a colleague in London who's been grumbling about needing a holiday in the country. I have no doubt he'll fill in for me. Besides, I fancy a holiday might be beneficial for us as well. Would you not enjoy the white sands of a Moroccan beach, walking barefoot beneath a canopy of stars with me?"

"Scandalous!"

"Exactly." The heat in his gaze, the promise in his voice, cast aside any further objections. This time when he pulled her body against his, his kiss did more than steal her breath.

And when he did break away, were it not for the support of his hand against the small of her back, she'd have fallen weak-kneed to the ground.

"Well"—she smiled—"I suspect I won't have much time for writing."

"Not if I can help it."

She laughed, as much for his intent as for the half-pirate gleam in his eyes. "Then by all means, to Morocco, Husband, we will go."

HISTORICAL NOTES

Mary Wollstonecraft Godwin (Shelley)

The spring of 1815 was a tumultuous time in the life of Mary Godwin (who was soon to be the renowned Mary Shelley of *Frankenstein* fame). She wasn't married yet and suspected her lover, Percy Shelley, was having an affair with her stepsister. Even worse, she'd recently lost her baby girl, who was born prematurely. The thought that she was in some way responsible for the death haunted her, and she spiraled into depression.

In an effort to raise her spirits, Percy Shelley suggested they leave London for the country. It was during this jaunt that she conceived her next (and only surviving) child. But her happiness was short-lived. Percy settled her into a home in Clifton, a suburb of Bristol, then left her to her own devices. She was alone, newly pregnant, still not married, and feared he'd gone back to her stepsister. Throughout her life, Mary kept detailed journals, but the one during this period is lost, rumoured to have been destroyed by her own hand years later, for such was the anguish of this dark time in her life.

And what better time or frame of mind in which to imagine a monster? For shortly thereafter, Mary Godwin Shelley began writing what was to become one of the most famous fiends ever created. I merely took the liberty of giving her a little inspiration in the tale *Lost in Darkness*.

Sir Humphry Davy

Born in 1778, Humphry Davy was a Cornish chemist and inventor. In 1799, he researched at the Pneumatic Institution in Bristol, where he experimented with nitrous oxide and discovered it made him laugh, hence the nickname "laughing gas." He wrote about its potential in a treatise entitled *Researches, Chemical and Philosophical—Chiefly concerning Nitrous Oxide and Its Respiration*. In this formal exposition, he discussed using the gas to relieve pain during surgery, so the properties were known, but nothing came of it as an actual anesthetic until 1844.

It was my artistic license to cause my fictional surgeon Mr. Peckwood to think outside the box and actually try using it.

Davy became a renowned speaker, giving lectures in London that were so well attended, traffic became an issue. He was knighted in 1812 and in 1818 was awarded a baronetcy, making him a peer. He died in 1829 in Geneva, Switzerland.

Nitrous Oxide

Nitrous oxide was first discovered in 1772 by Englishman Joseph Priestley, but research didn't really take off until the early 1800s at the Pneumatic Institution in Bristol. There, Humphry Davy experimented with what became known as "intoxicating gas," "Gas of Paradise," or what we know it as today, "laughing gas." Davy organized gatherings for his friends, asking them to record their experiences with the gas, and from there it spread. Members of the British upper class often engaged in what became known as laughing gas parties. Eventually the idea spread across the pond to the United States, where the anesthetic effects of nitrous oxide were recognized.

Joanna Baillie

Joanna was a nineteenth-century Scottish poet and dramatist who had a flair for gothic themes. And no wonder, for she was a descendant of the famed Sir William Wallace of *Braveheart* fame. Though she didn't learn to read until the age of ten, that didn't hinder her writing abilities. Once she caught ahold of words, she began writing plays and is best known for her *Plays on the Passions*. She also penned many religious pamphlets and diverse poems, one of which—"A Sailor's Song"—is featured in chapter nine when Graham Lambert dramatizes it with a series of sailor's knots. It is by my own artistic license that Graham recites this poem since the work was not first published until 1840 and this story takes place in 1815, a full twenty-five years before it became public.

Colston Buns

The character Mrs. Bap (a play on words because a bap is a soft bread roll dusted with flour and eaten for breakfast) was known for her

Colston buns before she fell on hard times. A Colston bun is a sweet bread made with yeast and flavored with currants, candied peels, and sweet spices. These treats are of Bristol origin, named after a local merchant—Edward Colston—who created the recipe. There are two sizes of these buns: "dinner plate," which has eight wedge marks to be split apart, and "ha'penny staver," an individual bun to stave off hunger.

Vade-Mecum

Graham Lambert, like other surgeons of the time, carried with him a *vade-mecum*, which in Latin means "go with me." *Vade-mecums* were small books, easy to carry in a coat pocket, that summarized facts pertaining to a particular subject and were quite popular during the Georgian and Regency eras. There were several titles of interest to the medical profession: *The Anatomist's Vade-Mecum*, *The Physician's Vade-Mecum*, and *The Surgeon's Vade-Mecum*, which is what my hero had tucked in his pocket.

Spilling Salt

Heroine Amelia Balfour is a superstitious person, so when salt is spilled at the dinner table, she immediately throws a pinch over her left shoulder. Why? Historically, it was believed that spilling salt was bad luck but tossing some over your left shoulder reverses that curse. The action was thought to blind the devil, who was waiting there to tempt you into acts of bad behaviour.

Blue Ruin/Geneva

Geneva was the Regency period name for what we call gin. It was probably not passed around the table after dinner by your average Regency gentleman because gin was notoriously the beverage of the depraved lower class. The nickname, "blue ruin," is applicable in that the overindulgence of gin ruined many a man and woman.

Resurrectionists

Body snatching, especially in the nineteenth century, was most often for the purpose of selling the corpse for dissection or anatomy study.

Before the Anatomy Act of 1832, the only cadavers legally available for anatomical purposes were from those condemned to death and dissection by the courts—which made for a limited supply. Men who dug up bodies by the dark of night were known as resurrectionists or resurrection men. They (and those who used the illicit bodies) faced a misdemeanor for interfering with a grave, which was punishable with a fine and imprisonment.

Physicians, Surgeons, and Apothecaries

You'll notice in this story that, though Mr. Peckwood and Mr. Lambert are surgeons, not once are they addressed as Dr. Peckwood or Dr. Lambert. That's because in the Regency era, there were three different levels of trained professionals, all of whom were referred to as doctors, but only physicians were addressed with the honourific Dr. preceding their name. Why the differences? Great question!

Physicians were the gentlemen of the profession. They studied medicine at a university or one of the more prestigious medical schools, where they earned a doctorate in medicine. As you may guess, this was expensive, so physicians were generally of the upper class and usually gentlemen by birth. Being such, physicians didn't stoop to touching their patients or caring for the general masses. They diagnosed by asking questions and attended those higher in society. They wrote prescriptions, but it was the apothecary who then filled them.

Surgeons were the next level of caregiver, having little to no formal university training. Instead, they apprenticed to an experienced surgeon. Though socially they didn't receive as much respect, these were the men whom most people relied upon. They treated everything from wounds to broken bones to malaises of all sorts. They were not considered gentlemen because they actually touched their patients. And like physicians, they wrote prescriptions for the apothecary as well.

But you'll notice that besides being a surgeon, our hero, Graham, was also cross-trained as an apothecary. This position held the lowest rank in the medical profession. These men were trained in the use and composition of herbs, potions, and medicines and were usually found more in rural areas. Physicians and surgeons generally practiced in cities.

ACKNOWLEDGMENTS

For this story, I did something completely different. I worked out a strict outline of the story instead of mostly winging it, and for that hard work up front, my full gratitude goes to Chawna Schroeder for suffering through the entire thought process with me. I cannot imagine how flat this tale would be without her insights.

Of course there are other integral critique buddies who keep me on the straight and narrow historically, grammatically, and creatively, so a huge shout-out to these intrepid women I am blessed to have in my life: Sharon Hinck, Tara Johnson, Julie Klassen, Elizabeth Ludwig, Shannon McNear, Ane Mulligan, MaryLu Tyndall, and first reader Danielle Snyder.

There are several publishing industry greats who make my stories possible...my awesome editor Annie Tipton at Barbour, my wordsmithing editor extraordinaire Reagen Reed, and my championing agent, Wendy Lawton at Books & Such Literary Management.

Readers, there are too many of you to name, but as always, I will highlight a few: Judi Cook, Stephanie Jenkins, Kristine Klein, Betti Mace, Candace West Posey, Vickey Burkhart Sluiter, Beverly Snyder...and those are just a *very* few. I would also like to give special mention to a dear reader who recently passed...Becky Morris, I have no doubt you are reading at the feed for your Savior, now. Until we meet next, my friend.

And as always, to my long-suffering husband, who never fails to help me out of a plot pickle or let me slam him around until I figure out how a fight scene will work.

ABOUT THE AUTHOR

MICHELLE GRIEP'S been writing since she first discovered blank wall space and Crayolas. She is the Christy Award–winning author of historical romances that both intrigue and evoke a smile. An Anglophile at heart, you'll most often find her partaking of a proper cream tea while scheming up her next novel...but it's probably easier to find her at www.michellegriep.com or on Facebook, Instagram, and Pinterest.

And guess what? She loves to hear from readers! Feel free to drop her a note at michellegriep@gmail.com.

BIBLIOGRAPHY

Seymour, Miranda. *Mary Shelley*. New York: Grove Press, 2000.

Florescu, Radu. *In Search of Frankenstein*. Boston: New York Graphic Society Ltd., 1975.

Shelley, Mary. *Frankenstein: or, The Modern Prometheus*. Avon: Heritage Press, 1934.

Foster, Shirley. *An Anthology of Women's Travel Writing*. Manchester: Manchester University Press, 2002.

Hamalian, Leo. *Ladies on the Loose, Women Travellers of the 18th and 19th Centuries*. New York: Dodd, Mead and Company, 1981.

Souter, Dr. Keith. *Medical Meddlers, Mediums and Magicians*. Gloustershire: History Press, 2012.

Fitzharris, Lindsey. *The Butchering Art*. New York: Scientific American, 2017.

McLean, David. *Surgeons of the Fleet: The Royal Navy and Its Medics from Trafalgar to Jutland*. London: I. B. Tauris & Co. Ltd., 2010.

Pfeiffer, Carl J. *The Art and Practice of Western Medicine in the Early Nineteenth Century*. Jefferson: McFarland & Company, Inc., 1985.

Priestley, J. B. *The Prince of Pleasure and His Regency 1811–20*. London: Sphere Books Ltd., 1971.

Coulthard, Sally. *Superstition: Black Cats and White Rabbits, The History of Common Folk Beliefs*. London: Hardie Grant Quadrille, 2019.

Adkins, Roy and Lesley. *Eavesdropping on Jane Austen's England: How Our Ancestors Lived Two Centuries Ago*. London: Abacus, 2013.

Don't Miss These Beautiful Stories
Penned by Michelle Griep...

Brentwood's Ward

Place an unpolished lawman as guardian over a spoiled, pompous beauty and what do you get? More trouble than Bow Street Runner Nicholas Brentwood bargains for.

Available as an ebook

The Innkeeper's Daughter

Officer Alexander Moore goes undercover to expose a plot against the king. And he's a master of disguise, for Johanna Langley believes him to be quite the rogue...until she can no longer fight against his unrelenting charm.

Paperback / 978-1-68322-435-8 / $14.99

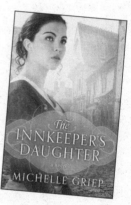

The Captive Heart

Proper English governess Eleanor Morgan flees to the colonies and is forced to marry to a man she's never met. Trapper and tracker Samuel Heath is determined to find a mother for his young daughter. But finding a wife proves to be impossible. No upstanding woman wants to marry a *murderer*.

Available as an ebook

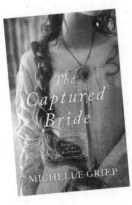

The Captured Bride

In the war-torn colony of New York, Mercy Lytton and Elias Dubois must work together to get a shipment of gold safely into British hands.

Paperback / 978-1-68322-474-7 / $12.99

Ladies of Intrigue

Michelle Griep pens the stories of three nineteenth-century ladies of intrigue who seek true love in the midst of secrets and seemingly impossible circumstances.

Paperback / 978-1-68322-826-4 / $12.99

The Noble Guardian

Lawman Samuel Thatcher arrives just in time to save Abigail Gilbert from highwaymen. Against his better judgment, he agrees to escort her to her fiancé in northern England. Each will be indelibly changed if they don't kill one another. . .or fall in love.

Paperback / 978-1-68322-749-6 / $14.99

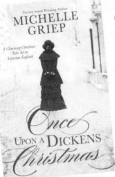

Once Upon a Dickens Christmas

Pour yourself a cuppa, get lost in the merriment of the season, and enjoy a Dickensian Christmas with fan favorite Michelle Griep. Three stories under one cover are filled with holiday romance, intrigue, and adventure.

Paperback / 978-1-68322-260-6 / $15.99

The House at the End of the Moor

She's on the run from her past, he's on the run from the law. . .but no one can run forever. And when the running stops, that's when the real trouble begins.

Paperback / 978-1-64352-342-2 / $14.99

The Thief of Blackfriars Lane

Newly commissioned officer Jackson Forge intends to clean up the crime-ridden streets of Victorian London even if it kills him, and it just might when he crosses paths with the notorious swindler Kit Turner—but Kit's just trying to survive, which is a full-time occupation for a woman on her own.

Paperback / 978-1-64352-715-4 / $15.99